as cool as i am

ALSO BY PETE FROMM

FICTION
How All This Started

SHORT STORY COLLECTIONS
Night Swimming
Blood Knot
Dry Rain
King of the Mountain
The Tall Uncut

NONFICTION
Indian Creek Chronicles:
  A Winter Alone in the Wilderness

PETE FROMM

as cool as i am

PICADOR   NEW YORK

www.picadorusa.com

Picador® is a U.S. registered trademark and is used by St. Martin's Press under
license from Pan Books Limited.

For information on Picador Reading Group Guides, as well as ordering, please
contact the Trade Marketing department at St. Martin's Press.
Phone: 1-800-221-7945 extension 763
Fax: 212-677-7456
E-mail: trademarketing@stmartins.com

Design by Nick Wunder

Library of Congress Cataloging-in-Publication Data

Fromm, Pete.
     As cool as I am : a novel / Pete Fromm.
          p. cm.
     ISBN 0-312-30775-6 (hc)
     ISBN 0-312-30776-4 (pbk)
     EAN 978-0312-30776-9
     1. Teenage girls—Fiction. 2. Mothers and daughters—Fiction. I. Title.

PS3556.R5942A7 2003
813'.54—dc21   2003049869

First Picador Paperback Edition: November 2004

10 9 8 7 6 5 4 3 2 1

For Rose, for everything.
M and P

ACKNOWLEDGMENTS

For reading early drafts of this manuscript and offering invaluable advice and opinions, I'm indebted to Dean Bakopoulos, Judy Blunt, Anna Cates, Dave Cates, Chauna Craig, Patty Fernandez, Steve Kissing, and Victoria Tilney. For fielding specific, frequently off-the-wall questions, Melissa Jette, Pat Jette, Meaghan Powers Ives, and Kathy Powers, as well as Brittney Morris, the clinic manager of Intermountain Planned Parenthood. And, for a couple of stories he'll recognize as lifted from his own, Jim Morrison. Thanks to the pros who looked after the details, Beth Thomas and Nichole Argyres. Greatest thanks, as always, to Diane Higgins, the kind of editor they say no longer exists. Also many thanks to my agent, Amy Williams, for bulling the whole thing along.

as cool as i am

CHAPTER ONE

Holding his truck door open was my job, dangling there waiting for him and Mom to get it over with. In winter, it was always dark, the reflection of the headlights all we had, the last-gasp reach of the porch bulb, exhaust fog thick and wreathy around us. It was summer now, the air heavy and green-smelling, the sun almost up over the High-woods, the sky white with it, but he was still leaving.

When they finally came slinking out of the house, I was still hang-ing off the end of his door like some kind of ornament. Even though Mom was all laughy and leaning on him, her legs these lethal flashes through the slit of her midnight skirt, Dad was looking at me, his usual what-in-the-world-will-happen-to-us-next grin gone AWOL. He kind of barely smiled, sad almost, and I knew Mom had ratted me out.

He peeled himself away from her, and I caught the narrowing of her eyes, her turn toward the mountains, her sudden interest in the day's progress.

"Hey, Luce," Dad said, bending down eye to eye.

I kept ahold of his truck door and looked out toward the mountains, same as Mom.

He brushed his thumb and finger down the sides of my face, stopping at my chin, gently turning my head. "Why the sourpuss?"

I rolled my eyes.

Letting go of my chin, he gave the top of my buzz cut a rub, the fresh-chopped hair stiff and bristly against his hand. "Mame here says you want me to stay."

I fired a razor-edged glance her way.

Dad waggled my head, making me look at him again. "This is what I do, Luce."

"Leave?"

He nodded. "Sometimes. I mean, I got to put the bacon in the bank, don't I? But every time I leave, what does that mean?" He waited, but I wouldn't say anything. "It means I come back, doesn't it? It means we get to have these great big partyland reunions."

Our it-just-can't-be-beat-to-all-be-together gala events. "We could do that every day if you stayed," I said.

Dad stood up, rummaging in his pocket, pulling out a handful of change. He thumbed through the pennies in his palm, pushing aside a bunch of dull ones until he found a brand-new one, shiny as, well, a new penny. "See this here?" he said, flipping the penny into the air with a flick of his thumbnail. "This is us, always new, always fresh, always fun." He caught the penny and held it out to me. "These others," he went on, riffling through the motley crowd of copper veterans, "never go anywhere, just stick around together all the time." He held them close to my ear. "Can you hear them? Yawning? Snoring? They haven't thought of a new thing to say to each other in years."

I took the shiny penny from him.

"You keep that," he said. "Lock it up in your private drawer. See what happens."

"Nobody's locking you up," I muttered.

"Ho ho," he laughed, rustling his hand over my head again. "Sharp as a bowling bowl, Mame, this kid of ours."

I couldn't help a smile. "You go to Canada and all I get is this lousy penny?"

He reached for his wallet and shook it upside down. Two singles fell free, floating to the ground. I picked them up. Leaving for months, driving hundreds of miles, thousands, to a place nobody would ever study in any geography class, and he had two dollars.

"You've raised a holdup artist, Mame," he said. "The two of you should take up stagecoaches, banks." As I stood studying the worn-out bills, Dad lunged at me, sweeping me up under his arm, holding me to him desperate-tight. "Don't shoot!" he yelled, "or the kid gets it!"

"Chuck," Mom said. Just the way she said his name, I could hear how I was too old to be swung around this way anymore. *She's as tall as I am, for crying out loud. All the figure of a snake, but still.*

Dad edged around to the passenger side of the truck, swinging the door open behind his back, turning to throw me in. Make his getaway.

I tightened my body into a torpedo, arms clamped to my sides, legs fused into a tail, not the least thing sticking out that might stop me outside that door. I had never in my whole life been as excited as at that one second, when I thought he might take me with him.

But at the last possible instant, Dad swung me up and away. "It's a trap!" he yelled. "She's wired! You thought you had me, didn't you?" He charged at Mom and, without a word of warning, threw me at her, yelling, "You'll have to get up earlier than that to eat this worm!"

Mom, though she's not what anyone would on her worst day call big, didn't have any choice but to catch me. She staggered back, gasping, "Chuck!"

He was already there, catching us, wrapping us up in his arms, keeping anybody from hitting the ground. He rocked us back and forth, like when we slow-danced in the living room. He was breathing hard, and I felt that warm, wet air tickling against the top of my skull as he said, "What you got to remember, Luce, is the coming home. That's all that matters. This leaving is nothing. The time away is nothing. You just remember the coming home."

He sounded like a hypnotist. A hopeful magician.

I squirmed, pancaked between the two of them. He didn't know all he thought he knew. He got to go, see everything out there, stuff we could only dream of. The whole time he was out there in the geography, we sat here, same as always. Waiting.

"I got to hit the dusty trail," he said, easing up on us, then squeezing in one last-second bear hug. "Hit it before it hits back." Then he let us go. He chucked me under the chin. "Remember that, Luce," he said. "Always throw the first punch."

He grabbed the sides of Mom's face the way Pepe Le Pew goes after that cat, and he puckered up for a smooch. They did it that way for a second, like cartoons, but then softened up and glued together and got all squirming and mashy. Right in the street. Mom and Dad were the only parents in the world who kissed like that. It was gross but fun to watch.

I slipped up alongside Dad and shoved the two dollars into his back pocket. Still all vacuum-cleanered to Mom, he rubbed the top of my head. Then he was away from both of us, bounding into his truck. He fired the engine, revving it a couple of times. He stuck his arm out the window, but not his head, not looking back. Starting away, he yelled, "After a while, alligator!"

I chased him down the middle of the street, him watching in the mirror, going just fast enough that I stayed a foot or two behind the bumper no matter how hard I ran. "Later, crocodile!"

"Adios, amoebas!" he called.

"See you, see you, wouldn't want to be you!"

He elbowed up his arm in a crisp ninety-degree, signaling right as he swung left at the corner, heading for the one-way. The two old dollar bills fluttered out into the street, and he accelerated, honking and waving and disappearing, leaving me gasping. Leaving me behind.

I stood alone in the middle of the street, hands on my knees, feeling each breath rasping in and out of my lungs until I heard Mom calling from in front of our house. "Lucy, get out of the street! You're stopping traffic."

There was a car idling in front of me, Dr. Ivers up ungodly early for some reason. I reached down for Dad's money, then stepped aside. Dr. Ivers smiled and waved, driving away, too.

I turned and walked back to Mom. "You're the traffic stopper in this family," I muttered when I got close enough I didn't have to shout. I couldn't believe she'd told him what I'd said. A violation of our number one unspoken rule.

She put her arm around my shoulders. "Would you look at the two of us? All dressed up and no place to go."

I was wearing a gray logoless sweatshirt, the sleeves cut off. Jeans. Running shoes.

She gave me a friendly shake. "Let's you and me go out and do up the town. Put on the Ritz." She started down the cracked driveway to our narrow, ancient garage, bending low and grunting as she reached to throw up the door. We skinnied around each side of our car, a sun-dulled blue Corvair Dad had found for us—"Spell it! It's practically Corvette!"

Mom shoehorned herself in, and by the time I did the same on my side, she already had her visor down, checking herself in the mirror she had tacked up there with clothespins. She smacked her lips, puckering in between, then gave up, reaching into her purse for her lipstick. As she worked it expertly around, I copied her contortions with my own lips. "No doubt about it," she said, "that man kisses like a plunger."

"Where are we going, Mom?" I asked. Put on the Ritz? We lived in Great Falls, Montana, what Mom called the last stronghold of the 1950s. It wasn't quite six in the morning.

"Tracy's, maybe," Mom said. "They're twenty-four/seven."

It was a tiny diner with a metal-plated jukebox on each table. The waitresses wore paper hats and smoked cigarettes they left curling smoke on the counter before bringing your food to the table.

"Maybe we should change into something nicer," I said.

Mom grinned. "Swines before pearls," she said, and backed out of the dark garage, careful not to break off the side mirror again. "Order whatever you want," she called out, waving her arms. "Anything at all." Then, in a side whisper, she said, "You got his money, didn't you?"

"Every last red dime," I said, both of us already filling in for Dad, saying whatever we thought he might. "Gutted him like a wish."

CHAPTER TWO

At Tracy's, Mom swung the door open for me, swishing me in with a dramatic wave of her arm. I knew without turning to look that she was doing her nose-curling routine, waving at the smoke in the air until she was sure both patrons and every waitress had seen her. I moved quick to a booth, feeling like a fresh-sheared lamb.

On Dad's first morning home last week, me sitting on his lap telling him everything that had happened since he left, the both of us waiting for Mom, he started petting my hair, messing with the few inches I'd managed to grow since the last time he was home. Same as always, I talked faster, trying to hold him off, but when I had to take a gasp or suffocate, he said, "Got something of a sheepdog look going here, don't you, Luce? A little long in the tooth?"

"You just got here, Dad!"

Mom walked in, and I could feel him wink at her as he pulled my hair up, started snipping at it with the scissors of his fingers. "Where's the motorboat, Mame?"

The motorboat was what he called the electric clipper, with its prow of teeth that kept the buzz to an even, overall quarter inch long. Like, if he could trim close enough, he might somehow be able to nip the leg off that second X chromosome of mine, shave it down to a Y. Boys "R" Us. Spent my entire childhood looking just like his one picture of himself as a kid; an indistinguishable face in an army of shaved-head kids, some team or something, a refugee gang, he never said what.

He called the haircut going water-skiing, hamming it up with jumps over my ears, carving turns around the spine bump, roaring outboard noises the whole time. Sometimes I couldn't help giggling, though it was my head, my hair.

So, at Tracy's I sat and scrunched down low into the booth, eyes down, feeling like my own refugee—someone to be viewed through barbed wire—and started twisting the jukebox knob, flipping through the selections, the metal pages clanking. Pretty soon Mom would get after me for whining about Dad leaving, and I thought finding something to play might get her humming, might put it off.

When Mom slid in across from me, she palmed a handful of coins across the table. "Play whatever you want, honey, as long as it's got nothing to do with lonesome highways or saying good-bye—any of that heartsick moaning and groaning."

After reading the name of every ancient song, I had to admit, "I don't know if there's much else in here, Mom. Bunch of sad love songs."

"Sad love." Mom sighed. "Sounds like something your father would say." She flipped through the pages herself. "They haven't changed these since before *I* was a kid. The Beatles are going to blow them away in this town." Before the waitress reached us, Mom said, "Don't let on that half of them are already dead."

"Dead? Who?"

"The Beatles." Turning to the waitress, she said, "Coffee, please," I said, "Two."

The waitress eyed me. I was fourteen years old, but at five-nine, and with how skinny I was, sporting my new crew cut, she probably figured I was sick or something, barely hanging on.

"She's my sister," Mom snapped.

The waitress walked off for the coffee, muttering "Sister, my ass" low enough that we could pretend she didn't mean for us to hear. When she came back, clapping two heavy white mugs on the table, filling them from her glass pot, Mom said, "Cream and sugar, too, honey. Plenty of it. Real cream, please. None of that powdered horse hoof or whatever."

The waitress gave Mom a look, her lip half curled. She was probably twice Mom's age, and ugly as a poke in the eye. She didn't want anybody like Mom calling her "honey."

When she pushed the tiny stainless cream pitcher across our table, the steel dull with frost, Mom gave her a wink. "Thanks," she said, nudging the cream my way. "We've been trying to keep her calorie intake up for thirty years. If it wasn't for that"—Mom snapped her fingers—"poof! Gone before our very eyes."

"Same as my hair," I murmured.

The waitress studied me. There was no way I was anything but a scrawny kid.

As the waitress started off, Mom raised her voice. "I'd like one egg, fried, loose but not slimy. No brown crust around the edges. One piece of toast, too, please, no butter."

The waitress turned around. "And your *sister?*"

"A full stack," I said.

"Lots of syrup," Mom added.

Once the waitress was gone, I chugged down my water and poured most of my coffee into the empty glass, then reloaded my cup with cream. Pretending to cover her eyes, Mom handed over the sugar. I held the spout above the cup until the whole mess threatened to overflow. Mom bugged out her eyes, sticking her finger down her throat. She called my coffee ritual making ice cream.

When I was done, Mom held her mug out toward me. I clinked mine against it, slopping some, and Mom said, "It's you and me again, baby." Taking a sip, she winced and put her cup down, setting her hands around it. Then she looked at me all serious, the peace treaty about to be broken. "The whole vanishing act is wearing thin on you, is it?"

Yesterday, in one of the rare seconds they were farther than a foot or two apart, Dad in the bathroom or something, I'd been stupid enough to say, "I hate it when he leaves, Mom. Why can't he get a real job? One where he works here?"

She'd gone straight to Dad with it. Our private conversation.

Even now I couldn't keep from picking at it, like a scab. "Well, what makes staying so impossible?" She eyeballed me like we'd never been introduced, but I shook my head, not playing that game. "I know you hate it, too. Why can't he just be like other dads?"

Mom stared at me long enough I had to look away. "That's what you want? For Chuck to be like other dads?"

"Well, no."

"He's a logger, Lucy. How's he going to stay in Great Falls? The place isn't exactly bristling with timber."

"But—"

"You know how hard it is on him? Leaving us? Did you ever stop to think of that?" She shook her head. "After all he does, you had to put that screw to him, didn't you?"

"Not *me*, Mom," I said. "*I* didn't say a word to him. *I'm* not the one sprouting stool-pigeon feathers."

She shook a fist at me. "Keep it up, sister, and you'll be wishing you had whole wings." Then she opened her hand and sighed, reaching over to rub the top of my head, feel the bounce of the bristle. "He does what he has to, Lucy. If there was a poorer state than Montana, I suppose we'd live there. He's just following the trees."

Following *trees*. Like they'd give you a good race. Only Dad. "Pounding the pavement," I said.

"Chopping down gold."

"Putting the bacon in the bank."

"Following the greenback's hard trail."

We could have gone on forever.

It wasn't until the ride home, cruising Central, that Mom showed any interest in my life. "How are you going to fill your day?" she asked.

I stared at the boarded-up Bon Marché building, where Mom and I used to look at clothes before making the Kmart run. I shrugged. "Drugs. Sex."

"Back in that rut, huh?"

I looked at her driving. We hadn't done much together before her job, though sometimes she'd load up a cooler and we'd tool around farm roads in the Corvair, going nowhere. We'd stop at creeks and have lunch. She loved making sailboats out of bark or wood and sending them off, saying, *"Bon voyage."* She said it "voy-aj-ee." Like Bugs Bunny. She pretended she was doing it for me, but long after I'd lost interest, she'd keep at it, standing on the bank, waving farewell to the boats as they headed downstream. She'd call out, "See you in Acapulco! See you in Cabo!" Then it was into the white water. No survivors.

Now we didn't even do that. With Dad gone an hour, I couldn't remember what I used to do on normal days. The ones without him. It was always like this.

Mom drove, waiting for an answer.

"I don't know. See if Kenny's around, I guess."

"Haven't seen much of him lately."

She sounded more bored than curious, but I realized that I'd dumped Kenny while Dad was home. Again. Even though I'd promised myself not to.

When Mom pulled over in front of the telemarketing world headquarters, she said, "Spent too long over our gourmet breakfasts. I've got some fast talking to do about missing last week as it is. Being late is not going to help."

She always said "There are no secrets in this house," usually when she wanted me to tell her something, but that all went out the window last year with this job. When she started, it was all hush-hush—"It's about my independence, baby. Not a word that goes over big with your father"—but then she switched tacks, telling me the job wasn't a secret so much as this special surprise she'd spring on him herself. Like I was that dim.

She jumped from behind the wheel, then paused on the sidewalk, smoothing her skirt. She always dressed nice, but not like this, not in her Chuck's-last-day, let-him-remember-this-while-he's-out-there-chopping-down-trees outfit. She finger-combed her hair as she walked up to the smoked-glass doors, and I imagined the eyestalks stretching out of the skulls of the guys in the office. If there were any guys. Mom had never let me come inside. "There are some places, Lucy, where a mother does not want her child to be able to imagine her. This is one. A rat hole with phones. Press the dial, the food pellet drops down."

I sat in the passenger seat, my hands sticky with syrup, waiting for her punch line, but when she reached out and flung open the office door, I couldn't stop myself. "Mom!"

She spun on her heel as if she'd been called back from the edge of a cliff.

"Did you forget?" I asked, not sure if this was a joke.

"About what?"

"Me."

She laughed, giving her watch a glance. Digging in her purse, she walked halfway to the car. When she found her keys, she stopped and launched them at me. "No cruising," she warned. "No picking up strange boys. Even normal ones. Straight home."

I caught the keys but stared at her, barely holding in my smile. "Mom!" I said, starting to laugh. "I'm not exactly licensed!"

Dad had made a big deal out of showing me the basics during the week he was home, working the stick, lurching figure eights around the light poles in the deserted Sunday-morning parking lot of the University of Great Falls, a tiny Catholic college just off the strip malls on Tenth Avenue South. UBT, Dad called it. University Behind Target. Mom had made me promise not to tell him we'd done the same thing tons of times. More secrets.

"Straight home," she said again, heading back to the office. "And leave it in the driveway. Don't go picking any fights with that garage."

"Really, Mom?"

"You're a natural. It's in your genes."

"But what about you? Tonight?"

She threw open the door as hard as she had before. "If I can't bum a ride in this outfit, I deserve to walk." Then she was inside, giving the huge rust-red buffalo statue a friendly whack on the rump as she charged past. The whole buffalo was made out of about a million horseshoes. But it belonged to the bank. Mom worked upstairs, where she said they didn't waste even a single horseshoe on decor.

I slid across the seat, settling in behind the wheel, trying not to smile. "Give a call if you need me to pick you up," I called, but Mom was long gone. I was talking to myself.

CHAPTER THREE

White-knuckling the knobbledy steering wheel, its back grooved for fingers as if somebody had already squeezed it halfway through, I got the Corvair up into third and left it there, timing all the lights. Home was the last place I wanted to go: the floors all echoey, doors booming behind me, each room more silent than the last. The vacuum Dad had left would fade, I knew that, but I was in no rush to knock around in that empty house by myself. I had to go by the park to get home, but it wasn't an accident that I chanced a look away from the road when I was near the playground, our ancient giant jungle gym. And I saw what I'd hoped for, Kenny spinning around at the very top, up in the stratosphere, only a knee and an elbow hooked over the bar. We were the masters of that move, the supersonic death spiral. Together Kenny and I were the undisputed masters of the entire jungle gym.

Only a block from the yawning hollow of our house, I pulled over.

At the last second I remembered to put it into neutral. I screeched back the parking brake, hearing how Kenny would have laughed if I'd jerked and stalled out at the curve. *Drive much?*

The jungle gym towered yards away, Kenny too high up to see anything but the empty passenger seat, the open window. It wasn't until I leaned over, peeking up, that I saw Scott there, too. Gross.

Kenny was still spinning, a blur, and they hadn't noticed me. Who would? Another car pulling up, some mom about to bail out with her snot troopers. Kenny would sure never expect to see *me* driving up to the park. I was about to swing my door open, say something slick and momlike—"You boys need a ride someplace?"—just to see the look on their faces, when I heard Scott's breathy, drooly voice. "Then there's undeniable kiss number seven. All tongue, no lip."

I sat back, invisible. No way I was walking into that.

"No lip *at all*," Scott went on. "Stick your tongue in her mouth, and she does it back, and you don't touch anywhere else."

I peeked over again, and just as I'd suspected, Kenny was still in the spin. Scott kept talking, all squirmy on his bar, and I missed Dad more than ever. Already.

Then Kenny stopped on a dime, back up on top of the bar. The world twisted in those first few seconds. "No lip?" he asked. "At all? Scott, an *anteater* couldn't do that."

Mom and Dad could, I thought.

Scott shook his head like Kenny would never know anything. "Anyway, then there's number eight."

It sounded a lot like licking out ear wax.

Kenny put the edge of a finger between his teeth, but I knew he bit his fingernails down the same way I did, and I doubted he had anything long enough to work at.

Behind the wheel, Mom's visor was still down, her mirror staring at me. I puckered up, all plunger, and made a cartoon smack. I almost laughed out loud.

Scott said, "If you're ever going to score with her, you got to pay attention, Kernel."

Kernel. Like that was the funniest thing in the world to call somebody, just because he was small. Once, after everybody started calling Kenny that, I passed him a note in school, spelling it "Colonel," like that was what I thought everybody was saying, like it was a cool name. Sometimes he called me General.

"I don't care about scoring with her," Kenny said.

Scott eyeballed him. "You should. Lucy Diamond is one of the best lays in town."

I shot back into my seat like I'd been horse-kicked. I had to remember to breathe. I listened to Kenny start down through the bars.

"What did you say?" he asked.

"It's true."

The hell it is! I wanted to shout. If Dad was here, he'd pinch Scott's fat head like a pimple. He'd do it in a second. Without a thought.

So soft I almost missed it, Kenny said, "I can't believe I ever told you I liked her."

"Oh, like it's not *so* obvious! People at the deaf and *blind* school can see it."

Sounding like he might puke, Kenny asked, "And I suppose you've laid her?"

I peeked out again. Kenny was almost down to Scott's level. Scott closed his eyes like he'd finally gotten to pee after holding it for days. "Over and over," he said. "In and out."

"God!" Kenny shouted. "Shut up! Just for once! Lucy wouldn't let you get close enough to touch her with an extension ladder!"

"That's about how big it is," Scott answered, giving his crotch a grab. "When it's ready for action."

"She'd break it off and make you eat it!"

Damn right I would. Kenny had told me Scott hadn't always been this way. "Big deal," I'd answered. "He is now. You should dump him like a bad rabbit."

"So, anyway," Scott kept going, "kiss nine is the one that does her every time. You lick up from her Adam's apple, all the way over her chin and up to her lips, then you—"

"You moron!" Kenny shouted. "Girls don't have Adam's apples!"

I reached up and felt my throat. Attaboy, I thought.

Scott was obviously struggling to picture a single part of a girl that wasn't supposed to be inside underwear. "You know what I mean. From her neck down there. Once you get through licking her titties."

"I thought these kisses were so you could get down there in the first place."

Scott stopped again. "Kernel, if you would try to listen, you might learn something. A whole new world might open up for you. Lucy Diamond might open up for you."

"You have never touched Lucy Diamond in your whole skanky, scurvy life!"

I smiled.

Scott eyed him. "True," he said. "Truth is, I wouldn't do Juicy Lucy unless—"

Kenny snapped around so fast I couldn't totally see. Spinning on his bar, he planted both feet in Scott's chest, kicking hard.

I popped out of Mom's car without knowing I was going to, the same way Scott tumbled over backward, way too slow to come close to grabbing any bar. He smacked an arm, then landed on the ground in the center of the gym.

The gym reached most of the way to the clouds. Dad said it must have been built before lawyers were invented. It had these two old metal signs bolted on down low, the U.S. star with the wings coming out to the sides, the air force symbol, the paint so faded you could barely see it anymore. Dad said it must have been part of some pacification program, winning the hearts of the natives. "Or else it's for recruitment. Any kid that survives, obvious air force material." Half the kids in Great Falls weren't allowed to go near it.

So when I started toward Scott, it was only to see if he was alive, but before I'd taken more than a couple of steps, it was easy to see that he only had the wind knocked out of him. It was kind of disappointing, not seeing any bones sticking out of his leprous skin. He did that fish-out-of-water thing until a bit of air squealed back in.

Kenny scrambled to the top of the gym. I stepped back to lean against the car. Glaring and gaping at each other, they didn't notice me.

Scott rolled onto his side, getting back more and more breath. "You little fucker." He propped himself up on an elbow. "You tiny little fucker." He knew it was hopeless to try to catch the Colonel up on the gym. But Scott was furious, and he was way bigger than either of us. He already shaved sometimes.

"Sorry," Kenny said, though I knew he wasn't. I mean, he had to try something. He couldn't stay up there the rest of his life. And Scott catching him on the ground would be like those lions sneaking up and getting between the baboons and their trees.

Scott climbed to his feet. "You are dead, Kernel," he growled, his voice lower than Kenny's would probably ever go. "You are deader than dead! You are going to wish you were dead! I'm going to rip your arms off and beat you to death with them. I'm going to . . ."

As Scott went on and on, Kenny sat up top and watched. Scott's face went red, purple, knowing how good it would feel beating Kenny's brains out all over the playground, knowing he couldn't catch him to start. Just like all his kissing dreams, seeing every detail but knowing he was way too disgusting to ever get a chance to try any of them on a real girl.

"I'll tear out your guts and feed them to rats! Rip off your head and piss down the hole!"

I couldn't stand it anymore. I stepped away from the car and said, "Hey, Colonel. Hey, Scott. You boys need a ride?"

CHAPTER FOUR

I stepped up on the jungle gym, climbing high, but not too close to Kenny. Both of them were dead quiet, watching me. "What happened, Scott? You got dirt all over your back."

Scott's eyes flicked back and forth between us.

"I knocked him off," Kenny admitted. "Almost an accident."

"Almost." Scott snorted. "You are dead, Kernel."

"Scott," I started.

"No matter how long I have to wait, I'm going to kill you!" he shouted. He wiped away some spit. "You can't stay up there forever."

I looked down at him, thinking of the way Mom could set men to squirming and then step on them like a nasty old worm. "Are you going to kill him because he kicked you off," I asked. "Or because he said you'd never kiss me?"

Scott tilted his head back to look at me. He couldn't think fast enough to say anything except "You stay out of it, Baldy. This is between him and me."

"Baldy," I said. "Good one. Kid's sharp as a bowling ball, isn't he, Colonel?"

"Why don't you go back to your concentration camp?"

"Camp?" I grabbed my ribs, pretending to laugh. "Stop. You're killing me."

"First I'm going to kill your teeny boyfriend, Diamond. Then maybe you. See how funny you think that is."

I looked down at him. "You'd hit a girl?"

"*You're* a girl?"

"You seemed to think so a minute ago." I hummed the way he had. "'Ooh. In and out.' You sicko."

Kenny said, "I don't think you're helping here, Lucy."

"He's a slug. Disgusting but harmless."

"You never got hit by him."

"You think I can't hear you or something?" Scott yelled. He sat down on the first crossbar. "I can wait. I got all day. First one down is a dead man."

We all three stared at one another. Scott started to whistle. Couldn't carry a tune in a bucket, but pretty soon I figured out he was trying "Lucy in the Sky with Diamonds." "Haven't heard *that* one since kindergarten," I called down.

After a while, Kenny asked, "Did your dad leave?"

I nodded, remembering again how I'd deserted him for Dad. No wonder he was with Scott. He didn't have any other options.

"So? Did you ask him? About staying?"

"I said something to Mom first. Wasn't a good plan."

Kenny shrugged. "He'll be back."

Which, I knew, was more than Kenny could say about his own dad. He had visiting rights, but he hadn't used them since Kenny and his mom moved to Great Falls, leaving him on the other side of the divide. Once, years ago, I asked Dad how far Kalispell was, and he said that if you had a good enough reason, you could make it in four hours. Kenny said it had been four years, and his dad still hadn't thought of a good enough reason. It had been about ten now.

Kenny tilted his head toward the Corvair. "You really drove here?"

"Mom forgot I was with her. She'd have been late for work if she brought me home."

"She forgot?"

"They say too much sex makes you absentminded."

Kenny blushed. "Maybe Scott will forget who I am."

"I don't think what he does with himself counts."

Kenny laughed, and Scott snarled, "Yuck it up, dead boy."

"So how'd it go with your dad?" Kenny asked.

"The same, I guess. He was as goofy as ever. As fun. We went fishing a couple of times. But it was different, sort of. Him and Mom. I don't know."

I'd caught them sitting at the kitchen table, just sitting there, looking at their coffee cups. I think it was the only time I'd ever seen them sit on opposite sides of the table. And it was as quiet as the second you pick to fart in school, nobody laughing, nobody even talking. I felt like I'd walked in on something, which wasn't a feeling I was used to. I'd backed away slow, no one stopping me.

Kenny asked what was wrong, so to change the subject, I made a show of spitting down at Scott, hawking it up, giving him all the time he'd need to get out of the way. But even so, he barely made it. My loogie hit right on the bar where he'd been sitting, and dangled there.

"Dead meat," Scott growled.

"Nice shot," Kenny said. He'd taught me how to spit like that. "Should get me a couple more smacks."

"We'll wait him out. I'll stay up here with you no matter how long it takes."

"Won't make any difference. He'll catch me sometime."

"I thought you guys were friends."

"Were," Kenny said.

I glanced down at Scott. He'd given up whistling. Just sat there like a vulture.

I thought of Mom and Dad this morning, how Mom put her lipstick back on afterward, how even a kiss like theirs didn't change anything, how Dad still climbed into his truck and drove away. I swallowed once, hard, and called, "Hey, Scott."

"What now, Baldy?"

"What if I *did* kiss you?"

For the first time in his life, the Colonel almost fell off the jungle gym.

Scott stared up, his mouth open. A mouth breather.

"If I give you a kiss, will you leave the Colonel alone?"

Scott, at last, had forgotten how to talk.

"Will you promise not to kill him?"

"Not even kidding, Lucy," Kenny said.

"You pick," I called down, making Scott squirm the way Mom could. "Any one of your nine." I started lowering myself, swingy like Mom, though I really was built like a slat.

"Lucy!" Kenny yelled.

I dropped the last bit, my feet slapping down in the dirt. "Promise me," I said.

Scott finally nodded, every dream he'd ever made up coming true before he could do anything about it.

"Say it out loud."

"I promise," he stammered.

"Promise what?" I was like one foot away from him.

"I promise I won't kill Kernel."

"Now or ever."

"Now or ever," Scott said again, like people do when they get married, only repeating what they're told.

"Okay," I said. "You can kiss me."

Scott's eyes bulged. He licked his lips.

"Which one?" I asked.

"Which one?"

He'd forgotten everything he'd ever said.

There was an inch or two between us.

"Lucy," Kenny called. "Don't!"

Scott kept gaping at me, but I don't think he was seeing anything.

"Lucy," Kenny said. "He won't kill me. We're friends."

Thinking of Kenny having to admit that, how I'd forced him into it, I closed my eyes and scrunched up my face like I was about to get hit, nothing like Mom and Dad. I jabbed forward cobra-fast. It was more head butt than kiss.

Scott jerked back, banging his head on the crossbar. But I truly hated him then, and I snapped a hand up and grabbed him by the hair, pulling him back. I tried to do it like Mom and Dad had that morning, without all their squirming or body mashing. I was trying not to touch Scott at all, like we were back in the boy-and-girl-cootie phase. This was, I realized, practically undeniable kiss number seven.

I heard Kenny yell, "Lucy!," but it sounded a long way off.

Scott revived enough that I felt his slippery hot tongue press between my lips, smashing up against the locked gate of my teeth. That was too foul, and I jerked his head back, my fingers still threaded through his greasy black hair. Even as I was doing that, Scott was snaking a hand up to give me a feel. Me and my acorn boobs.

I grabbed his wrist and almost spun him around in a hammerlock, this wrestling move Dad had shown me, but then I couldn't stand touching him any longer, even to break his arm. I threw his hand away like it was some kind of new disease. Ebola cooties.

He had this start of a smirk across his face, and I jumped away as fast as I'd crashed into him. I hawked up another loogie, like I'd been drinking acid, and spat it out between us. Then I scooped up a handful of the dust-dry dirt that was supposed to save you if you fell. Scott turned his head, like I was going to throw it at him, which, to tell the truth, I was. Instead I whisked it straight into my mouth.

Dirt spilling out of the corners of my mouth, I choked, "Undeniable kiss number ten. The maggot-gagging slimer of Scott Booker."

Scott stood there. He looked once at me, then away. Carefully, he ducked beneath the bars, out of the jungle gym, and walked off. As he got farther away, he turned and walked backward, retreating, like he was trying to think of some last great thing to say. After a few steps, he turned back around and kept going, getting smaller with every step.

I spat out all the dirt I could, twisting my head around to rub my tongue on the shoulder of my sweatshirt. I hacked and gagged and retched like a cat with a hairball. The whole time I was afraid my legs might fold up like an accordion. Like I'd drop right there. Die puking.

When I caught my breath, without looking at Kenny, I climbed slowly up like I always used to, without paying attention to where he was, how far away I had to stay.

We sat together at the very top. You could see the Highwood Mountains from up there, the Little Belts to the south. There was still some snow. We used to think it was the highest spot in the world.

I tried spitting once more, but I was out of juice. "I can't believe the first boy I ever kissed was Scott Booker," I said. "That I'll have to live with that the rest of my life."

Kenny nodded, trying to say something but having to clear his throat and try again, like he'd been the one eating dirt. "Maybe you and me could kiss. We could pretend we were the first. Like Scott never happened."

We were sitting so close we were almost touching. "I got to get this dirt out of my mouth," I said. Kenny flinched, and I added, "I don't know how worms stand it." I looked over at him a second. "I couldn't kiss somebody I wanted to now, Kenny."

"I know," he said. "That's what I meant. I didn't mean right now."

He was the world's worst liar.

But I leaned in to him, the way Mom and Dad would sit on the couch, my shoulder touching his. Our shirts, anyway.

"Was that really the first boy you ever kissed?" Kenny asked.

I snapped my head back. "Of course!" I blurted. "God!" I put my face in my hands, barely balancing. "How about you?" I asked, though if there was a person in the world who'd done less kissing than me, it was Kenny.

"I still never kissed a boy," he said.

We sat that way a long time before Kenny said, "You got a little on your teeth."

I ran my gritty tongue around. "So, want to go someplace? I got the car."

Kenny leaned against me maybe a touch harder. "This is fine with me right here."

We sat there awhile longer, but neither of us could think of anything else to say. I grabbed the next bar down and swung away. "I got to get moving, Kenny, or I'll grow roots." I kept going, one bar at a time, to the ground. "Hard to get shoes on over *them*. And don't even think about socks." Dad's lines.

I walked around Mom's car to the driver's door. "Kenny," I called over the dull blue of the roof. "I'm never cutting my hair again. I'm not letting him do that to me anymore."

"I always thought it looked cool." Kenny was not anybody's consultant for cool. "You look good," he insisted.

I couldn't help but smile. Shaved bald, a chocolate face of mud smeared around my mouth—looking good. I gave the roof of the car a slap, the way Dad did. "Come on, Colonel. I'll give you a ride home."

He raised his hand, pointing down the block, all gap-toothed without the elms. "I live right there, Lucy."

I swung open my door, then slid across and popped his open. "I know where you live."

CHAPTER FIVE

Kenny climbed slowly down the jungle gym and edged into the passenger seat. He kept his head down, searching for a seat belt.

"No belts in the Corvair," I said, like it was some kind of built-in advantage.

He glanced at me.

"Trust, Colonel. Makes the world go round."

I checked my mirrors and scanned the dashboard instruments. Stuff Dad had taught me. Things I'd never once seen him do. I turned the key, the engine whining. Not a soul in sight, I pulled away from the curb. "Got to hit the road before it hits back," I said. "Remember to always throw the first punch."

Getting it into second, I drove past my house, then, across the street, Kenny's, where he lived with his mom. Same as me in mine, except his was a duplex. This crumbly stucco place the color of scrambled eggs, with Mrs. Bahnmiller, his little-old-lady neighbor, already perched in her chair on the tilted porch. Kenny called her his built-in crazy grandmother.

"Missed it," he whispered, waving back at Mrs. B.

"By a mile." I kept driving straight, not risking anything in the way of turns. "This is cool," I said. "Maybe I'll teach you someday."

"Like once my feet reach the pedals?"

I glanced his way. "You're not so short."

"No, they call me Kernel because I like corn."

" 'They' is Scott, and he's a turd."

"A *big* turd."

I tried sticking my elbow out the window and resting my arm there, then hauled it back in, concentrating on the S-turn at the end of First. "We'll be doing this all the time in high school."

"They give you a car?"

"I mean, you know, adult stuff."

Kenny and I were geeks, we knew that, but at least in middle school everybody else knew it, too. We got left alone. Kids knew I got my head shaved now and then, that I always had. It wasn't something they gawked at or even noticed anymore. But high school. A whole new world of kids. Brand-new heap to slide to the bottom of. Every time I tried finding something to look forward to, Kenny gunned it down. He said we probably wouldn't even be friends anymore. He had this thing with the way I looked. This crackpot idea that I'd be the next thing in cool. So, of course, to make it that much harder, I spent the summer growing a few more inches taller than him, and growing out some, too, not quite a slat anymore, not quite acorn boobs, my body with a treacherous mind of its own.

I got the Corvair up to fourth on the long straightaway out to nowhere, where the air force base anchored the edge of town before the wheat took over. Great big fence all around it, like we had to be separated, jetters from townies. I knew a girl, Rabia Theodora, a year older than us, already through the gauntlet of freshman year, who was going out with one of the jetters. Twenty-year-old guy who sat in a hole all day with a nuclear missile, and he was dating a fifteen-year-old. She wasn't even pretty. Maybe not as bad as me, but definitely no looker. I was about to mention her to Kenny, but he knew her, too. She used to play on the jungle gym with me, before Kenny moved here, and then for a year or two after. Her mother hardly spoke English. Probably thought it was great that her daughter had found herself a soldier. In Kejerkistan or wherever, that was probably a great thing to do. A catch. Somebody armed once the cleansing started. Made me sick whenever I saw the guy pick her up at her house, his head sheared closer than mine. There was only one thing he could have seen in her. Same thing Scott Booker saw in everybody.

I got the car going, feeling the wind. Right before hitting the base, I said, "You want to keep going? Wind this baby out? See what's happening in North Dakota?"

Kenny pointed up ahead, at the gate and the guardhouse, the jarhead with his black beret and machine gun. "I don't think he'll let you cut through."

Slowing down, I waved at the guard. Mom said the base, all those guys underground with nothing left to shoot their missiles at, was what single-handedly kept Great Falls stuck in the 1950s. When they were shutting down bases all over, we had this parade downtown, everybody marching to show how much we wanted to keep our missiles. In the paper they quoted some grandmother saying she thought it would be horrible to spend all that money on the missiles and then never use them. Mom had read it out loud to me, muttering, "Great Falls!"

I waved once more at Machine Gun Joe, but he wouldn't wave back. Right in front of him, I hauled us through a left, forgetting to downshift, jerking and almost stalling, then getting it going again, pointed at the river. The road falls apart there, and the Corvair bounced through the chuckholes, gravel pinging under us. The wheel jerked in and out of my hands, the grips washboarding under my fingers.

Then we were on real asphalt again, and the ride smoothed out. Screwing up the shifting, and feeling the wheel drive the car itself, spooked me, and I pulled off above Rainbow Falls. The car bucked and died. "Still getting the hang of this," I said.

We sat and looked out. Though they'll always call this place Great Falls, there's nothing left of the falls but dams. The cliffs below the concrete were mostly dry. A little white gush of water over one gate at the far side. Beyond that, nothing but strips of wheat and stubble stretching away to Canada, the frozen tundra. Brown, green, brown, green. It wasn't ten in the morning, but at night the word was that this place got crowded: full of people come to watch the river, the lights of the dam, the city upstream. To neck and grope. That was the word, anyway. "Going to the falls" did not have anything to do with watching water.

Kenny knew this as well as I did. He said, "Want to go down there and wash your face?"

I laughed. The river was like a mile down over the cliffs.

Then we were still. Quiet.

"I didn't plan on coming here," I said. "Just happened."

"My mom took me here when I was a kid," Kenny answered. "Right after we moved here. Remember that comet? The one those people killed themselves to hitch a ride on? We used to come here to watch it. Almost every night."

"That's what going to the falls with me reminds you of? Your mom?"

"She thought that comet was about the coolest thing in the world."

"Well, how about here and now?"

Kenny faced the window. "How about it?"

"Do you want to 'go to the falls'? With me. Not your mom."

Looking downriver, where the water poured on to the next dam, Kenny started spinning the window-crank knob around and around. "Scott's still going to kill me, you know."

I leaned toward him. "You don't want to die without getting kissed."

"You said you didn't want to."

"I changed my mind." And I had, sort of, but gulping and licking his lips, Kenny didn't look all that different from Scott. "It's up to you," I said. "I'm not kissing you. You have to do it."

I didn't close my eyes. That seemed too corny. But I looked down, giving him a chance. He surprised me, moving fast, like it was a dare he had to get over with. A peck on the cheek.

I blinked. "Did I fail to make it clear that I am not your mother?"

"What?"

"That's how you kiss your mom. Or your sister."

"I don't have a sister."

"Kenny, kiss me like a woman."

"How'm I supposed to know how a woman kisses?"

"Kenny!"

"Are you pretending to be a woman now?"

I glared at him. "On the lips, Colonel. Now or never."

We moved toward each other, our eyes open until our lips touched, till we were too close to focus, his eye huge, like something peering through a spaceship door. Then I closed my eyes.

We mashed our lips around till breathing got to be something to think about. He never tried anything gross with his tongue. In fact, though I had never ever in my life thought I'd kiss Kenny Crauder, there wasn't anything gross about it. It was just warm. Kind of tingly.

When we slipped apart, breathing hard, I whispered, "So. Colonel."

"General," he answered. I was afraid he might salute, but he said, "If this is more of that adult stuff you were talking about, you're right, high school is going to be great."

I gave him a look, and he whispered, "How'd I do?"

"How am I supposed to know? You beat Scott Booker with a big stick." I looked away from him. "What did you think? How was it?"

He seemed to consider it before saying, "Dirty."

I saw the dirt smudged around his mouth. "Dirty" was what they called girls like Rabia Theodora. We sat there next to each other and laughed.

We stayed at the falls all day, not saying another word about kissing or going to any dams. Finally, we scrambled down to the river, something neither of us had ever done. I washed the dirt out of my mouth. Kenny, too. We guessed we'd probably die of giardia before Scott had a chance to kill us. Kenny said that would be fine as long as it happened before high school.

We didn't go home until I had to, to get the car back before Mom got home. I dropped Kenny at his house, afraid he'd try to slide over and give me a kiss good-bye, like they do in the movies, then mad that he didn't. He only said, "See you tomorrow, Lucy."

Then there was nothing else for me to do but park in our driveway, our empty house inches away, peeling white flakes of paint. Rabia Theodora lived down the block, and though we hadn't been friends in years, I wondered about her now, her and her jetter. I wondered if I'd be the next Rabia Theodora. If kids on the jungle gym would one day be talking about me: *Once there was this one really skinny bald chick.*

She used to kiss anybody. They'd point at the dirt beneath the gym. *She once made out with this giant skank-master right there.*

I clapped my hands against my temples and slid down low in the car seat, wishing it was that easy to disappear.

CHAPTER SIX

When I crawled out, ducking beneath the picture window like somebody might be inside looking out, then up onto the porch, kicking open the sticky door, I crept through every room, making sure Mom wasn't home, that Dad was still gone. No matter which room I wandered through, the huge vacancy snugged down on me like a coffin lid. Even with that, I couldn't stop the running tingles of hope at every closet door I opened, every bed I looked behind. When I'd been a kid, Dad played this game sometimes, going through the whole leaving act only to sneak back in and hide on me, come flying out of some cupboard just when I'd started to be afraid he was truly gone. He saw it as this whole new partyland reunion, but my breath always came in hiccups, my face twisting with the effort to keep laughing.

In the kitchen, I found myself standing in front of the phone, mumbling Mom's emergency work number. Though I knew I never would, I felt ready to tell her everything. I imagined gushing it out breathless, like a girl, like Kenny and me kissing had been something Mom and I'd talked over for years, Mom giving me pointers, showing me how a kiss works, having me practice on the back of my hand, a piece of fruit, a plunger. Something maybe real girls actually did with their mothers.

I just wanted to hear her voice. Have it push back the emptiness. Lame excuse though it was—I always did the cooking—I could tell her I couldn't think of anything to make, was wondering if she had any ideas. I punched in the emergency number.

The phone rang and rang. Her phone at work, in her cubicle. Where she said they kept her chained by the ankle.

Hanging up, I walked into the living room and threw myself down on the couch, wondering why I had kissed Kenny. Scott had been heroic. Diamond Girl to the rescue. But Kenny? That had been for me. To see. "Harmless curiosity," I said out loud. I hadn't expected to like it.

I wished I could tell Mom so she could tell me what to do next. Stay away from Kenny for the rest of my life. Become a nun. Cover my lips with tar, sew them shut. Anything.

Kenny and me kissing? Going at it like Mom and Dad? It was all I could do not to bust out laughing. A long time ago, years and years, when I'd known Kenny maybe a few months, I thought how nothing could be better than if we adopted him. I thought it would be cool having a brother, but really I had this idea that maybe by having a son, Dad would decide to stick around more. All of us being this normal family. All those years, that was why I'd let him shave my head, so if the one thing missing here for him was having a boy to do stuff with, I'd be almost as good, the next best thing. Somehow I missed the fact that it never did any good. Same as Mom's kisses. He still always left.

The idea of having Kenny as a brother didn't seem like a bad one. Having him here with me now. Except for the kissing part. That would be extra sick.

After what seemed about a hundred hours, and this day one of Dad's absence, I heard a car stop out front. I spun around, just short of pressing my nose against the glass. If I was a dog, I would have been jumping in circles, wetting the carpet.

What I saw stopped all that. More what I didn't see, like Mom's door popping open an instant before the car came to a stop. Like her laughing dash up the steps, a careless "Thanks tons" wave over her shoulder at whatever schumck she'd allowed to drive her home.

The door stayed shut. I could see right in. They were talking. Mom was smiling. Then she opened her door. She put one foot out on the curb, the slit in her skirt doing its thing, though Dad was a thousand miles away.

The driver laughed at something Mom said. He had a mouth like a horse. I could see his teeth. "Clap your piehole shut, Mr. Ed," I whispered. "Eyes on the road, hands on the wheel."

Then, as Mom straightened up beside his car, the driver leaned over. He wasn't grabbing at her or anything, just extending his view, saying one last thing to make her linger.

"Take a picture," I said. "It lasts longer." It was something Dad said when we were all out walking. Made both of them laugh but it made me blush, and now it even made me nervous. At the state fair last year—the three of us dizzy and woozy from slingshotting through all the rides together, mashing into seats meant for two—somebody hadn't thought it was so funny. He came after Dad, asking what the hell he thought that meant.

Dad didn't even stop smiling, just unwrapped his arms from around our shoulders. Then, faster than any of us could see, he dropped the man down cold. Mom shouted, "Chuck!" but Dad already had his arm around her again, pulling her along. I jerked away from his other arm, and by the time I quit gaping at the man, at the way the blood from his split lips filled into the cracks between his teeth, how his eyes rolled back down in his head as he struggled to get himself up to an elbow, Mom and Dad were disappearing into the throng by the midway.

I tore after them, found Dad winking, teasing Mom, "You're positive that wasn't your Mexican dreamboat?" He tucked me back under his other arm.

Mom said, "Oh, for crying out loud, Chuck."

That guy was as Mexican as me. Or Mom. Some blond crew-cut guy from the base.

Dad pulled the roll of red ride tickets out of his pocket and handed them to me. "We got to lay low awhile, Luce. Meet you at the west gate. Nine sharp. Ride everything twice for us."

"But—"

He dug in his pocket, following up the tickets with a wad of bills. "West gate. Don't let anybody follow you."

"Stop it, Chuck. You'll scare her."

"Too late for that," I said.

"He had designs on your mother, Luce. And you, too."

"Oh, he did not," Mom said.

"Eyes got any farther out of his head, he'd be looking for them on the ground."

I managed to say, "How would he see them if they were on the ground?"

Dad chucked me under the chin. With the same fist. "Did I tell you, Mame? Sharpest bulb in the drawer!"

They slipped through the gate, Dad once more saying, "Nine o'clock." Watching them go, glued to each other like flypaper, I had little doubt what they'd be doing for two hours. Back at our house, going to the falls. I sat down on a curb and waited for nine o'clock. Gave my tickets to some kids I recognized from school.

Now, in front of our house, Mom turned back to the man in the car, saying something else. She walked away backward, facing him, not me or our house.

The driver gazed after her. His black hair shone like a crow's, some kind of weasely predator.

"If Dad was here," I said, making a fist, slamming it into my hand, "Pow! Zoom!"

Then Mom was in the house, our door clicking shut behind her. The man leaned out even farther to grab the handle and pull her door shut. Mom had left it open for the view. Then he straightened up behind the wheel but kept staring at our house, like he could see her through walls, like those few minutes with Mom had imbued him with true superhero powers. "Clark Kent wanna-be," I muttered.

From the front hall, Mom called, "Home again, home again!"

"Riggedy jig," I answered, and though I waited for her to follow my voice into the living room, when she waltzed in, I was spinning away from the window as if I'd been caught at something.

"Yes?" she asked.

"To market, to market, to buy a fat pig." That was what she said when she left in the morning, then "Home again, home again" when she got back. All I had to come up with was "Riggedy jig." Today, though, she hadn't said a word about the market.

I eyed her. Everything in place. Her hair. Her lipstick. Her blouse. Tucked in tight to show both her flat tummy—salvaged the way most mothers never managed, she told me—and her jutting breasts, forever unconquerable, she promised, by that bastard gravity.

She'd had me when she was just a kid. She still said she wasn't thirty, which was almost true. Gravity had hardly had time to gain a foothold.

"You're late," I said.

She glanced around. "Am I?"

"I called you. On the hot line."

"When?"

Not why but when.

"I got back late after lunch. Tato had a fit."

Her boss. Mr. Potato Head. Head like a big Idaho baker.

It wasn't until then that Mom thought to ask, "Why the call? Where's the fire?"

"No fire."

Mom tilted her head. She clapped her hand against her leg, and I slid off the couch and crossed over to her, leaning against her side, under her arm. Even being as tall as she was, I could still feel small there.

"Miss him already?"

I nodded beneath her hand.

"Me, too."

She kept petting me. "We'll get our sea legs back soon enough. Don't worry."

I nodded again but couldn't help ask, "Who gave you a ride?"

"Just another cubicle filler."

"He had nice hair," I said.

"Did he?" Mom asked, like she didn't know, like she would never notice such a thing about any other man.

I smiled. "Mom? What's it like? Kissing somebody?"

I could feel her rearing back to look sharp at me. She needed glasses but would never be caught dead admitting that.

"Kissing? A hot-line call? What exactly went on here today?"

"Same old, same old."

She sighed. "Thank God you're an only child," she said, slipping away from me to head for the kitchen. "So. What's for dinner?"

I watched her go. I was never going to say another word about kissing. Anybody. Ever.

CHAPTER SEVEN

The next morning, as Mom tore out the door, hair still wet, a banana—minus the bite in her mouth—clutched in her hand with her keys, she managed to sing out, "To market, to market."

I sat in front of my soggy Special K, sickly blue skim milk lapping around the flakes. Mom's new cereal choice. Not a good sign. We used to eat Cap'n Crunch. Lucky Charms. "To buy a fat pig," I whispered.

The door banged shut. The Corvair roared. We were back on our schedule.

My cereal made a disgusting wet plop in the sink. The day stretched ahead of me forever, Kenny out there with his lips.

Ignoring my butterflies, I whipped open the door like it was any other day, deciding to get it over with quick, face the new us. See what we'd done to each other. Mom and Dad weren't much older than we were when they got married, and I wondered if they'd started like this. A kiss and then panic. Just not quite enough panic to do them any good.

When I reached the park, Kenny wasn't there.

That never happened.

I climbed up the gym to wait, but the playground was already busy, and without Kenny, all the mothers and their little kids left me feeling more oddball than usual. Someone whose welcome had long since worn out. I was taller than most of the mothers.

On a normal summer day, I'd see Kenny every morning at the jungle gym. It was where we met. We practiced moves that would leave mere mortals broken and bleeding. At least staggering and puking dizzy. Sometimes we walked around town. Grabbed bikes and rode down by the river. Watched the geese and their babies. Kenny brought a fishing rod once in a while, and once in a blue moon, we'd catch a trout. We'd stare at it, all silvery and eyelidless, then put it back. Dad had taught me how to fly-fish years ago, on his longest visit ever— almost a whole summer—but Kenny was happy drowning worms.

None of this was anything to look forward to by myself.

Even as I climbed to the ground, I kept looking down the block for Kenny. I couldn't shake the idea that after the kiss he didn't want to see me. That maybe he thought it was gross. One kiss and I'd screwed up my whole life. Okay, two kisses. One and a half.

But I didn't see Scott, either, and I wondered if maybe my kiss had powers I hadn't dreamed of. Dark powers.

Glancing at Rabia Theodora's house, I wondered if she'd felt this alone after discovering her jetter: her world narrowing to that one sharp point.

I started toward Kenny's. When I was a kid, even before he lived there, I'd watched the men work day after day cutting down the elm trees; but the roots were still under the ground, heaving up the sidewalk like we hadn't quite survived an earthquake. Not a chance of leaving your mother's back unbroken.

Glancing up from all the cracks, I saw Mrs. Bahnmiller in her chair, already craning my way, dying to talk. I spun and crossed the street, banging through our gate.

I schlumped around our whole house again. Why couldn't I be one of those kids who slept till noon? Half the day gone before they even crawled out. In the bathroom I peeled out of my clothes and stepped into the shower to kill time.

I stayed in till the hot gave out, but the day was still there, hardly begun. After drying off, I wrapped up in a towel and tried to give myself a once-over in the steamy mirror. There was nothing left for me to do, none of the stuff I figured most girls spent long hours over. I didn't have any hair to dry or curl, mousse or style.

I flung open the vanity drawers. The stiff cords of Mom's hand-me-down blow dryer and curling iron tangled through everything, enough of her old makeup to prep a Volkswagen load of clowns. I scrubbed a circle out of the mirror's fog with the side of my fist. That was what I'd look like. A clown. Blobs of mascara drawing attention to my fish eyes. Lipstick making my teeth stick out even more. I needed braces, no matter what Mom said about my perfect teeth. They could always be straighter, couldn't they? Couldn't everything?

I settled for pinching my cheeks the way Mom did. Getting the blood flowing. Something I did in secret every day, ever since Mom said I had perfect plains for cheeks. Great bones. I rolled my eyes, thinking of the Great Plains, the most boring feature of an entire nation; of this picture from our history book of buffalo bones stacked and bleaching as far as the eye could see.

My natural beauty.

Back when Rabia and I still did stuff together, years ago, she came over one day with this armload of magazines, *Cosmo* and *Seventeen* and *Mademoiselle*. It was late in the summer, and when I looked down at the magazines, she said, "I'm going to Paris next week."

"You are?"

She nodded in the direction of Paris Gibson Middle School. "Thought I better look the part," she said. "I can be a new me."

She tumbled the magazines onto my bed. That's how desperate she was. She wanted *me* to glam her up.

We flipped through the glossy pages while I wondered if Rabia

thought she could ever come close to looking like any of these crea-
tures. Her mouse-colored hair hung limp over her face, trying to hide
her red, raw skin.

Maybe she started to realize the same thing. She caught me looking
at her, and her red face got even redder. "Hopeless, huh?"

I denied it flat out, but she shrugged, and we wound up reading
out loud about what men really want. We took a quiz. We laughed our
heads off, partly because it seemed so ridiculous, but mostly out of hot
embarrassment. I wanted her to go home. And when she did, as soon
as I closed the door behind her, Mom was standing there, her eyebrows
halfway to the ceiling. "What was that all about?"

I didn't give Rabia up. Didn't give Mom a chance to guffaw, blurt
anything about silk purses and sow's ears, about how Rabia's best
chance might be a long dress and a polka-dot scarf, hope to catch the
eye of a nice young Hutterite boy come to town from one of the colo-
nies. I did at least that much for her.

Now, fleeing the bathroom, I scampered quick down the hallway
to Mom's room, peeking out the window at the playground, but the last
surviving elm hid the jungle gym. Maybe Kenny was there by now. I
turned to get dressed and give him another try, but I caught my reflection in the steam-free torture of the full-length mirror on the inside
of Mom's closet door. It reeled me in like a magnet.

She'd left the door gaping, her knock-'em-dead outfit sprawled on
the floor in front of it. Wouldn't be needing that for a long time. Keeping
my eyes on her dress, I let my towel drop down beside it. I stretched
my arms over my head, coiling them together, throwing a hip to the
side. My own Victoria's Secret catalog. Then I glanced up, hoping to
catch the full effect.

I couldn't stifle a laugh. Not a funny one. I had bones poking at
my skin where most people didn't know they owned bones. Dropping

my arms, I hunched my shoulders, pressing my arms in, scooching up my cleavage. I sucked in a breath to expand my chest. Pretty soon I let it out in a long, stale sigh. God, cleavage. I was practically still a boy. I waggled my hips from side to side, studying the wispy patch of hair, imagining a boy's equipment swinging around down there. Leaning forward, letting my forehead touch the cool, hard glass, I whispered, "At least you don't have that to worry about." All those dangling, embarrassing appendages.

I pictured Kenny over at his house—a place, in all these years, I'd never been inside—dripping wet himself, leaning against his mom's mirror, looking at his parts, thinking of mine, wondering what it would be like to be all slick and streamlined.

Resisting the urge to slip Mom's showstopper over my head—it would hang on me like a sack, some biblical punishment, what they were wearing with ashes this year—I reached up, curling my fingers over the dusty top of the door, steadying myself. I pressed against the mirror, my nipples touching first, my whole body goose-bumping against the glass. Kenny thinking of me naked. My hair prickled against the mirror, and I looked myself in the eyes. Blue, with a dark ring around the outside. Milk blue more than sky blue. Skim-milk eyes.

When I stepped back, there was a fog outline of me on the glass. It only lasted a second. As it faded, I whispered, "Mirror, mirror, on the wall," but I couldn't finish. Instead I swept up my towel and wrapped it tight around myself, trudging down to the kitchen to dig through the fridge, see if we had anything to eat besides Special K and blue milk.

The knock on the door froze me, standing in my towel at the open refrigerator door.

People did not knock at our door. Except Mormons, maybe. Who else pounds on a door at ten o'clock on a Thursday morning? Dweeby boys in white short sleeves and black ties, killing their two years. I grinned, picturing swinging open the door in my towel, saying, *Oh, do come in. Puh-lease.* Watching them tear down the street. Lead me not into temptation.

The knocking came again, not as hard as it seemed the first time. Then I heard Kenny calling into the mail slot. "Lucy? It's me."

I stepped quick. Cracking the door, I hid behind it, peeking around. "Where have you been? Fall down a well?"

Kenny stood on the porch. "What are you, naked?"

"Well, Scott's here, and—"

Kenny's jaw about separated itself from his face.

"Shower, Kenny. Jeez." I pulled the door open wide, showed him the towel reaching from my armpits to my knees. Modest as a straitjacket. "Come on in. I'll go get dressed."

Tearing upstairs, I had shorts and a tank top on in seconds. I slid down the banister, one cheek up on it, kicking against the steps to shove down faster.

"Where've you been?" I shouted, only remembering about the kiss—that I might not want to know his answer—after I shot off the banister and staggered into the front hall.

Kenny looked at me from the living room and shrugged. He was sitting on the couch, up straight, like some kind of salesman. He didn't look right at me.

"Colonel," I said.

"General?"

"Where've you been?"

"Just around is all."

I turned to the window. The empty street. "Not around me."

"Well, I—"

"Yeah, me too," I interrupted. "I looked for you at the jungle gym. It wasn't the same."

Kenny nodded. "What are we going to do?"

I shook my head. "Mom took the car. We're stranded."

He kind of smiled. "No wheels? Shit."

"Can you believe it?"

"Want to try the jungle gym again?"

"Could."

"Only if you want."

I sat down on the other end of the couch. We looked around the room. "We only kissed each other," I said at last.

"I know."

"So don't say stuff like 'Only if you want.' What kind of way is that to talk?"

Kenny picked at a fingernail.

"It's not like we hurt each other or anything." And then, to prove it, I leaned forward and planted one on him. A real one. On the lips. I stuck my tongue in his mouth. He didn't bite.

I liked the way he tasted. His lips. His mouth. My heart went all gallopy.

Kenny sat back long enough to blink, to gasp, "Holy shit!" Then he moved back in for more.

Jungle gym, schmungle gym.

CHAPTER EIGHT

Of course, this wasn't something I went racing with to Mom. *Gosh, Mom, Kenny and me, we discovered this whole new thing! Way better than the jungle gym! Why didn't you ever tell me? I mean, what a way to pass the time!*

She kept coming home every evening same as ever. Home again, home again. Riggedy jig.

After I noticed how puffy my lips got from mashing them all over Kenny's face, I started running cold water on them before she got home. She caught me once, hunched over the sink like a kid drinking out of the faucet. She looked sideways at me, then said, "We use cups, honey. Even in Great Falls."

Kenny and I got to be masters, going way, way past Scott Booker's nine undeniables. One afternoon, when we were going at it hard on the couch, the mail slot's rattle about sent us through the roof. We both checked the clock. Mom wasn't due for a couple more hours. All locked up with each other, time and everything else got tough to keep track of. We giggled nervously, and, still shook, I got up to find the mail scattered across the hallway floor, Dad's first postcard mixed in with the bills and junk. It was a black-and-white picture of two huge naked people hugging. They were kissing, too, we guessed, face smushed to face, their feet yards apart. They were so fat you couldn't see anything but creases and rolls. If they'd had those diaper deals on, you would've guessed they were sumos, not lovebirds.

Without saying a word, Kenny and I took a couple of steps away from each other, then leaned in, hugging, trying to kiss the same way. We tipped over and lay on the floor howling.

I left the card on the table that night for Mom, but she curled her lip as soon as she saw the picture. She flipped it over and read aloud, " 'I love you *this* much!' " then tossed it back down. "What the hell is that supposed to mean?"

"Don't ask me. I didn't write it." Till I saw her read it, I'd thought it was hysterical. It was the only thing we'd heard from Dad since he left.

"Well, it makes me feel better knowing he cares. Doesn't it you?" Mom said.

"We know he cares."

"But look at those people. Is that supposed to be a hint?"

"What? Do you think you're getting fat? Is that what these breakfasts are about? I thought maybe you'd decided anorexia was the next step for my figure."

Her eyes narrowed in on me. "Just wait till your metabolism slows down, honey. See how funny you think it is then."

I didn't have any idea what went on in her head.

The next morning, I didn't have the heart for another mother/daughter diet breakfast. Though I never slept in, I stayed in bed, listening to Mom rummage around downstairs. For a while I thought she'd never leave. When she roared out at last, all I did was keep staring at the ceiling. I thought about lying there in my Supergirl T-shirt until Kenny came over, call him on up to my room. Let him see me in bed. But saving him the heart attack, I climbed out and got dressed, then sat on the porch to wait for him.

As soon as he walked up, he said, "Where's your mom?"

"At work." Like, duh. Where did he suppose she was? If there was one person who knew more about me than I did, it was Kenny.

He slid down next to me. Our sides touched knee to shoulder. "It's the Fourth of July. Nobody works today."

I jerked to my feet, almost dropping him down the steps. Without a word, I banged through the door, dashed upstairs to Mom's room, checking for some clue that, for the first time in my life, I'd missed Dad's arrival, that they'd sneaked out on me to plan some great surprise.

There was nothing. No boots. No gas-smelling black jeans. Just Mom's stuff in its usual crumple on the floor. Not the way she'd leave it if she guessed Dad was coming home.

I stood and turned a circle, glimpsing my reflection in the mirror. Almost like Mom hiding in there, catching me looking. I turned away fast, leaving the empty room.

Kenny stood on the porch, waiting.

"This is too weird," I said. "She blew out of here like any day." At least I guessed she had.

Kenny smiled. "So the house is ours?"

"Yeah, till she comes home. Whenever."

He saw what I meant.

"We better blow this pop stand," I said. "Get the hell out of Dodge. Get a Dodge and—"

Kenny jumped after me, and I popped the leaning gate with my foot. We were off.

But we'd spent so much time on the couch that we didn't know what else to do. We walked to the railroad tracks, cutting down past the grain elevators and the baseball field, out onto the bluff above the muddy little rapids below Black Eagle.

"This is like when we drove to the falls," Kenny said. "That day we first kissed."

We'd kissed maybe a thousand times since then. Ten thousand. We did it again, right there in public, the truck-route traffic roaring by. Some guy gave a long blast on his air horn, and Kenny pumped his fist like an engineer pulling his whistle cord.

We walked all over, down to the park where they were getting ready for the fireworks, putting up plastic fencing, some bleachers in front of the bandstand. Some old guy gave us the last of his bread so we could feed the ducks in the pond. Like we were little kids. We laughed like crazy over that. All the same, we fed the ducks, Kenny throwing his chunks over the piggiest to the smaller, shy guys hanging at the edges.

We made the long walk back to my house for lunch—Mom was still gone—and took a couple of chances on the couch. Kenny got his hand under my shirt, scratching against my bra, but with Mom out there anywhere, it wasn't something we could get into.

After hanging all day, we wound up at the park again in time to find a decent place for the fireworks. The band puffed away in its shell, the same tunes as every year, like we were all supposed to be marching until the first rocket launch. Without the car or parents, we didn't have blankets or chairs like everybody else. And, the river park's playground was brand-new, all red and blue plastic-coated metal, a jungle gym about six feet high. Pathetic. Kids crawled over it like ants. We just found a chunk of grass and sat down. There were kids roving everywhere. Bottle rockets zipping up and popping. Firecrackers and Roman candles. Buzz bombs. Enough gunpowder smoke to choke a goat.

On our chunk of brittle, dry grass, Kenny and I sat maybe a bit closer to each other than was safe. All day I'd been guessing at what Mom was up to, the likeliest being that she'd find us down here, that maybe she was cooking up some kind of surprise. I threw Dad into a lot of these fantasies, but Kenny gave me a look when I said so. It was, I had to admit, awfully soon for a return.

Kenny touched me, his hand between my shoulder blades, rubbing circles. "She probably had stuff to do," he said. "You know, how Saturday you go to the store, clean the house, how—"

It was like he was preparing me for her not showing up, letting me down easy. "It's no big deal," I said. "It's just that she never leaves without me knowing where. She never leaves period. It's just weird is all."

Kenny raised his eyebrows.

"And that's not how we do it, anyway. I do all that while she's at work." I remembered Mom explaining my role after the house fell apart when she started working: "Clear the decks for Saturday!" she'd boom, like we were pirates or something. "If you keep up the house, we'll have time on weekends for you and me. Like always. Instead of being anchored here cleaning." More boats cast to the rapids.

Years earlier, she'd turned the cooking over to me the same way. She hated it. Swore up and down she couldn't do it. She was right, but all you had to do was read the recipes. It wasn't hard. You only had to try.

She'd said, "It's a fair trade. You hate cleaning the toilets. 'It's *so* disgusting!' So I'll do the toilets, and you do the cooking."

"Two ends of the same job," I'd answered.

It wasn't till later that I figured out you cook three times a day, clean toilets once a week. It wasn't more than a year or so before I had to start cleaning my own toilet anyway, Mom insisting that I didn't want her snooping around in my bathroom.

Kenny moved his hand up and down. Still comforting more than moving in for a kiss. It was disappointing. I leaned over to kiss his ear right as a sparkly flash arced over his head and landed in his lap.

The firecrackers were going off before I was sure what I'd seen. Kenny and I both jumped, slapping at the crackers, a whole pack of them dancing as they exploded, shredded paper littering our spot in the grass, sticking to the tiny hairs on our legs. They couldn't hurt you much, but they sure got you dancing.

From behind us we heard, "Another second and you'd've been humping right there on the grass."

Scott.

"Had to stop that. Whole place would've been puking."

He stood only a few feet away, another pack of firecrackers in his hand, a glowing punk in the other.

"So I suppose that's all you guys do now. Screw." He held the punk to the fuse, waited for the flare, then threw the pack at us. "I should have known."

The firecrackers popped and hopped at our feet.

A mother on a blanket beside us, her kids wide-eyed and pressed against her sides, said, "Hey, there are kids here!"

Scott ignored her. "I've been looking for you," he said, pointing his punk at Kenny. "Don't think I haven't." He kept digging in his pocket. For another pack of firecrackers, I hoped. But before he could haul it out, a man touched his shoulder and said, "I think that's enough."

"Who the hell do you think you—" Scott said, sort of belligerent, but shrinking from the man's touch, no longer digging anything out of his pocket.

I took my eyes off Scott. It was a man with sleek black hair. Horse teeth. Mr. Ed. Our cooler dangled from his hand. Mom stood behind him. Smiling.

I doubted Mom knew Scott's name, but I knew he'd already memorized every detail of her. Every man in the park must have wanted to stand next to her. Every boy. Hell, *I* did. She was wearing the same thing I was, a halter and shorts, but I felt like one of those mannequins they have, dressed to the teeth but without real bodies, only sticks and a flat, smooth gray cutout of a head.

I stepped a little behind Kenny.

Mom smiled. "I knew I'd find you kids down here."

"*We'd,*" I corrected.

She looked at me, tipping her head.

"*We'd* find you here. Not *I'd.*"

Keeping her head in that quizzical tilt, Mom said, "This is my friend Guy."

I wanted to ask, *What kind of person calls their kid Guy? You got a sister named Gal? Why didn't they just name you Hey You?*

Mom said, "At this point, Lucy, it's customary to introduce your friends in return."

I stared at Mr. Ed the Guy.

"Guy," Mom said, "this is my charming and lovely daughter, Lucy. And that's her friend Kenny she'd hiding behind. And this," she went on, with a dismissive wave toward Scott, "this gem I am not acquainted with."

I wished I could give a wave like that. One that says you are not so much as fly poop. I followed Scott's stare. Mom wasn't wearing a bra. Her nipples made bumps.

"You leprous toad!" I blurted. He was so busy loading his memory bank with Mom's boobs, I snatched the glowing punk right out of his hand. I reared back with it, like I was going to jab it in his face. "I'm going to put your eyes out once and for all."

Mr. Ed grabbed my wrist. Not hard. Just in case. "Looks like we got here in the nick of time, Lainee," he said.

At least he didn't call her Mame. It would have been his eye smoldering on the end of my punk if he had.

Breaking his gaze, Scott said, "See you around, Kernel." He stepped around the blankets. "Count on it. You, too, Baldy."

Mr. Ed let go of my wrist. *Excitement's over. Nothing to see here.*

Mom sat down on the firecrackers' snarled confetti, waving her hands around her legs, pretending to flounce wide skirts. "Well," she said, all southern sorority, "what an absolutely charming young man. And this young lady," she went on. " 'Leprous toad?' What an unusual command of the vocabulary. How proud your parents must be."

I looked down at her. At where Scott had looked, then away. She was not a person who wandered around braless.

Mr. Ed cleared his throat. "So, Kenny," he said. "What do you do for a living?"

"Me? I'm a kid."

"Where were you all day?" I hissed at Mom, trying to be private.

"We were at Guy's cabin, up on the Smith River."

"You went to his *house*?" My voice went so high it squeaked.

"Cabin," Mom answered. She squinted, studying me. "Where are you letting your mind take you? What have you conjured up?"

"Mom!"

"There was a whole party there, Lucy. Everybody from work."

"Then why'd you sneak off like that?"

Mom looked blank, and I thought I had her.

"You were in bed, Luce. I left you a note."

"You did not. Where?"

"On the back of that lovely postcard. He always leaves plenty of space for actual communication."

I couldn't believe she'd bring Dad up right in front of Ed. "How on earth was I supposed to find it there?"

"Maybe not the best place," Mom admitted.

"Why didn't you come upstairs and tell me?"

There was a loud crack then, like thunder but sharper. The first firework, a banger, no colors, letting you know things were about to start.

Mom ignored the empty sky. "Because, Luce, I knew you'd be like this. And just once, I wanted things to be easy."

"Easy? What is so hard?"

"Can't I have friends, Luce? Even for one day?"

"*Friends,* or *a* friend?"

She let that go. "You've got Kenny. Why can't I have a day off with friends?"

"Three words, that's why. D. A. D."

A real shot went off over our heads. I didn't look, but the crowd oohed.

Mom shook her head. "What did you do all day?" she asked.

I watched her face light up as the fireworks burst above us. "Kenny and I made out."

Kenny grunted as if he'd been punched.

Mom was unfazed. "All kinds of heavy petting?"

"Teens left alone . . ."

Mom nodded. She picked up a piece of firecracker paper, shredding it finer still with her long nails. "Put it off, Lucy," she said. "As long as you can. You're not ready for it, and believe me, not one thing will be the same once you've turned Pandora loose. There's no getting her back inside that box."

"Yeah, well, I wouldn't know about that."

"I hope not." Mom looked over my shoulder. "Come sit down, Guy. Watch the fireworks. The ones in the sky." She gave me one more look. "You, too, Lucy. Remember? We're a team."

I chewed my lip, then, grabbing Kenny's hand, I pulled him down next to Mom so he was between the two of us. Mr. Ed sat down on Mom's other side.

I didn't let go of Kenny's hand but moved it up onto his leg, where Mom couldn't miss it, my long fingers twisted up with his short dirty ones. He didn't move a muscle in his hand or arm. I could feel him sweating.

But Mom was leaning back on her elbows, her head tilted back, smiling at the swaths of color flashing across the night, the booms rumbling inside our chests. I had to stop myself from burying my head against the cool, long line of her throat.

Instead I gripped Kenny's fingers tighter and tighter, making him squirm.

CHAPTER NINE

Mr. Ed had his own car down at the park, and after the fireworks, I watched him drive away, making sure he didn't try to touch Mom. Once he was safely gone, we loaded into the Corvair, me stealing the backseat before Kenny had a chance.

Mom stopped at Kenny's house—Mrs. Bahnmiller's chair empty for once—and Kenny skittered out of the front seat like it'd been scorching him. " 'Night, Lucy," he yelled as he pounded up the porch steps. "You, too, Mrs. Diamond. Thanks for the ride."

Mom lifted her hand in a wave and pulled out. "He's a good kid," she said, like he was six. Then she turned around to me slumped against the window. "Making out!"

I stared out at Kenny's empty porch. She didn't know one single thing.

U-turning back to our house, Mom slid the car into the dark garage like it was greased. But then she sat there, not making a move for her door. "It's been a long time since I've seen Kenny. I thought maybe something had happened between you two."

Something happened, all right, I thought. You haven't seen him because he scrams at four-thirty every day to make sure you don't see him. We knew there was no way we could face her together after a day of mauling. She'd take one look at us and know in an instant. It was the way she was.

"And here you've been making out all this time." She said it like it was a joke, the furthest thing from possible.

"We weren't making out," I muttered.

"Still tearing up the jungle gym?"

"I'm fourteen, Mom. Think maybe I might be outgrowing the jungle gym?"

"Oh, this is serious." She paused, like she was still kidding around, though she was fishing hard. "You're not holding out on me, are you? You and Kenny? You're not keeping any secrets? You know, there are—"

" 'No secrets in this house.' Yeah. I know."

Which, really, was total bullshit. We both knew that. Even before she started appearing braless with strangers. In fact, it always had been, no matter what Mom wanted to pretend. A long time ago, like half my life, I'd been playing dress-up, digging through Mom's underwear drawer for anything slinky, when I came across a thin handful of postcards stashed at the bottom. I was old enough to read, but what they said didn't make any sense. "Hola, Lola," they started. Mom's name was Lainee. And what in the world was "Hola"? And why weren't these taped up on the refrigerator like Dad's? The pictures were of huge deserted beaches. They said things like "The sand cries for you" or "It's just not paradise without you" or "Corona mornings, lobster afternoons. What's not to like?"

When I carried them down to tape them up with the rest, Mom went all white and snatched them out of my hand. One of her bras was strapped around me like a vest, she didn't need to ask how I found them. She never said a single word. She hid the cards someplace else after that. Or threw them out. I never found them again.

For a long time, when I thought about it at all, I'd guessed that Mom had a crazy sister or something, an aunt maybe, someone locked away who didn't know her real name, who couldn't even spell "hello." Who would scare people. A secret she had to keep.

"Lucy?" Mom said, serious now. "That hand-holding at the park?

The making-out crack? Is there something we need to talk about?"

"Kenny, Mom? Me and *Kenny?*" I said it like "What could be more ridiculous," but I was fiddling with the cooler handle, pushing it open, lifting the lid, like there was something in there I had to find. And what I found was a knotted plastic bag. How Mom stored anything wet. I picked it up, but it felt empty.

The dome light flashed on, Mom no longer interested in what we might need to talk about. She wriggled out her door. I followed her into the house with the bag.

As soon as I got inside, I picked up Dad's postcard. Sure enough, Mom's note was scribbled across the back: "Out on a company picnic. Thought I'd let you sleep. See you at the fireworks. XXOOXX."

I heard Mom upstairs.

I tugged at the bag's knot, and when I got it untied, sure enough, there were the two tiny slips of black Lycra. The thong bikini that Dad had dared her into buying but we'd never seen her wear. He called it her howl-at-the-moon outfit, and he'd howl himself whenever he tried to get her to put it on.

"Down, boy," she'd say, smiling.

He'd howl some more. Pant.

"It's indecent," she'd say. "I can't wear it in public."

But Dad only howled louder, drawing it out, sounding like he might die of longing.

Mom pointed her finger at him. "Wolves are an endangered species, bud. Settle down, or they'll be extinct."

I tied the neck of the bag back shut, pulling the knot as tight as Mom had. She'd worn it in front of all her fellow cubicle dwellers. Mr. Ed.

Counting back, I realized we'd been on the Special K rations for a month. That, I guessed, was how long, to the day, that she'd known about this party. The chance somebody would say "How about a swim?"

The time she had to work her body up to peak thong shape.

I thought of her sneaking out. Leaving me to sleep. If you were going to wear the howl-at-the-moon suit, you sure wouldn't want a bag of sticks like me standing beside you, drawing off the commotion, making people storm down from the grill to push hot dogs and hamburgers and chips and s'mores at me while you're standing there all gorgeous and ignored. What would be the point of that?

One by one, I climbed the stairs. Seventeen up to where we slept. When I reached her door, she was already in her bathroom, the door left open, the light on.

"Lose your underwear at that party?" I asked, like it was one of those things always happening at the most annoying times.

"I had my suit on underneath. Then some of us went swimming, and I realized I could either swing free or have wet blotches over my boobs the rest of the afternoon."

She couldn't swim across a puddle.

"You want looks, Lucy, but not because you look like a milk cow that's lost her calf."

"Guess you'd cause a commotion either way."

"I should hope so," she said, her voice echoing off the old tiles. I heard her flush, and a moment later she came out wearing one of Dad's T-shirts. "Is this a truce?" she asked, slipping into bed. "Are you done with your tantrum from the park?"

"Are you done walking around half dressed with strange men?"

She fluffed her pillow. "Oh, Guy's not all that strange. A little odd, I guess, but I'd draw the line at out-and-out strange. No stranger than any of them."

She was always doing that, talking about men like they were another species. I stared at her, and she said, "That's a joke, son."

She watched me, then puckered her lips into an air kiss. "Good night, Lucy," she said. "Get the light, would you?"

I held out my hand, the plastic bag with her suit dangling from my finger. "Bet this caused a whole ocean of commotion."

She waited, then said, "So what? I look good in it. You should have seen the looks on their faces."

"I can imagine."

"Truce over already?"

"You wouldn't even wear that suit for Dad."

She squinted at me. Why didn't she admit it and get glasses? "What do you think, Lucy? That I like him hitting people?"

I thought of the man at the fair, the blood between his teeth. The man who was not her Mexican dreamboat. I'd learned what "hola" meant a long time ago. "No," I said.

Then we were quiet. I wanted her to pat the bed, call me in. I would have slept there in a heartbeat, listening to her explain everything. Something.

But Mom eased herself down, her head sinking into the pillow. "Go to bed, Luce," she said, sounding tired. "Nothing's changed. Only you."

CHAPTER TEN

By the time the joys of freshman year started that fall, Dad's postcards had peaked and were already tapering away, usually a sign he'd be back soon. I worked harder on the house, scrubbing it out, keeping it tidy, getting ready.

Despite all our worries, Great Falls High was hardly different than

Paris Gibson Middle School. More kids. Bigger ones. The first day I sat in my bathroom at five o'clock in the morning, wishing for a makeover. I even hauled out Mom's old makeup, nervous enough I'd let myself start thinking like Rabia Theodora—that I could get a whole new start, completely reinvent myself. But after looking at all the colors and myself in the mirror, I slammed the drawer shut. Invisibility was definitely the way to go.

And, like usual, Kenny and I fell through the cracks. I heard "Who's the new dyke?" a few times but let it bounce off, knowing they were admiring my hairstyle. No matter what Kenny had thought, I wasn't swept up as the poster child for cool. There were enough kids trying their best to look weird that I hardly stood out at all. In a way, it was kind of disappointing. We staked out our spots at the bottom of the pecking order without a fight.

Schoolwise, the tests were the same, codes you had to break. Even if I hardly knew anything, I did better than scrape by. Teachers thought I was smart, which I told Kenny I thought was a gas, but he said, "You *are* smart."

On our way home every day, Kenny and I walked past the park, our old jungle gym, and I'd think of seeing him up there, spinning like a top. One afternoon I couldn't keep from giving him a shove, yelling, "I am the undisputed universal master of the jungle gym!" We both used to crow that from the very top.

He laughed, stepping back onto the sidewalk, putting his arm back around my waist. I stuck my fingers in his rear pocket. It wasn't that comfortable, but I liked feeling his butt flex.

Kenny came to my house every day. We'd grab something out of the refrigerator or nuke ourselves a couple of Pizza Pockets. Neither of our moms got home till after five.

Days I had to clean—vacuuming or dusting, mopping, whatever—Kenny got into the habit of helping. I thought it was weird, but it was also kind of cool to see him wipe a rag over the TV screen as the roar of the vacuum drowned us out. It was like a silent movie of us married or something. Grown-ups. I knew that was why he did it. That we were playing house.

Most days, though, we'd head straight for the couch, pretending we were going to watch a movie. We hardly ever got the TV turned on.

The first time my fingers slid under the front of his jeans—an inch in, at most—I thought I'd somehow hurt him. He stiffened up all over, and shook like a horse shooing off flies. I sat up, whispering, "You okay?" thinking, Oh, Christ, he's epileptic, and I just gave him a seizure. No wonder he's so scrawny. Maybe he's never been right.

He nodded. He couldn't talk.

I pulled my hand back up, outlining his belly button with my fingertip. He started breathing again and kissed my ear. He stuck his tongue in a little, which usually almost made me forget to breathe, but this time, for no reason at all, it made me think of Scott Booker, who we never saw at all anymore, and I couldn't stop a giggle fit.

Kenny sat up. "What?"

"Undeniable kiss number three-oh-eight." I laughed. "The Amazing Creepo Man. What ever happened to him?"

"Catholic school. His parents were that desperate."

"He'll make a great priest."

Laughing, we started back down, but the timer buzzed in the kitchen. Kenny groaned. So did I, but I pushed myself up. The timer was my idea: the only way, once we started, we could keep track of the world. "I have to start something for dinner. You hungry?"

He shrugged, and I went off to the kitchen, leaving him with the bewildered look he wore whenever I left him on the couch. "Mom will kill me if I eat now," he yelled after me.

"Why don't you stay?" I yelled back.

He stepped into the kitchen, holding out a handful of mail I hadn't noticed lying in the hallway. I shook my head. We hadn't even heard the mail slot rattle this time.

"She doesn't like me to. She hates the house empty."

"Well, who doesn't?"

"I don't," he said. "Not really."

"It gives me the creeps."

There was another card from Dad, the first in a couple of weeks. It had a picture of these five babes sitting on stools in front of a bar, their butts, which were naked, facing the camera. They had on cowboy vests and cowboy boots. It said, NO SHIRT, NO SHOES, NO SERVICE.

Before I could read the back, Kenny said, "Mind if I keep that one?"

I slapped my rear. "This is the only one you need to be looking at."

Dad had written, "Mame, how'd they find five of you?" then, in an unusually informative sentence, "Think things may wind up here soon." As always, he signed it "Chuck," like maybe we got cards like this from all kinds of people.

Kenny looked at me, seeing how things would be as fast as I did. Playing house would be over. Watching movies.

I bit my lip. "No telling when," I said, making myself feel terrible, like I hoped it'd be later rather than sooner. "He never stays long, anyway," I added, making it worse.

"Except sometimes in winter."

It was already October. "He might try for my birthday," I said. Next week.

I ran my fingers through my hair, which was long enough that I could get it down on my head instead of leaving it sticking up like a Chia Pet. "We'll have to come up with a plan," I said. "Some way to keep him away from the motorboat."

Kenny smiled. "You never believe me. I like the way he cuts it."

"You don't like it now?" I'd actually spent time on it this morning, slathering on Mom's gel, combing and blowing.

He stammered: "I like it all ways."

I gave him a look. "I got to cook dinner."

"Okay." He dove in for a kiss, but I turned my head, taking it on the cheek. I couldn't let that get started again.

"See you tomorrow," I said. "Hope you get a good batch of Helper." He said they ate it every night. Hamburger Helper. How could anyone stay so skinny eating that?

That night Mom tapped the postcard against the table edge. "Lovely," she said. "Just lovely."

"At least they're slimmer than those first two." Since I was a little kid, I had taped Dad's cards together, picture side out, down the front of the refrigerator. The day he'd leave, I'd take down the old string and wait to start the new one. I had them all saved in a box under my bed.

Mom looked at the top card, the enormous lovers, then back at the five cowgirl butts. "True," she said. "Some fine derrieres there."

"Nothing we don't have," I assured her.

"Honey, everybody's got an ass."

" 'Just because you have one doesn't mean you have to be one.' "

Mom smiled. "Or marry one."

"Think it'll be soon?" I asked.

"Never can tell with that man."

She sounded the way I had with Kenny. Like Dad's arrival was something that had to be prepared for. Like things would have to be put on hold. Like this wasn't the day we'd been waiting for since he last stuck up his hand for a right turn and swung away left.

The way it used to be.

Mom handed over the postcard. "You've been keeping the house nice," she said. "At least that's ready."

"Kenny helps."

She swung her gaze back to me. "He does?"

It was a slipup, mentioning it. A violation of my new rule: allowing out only the minimum of information. Tit for tat. Tick for tock. Mom hardly ever said what she did anymore. Twice since school started, she'd called at five and told me she wouldn't be home for dinner. Me standing there with it cooked. Or practically. When she got home, all she'd say was that she'd worked late, happy for the overtime. I could picture the way Dad slammed the phone down on telemarketers calling during dinner. How it made me jump.

"Why would Kenny help you clean?" she asked.

"He's a 'nice kid.' Remember?"

"He's a boy." She leaned in close, studying me. "A *teenage* boy."

"What?" I insisted, all innocent.

"That's what I'd like to know. What exactly goes on here?" She sighed, like knowing was the last thing she wanted.

"The house *is* clean, Mom. If we spent all our time power boinking, how could it get clean?"

"Power boinking? Good Lord." She dropped her face into her hands, rubbing at her eyes, her forehead.

I laughed a little. "Well, what do *you* call it?"

"Power boinking? Where on earth did you get that?"

I giggled. "Well?"

Mom pointed a finger at me, smiling. "Listen, young lady, you better not even be *thinking* about boinking. Power or otherwise." She curled her finger in with the others, making a fist. "I'd show you a thing or two about boinking."

"Pow, zoom?"

"You better believe it, honey. Straight to the moon."

She pushed back her chair and slid her plate onto the counter.

I thought we were done, that I was off the hook, the best defense a strong offense, but Mom dinked around at the sink, and said, "Luce, I think if Kenny's going to be around, you might want to do him a favor. Wear your bra. For his sake."

I didn't get out "What for? What would I put inside it?" quite fast enough. My face went hot.

Mom rearranged some dishes. "You're growing up, Lucy. You know that."

I was about to strike back with her Fourth of July attire, but she turned from the sink. "It's not fair to him. Driving him wild like that." She smiled. "You don't even know the effect you have yet."

I tried to smile back. I knew exactly what kind of effect I had on Kenny. Shelving my plate with Mom's, I turned for the living room as nonchalantly as I could. There, sticking out from between the couch cushions, was the tail end of my bra. I snatched it up, stuffing it into my jeans as I headed for the stairs.

In my room, I kicked the door shut behind me and slid my arms out of my sleeves. I worked my bra on and hooked it without taking off my shirt. Same way I'd wriggled out of it while Kenny panted beneath me. No matter how much he fumbled, he could never open it himself. He'd have been useless as a girl.

Down the hall I heard Mom's door close with a solid click.

CHAPTER ELEVEN

Dad didn't get home for my birthday. Mom took the day off, trying to make up for it, but that only kept Kenny away, and Mom and I didn't know what to do with each other anymore. No more than Kenny and I did, if we weren't mauling each other on the couch. She ordered a pizza for dinner, giving me the night off, and afterward she gave me a beautifully wrapped box. Definitely a store job. I tore into it, and found a Victoria's Secret bra and panty set; sheer baby-blue see through, edged with this like black lace piping. Would have been a struggle to cover a freckle with the pair. "Mom," I said, "these are obscene." They'd stop Kenny's heart.

She winked at me and shrugged. "If you've got it, flaunt it."

She'd spent half the afternoon making me a cake, refusing to let me help. After I blew out the candles, we tried our best with it, but she'd left something out. The sugar, I think. When we glanced at each other at the same time, Mom spat her bite out onto her plate and we burst out laughing. We practically suffocated. It was the best part of the day.

The next morning, Kenny showed up the second Mom left. He gave me a necklace. This tiny golden necklace, with an even smaller golden heart. Mine. A necklace. Me. Like I was some sort of girl. I hit him over the head with the box. But really it was the best present I ever got. Like I was a girl.

A couple of weeks later it was still just me and Mom. Not another postcard. Kenny and I watched a few movies, but I couldn't get into it, not thinking about Dad sneaking through the door, planning one of his big surprises, finding me with my fingers inched under Kenny's waistband, Kenny's hand inside my shirt. I left Mom's birthday present in my drawer, for Kenny's health. It made me almost sick to my stomach, thinking of how Kenny would sound hitting the floor. The snap of his bones. *Fe fi fo fum, I smell the blood of a little man. Grind his bones to make my bread.*

Then Mom missed another dinner. She called at quitting time. More overtime.

I asked, "How are you going to hide your job from him when he's home?"

There was silence.

"I mean, if you can't even make it home for dinner?"

"You've got your own arrangements to worry about, Luce. Leave mine to me."

Steam trembled the lid I'd cocked ajar over two potatoes. Two chicken thighs sat in soy sauce. I'd been planning to barbecue. "What should I do with all this food?" I asked. "Couldn't you think to call before I started cooking?"

More quiet. I knew, if she was calling from work, she'd have her headset on. I could imagine the way she'd rub her forehead, her eyes. "These things pop up, Lucy. It's not like I come to work planning them."

"Your overtime?"

"What else would I be talking about?"

I didn't chance an answer.

"Maybe Kenny could eat with you."

Now she *wanted* him here alone with me. "His mom likes to eat with him."

"So do I, honey."

"You like eating with Kenny?"

I could hear her blow air past the mouthpiece. "I'm sorry about dinner, Luce, but I have to go."

"Go?"

"Get to work. God. Would you leave me alone!"

The lid had slipped down over the potatoes rattling with the escaping steam. "You're leaving *me* alone," I said, too soft on purpose.

"What?"

"I got to go, too, Mom. Run over to Kenny's to see if he can use some of this dinner. Maybe I'll take it all to them. Start my own catering business. Call it Dinners for *Two*."

"Twist the knife, Luce," she said.

I heard her click off, but I shouted, "When will you be home?" Like shouting would get across the severed connection. I hung up, then went out and started the grill. Warming it up. A wasp was hovering over the chicken bowl before I got the match blown out.

I walked over to Kenny's. Even though Mrs. Bahnmiller had the porch staked out, I pushed on. "Is he home?"

She nodded. "I like your hair. You should let it grow out."

"Jeez, I never thought of that."

She narrowed her eyes, studying me. "You're going to be one of the pretty ones, aren't you?" She shook her head. "Poor little Kenny."

"What's that supposed to mean?"

"If you don't already know, you will soon."

"I just came to see if Kenny wanted any dinner. A break from hamburger."

I saw Kenny standing in his doorway, shadowy behind the glinty black screen. "Hey, Lucy," he said, the only person in the world who never called me Luce, who always took the time.

"Mom just called," I said. "She's got to work, and I have dinner going. Want to eat?"

Kenny stepped out onto the porch.

"Feel free to join us," I said to Mrs. B. I'd never seen her anywhere besides this porch. She didn't even smile.

"Mom doesn't like me to—" Kenny started.

"Oh, come on," I said. "For once."

Kenny hesitated. "I'll leave her a note."

"I'll let her know where you are," Mrs. Bahnmiller said.

But Kenny was already inside. I followed without thinking. Anything was better than staying out there with her.

Kenny jumped at the second bang of the screen. "What are you doing?"

"Getting away from her."

"She's not so bad."

"Didn't you hear her?"

Kenny shrugged, and I knew he'd heard at least "Poor little Kenny."

I stepped up and kissed him. Full on the mouth. All tongue. Undeniable kiss 524. Poor Scott hadn't scratched the surface. I ground my hips into Kenny's making sure he didn't feel like a poor little anybody.

When I broke it off, he stood there with his hand moving over my butt, absentmindedly, like you'd pet a dog while you talked to its owner. "I better write that note," he said, and started sifting through a pile of stuff on the kitchen table, searching for a piece of paper. The table was inches deep in it. He found an envelope, scribbled something, then looked for a place to leave it.

I'd been trying to find the same thing. Their house was an absolute hole. Smaller and dingier than it looked from the street. The pattern on the linoleum was worn through, or it seemed like it might be, through the dirt. A pot handle stuck out from the sink. A line of empty green wine bottles bordered the refrigerator. No wonder he never let me in here.

Kenny cracked open the refrigerator, then closed it, pinching the note under the door's rubber gasket.

"You ever think we should clean *this* place once?" I said.

Kenny turned, totally not amused. I followed him into the living room, where a blanket lay crumpled on the floor in front of the couch. A pillow slid halfway after it. His bed? His mom's?

For some reason, that made me think of Dad gone, Mom not coming home. "What happened with your mom and dad?" I asked. I'd known Kenny practically my whole life, and I'd never asked. "How'd it start?"

"I don't know," he said, and he was quiet a long time before saying, "I think they just didn't like having me. Dad, I mean. It wasn't what he thought it'd be."

"What? You?"

"Having a kid. I think I screwed up his 'lifestyle.' " He smiled this tiny smile, letting me know his dad was not someone he expected a lifestyle to ever happen to. But Kenny thought my dad was the greatest guy in the world. Once Dad found me and Kenny in the park, and he called, "Dinnertime, Luce. Bring along your compatriot. We could use some fresh meat."

But after Kenny went home and I was doing the dishes, I heard Mom from the living room. "Well, think about it, Chuck. If he's here, where is she?"

My hands went still in the hot water.

"Sitting alone in her house is where," Mom answered herself.

"You think she doesn't enjoy a night off now and then?"

"Sitting with the dinner she made for both of them because you ask him over two minutes before dinnertime? You think that might bring back some memories? You think that might make her feel that much more abandoned?"

"It was just a dinner, Mame."

"Well, think first. That's all I'm saying. If you'd planned it for one second, we could have asked her, too."

"Oh, that would be great fun."

Mom must have given him a look, because the next thing I heard was Dad's laugh. "Come on, what's her name? Quick!"

"I don't know, but—"

"Hello, Lenny's mom? This is Lucy's dad, and I was wondering if you'd care to—"

"For Christ's sake, Chuck, it's not a date."

And then they were off, laughing, going over different ways to ask each other out, calling each other so-and-so's mom, or dad or sister or child. "Hello, madam, you don't know me, but your son has designs on my daughter, and I think it is high time we had a confatuation—"

"A *what?*" Mom giggled.

The whole time Kenny was walking back to this mess. His mom waiting, doubly abandoned.

And I was asking him to do it again. Leave her alone. Here.

Kenny walked down the dark hall. "Come on," he said. "We going or not?"

CHAPTER TWELVE

By the time we reached my driveway, we could see the smoke. We ran back, and Kenny whipped open the smoking barbecue lid. "Guess that's hot enough," I said, trying to make him smile.

He said, "So, now you know."

"Know what?" I asked, but I knew what he was talking about. "Well, so you spend all your time over here, helping me clean. Let's trade shifts. Don't think I haven't ever let our house go too long." We both knew my house had never looked like his.

I turned back to the grill, forked on the chicken, then remembered. "Oh, shit, the potatoes!"

Inside, I yanked the pan off the stove, the water only a few starchy bubbles on the bottom. "Another second, the place would've been up in flames."

"That would be the only way to fix my house."

I splashed a shot of water into the pan to keep the spuds from scorching, then took Kenny's hand and pulled him into the living room, down onto the couch. "You think it's easy for your mom?"

"It's not her fault," he said. "It's mine."

"It's your dad's," I whispered, licking his ear. He kissed back, and pretty soon I had my finger inside his waistband. More than an inch. For the first time ever, I was holding it. I could feel Kenny's heart racing right against my chest.

I scrunched down, kissing Kenny's chest, then his belly, my hand working open the buttons of his fly. I thought he'd die, but I suddenly wanted to actually see it. I pushed down his boxers, and it popped out alone in the open.

Kenny was paralyzed, quivering and frozen, a bank-tossed trout.

I gave it this tiny kiss. Undeniable what?

It's what the girls at school always talked about, how it wasn't sex but the boys still loved it. I could hear the boys teasing. "Suck! Suck! Blow's just an expression!"

I felt so bad for him, running away from his house like a little kid, that pretty soon I wasn't just kissing it. I was into a real Lewinsky. Or so I guessed. I didn't know a thing about it.

But Kenny's breath was coming in these huge gasps, and for a few minutes, I knew it made no difference where he lived, what his mom was like. I almost smiled, even doing what I was doing. Like I was doing something good. Diamond Girl to the rescue.

Then Kenny squeaked, "Lucy, look out."

His head was tilted back over the arm of the couch. I could only see his chin, the stubs of a few black hairs, a couple of ingrown red bumps starting to swell. He shaved.

Then his thing erupted.

I jumped back, some of it in my mouth. My eyes wide.

Kenny covered his thing with his hands. "I'm sorry, Lucy."

I looked around like I might suddenly find a sink sprouting from the couch.

"Mean people suck!" the boys would shout at some girl they'd surrounded. "Nice people swallow!"

I ran to the kitchen and spat into the sink, gushed water all over. Took mouthfuls out of the faucet.

It wasn't so horrible, really. I mean, if you'd been expecting it.

What in the world had I been expecting?

I'd only pictured that house of his. His mother holed up in there. Just the two of them. Mrs. Bahnmiller already knowing more about me than I did.

Then I had this image of Dad coming in, me on the end of Kenny's deal. I had to hold on to the sink to stand up.

Kenny touched my back. "Lucy?"

I could feel the tears coming. I turned off the water, ran my hands over my face.

"Oh, Christ," I said. "The chicken."

What was left looked more like raisins. I jabbed the long tines of the fork through the black crust of one piece, then the other. I walked into the alley, opened the dumpster, and scraped them in.

I wiped my eyes and looked across the length of the backyard to the house. Kenny was at the grill, turning off the gas.

"I wasn't hungry anyway," he called.

"There's still potatoes."

Playing house.

As I walked back toward him, I couldn't help a glance down at his fly. All buttoned up safe. Then I found I couldn't lift my eyes. Couldn't meet his. I was afraid he was going to apologize. "You want a potato?" I asked.

He didn't answer. In a minute, he said, "I suppose I should get home."

"Okay," I said, and slipped past him through the back door.

I didn't expect him to follow me, but he started again. "Lucy—"

"So, what is it?" I interrupted. "She won't clean, or she can't, or what?"

Kenny took a step back. "She's tired is all." He ducked his head. "She comes home and collapses. Spends the weekends saying she's got to rest up for the week."

"Drinks," I said, remembering the long row of green bottles in Kenny's kitchen.

Kenny shrugged.

"You could do it," I said. "Help out."

"I'd rather be over here."

I waved my hand around. "Palace like this, who wouldn't?"

Kenny stopped. "Why do you always do that?"

I raised my eyebrows, still not quite making eye contact.

"Why do you always have to make fun of everything?"

"Genetics."

"Well, you should think about it first. Think about how good it really is over here before you start pretending it's not."

I did look at him then. Skewered him with my eyes. "Maybe you should stick to talking about what you know about."

"I know I'd move over here in a second. That I'd give anything to be like you guys."

"Trade places with *me?*"

"I didn't say trade. I wouldn't even do that to Scott. I mean join, not trade."

Him wanting in on this. Mom gone. Me spitting into the sink. Dad hovering out there somewhere, keeping us guessing. I shook my head. "Overtime, my ass."

Kenny tilted his head.

"Never mind. You sure you don't want a potato?"

"No. I got to go."

Maybe I'd grossed him out. "How come? What's the sudden rush?"

"Mom," he answered, making it sound like that explained everything. "It helps if I'm home."

"She can eat alone now and then. I mean, what's she going to do if you're gone?"

He widened his eyes. "Drink," he said at last, like "Duh!"

"Oh," I said.

He was already backing toward the door. He left without saying anything else. There wasn't even a stab at a kiss. I thought of my lips, my tongue, my mouth. *Don't touch that thing! You don't know where it's been!*

But Kenny knew.

"I was only trying to help," I said, but he was already gone.

I wandered into the kitchen. The potatoes had scorched, the bottoms flat and black. I carried the pan out to the Dumpster and just resisted throwing it in after the chicken and potatoes.

"I'm a good cook," I whispered, looking back toward our empty house, the scorch of our dinner overpowering the usual garbage reek. I gave the Dumpster a whack with the pan. "I am."

CHAPTER THIRTEEN

It snowed, and still no Dad. I went to school. Mom went to work. Sometimes she worked till ten. Eleven. She'd poke her head into my room on her way to bed and whisper, "Sweet dreams." I'd pretend to be asleep.

Telemarketing at eleven at night. Sales in Outer Mongolia must be skyrocketing. Who on earth did she think she was fooling? Kenny and me doing what we were doing made it seem pretty obvious what she was after, with all her sneaking around. Sometimes Kenny and me would practically run home from school to get at each other that much quicker. In history, my last class, it was all I could think about. I'd get all squirmy, at the same time I wondered what was wrong with me. Even with Dad headed our way, Kenny and I couldn't keep from grinding each other into the couch like we were trying to erase something, underwear our last thin line of defense.

At school, I never let Kenny touch me, no walking arm in arm, all slouched over each other like some of the more pathetic specimens. But what we did after school must have given off pheromones, drawing the boys in to my flame. Even Justin Haven, the head rooster in the school's every pecking order, one day suddenly stood blocking our path down the hallway. "Hey, Lucy," he said, like I was completely alone and waiting for this chance. Like it was perfectly normal that he'd know my name. Him *the* senior. Me a freshman. We had of course, never spoken a single word, exchanged a single glance.

"Hey," I said back, stepping around him, bumping shoulders with

Kenny, who had to kind of jump to get back in step beside me.

Justin one-eightied without a hitch, as close to me on one side as Kenny on the other. "Where've you been hiding?" he asked.

I dropped my jaw wide the way Mom would. "Me?"

Justin smiled. "Yeah, you. I keep hoping I'll see you around. At a party or something. After a game."

His letter jacket was covered with pins and badges and stripes. It was so old the sleeves didn't smell like leather anymore, the way the new kids' did. Like he'd been born in it or something. "Are you in sports?" I asked.

He laughed, bobbing his head the way Dad would, admitting he'd walked into one.

Kenny stomped along beside me, hands bottomed out in his pockets, glaring at the floor, his feet, his every step. A red splotch the size of a quarter blazed on each cheek.

"I never go to parties," I said. I stopped right before asking why he'd look for me in places I'd never been. Why he'd look for me at all. "I never go anywhere."

"Well, you should start. It'd be good seeing you around. Be good seeing more of you."

He started to veer off, then hesitated. My steps faltered, and I could feel the automatic bloom of my own cheeks.

Justin looked puzzled. "It's not true, is it? What they say?"

I rolled my eyes, but I waited.

"About the kindergartner you hang with. What do they call him? The Kernel?"

Kenny not inches away. Completely invisible to Justin Haven.

"It's all true," I said. "I mean, who could ever lie to you."

Justin nodded, still smiling. "Not to these big blues."

"Exactly what I meant," I said, tapping my temple.

I started walking again, away from him. He walked backward, watching me, knowing the crowds would part for him. "Well, see you around, I hope," he called.

"See ya, see ya, wouldn't want to be ya," I answered, turning completely away from him, heading to class. "Adios, amoebas."

Kenny was like this nuclear-waste dump beside me, glowing deadly radiation. I could almost hear the grind of his molars.

"Isn't he the greatest!" I said, all smitten.

Kenny didn't bite.

I got to the door of my next class. "Well, see you."

It was like saying the sky was blue. Kenny, no matter how far apart our classes might be, was always waiting for me when I got out, to walk with me to my next class.

Down the hall, the crowd was thinning into different doorways. I leaned forward to give Kenny a kiss, our first ever in school, but he took it on the lips like a grandmother, without budging a muscle to kiss back.

He looked somewhere down near my feet. "Maybe now you'll believe me when I tell you how beautiful you are."

"Yeah, me and the Elephant Man. You and your cataracts."

"Would you shut up for once! Justin Haven. You're the only one who can't see it!"

"What do you think just happened?" I shot right back. "Think I just gave him a blow job in the hallway?"

Going into class, Carly Blount almost walked into the doorway.

"You think I started that?" I asked Kenny. "Did you hear me say, 'Hey, Justin, where've you been keeping yourself?'"

"No," he had to answer.

"Well, get over it then. Justin Haven. Give me some credit for taste."

"Oh yeah," he muttered. "A fate worse than death. Like the whole school would mourn for you."

"Since when do you care what anybody in this school thinks?"

He stared down.

"I got to go," I said. The hallways were empty. "So do you. You're late."

He just stood there. The mope.

"Thanks for the great kiss. Undeniable number zero."

I turned in to the classroom, Mr. Mueller already talking, giving me a look. I barely heard Kenny say, "See you later, crocodile."

But he was right there after my last class, like he'd never left, like always, walking close enough that you'd think somebody was trying to pry us apart. My very own barnacle.

CHAPTER FOURTEEN

Spaghetti for dinner that night. That I ate myself. Not even a call from Mom bitching about her overtime. I called Kenny, but he said his mom was home.

"Okay," I said. "I did mention that this was my world-famous spaghetti? Not SpaghettiOs. Not Hamburger Helper."

"Mom's home," he said again.

"Bring her along."

There was a long silence.

Holding the phone away, I called, "Forget it, Justin, he's got to eat with his mom."

The silence stretched until Kenny said, "That's pretty hysterical."

"Justin says he's got to eat it all anyway, what with the big game and all."

"I got to go, Lucy. Before I die laughing."

I waited for him, then hung up myself. Okay, so that was not a laughing matter, me and Justin Haven, though it was pretty hysterical if Kenny had actually thought about it.

I sat down in front of my spaghetti and spent most of the rest of that night thinking about it. Me walking down the halls with Justin, everybody oozing envy instead of recoiling, wondering who the bald chick was. Not sneaking around with Kenny. Or even getting Justin on the couch, somebody built like that, a man's body pressed against mine instead of Kenny's little-boy one. It wasn't the worst thing I'd ever thought about.

But it was only thinking. I didn't have anything else to do.

Mom didn't come home.

I went up to bed eventually but woke sometime in the middle of the night, realizing I hadn't heard her. I staggered out and checked her room. Bed unmade but empty. The way she always left it.

I went in and sat down on the rumpled blankets. Checked her clock. One-twenty-one A.M. "Mom?" I said.

I sat awhile, trying to think. Making sales calls at 1:21. That kind of initiative could cost a person her job.

I shivered but resisted the urge to lie down and pull up her blankets. I didn't want her to think anything but that I'd been up waiting. So I turned on her closet light, searching for the big terry-cloth robe Dad had brought home for her once, a hotel's monogram across the pocket. Her buffalo robe, she called it, because it was so thick she said that's what it made her look like. She never wore anything that made her look big.

I saw myself in the mirror, pulling it on. There was a glimpse of pale blue panties, a flash of tummy, then my Supergirl T-shirt, the robe tied down over everything. Buffalo girl. My hair was flattened on one side and sticking up on top.

I stuck out a hip. "Call room service, would you, Justin?" I whispered. "Be a dear and order me a full stack." I stretched. "You know how hungry it always makes me."

I couldn't quite smile. I stared at myself, my fish eyes. "What are you ordering, Mom? What's Horse Teeth calling down for you?"

I tugged the bulb's pull string and stood still, trying to adjust to the darkness.

I walked back to her bed, stuck the pillows up against the headboard, and sat down to wait. I started lining up my questions: *Where on earth have you been? What do you think you're doing? Don't you think of anyone besides yourself? How could you do this to us?*

"Shit," I whispered. "This is supposed to be *your* job, Mom."

I kept staring at the clock, the automatic switch of its square red numbers. By four my eyeballs were scratchy, my stomach gnawing on itself. My hands trembled. I thought about going down and starting coffee, but even that would look too ordinary, too comfortable.

"Mom," I said, something to break the quiet. Then I said it again. I practically yelled it, my voice thin and spidery in the empty house.

So this is what it's like for her, I thought, sitting here alone without Dad. Me out cold in my room, or sitting up just as alone, wanting nothing more than to get my hands back on Kenny. Or Justin. Suddenly, instead of being mad, I felt rotten for always leaving Mom here on her own. This was what it was going to feel like for me now, too, I realized; being alone, Mom off finding some life of her own, Dad wherever.

It wasn't a lot to look forward to.

I was still kind of awake when I heard the door scrape open. I had missed the car pulling in. It was dark outside, the window black and blank. I rubbed my face, sat up straighter, pulled the pillows out from behind me.

Mom moved quietly. I heard the rustle of her coat as she hooked it over the banister, something I'd seen her do so many times I could see it even in the dark. I turned enough to glance at the clock. Five-forty-seven.

I heard Mom take her first steps up the stairs, then turn at the top. As soon as she was in the doorway, I said, "Home again, home again."

I heard the catch of her breath. "Lucy?"

I didn't say a thing.

She clicked on the closet light, not blinding us with the overhead. "What are you doing?"

"What am *I* doing?"

She had her shoes in her hand, that ready for stealth. "Unbelievable night," she said, blowing out this exhausted breath. "I wound up sleeping down there. Then realized how I would look this morning. Sneaked home for a shower and a change of clothes. Then back to start the whole thing over by eight."

"Riggedy jig," I said.

Mom tossed her shoes in the closet, looking around me instead of at me.

"Working all night?"

She nodded. "I have got to hit the shower, Luce. Would you mind putting coffee on? Bless your lifesaving heart."

"You were *working* all night?"

She nodded again, turning her liar's face away from me, heading for the bathroom like a kid playing tag, pouring it on for base.

I snorted out a laugh. "Come on, Mom. You're going to have to do better than that. Where were you calling? Uzbekistan? 'I understand that you don't have electricity, but this Mixmaster will be what everyone wants first. You don't want to fall behind the curve.'"

She stopped in the doorway, leaning a shoulder in to the jamb as she turned to really look at me. For the first time, it seemed, in ages. "Nobody wants to be the one left behind."

"Especially at two in the morning. Three. Four."

"You stayed up all night?" She seemed sorry about that. My sleep. "I should have called," she said.

"He didn't have a phone?"

Mom studied me. "Nice robe," she said. "Looks good on you."

"Buffalo Bob. That's me."

She smiled. "You can get away with it. The way you're put together these days."

"Think Horse Teeth would like it?"

She didn't answer.

"If you think he might, you should take it with you next time. I'll get by without it. Here. Alone. I don't mind."

"Don't mind the robe or Horse Teeth?" She caught herself. "Guy."

I threw back the blankets and sat up straight. "Why are we talking about this stupid robe?"

Mom raised an eyebrow. "Is there something you'd rather talk about?"

"You. You and what you think you're doing! What you're planning on doing to us!"

"No plan," she said easily. "I wish there was."

I gaped. Her hair was ratted up in the back. Like from a pillow. She had bags under her eyes. She never went out looking like this, ever. "You look like you got something to sell." One of Dad's least complimentary lines. "What do you think Dad'll think of *that* new job?"

Mom started tapping the doorjamb with her knuckles. "You think I need to explain myself to you?"

"Me or Dad. Maybe just yourself."

"Don't you start worrying about me, Luce. You've got plenty to keep you busy right here your own self."

I threw my legs over the side of the bed. "What is that supposed to mean? Am I the one sneaking in at the crack of dawn? This is not one bit about me!"

"Am I the one leaving my bra in the couch?" she fired back. "How do you suppose that happened? Just lying there one day and decide, 'Jeez, I guess I'll take off my underwear while I watch this movie.' "

"That has nothing to do with this!"

"Are you using protection, honey? That's what I want to know."

"Are *you?*" I blurted.

"It's not like it used to be," she said, calm as an oil slick. "Sex can kill you now. Not to mention all those hideous diseases. Warts in your crouch. And pregnancy, that's not all it's cracked up to be for a fifteen-year-old, either."

"You'd know, wouldn't you!"

She eyed me. "None of this is anything I have to answer to you."

"Well, you better start thinking about who you do have to answer to."

"And that would be?"

I slapped my hand to my forehead. "Hello? Dad? Remember him? 'Take a picture, it lasts longer.' "

"Tallish guy, sandy hair? Built like he's made out of bricks?"

"Bingo."

"I remember him."

"Not so often anymore, it doesn't seem."

Mom rapped her knuckles against the doorjamb once more, then held them there, her hand a fist. "Luce, I don't have to explain anything to you, but listen, your father and I, we've, what, I mean . . ." She blew out this big breath. "I see him what, a couple times a year? You think you can call that a marriage? It's like we've been, I don't know, *dating* for fifteen years. This long-distance-romance thing. Those never work out."

"You never seemed to mind before."

"Maybe I'm growing up. At last."

"And you're going to tell him that? That you've outgrown him?"

She stared at me. "You make sure I'm the one telling anything to him, Luce. Okay? You make sure I'm the one who does any of that."

"How on earth are you going to? You'll end up like that guy at the fair."

"Your father would never, ever raise a hand to me."

"Well I sure don't like Horse Teeth's chances."

"His name is Guy."

"Whatever."

"And there is nothing going on."

"Do you think I'm two, Mom? That I don't know a thing?"

"Leave alone what you don't understand, Luce. Loose lips sink ships."

"Loose or Luce?"

We stood there then, until at last Mom said, "Okay, Luce, like I said, it's been a long night. And it's morning now, and I'm going to be late for work."

Then she turned and shut the bathroom door between us, and I heard the first knocking rush of water and air through the pipes.

CHAPTER FIFTEEN

Mom made it home for dinner every night after that. Like it was some kind of penance. I served out whatever I'd cooked, and I tried to make it kind of special, but we sat and ate like strangers. Nobody bothered with home again, home again. No more riggedy jigs.

She helped with the dishes, though that wasn't our agreement; then we'd sag into the living room, turn on the TV. Mom read magazines and catalogs, glancing up now and then when the canned laughing peaked, as if she could make out the joke then.

After the news, which she'd watch till the weather—continued arctic blasts—we'd tromp upstairs. She'd say, " 'Night, Luce," and I'd answer, "See you," and her door would snick shut. It was like she was trying to show me how much nothing we had with just the two of us.

Then, in the middle of all that, I woke up in the dark one night like I had the time she didn't come home. I had the same feeling, of something not right, but I'd seen her go into her room. I sat up, straining to hear.

There were footsteps outside, screeching across the snow on the walk, the porch. Then the front door opened, and I lay in bed, frozen myself.

The door closed quietly, not sticking the way it did in summer, and I heard someone slap himself, trying to warm up after the dash through the cold. Then the creak of the stairs, somebody big, on tiptoes. I eased back down to my pillow, smiling.

He cracked open my door, peeking in at me pretending to sleep, before sliding down the hallway to Mom. I heard him laugh once in their room, then Mom's sleepy voice asking, "Chuck?" like it could have been anyone creepy-crawling into her bedroom.

I heard him say, "You didn't have to get all slinky just for me."

Cold as it was, she must have been wearing one of his frazzled old sweatshirts.

Then there were the usual sounds.

I sat up in bed, unable to keep from picturing Kenny, how he had a hard time breathing just because I could see his. I pictured the two of us like Mom and Dad, bouncing the bed around, making all those noises. It was not, if you'd heard it off in the night somewhere, anything that sounded like love.

I wanted to grin at having him back, but those noises, knowing what they were doing, knowing I hadn't done anything like that yet myself, made smiling the wrong thing to do. I kind of tingled instead, like I was some kind of sicko. The next Scott Booker waiting to happen.

I turned to face the window, its blackness, the stars cold and tiny out there, the snow down like a guard around our house, squealing at the slightest trespass. I started to hum quietly, something to fill up my head with sound, block out their noise. I wound up with "Twinkle, Twinkle Little Star." It was the only song I could think of.

Maybe I dozed a few minutes the rest of that night, but it sure didn't feel like it. It was still black outside, those burning cold pinpricks of stars, when I edged out of bed to rummage through the floor of my closet. Kenny and I had come up with a plan to save my hair.

At last I found it, the bike helmet Dad had given me three Christmases ago. He swore it was from Santa. He still insisted there was a Santa Claus. Wouldn't hear otherwise.

Though it felt silly, I strapped the helmet on, something I would have done for real years ago, back when Kenny and I were still the undisputed universal masters of the jungle gym, before we knew what it did having a hand inside your shirt, your pants, to grind up against each other so desperately. First time I ever wore it. Dad said Santa brought it to protect me from the knocks of the world.

I was freezing. I threw on my old robe over my Supergirl T-shirt and stepped into my giant sheepskin slippers. Then I went downstairs to wait for him.

But somehow he was there first, like always. He had his cup to his lips, trying to look like he was there every day, the paper out in front of him—a Spokane paper this time, so I knew he'd been out that way—but this time it was *his* face that couldn't quite hide the surprise.

Me standing there in my bike helmet was part of it, but I watched his eyes, how they slipped up and down me, widening, taking in the changes. I hunched my shoulders, making my boobs stick out less against my thin robe, the tiny thread loops worn off in too many spots. I shifted my legs, trying to look less curved, more the same old safe, straight slat of a kid he'd left in the spring. I wished I'd taken the time to pull on a pair of sweats.

He got this fake confused look, tilting his head to the side like a flummoxed dog. "And you would be?"

I smiled, said, "Welcome home," and slid into his lap. No matter how old I got, I'd always fit there. He curled his arms around me and said, "Well, tell me all about it."

It was what he always said, waiting for me to recite everything that had happened since he left, but there was already something different, something besides all I couldn't tell him this time. His arms held me more like barrel bands than a hug. His hands, which always used to be petting and stroking, were still; afraid, I realized, to touch me any way wrong. Dad was afraid of what I'd become.

It wasn't like I was naked or anything, but it felt that way.

I could feel his head tip forward, his cheek pressing down on top of the glossy black helmet keeping him from rubbing my hair, from mowing me bald.

"You signaled right again," I said, trying, "but turned left."

He laughed, his stomach muscles bouncing me. Across the room, on the counter, wrapped in plastic and thick frost, sat the biggest turkey I had ever seen.

"Are you going to stay for Thanksgiving?" I asked before I'd told him a thing. All out of order. Thanksgiving was a week away.

He said, "You bet. Got to get that thing into the freezer." Then he asked, "Did you and Mom have breakfast?"

He meant the day he left. "Uh-huh," I answered. It seemed this whole tradition was something from another life, an ancient culture I had to struggle to remember. "At Tracy's. Mom called this hatchet-faced waitress 'honey.' She wanted to kill Mom."

"Then what?"

"I drove home," I said. I wasn't thinking.

Dad's stomach bounced me a little more. "You did, did you?"

"Mom told me to go straight home, but I stopped at the playground."

"Meet your friend there? Lenny?"

"Kenny."

"What did he think of that?"

I moved my hand down to one of Dad's and spread his fingers open, sizing mine up against his. All the lines in his hands were grimed black. My fingers almost reached the ends but were twigs compared to his.

"Was he impressed that you were driving?"

"Not so much," I said, remembering what seemed years ago. "There was another guy there. A creep."

"And?"

"After he left, Kenny and I just sat around on the jungle gym. Then I drove home."

"That's all? You get the car when you're thirteen years old and you drive home?"

"I was fourteen, Dad. The last time you left, I was still fourteen."

"Just seeing if you're on your toes," he said, patting the top of my helmet. I knew he wanted to get in there at my hair. "Sorry about the birthday. You know how it gets in summer. Got to do what you can while you can."

I pictured trees dropping all over the place. Leveled forests wherever he went. Dad screaming, "Timber!"

"The car all to yourself and you drive straight home," he marveled. "I can't beat that with a stick. If I'd had that chance when I was a kid, I'd *still* be driving."

"You still are."

Dad stopped patting my helmet. I could practically hear that turkey thawing.

"I didn't drive straight home," I said, just to be talking. "Kenny and I went to the falls."

"Oh, really."

"I kissed the creep." It just popped out.

Dad sat up straight, his lap disappearing. I scooted out onto his legs to keep myself from falling onto the floor.

"Kenny?" he asked.

"What? No. The creep. At the playground."

"What?"

"I had to."

"Why?"

"He was going to kill Kenny if I didn't."

"He held a gun to Kenny's head and said 'Kiss me'?"

"Practically," I said, but Dad put his hands on my shoulders, push-ing me far enough away that he could focus on my face, the same way he did with the newspaper.

"From the beginning," he said.

So I told him. Most of it, anyway. "He was talking gross, Dad. Then he started talking about me, like me and him did things."

"Who is this bright boy?"

"When he started doing that, Kenny kicked him off the gym. Al-most broke his neck."

"Always liked that Kenny," Dad said.

"He only talked about me like that 'cause he knew me and Kenny are friends."

"Who is this kid?"

"After he hit the ground, he was crazy mad. He was going to wait until Kenny came down, no matter how long it took. He was going to clean the playground with him, Dad. Kenny's a shrimp. He would have been dead meat. So I made him a trade."

"Who?" Dad said, listening for a name.

I couldn't believe I'd started this. I talked faster and faster. "It didn't cost me anything, Dad. One lousy kiss. I tried pretending I was you and Mom. It was gross, but it didn't hurt me or anything. Like after you leave, when Mom redoes her lipstick. Doesn't change any-thing."

Dad squinted at me. "Is that what she does?"

"Of course. After you two go all plunger, she has to fix it back up."

"And she goes on from there?"

"Did you think we hung ourselves up in a closet or something?"

"I sure didn't think you were out driving around, kissing creeps."

"That was once, and I already told you why, and—"

Dad slipped his legs to the side, grabbing my shoulders and setting me down on my feet. "Is that what your mom does, too? Drive around kissing creeps?"

"*What?*"

"Sorry," Dad said. He said it again. He got up and strode across the room, slapping an open hand down on the turkey. Frost flaked off, making a white ring on the counter. "Can you believe the size of this bird? No wonder they can't fly, big lump like that."

"Turkeys can fly, Dad. We're not talking dodoes."

He cracked a tiny smile. "No. I suppose not." Taking a step back toward me, he pulled my head against his chest. "So, what's the deal with the hard hat?"

"No deal," I answered. "Utterly nonnegotiable."

"What's that?"

"The helmet. It stays."

He rapped his knuckles against the hard plastic. "A regular Fort Knox of a kid."

"A Fort Knox with hair."

"Now tell me," he said. "Who's the creep?"

"Don't know. Haven't seen him since. I don't think anybody recovers from my kiss."

"Just like your mother." He laughed. "And where was she during all this driving and kissing?"

"I dropped her off. She was going to be late."

"Late for what?"

I closed my eyes. Loose lips.

"For what?" Dad said.

"She had a meeting." It couldn't have sounded more like a lie if I'd tried.

"The day I left? First thing that morning?"

I could feel him peering down, trying to see through my helmet, though I didn't dare peek out from under its edge.

"What kind of meeting? With who?"

I whispered, "For her job." It was better than what else he could think.

After a long while, standing there holding me, he said, "So, you've had enough of the buzz cut. Driving. Kissing creeps. Guess you want that hair falling all over your face. Something to hide behind."

Easing away from him, I unstrapped the helmet, let it hang by my side. My hair was inches long now. I could feel it sticking up all over, bed-head and helmet-head wrapped into one glam package. "This was a joke. Something to make you laugh."

"So you're still good with the buzz?"

I shook my head. "I'm done with that. And I don't need any helmet to prove it. I'm just done. I'm not a kid anymore, Dad."

He smiled, held out his arm for me to slip back under. "You'll always be my kid," he said. "Can't change the facts, ma'am." He finally got to rub his hand back and forth across my head. "I guess, with a do like this, I understand why you'd want to stick with it."

Standing there under his giant, quick arm, his hand on my head, I heard Mom coming down, felt the stiffening in Dad when she came into the kitchen. He didn't say anything to her, didn't call her his dreamboat or beautiful baby, any of his usual things.

Mom said, "Good morning, everybody," like we were a crowd. She whisked open the refrigerator, pulled out eggs and cheese. "If you'd called, we'd have had bacon."

Apparently this was not a Special K kind of morning.

Dad swiveled enough to keep watching her, me twisting under his arm. "Don't make yourself late for your job."

Mom was at the stove, her arm up, ready to bring an egg down against the side of the pan. She hesitated, looking at the egg. "Later, huh, Chuck?"

"Don't I send enough? You want me staying out longer? Sending back more?"

"That's not it."

"Well?"

She turned slowly from the stove. "It's something to do, Chuck. What exactly do you picture the two of us doing while you're gone?"

"I picture the *two* of you, that's what. A kid with parents. I picture you free to raise Lucy right. Every tree I put a saw to, I picture you having that chance. Not letting our daughter raise herself, not letting one more catch-key kid loose on the world."

"Latchkey," I whispered.

"She's at school all day," Mom said.

"You're supposed to be here when she's not. Lunches."

"She eats at school."

"After school. In the summers."

"And what am *I* supposed to do? What am I here for?"

"To watch out for her!" Dad said, his voice getting too loud.

Mom laughed, nothing funny. "Hell, Chuck, if you were around enough to know her, you'd want her watching out for me!"

My parents did not fight. I swung out from under my dad's arm to watch.

"This is something we figured out a long time ago," Dad said. "Why do you have to screw it up now?"

"A long time ago?" Mom waved in my direction. "No kidding!"

"Yeah. Seemed to work fine the last fourteen years."

"Fifteen," Mom snapped. "Don't you think anything changes? Hell, we were her age then."

Mom still shaving off a few of her years.

Dad ran a hand through his hair, taking a deep breath. "What is it exactly that you do?" he asked, trying to sound normal, like this was an everyday breakfast chat.

When it seemed that Mom wouldn't answer, that it might be more likely she'd say something along the lines of *"None of your business,"* I blurted, "Telemarketing, Dad. That's all."

"When did this happen?" he asked, still to Mom, like I was on some other planet.

But Mom had her back turned and was cracking too many eggs into the pan. They spattered in the hot butter.

"While you were gone, Dad," I said, shaving my own year. "A month or two ago."

Dad looked over at me. "Why don't you go on up and get ready for school, Lucy. You still go to school, don't you?"

"Dad, it's no big deal, nothing's changed. I can take care of myself. I'm fifteen."

"Go get ready," he said.

I wondered if he thought classes started at six, but I kept my mouth shut.

Though she usually fried Dad's eggs, Mom started whipping them around with a fork, the steel making hard, skittering sounds against the pan.

"Here, Mom," I said, stepping up beside her. "You might want this." I held the helmet out to her.

She glanced at me but wouldn't smile. "That didn't take you long, did it, Luce?"

CHAPTER SIXTEEN

I walked into the living room, then heard the swish-swoosh of the push-through kitchen door we always left stuck open against the wall. Picturing Dad, his quick wrist flip pitching the door shut behind me, I turned to see its dusty white face swing once more, then stand shut. Behind it their voices went up, and I walked away so as not to hear.

It was just dawn, but I snagged my coat and pulled it on over my robe and walked outside. My nose pinched shut with my first cloudy breath, and the snow squeaked so loud I thought they'd have to follow me out and bring me back. I wished they would. I wished I'd brought a hat, too, mittens, at least sweatpants, my boots instead of slippers, but rather than risking a return, I dashed down through the gate Dad had left open in his hurry last night, out past his pickup, now glazed over with frost. I went straight to Kenny's. No Mrs. Bahnmiller. They'd have to chip her out of her chair in weather like this. I wondered what she did for entertainment all winter.

I stood at Kenny's door a minute, thinking about how early it was, then tapped on it anyway. I danced around, waiting, trying to stay warm. No answer. I knocked again. Then I tried the knob. Open. I stepped in, whispered, "Kenny?"

As much as I could see, the place was the same as it was before. Except this time his mom was on the couch with the blanket. I could see her hair poking out. The TV was on with no sound but she wasn't watching. She was turned in to the back of the couch.

I tiptoed to the kitchen. I didn't even know where Kenny slept. I'd guessed he used the couch. I found the bathroom on the back side of the kitchen, and beyond that, Kenny's room. I saw him in the tangle of blankets and softly said his name, but he didn't move any more than his mom. "Kenny," I said again.

Still nothing.

Their house didn't seem much warmer than outside. I hugged myself, looking at him all wrapped up tight. I crept in and lifted the edge of his blankets. He didn't move until I started to slide in there with him.

"Mom?" he mumbled. "Are you okay?"

"Shhh. Your mom's asleep."

"Lucy?"

"No. Britney Spears. Move over."

"What time is it? What's going on? What are you doing here?"

"Shhh," I said. "I'm freezing. I need to warm up."

He let me stretch out next to him. Cautiously, he put his arm around me. I still had my coat on, my robe. "What happened, Lucy?"

"Dad came home."

He waited.

"Mom and him are fighting. He found out about her job." Even under the blankets, I kept shivering.

"You're freezing," he said.

"I noticed."

"You can stay here as long as you need."

I kissed his cheek. Me staying here. Out of the fire into the frying pan.

"I can't believe you came here," he said, his amazement not quite hiding his joy.

"It's no big deal. I mean, it's not like they're throwing things at each other. I never even heard them shout before."

" 'It's no big deal'? Lucy, this is the first time you've ever been in my house."

"Second," I said.

"Okay. Right. Definitely first time in my bed, though."

"Probably should have made an appointment, huh."

"Pretty darn lucky it was empty."

Only Kenny would call a bed he was sleeping in empty.

He ran his fingertips over my cheek and neck, the only exposed skin. He always touched me that way, lighter than tickling, like he was afraid that if he pressed too hard, I might realize he was there, might come to my senses.

We started kissing. Just to warm up.

It didn't take long to find out he slept naked. Totally. His thing jabbing all over the place.

I took my jacket off. Then my robe. It was getting way too hot.

Later, after he found out I wasn't wearing any pants, I asked, "How long's your mom going to be asleep?"

Kenny craned up on an elbow. "Half an hour, maybe longer. She's got to be at work at eight." He had his hand inside the elastic band of my panties. Pretty soon they kind of slid off. It just kind of happened. Our only protection.

I sat on top of him. Kenny's hands went up under my Supergirl shirt, still touching that way, like breezes.

I wanted to tell him about Mom and Dad at night, how I heard, how I thought of him. I put a hand on either side of his head. If I'd had hair, it would have been tumbling into his face.

His hands drew feathery circles around my nipples.

I shifted my weight, sliding my knees up alongside his waist.

He kind of slipped into me before either of us expected it. Almost like it was a surprise. Not something we meant.

It hurt a little. I bit my lip. I thought of Mom and Dad last night. I moved up a bit, then down.

"Lucy," Kenny said, his words hardly making it out. "Are you all right?"

I moved again.

Then so did Kenny.

Then me, then him, both of us starting to move together.

We didn't make any noises like Mom and Dad. I wondered what we were doing wrong.

Just as we started to figure out maybe our first things, me up while him down, then coming back at each other, then away again, Kenny kind of jerked backward, out of me. He rolled fast to his side, his breath gasping out. I was still trying to move right. I came down on the edge of his hipbone.

"Ouch," I said. "Christ." .

Kenny apologized.

The first time you'll remember the rest of your life. Lasted maybe two minutes. If that. Stung. Kenny apologizing. The whole time me wondering what the hell I was doing. Kenny. The Kernel. My best friend.

Then I realized what he was doing, what he'd done. Early withdrawal. What we'd learned was not an effective form of birth control.

Birth control.

Pregnancy.

This all comes faster than it ever should. I mean, you can test-drive a stupid car.

I swung a leg up over Kenny and sat on the edge of his bed, burrowing for my panties in the crumple of blankets.

Behind me, Kenny said, "Lucy, you know I love you, don't you?"

"Love?" I said, strangling over it. "For Christ's sake, we're fifteen years old."

I pulled my panties on. I still wore my shirt, and I whipped on my robe, then jammed my arms into my coat sleeves, the robe bunching up thick in the elbows. I stepped back into my slippers. "I got to go," I said.

"Lucy, what is going on?"

"I had to get out of the house. I was freezing."

"And the rest . . ."

"I don't know," I said, wiping at my nose. "Shit, Kenny. I don't know. I got to go."

I walked as fast as I could in the dark without tripping over all the crap on the floor. When I went past the TV, I saw Kenny's mom squinting my way. "Hello?" she said.

I could see the hallway by then, and I didn't slow down. I slammed the door behind me. Snow and ice everywhere, I was on my ass before I made the sidewalk.

I think I started to cry then. Maybe.

Staggering up, I wiped at the snow stuck to my robe, my naked leg, with my bare hands.

When I got back to my house, I blew straight in, shooting up the stairs for the shower, hoping not to see anybody. I had my hand on the bathroom door when it occurred to me that there wasn't anybody shouting anymore.

I stopped. I couldn't believe what I did hear.

They were up here. In their room. At it again. The two of them. Mom making these breathy sighs. The rhythm they had was something you could feel in your insides, straight through the walls. Like this huge, urgent heartbeat.

There was no way they could know where I was. Where I'd been. I could be out in a snowdrift, frosting over white as Dad's truck.

And this was what they decided to do about it. Power boink.

I turned on the shower. By then I knew I was crying.

My legs went all weak, and I sat down on the floor of the tub, the water drumming down. What was wrong with them? With me? Why in the hell had I rushed off to join their club? I remembered Mom saying there was no going back once you'd started, and I sat there with the soap, blubbering, "Bullshit" over and over, scrubbing at my crotch until there was nothing but a sliver of soap left. There was some blood, but not much, and it washed away quick.

CHAPTER SEVENTEEN

I was still sitting in the shower when Mom knocked on the door. "You're going to be late, honey."

Twisting off the water, I swept back the curtain and wrapped myself tight in a towel. They never knew I'd been gone. *What about you?* I wanted to shout. *What about Mr. Potato Head? Horse Teeth? All those vital overtime calls to Kamchatka?*

I waited long enough that she'd be gone, then slipped into my room. Even after the shower, I was freezing, so I pulled on long johns, jeans, a T-shirt, two flannel shirts, and the jacket I'd dragged out of the bathroom.

I peeked out, making sure the coast was clear, then tore down the stairs. Only then, fumbling into my big boots, did I notice the smell hanging in the air. Burned eggs. Had they argued so wildly that they hadn't noticed? Or had they been in such a rush to get upstairs?

I pulled open the front door, Kenny was waiting at the gate.

I wished I'd thought to look. To sneak out the back.

I stomped down to him, dodged around his reaching arm, and sidestepped him onto the sidewalk. I walked fast, Kenny almost keeping up.

"Lucy?"

"We're going to be late."

"Lucy," he said, much less a question.

I didn't slow or turn.

"Lucy!"

I lowered my head, kept going hard, a car off a cliff. When he grabbed my sleeve, he almost jerked me off my feet. Little Kenny Crauder.

Whirling, I hissed, "Just leave me alone! Okay?" My breath made great steamy clouds between us. "Is that so hard?"

His mouth dropped open like a nutcracker's. I took my chance to escape.

Poor Kenny. It's not like any of this was his fault. I turned, walking backward a second, and yelled, "Look, I'm sorry. Okay?" Then I spun around and started to run. In my clomping boots, Frankenstein had nothing on me.

I kept checking behind me, but Kenny didn't try to keep up. By the time I reached school, he was nowhere in sight. I zipped up my coat clear past my chin as I walked past school, against the flow of kids, a fish upstream. I sank as deep as I could inside my coat as I walked the twenty frozen blocks to Planned Parenthood. When I got there, I practically fell against the smoked-glass doors, the whole place too fancy-looking, like I was entering the lobby of some exclusive hotel. In Great Falls, it stuck out like something dropped from a tornado.

Inside it was the same, only warm. It resembled a hotel in a movie, plush and welcoming. Something black and white dancers should be twirling through.

A girl behind the receptionist counter, maybe all of two or three years older than me, glanced up and smiled. "Hello."

I wished she would have asked something: "What can we do for you?" "How can we help?" or even "Do you need help?" Maybe then I wouldn't have just stood there, pressing back against the doors, wondering what to say. I glanced both ways down the halls. There was a woman at a big desk in a room behind the receptionist. There were flowers next to her. She looked like a businesswoman. But on her name tag I saw the letters "RN." I chewed my lip.

The girl kept smiling. She said "Hi," this time.

"Hi," I croaked. A shiver racked me, and I shrugged, trying a smile. "Colder than a well digger's brass monkey out there."

She looked at me blankly.

I shook my head. "Something my dad says."

"Oh."

I took a step forward, halfway to her desk. I tried to stop the words, but out they came: "Do you work here?" Did sex, just once, rot your brain?

She smiled wider, dipping her head to hide it, maybe. "They pay me, anyway."

"A friend of mine," I started, my face red from a lot more than the cold. "Sort of a friend, somebody I used to play with . . ."

"Are you here for a friend or for yourself?"

Behind her, the nurse at the desk looked up.

"Me," I admitted.

The receptionist spun her chair around to a file cabinet, zipping out two forms. "This is a consent form, and this is a health history. Fill those out and then a nurse will talk with you." When I took the forms from her, she asked, "What's your name?"

"Luce," I answered automatically. "Lucy."

"I'm Kelsey. You're okay here."

"Thanks," I said, then stood at the counter with her pen and forms.

I bent over them, never thinking to look for a chair. On the health history, I checked off a long row of no's. I was a picture of health, but I felt like writing in, "Should have head examined."

The first question under family history was "Is there an inherited medical condition?" I thought of Mom and Dad going at it as soon as I'd dodged out to Kenny's. My pen hovered before I checked "no."

Then I got to sexual history, and my face flamed again. "Are you currently in a sexual relationship? If yes, how long?" I wrote, "A few hours." Then added, "Beginning to end." I underlined "end."

Beneath that was "Have your partners been_male,_female,_both."

"Jesus," I whispered. *"Both?"*

The receptionist looked up, and I lowered my head till my nose was practically on the paper.

"Have you or your partner had a new partner within the last year?" New? Besides each other? Kenny? I almost laughed.

I signed it.

A minute later, it was like any trip to a doctor. Weight. Blood pressure. Wait.

The place was practically wallpapered with pamphlets. "Contraceptive Choices." "Your First (or Twenty-third) Pelvic Exam." That one was subtitled "How to Turn an Embarrassing Moment into a Positive Experience," which almost made me reach for it. "Emergency Contraceptive Pills." That one looked good.

By the time the nurse came in, a different one than the one I'd seen at the desk, I held up that brochure.

"So," she said. She held the history I'd filled out. "You had your first sexual experience a few hours ago?"

I looked at the floor and nodded.

She waited, then asked quietly, "Was it consensual?"

I shrugged and nodded. "It kind of wasn't really planned."

"Were you with your boyfriend?"

I pursed my lips, thinking. Kenny my boyfriend? "Sort of, I guess." Hell, Kenny was my only friend.

"And you used no protection? No contraception?"

"No," I whispered.

"And you'd like emergency contraception?"

Just to keep from nodding again, I said, "Pregnancy wouldn't really fit my lifestyle now."

She gave me more stuff to read, then read it over with me, like maybe I was illiterate. "We'll get your pills for you," she said. Then she asked if I'd had a chance to read any of the other brochures.

I said no, and she started flipping them out of their slots.

"What do you plan to use for contraception in the future?" she asked.

Future? I almost said. I was holding the "Choices" brochure on top, opened so she'd think I was reading. I pointed down at the heading "Abstinence."

"Not always an easy thing to stick to. No easier than this morning."

"It'll be easy," I promised.

"The choice is yours," she said. "But I want you to look at all this information so you'll have the knowledge you need to make an informed decision."

I nodded.

She was silent for a moment. "Are you completely sure your partner is monogamous?"

"Kenny? The definition of it."

"We could test you. If there's any doubt, we should check for STDs. Have you ever had a pelvic exam? Have you ever had a Pap smear?"

When I said no, she handed me that pamphlet, too.

"There's really no way," I said. "This was his first, too. I know. I've known him forever."

"It's not only about that," the nurse said. "It's your health, your body. The more you know about it, the better off you'll be, the more in control."

I was still looking at the contraception information. "Maybe," I said, "maybe going on the pill wouldn't be such a bad idea."

That launched her into the whole thing about condoms, and I wound up with a six-pack of those, too. A lifetime supply. She was nice as could be, but I began to fear I'd never make it back out to the front desk. I held firm on the exam. The word "relax" was in bold print on almost every page. Like screaming "Don't panic!" in a smoke-filled theater.

When she asked if I wanted my parents to know about any of this, I was sure I couldn't get out of there fast enough. "No way!" I gasped.

She smiled. "In my experience, your mother already knows a lot more than you think she does."

"No," I insisted. "Not a chance. You don't have to call them or anything, do you?"

"State law says we can't without your permission. You're safe. If she called us, we couldn't even verify that you're a patient."

"Good."

She watched me. "Again, it's your decision. But if you've got a relationship with your mother that will stand it, talking usually helps. A lot."

"She's an expert on this stuff," I said, waving at the pamphlets in my lap. "But not on me."

She nodded and dropped back into her talk on the pill, how I'd *have* to get an exam in three months. Finally, she walked me back out front and wrote out a pair of prescriptions, and I got my pink dial-a-pill pack and my two white emergency pills. One now, one in twelve hours.

Then I said thanks, more than once, and good-bye, and stepped out into the cold, dirty, windy gray of Great Falls, my resort-hotel stay over.

CHAPTER EIGHTEEN

By the time I made it all the way home, I was frozen solid again. My brain, too, I guess. I stomped right in, eleven in the morning on a school day. Before I got the door closed behind me, I heard them laughing. "Luce?" Mom called.

"No, Britney Spears," I whispered.

"We're in here," she said from the living room.

She didn't sound the least bit surprised to hear me home. Or curious. When I got to the living room, she was smiling, saying, "But that's horrible."

Dad was in the middle of the room, dancing around like a boxer, his hands up in front of his face, guarding, ready to swing. All stuff he'd tried teaching me.

I got the abbreviated version. Seems some guy Dad worked with got in the way of a load of logs being lifted off by a helicopter. "The load pivoted," Dad explained. "One log sticking out clipped this guy right upside the head." In an aside, he said, "A new guy standing around with his teeth in his mouth. No business being anywhere near there. So, down he goes, poleaxed like a ton of bricks. Deader than a keg of mackerels. Tumbles down the side of the hill, ass over teakettle. Comes up short against a stump." Dad clapped hard and sudden. "Wham!" He slithered one hand down off the other. "That alone should have cleaned his locker, if the butt end to the melon hadn't finished him off at the start."

Dad stood shaking his head, and I wondered what about this story could have gotten Mom laughing.

"We all went bailing down the hill after him, but as we're piling up around him, standing there gaping like a bunch of fish at a car wreck, this guy—you could hardly make out his face for the blood—springs up like Satan's jack-in-the-box, launching haymakers for all he's worth." Dad leaped off the floor and thundered back down in his boxer stance, arms windmilling. "Coughlan steps in to help and just gets his onion peeled."

He laughed. "So we all pile around Coughlan instead, while this new guy's still cartwheeling his arms around, head whipping this way and that, screaming, 'Come on, you pussy little shits!'" Apologizing for the language, Dad went on, "'I'll kick *all* your asses!'" He shrugged, smiling. "Turns out he was from Butte. His dad probably whupped him every night he came home *without* getting in a fight."

"Was he all right?" I asked.

"*All right?* He felt great for taking such a shot! You'd have to pile-drive his head with a whole log truck to put more than a dent in it. Coughlan, though, he had to get his jaw wired shut. Drank protein milk shakes for a month."

I watched Dad making our whole living room about the size of a matchbook, and I wondered what we could do for him here that would match up to that kind of entertainment.

I didn't have to wonder long. As Dad started, "So, tell me about your day in higher education," there was a knock at the door, a soft, timid tapping—something a shy kid forced to sell Girl Scout cookies might make. More hoping nobody would answer before she could shrug down to the sidewalk at her mom or dad and slump off to the next door.

We all turned, but Dad jumped first. I don't know who or what he expected to find. Mom and I exchanged a glance, holding our breath.

Then Dad boomed, "Lenny! Come on in."

I heard Kenny say, "Thanks, Mr. Diamond. Welcome home." He came slouching in beside Dad. I couldn't look at him.

"So, I see Luce isn't the only one putting on a growth spurt. What are you now? Six-one? Six-two?"

Kenny nodded. "Getting there, Mr. Diamond. I'm getting there."

He hadn't broken *five*-two and didn't have any assurances that he would.

"Good for you," Dad said, talking too loud, like he did when anyone came over. "So, what brings you to these parts?"

"He lives down the block, Dad."

"Just wanted to see Lucy," Kenny said. I had this horrible thought, this like standing nightmare, that he was about to tell them what we'd done that morning.

"Well, I can see why. Turned into quite a looker, hasn't she?"

Kenny blushed, but he said, "She always has been, Mr. Diamond."

Dad clapped him on the back.

I rolled my eyes, but Kenny was in with Dad now, and he chanced, "I heard about this party Friday night, Lucy. After the game. I was wondering if you wanted to go."

A party? I could still picture Kenny standing alone on the sidewalk, watching me leave. How lost he seemed.

Mom and Dad waited for my answer. Their daughter was being asked on her first date. Precious.

"Well?" Dad prompted.

"Jeez!" I huffed, marching straight at Kenny, grabbing him by the arm, and hauling him out of the room. "Privacy," I hollered behind me. "It's in the dictionary."

I flung Kenny onto the front porch, then slammed the door behind us.

"Where did you go?" he asked first thing. "I looked everywhere."

"What are you, the hall monitor?"

"Lucy," he said. "I didn't plan what happened this—"

"Don't even start," I interrupted. "I do *not* want to talk about it."

"But," Kenny went on, urgent, "you can get pills to keep from getting pregnant."

"If you think that's going to happen again—that that's going to be some regular thing—"

"Pregnant from this morning!" Kenny said. "I went to Planned Parenthood." He stared at the porch. "You have to get the pills before seventy-two hours."

I thought of him opening those doors by himself, standing in front of that pretty girl, those women. "You went there?"

Kenny nodded.

"When?"

"I skipped out at lunch."

I looked down the block at our bare white street. "You must have just missed me," I said. "I already took the first pill. I take the other tonight."

"Want me to be there?"

"You think that would be romantic?"

"No, I—"

I gave him a push on his shoulder. "Kidding, Kenny."

"I'll come over if you want. If you don't want to be alone."

"You know what my dad would do to you if he caught you sneaking into my room?" I shuddered. "There wouldn't be enough of you left to grease a pan."

"He likes me."

"What difference does that make? He thinks you're harmless."

"I am."

I let my mouth hang open. But then I smiled. "I can't believe you sleep naked."

That caught him. "What's wrong with that?"

"I don't know, just, you know, with all your parts flopping around."

" 'All my parts'?" Kenny couldn't stifle a laugh. " 'All my parts'?"

"You know what I mean." I hit him again. "What was it with the party?"

"It was the only thing I could think to say around your dad." Kenny looked down the street toward his house. "But there is one. Want to go?"

"Where?" I asked. We'd never gone to a party in our lives.

"Jaimie Tilton's."

I laughed. Jaimie Tilton was cheerleader material but too hip to actually be a cheerleader. "How on earth do you know about a party at Jaimie Tilton's?"

"As cool as I am?" he asked, all insulted. Then he admitted, "Justin told me about it."

I laughed again. "Justin? Haven? Why on earth—"

Kenny raised one eyebrow, letting it dawn on me. He said, "We could go to the game first. Freeze our butts to the bleachers. Feel the school spirit."

Man, it felt good to laugh. "I don't know. Maybe. Ask me Friday."

"Okay," Kenny said, then, "About this morning, Lucy—"

"I got to go, Kenny. They still haven't figured out enough to ask what I'm doing home." But I knew that they wouldn't, that we were still in grand partyland reunion phase.

"Okay," Kenny repeated, moving in close, reaching to hug me. "You don't want to talk about it, I know, but—"

I stepped back, lifting my hands to block his arms. "They're probably watching." I lowered my voice. " 'Come on, now, you two, break it up. Let's see some air between you.' " It was what Mr. Sledden said if he caught anybody going at it in school.

"It's the only way to keep warm out here."

"I warmed up with you once today."

"All right, Lucy," Kenny said, taking a step down the porch. "See you tomorrow?"

For the first time, it was a question rather than an unassailable fact.

"Yeah," I said. "I'll see you tomorrow."

CHAPTER NINETEEN

So Kenny and I wound up going to the game. There was a chinook, this warm wind that comes screaming out of the mountains, so we didn't quite freeze ourselves to the bleachers, but the blast of the wind made it almost as bad. We huddled in what shelter we could find, Kenny careful not to touch me in the crowd. I watched maybe two plays.

We won. Rah. Go Bison.

We hardly said two words to each other. Since we'd had sex, there was only one thing to talk about, and I wasn't going there.

The snow on the ground had gone squishy rather than squeaky, and we tromped through it, me and Kenny, on the way to Jaimie Tilton's. We had to look up the address. It was not a place either of us ever considered looking for. In fact, I asked Kenny what made him think they'd let us through the front door instead of laughing in our faces. "For crying out loud," I said. "We're *freshmen.*"

"You," he answered. Though this whole night had started as a joke, he'd gone all serious on me. "They'll let you in anywhere."

I stared at him.

"And I'm with you. So they'll probably let me in, too."

"Exactly who is it you think I am?"

"The cutting edge," he said. "You're so much the next thing in cool, you don't even know it yourself yet."

I did this exaggerated cartoon gape at him, but it wasn't anything he could see in the dark. "And then what?" I asked. But I had an idea, a thought. I leaned over to stare at Kenny. "What do you think? Do you think that by coming here, where Justin Haven can see me, he'll quit looking for me in school? I mean, what is your plan?"

"No plan," he said. "Just trying to integrate with high school life." It was what the counselors were always advising. Kenny made it sound like a science experiment.

When we arrived, there was only a handful of cars on the street. Through the window, the house didn't look half full, and I smiled to see Jaimie Tilton could throw a party that flopped. But I knew better. "Football players are still showering," I said. "They won't show for a while yet." The main attraction.

We hesitated at the door, peering inside. "Think we can walk right in?" Kenny asked.

"They'll tell us to leave if they want." Jaimie or any friend of hers would not be worried about any possible rudeness to the lesser classes.

Another car pulled up, four kids piling out, the boys shoving at each other, the girls giggling.

I opened the door and stepped in. The warmth of the house struck like a hand. "Come on," I said to Kenny. He glanced at the kids coming up the walk and followed me in.

Inside, some girl walked past, and I said, "Hi."

"Hey," she said, not slowing down. Behind us, one of the girls from the car called, "Brie!" The girl who'd blown me off whirled, shrieking, "Cassie! Did you just get here?"

Cassie laughed. "No, we've been practicing walking through the door. *Hello?*"

Everybody laughed, and they flowed around us, disappearing into the living room.

Kenny and I glanced at each other. "This is going to be *so* much fun," he said. "Lucy! Did you just *get* here?"

I said, "Don't forget whose idea this was," and took a step toward most of the noise, the kitchen, I guessed. "Walk the plank with me?" I asked, but Kenny was right beside me, not wanting to be left alone behind enemy lines.

We didn't get thrown out. People studied us for a second but mostly smiled, nodded, and turned away. I caught a smirk or two, some talk as we moved on, but nothing much. Some guy even offered us beer from a keg on the back porch, but we shook our heads like puppets, and he went off pinching four cups, a finger in each.

"How do you suppose they scored a keg?" Kenny asked.

"The Jaimie Tiltons get what they want."

"Where are her parents?"

I stared at him. *Where are her parents?* For crying out loud. Where were his? Mine?

Then, all of a sudden, there was a rush in the party, everyone talking louder, laughing louder, moving more. Kenny and I turned, and here came the football team. Victorious warriors, you'd think, by the way they took over the room, by the way the girls surged forward, the boys fell back.

I turned to smirk at Kenny, saying, "What, again, are we doing here?"

Kenny didn't answer. He stared straight ahead, falling back as sure as the other boys who weren't part of the select.

I followed his gaze and saw the last of Justin Haven's beeline to me.

"Hey! I can't believe you're here." He put his hand on my arm, between my shoulder and elbow, and gave it a squeeze. He left it there, stroking, kind of, until he noticed me staring at it like some kind of a lizard, some slinking, slimy salamander. He let his hand drop, but I could see it would never occur to him that my presence had nothing to do with him. His friend Tim Shaughnessy, this enormous carrottop redhead, cut from the same blocky mold only bigger, gave him a shove, laughed, and said, "I'll get us beered." He gave Kenny the same friendly shove, saying, "Hey, Junior."

"So, did you go to the game?" Justin wanted to know.

"You were marvelous," I gushed, but he beamed. "We hid behind the press box," I explained. "To get out of the wind."

"Yeah, you don't feel that kind of thing out on the field," he started, but then my "we" caught, and he turned his gaze to Kenny. "Hey, how's the weather down there?"

Kenny said, "Ha. Good one."

Then Tim was back, carrying four beers the same way the other kid had. This time Kenny and I took ours. The foam on top had settled into round patches, like mold cultures on a petri dish.

Tim sucked the beer from his fingers and shouted, "To victory!" He tilted his head back, draining his cup. "Helena losers." He grinned and belched. "You ready?" he asked Justin.

Kenny was behind me, so I didn't see anything more than his arm sticking out with an empty glass. "I am," he said. I turned to see him wipe the side of his thumb across his lip. He shrugged at me and smiled.

Justin drained his own beer. "Wow, two seconds in, and I'm already playing catch-up. Way to go, boy."

I took a single sip of my own beer, my first taste ever. Awful. I tried again. Just as bad. Yeasty and tingly and bubbly. "Don't you have any straight poison?" I asked. "Does it have to be this long drawn-out misery?"

Tim grinned. "I'll see what I can do." He disappeared, taking the three empty cups.

Jaimie came by then with some of her entourage, but Justin straight blew her off. I mean, he said hi and all, great party, but as she started asking about something else, he grinned at me. "I can't believe you actually came. Lucy Diamond. Makes my whole night. My whole week."

Jaimie stopped in midsentence, her mouth open. She stared straight through me, and I made a note not to use the bathrooms at school until after she graduated, not to get myself anywhere alone. Then she and her group swirled away as one, like a school of fish. Bait.

Justin laughed again. He hummed a few bars of "Lucy in the Sky with Diamonds."

"Where have I heard that before?" I said.

He laughed more. The guy was impervious.

Tim was back, and this time Justin beat him to the toast, holding out his cup and saying, "To Lucy, my diamond." He held his cup up, waiting for the click of the others, but Kenny's cup, when he reached over me to touch rims with Justin and Tim, was already empty.

Tim looked from the cup down at Kenny. "Puking before midnight."

"Before eleven," Justin said.

"I'll make it longer than either of you," Kenny answered in a voice so flat and assured that I wondered if those wine bottles in his kitchen were all his mother's.

With this elaborate flourish, Tim whipped a small bottle out of his back pocket. He held it out to me. "As you requested, ma'am. As close to pure poison as I could find."

Kenny laughed. "It's peppermint schnapps. That's closer to pure *candy*."

Justin shook his head. "We got a man on a mission." He took the bottle from Tim and unscrewed the cap, breaking the paper seal. He threw the cap over his shoulder. "Won't be needing *that* anymore!" He took a swig and roared out this kind of sigh. He handed it to me.

"You have got to be kidding," I said.

"You were the one looking for poison." Leaning in close, Justin said, "Here, smell, it's peppermint, like candy." He was only a few inches away.

"Smells more like toothpaste."

"Taste," Justin said, leaning even closer. He wasn't offering the bottle.

I wasn't going to bend any farther for him. Instead I stared, my lips shut as thin and tight as scissors.

Kenny jerked the bottle out of Justin's hand. Justin tried pulling it back, but Kenny had caught him off guard. All Justin did was manage to spill some, on me, before Kenny had it. I smelled like I'd been swimming in it.

"Kid stuff," Kenny said, choking down a gulp.

Justin straightened up, away from me. "Man," he said, "make sure you go outside before you blow chunks. Jaimie's parents will have a fit."

I reached for the bottle, having to pry it away from Kenny. I took my own sip. A tiny one. "Not bad," I said. It really was more like candy, burning candy, than anything else.

Somehow, while we were passing that bottle around, we became the center of a gang of kids, Justin and his sidekick, me and mine.

Things got loud and swirly around us, but as much as Kenny was trying to walk the walk, he was fading fast. Only the wall, I think, was holding him up. Tim planted the empty schnapps bottle neck-down in the dirt of a large rubber plant. "Go on, little buddy, grow some more quick," he said.

The group took this as the highest humor. Even Kenny laughed. Beer got passed around like pop, most everybody drinking it, not just making a show of how cool they were. I had a few more sips myself. Maybe it was a different kind. It wasn't as bad as the first.

The whole party wasn't as bad as we'd figured it would be. Some of these kids seemed sort of nice, sort of fun. Even Tim, big doofus clown that he was, was pretty funny. We all got laughing.

When Kenny put his arm over my shoulders, Justin wasn't mean about taking it off and giving it back to Kenny. "Now, now," he said. "None of that. Break it up. Let's see some air between you. It's not that kind of party." Behind him, on one of the couches, there was a couple groping and mashing.

I laughed. "Get a room!" I called, one of Dad's.

Though Kenny's eyes were only half open and his lips looked as heavy as plates, he managed a glower. He slid up against me. "I love you, Lucy," he slurred. "I love you."

I'm sure he thought he was being quiet.

Justin burst out laughing, spraying a bunch of us with beer. I fixed my eyes on the floor, looking for a crack in the hardwood to disappear into.

"I luff yoo, Lushie," Justin cooed.

I let him have it with all the beer in my glass. Somehow it was only about a teaspoonful. That got everybody laughing twice as hard. Tim had to wipe the tears in his eyes.

Only Kenny wasn't laughing. It was like, for him, the two of us were in our normal vacuum. His whole face begged me. "I do," he said. "I'm the one."

"Sure, sure, little man." Justin had him around the shoulders, steering him away. He passed him to Tim, who passed him to somebody else, saying, "Make a hole! Vomit Express!" Justin transferred his arm from Kenny's shoulders straight to mine, looping me back, keeping me from following. "He'll be fine," he said, his lips practically touching my ear, his breath hot.

I twisted around to see people jumping back from Kenny. The last I saw, Jaimie Tilton had him by an arm, aiming him toward the front door. He stumbled on the threshold. I hoped Jaimie could keep him from bashing down the steps.

Justin said, "Just needs a little fresh air. You don't have to baby-sit him anymore."

"I'm not—"

"Whatever you call it, then," Justin went on. "Your civic duty or whatever."

"He's my friend."

Somehow Justin had me in a corner, and was standing in front of me. There was no air between us.

"He's giving you a bad rep," Justin said. "Shit, he looks like he's in fifth grade. Following you around everywhere."

"But he's—"

"Is that why you came here? To talk about the kid?"

"I came here because he asked me to."

Justin laughed. "You came here because I asked him to ask you. And I bet that's a move he's rethinking."

Then he kissed me. Right on the mouth. His beery tongue on mine before I could clap my teeth shut. His hands moved from my shoulders to my neck, pulling my head toward his. Like it could get any closer.

I didn't quite break away from the kiss. Maybe I even gave it back a little. Just for the hell of it. To think of Jaimie Tilton seeing this. I mean, I could hardly believe it myself. Justin Haven kissing me. It was like a souvenir from a place I knew I'd never be again. It was so ridiculous I laughed out loud.

Justin pulled back. He was smiling, but you could tell laughing was not the usual reaction to one of his kisses. I suppose I should have been all aswoon.

"What?" he asked, his voice huskier but quieter than it had been a moment before.

I shook my head. "Just something I thought about."

"You know what I was thinking about?" he asked, then moved in for another kiss, our tongues dueling.

"What?" I asked, coming up for breath.

"About what you said before."

"What was that?"

"About getting a room."

He had his lips all over mine again. His hips were trying to drive me through the wall. His hands were wandering, too. He got ahold of my boob and started cranking on it.

I pulled my head back, and grabbed his hand, gave him this long sideways look. "A room? You and me? Is this like the second time in your life you've talked to me, or do I have myself confused with somebody else?"

"No time like the present," he said, so damn positive of the outcome.

"Indeed," I said. "And it's time for me to go."

I was holding his wrist, his hand still cupped like it was molded to my curves. "This is yours," I said, and I started to slip around him, out of the corner. He only pushed his hand against the wall, blocking my way.

I tried to burn a hole through him with my eyes. I tried not to smile. "If you ever want even the slightest chance of getting your hand back where it was, you'll move that arm out of my way so fast I'll forget it was ever there."

Justin grinned but slowly lowered his arm. He reached in for a kiss as I dodged by, but I blocked it with a hand held up like a policeman's.

From somewhere off to the side, Tim howled. "And the final score: ex-bald girl, one; Haven, a big fat zero."

"Final?" Justin called, turning his back on me. "Final?"

I was almost to the door. I had no idea where my coat was. I couldn't remember taking it off or anybody asking to take it for me.

"*Final* score?" Justin shouted. "I haven't even gotten warmed up!"

I left without the coat. Cutting losses. By the time I made it through the door, I was running.

CHAPTER TWENTY

I didn't run more than a step or two. Because there was Kenny, alone, lying in the snow, puke all over the place. Somebody'd pitched his old coat down after him. It lay half over his chest, one dark sleeve draped across his leg.

"Oh, Jesus, Kenny," I said, stooping over him, petting his messed-up hair.

He groaned something. An eyelid flickered open. He tried to lift his head. There was blood in his nose, and I knew Jaimie, besides not keeping him from falling, had pitched him down the steps.

"You fucking bitch!" I screamed at the house, but the door was already closed, the music loud enough I could feel it in the hollow of my chest. I stumbled, trying to pick Kenny up. "Come on, Kenny. Let's go home. It's time to go." I got him to his feet, and he turned to me and smiled, murmured something about me being the best.

He was wet from the snow and could hardly walk. I held him up, trying to drape his coat over both our shoulders.

We did not make great progress. Kenny was cold enough and wet enough that he was freezing me, too. Then he had to stop and throw up some more. Well, not actually more. He seemed to be pretty well puked out, but he tried, on his hands and knees, retching and rasping at the edge of the sidewalk, while I tried keeping him off the ground.

When he got done, he was crying.

"For God's sake, Kenny. Don't do that."

"You love him now."

"What? Who?" I tugged at his coat to move him forward.

"Justin," he sobbed, almost sounding like he was throwing up again.

"Wow, you are shitfaced. Me and that gorilla?"

"I saw you," he said.

I tried to imagine how he could have seen anything from out in the front yard, lying in the snow and the puke.

"See?" Kenny said.

"Yeah, sure, Kenny, whatever you say. But you've got to help me here. Walk, okay? You remember. Left foot, right foot. Red foot, blue foot."

He laughed at that, and we staggered on.

By the time I finally, finally got him up the steps, past Mrs. Bahnmiller's abandoned post, Kenny hadn't said anything in a long time. He was shivering, moving his feet in an automatic shuffle. It wasn't till I got him into the long hallway that I thought of his mother. There was a light on down there, a dim one, maybe only the TV.

"Kenny," I said right into his ear. "Kenny? What should we do?"

But he was out of it, his head hanging, mouth more open than his eyes.

No one had come down the hallway, so I went ahead. "Please," I said to myself. Then I said it again.

Kenny's mom was on the couch, a small light on beside her, as well as the TV with its sound muted. She was sitting up this time and, turned to look at us as I stepped into the room.

"Kenny's sick," I said.

She looked at me a long time before turning to Kenny. There was a glass of something dark beside her on the table. Half full. "Drunk?" she asked.

"Well, sort of. He drank too much."

She nodded in this heavy way, then focused on me. "Where's your coat, sweetheart?" she asked.

Mom sometimes called me sweetheart, but not the way Kenny's mom did, a way that made you feel she was searching for your heart with an ice pick.

"I left it behind."

"And you drove Kenny home? Carried him in here by yourself?"

"I can't drive yet." Her eyes widened, and I shrugged, Kenny's head wagging beside mine. "He's not very heavy."

"Dead drunk, everybody's heavy."

"I'm going to put him down," I said. "He's heavy enough." I started toward the kitchen, his room, and that's when it dawned on her.

"You've been here before," she called after me. "I saw you sneaking out that morning."

She stood up behind me. I kept moving.

"What in the world is going on here, anyway?" she asked. "Kenny?"

I banged Kenny into his doorway, and she caught up to us as I was trying to fit him through. She flicked on the light, making all of us squint. Kenny's floor was covered with clothes, the blankets stretching from the bed halfway across the room.

"Who are you?" his mom asked, craning to see my face.

I almost said "Jaimie Tilton," but that might have woken up even Kenny. "Lucy," I said.

"You? That little crew-cut girl Kenny used to play with?" She laughed. "Go on!"

"Lucy Diamond," I said.

"And what were you doing sneaking around here the other morning?"

"Nothing I'll be doing again."

"I should say not."

I stumbled through the clothes and dropped Kenny on his bed. His mom followed. I forced myself to look at her. "Really, Mrs. Crauder, I don't know anything about this. Is he going to be okay? He's freezing. Should we make him drink coffee or something?"

"What makes you think I'm such an expert? What's Kenny been telling you?"

I blinked. "Nothing. I mean, just that you might know. I've never been drunk in my life."

"Well, aren't you perfect," she said. She sat heavily on the edge of the bed. Kenny rolled into her, and I stood to keep from doing the same. At last she touched Kenny, seemed to care what happened to him, remembered that she was his mother. "Damn," she said. "What did you do? Drag him through the snow?"

"I found him outside."

"What the hell were you doing while he was outside?"

"I was—I was looking for him."

She tugged Kenny back to his feet. "We have to warm him up."

We staggered out of Kenny's room into the dingy little bathroom.

Mrs. Crauder cranked on the shower and sat on the edge of the tub, the curtain pinched beneath her. "Help," she said, starting to tug his sweatshirt over his head, like a kid.

I hesitated, then went to work on his shoes, old runners, the laces knotted with water. I peeled his socks off, his feet white and cold and pruny.

His mom had his sweatshirt and T-shirt off and was already working on the buttons of his jeans. I straightened up. He was so white and skinny, you could practically see the skeleton of him inside there. Steam was rising up around us.

Mrs. Crauder lifted her face to me. "Pull on the legs."

I bit my lip, still looking at Kenny.

"Come on, now, sweetheart. Tell me there's something there you haven't already seen."

I bent down and tugged at his jeans. Kenny gurgled something. I never looked at anything besides his wrinkled feet.

"Hang on to him," she said. "Don't let him fall."

She stood up and tested the water, fiddling with the faucets until she said, "There, that won't burn him."

She grabbed Kenny by the shoulders, and said, "Can you stand up, Kenny? Can you try?"

It was the first time she sounded as if she might like him.

She turned to me without a trace of a smile. "Thanks for bringing him home."

I nodded.

"I can take it from here," she said, pulling back the curtain, testing the water one more time. "His father gave me plenty of practice."

Kicking off her slippers, she pulled her own sweatshirt over her head, wriggled out of her sweatpants. She stepped quick into the shower, trying to hide, but there was a second while she coaxed Kenny in beside her that I couldn't look away. She was as scrawny as I'd been last year, before my body started its mad dash. Her shoulders looked like round rocks squeezed in under her skin, her ribs like the sand ripples at the edge of a fading river. She wore a bra the way I used to, as if in the faint hope that something might someday fill it out: two flat white triangles against her chest. Her sunken belly had one tuck of wrinkly, overstretched skin at the edge of her panties, maybe the only reminder she had that she and Kenny had once been a part of each other.

The water drummed over them, Kenny naked and tiny, curling in to her side. She put her head down on top of his and said, "You'll be okay, baby."

It sounded like something she'd said to him often enough before.

I stepped backward to the door. As if just remembering I was there, she reached out and whipped the shower curtain closed. From behind it, she said, "You and I are going to have ourselves a little sit-down, sweetheart. Sometime soon."

She wasn't talking to Kenny.

I didn't say anything, just kept backing out of the bathroom, then the house.

CHAPTER TWENTY-ONE

Mom and Dad had left the porch light on for me, a dim beacon guiding me back from Kenny's. Inside, the light over the stove was on. I snapped it off and saw the glimmer from the top of the landing. After climbing the stairs, I flicked that off, too. From my room, the bedside lamp glowed. It was like they'd mapped out my every step. The first night I'd been out after they went to bed.

I clicked off my light and lay flat on my bed, my bones sinking toward the bottom of the springs. My mouth felt dry, my tongue thick, sticking to my teeth, but I was too exhausted to crawl out for a drink of water.

I woke up the next morning in the same position, still in my clothes, my comforter pulled sideways across me but the sheets and blankets beneath me. It was light outside, and I could hear somebody moving around downstairs. Probably Dad expecting me down early for cartoons.

I sat up at the edge of the bed. Tried my feet on the floor. Instead of aching, my head felt more filled with cotton or wool: something thick and scratchy.

So this was drinking. Another milestone. It, along with sex, I figured, could now go into some kind of keepsake box. "Milestones Passed." Rattling around like my baby teeth in Dad's old Copenhagen tin. Been there, done that. It was funny, but the more things I did—like kissing Justin Haven in front of the whole world—the emptier I felt. Like you started out full and kept throwing things overboard instead of the other way around. It wasn't how I thought it would work.

I stood up, testing my legs. Though it didn't feel like a brilliant idea, I tottered to the door, thinking only about a chance to brush my teeth. I moved as quiet as I could, but even so, as soon as I poked out from behind my door, I was looking straight at Dad standing in his doorway, the phone pressed to his ear, the cord stretched way out so he could look right back at me.

I had this sudden picture of Mom's job, thousands of men around the world looking exactly like Dad, everything pulled that taut just to stay near her voice.

Dad gave me a wink, did this yadda-yadda-yadda head bob at the phone, but it wasn't quite the same as it always was. He had this different look. Anxious, somehow.

Work.

He was getting called by somebody to go back to work. Some super job somewhere. Borneo or someplace. A whole rain forest with my dad's name on it. Meanwhile, a turkey the size of a Volkswagen, and every bit as hard, spends a year in our freezer. I wondered if, with him gone, Mom would be here or off someplace with Horse Teeth. Leaving me to whittle slivers off the turkey carcass. Suck them enough to thaw and swallow.

Dad listened and listened, but rather than easing back into his room, where he could make his plans in secret, out of my sight, he stayed where he could watch me, memorize me, maybe, since there was no telling when he'd see me again.

At last he said, and you could tell he was interrupting, "Listen. I've got a better idea. Why don't you come over here for Thanksgiving dinner? We got a turkey that'd stuff a pope."

He smiled. That had stopped whoever he was talking to in their tracks. "We'll dust off all our skeletons, and you bring yours. We'll get to know each other."

I mouthed, "Who?" We'd never met anybody Dad worked with.

"Well, of course both of you. What? Did you think I'd want you to leave Lenny home?"

My eyes went wide, then shut completely.

He said a few more jokey things I didn't have the heart to listen to. I backed into my room and sank down on the edge of my bed.

A few seconds later, he was at my door. "That was Lenny's mom."

"I thought it was work."

Coming up the stairs, Mom said, "*Kenny*, Chuck. For crying out loud, it's *Kenny*."

Dad shrugged. To me, he said, "Sounds like *Kenny* did his share of drinking last night."

"More than his share," I said.

"She sounded a little upset. She's a bit of a shrieker, as a matter of fact." He stuck his finger in his phone ear, squeaking it around like in cartoons.

Mom stepped through the doorway, closing the gap. "What happened, Luce?" No trace of Looney Tunes about her.

"Some of the football guys. They made this game out of making Kenny drink."

"Making him?"

I caught my thumbnail between my teeth. "You don't know what it's like."

"And you?" Mom asked.

"Nobody can make me do anything."

Dad smiled. "Atta boy." But Mom said, "Only poor Kenny had it forced into him?"

"He did it for me!" I said, my voice going sharp. "Okay?"

Dad pursed his lips, his thinking-hard look. "Not sure I follow you, Luce. Kenny drank to protect you? Would this be the same way you kissed the creep to save Kenny?"

"What?" Mom asked.

Dad waited.

"I can't believe you asked her over for dinner," I said.

"Kissed what creep?" Mom asked.

"How exactly did Kenny's drinking protect you?" Dad asked.

"She didn't say yes, did she?"

"Luce?" they both said at once.

I ran my hand through my hair. "It's complicated."

"I don't doubt that," Dad said.

"Chuck, what creep? What are you talking about?"

"Have her tell you."

"I thought we were going to get a Christmas tree today," I tried.

"Lucy!"

I rubbed the side of my face. "He'll tell you, Mom. I'm sure it's better his way."

"Chuck?"

"Seems some creep was going to kill Lenny. The only way to save him was by kissing him."

"Kenny?"

"No, the creep."

"Kenny kissed the creep?" I said, saving Dad the trouble.

He smiled, but Mom stared hard at him. "Lucy had to kiss the creep to save Kenny," he explained.

"How on earth did that work?"

"Apparently, her kisses are from your side of the family."

Mom narrowed her eyes, but Dad turned to me. "Let's get back to last night. Kenny drank himself into a stupor to save you. From what? Kissing more creeps?"

That's the one thing it didn't save me from, I thought. "It's complicated," I said again.

"Hell's wells, Lucy! Everything's complicated! You're a teenager."

"I know how old I am."

They stood there, silent for once.

"Look, Kenny wants to be my boyfriend, all right? Like we have to be this whole new dumb thing." I was so close to cracking, I made my voice go all stupid. "Just 'cause we're *teenagers.*"

It didn't faze them.

"He thought he could keep the other boys away from me by drinking with them."

"*Away* from you?" Dad asked.

"Boys," Mom said, like a swear word.

"How'd his plan work?" Dad said.

"Well, I carried Kenny home. So I guess that saved my virginity one more day."

"Hey!" Dad burst out.

Mom shook her head. "Lucy, for Christ's sake."

"Well, I didn't say it was my plan. I never commended its brilliance. It's just what Kenny did. You wanted to know. Now you do."

They stood there, looking at each other. Looking at me.

"Did she say yes?" I asked.

"What? Who?"

"Kenny's mom. About Thanksgiving."

Dad rubbed at his jaw. "What exactly has been going on here while I was gone?"

"Don't even start that 'while I was gone' crap," Mom snapped.

Dad held up his fingers. "Okay. Let's see. Mame's got a job." He thumbed down one finger. "Lucy's kissing creeps." Another finger.

"That was one time. One disgusting kiss."

"I still haven't heard enough about that," Mom interrupted.

Dad kept working his fingers. "Lucy's carrying home drunks. She's got a boyfriend."

"I do not have a boyfriend!" I shouted.

Dad paused with another finger poised to go down. "Anything else I should know about along those lines?" he asked Mom.

"Oh, grow up, Luce," Mom said. She waved her hands in the air. *"Boy germs! Ahh, cooties!* You're not six anymore."

"I wish I was," I said, and Mom looked like she knew what I meant, like she wanted to go back there with me herself.

"Kenny's mom didn't say yes, did she?" I asked one more time.

Dad nodded. "She and Kenny will be over in time for the second football game."

Mom laughed. "She said that?"

"Not exactly. But I could tell. She's definitely a fan." Football was the one thing Dad watched on TV. It was about the only time he ever sat still. Mom and I couldn't stand it.

Mom shook her head. "We don't know her from Adam, Chuck."

"Luce and Lenny are tight, though. We should get to know his mom. It'll be fun."

"Fun?" I blurted.

Dad glanced at me but kept on at Mom. "And it won't be any more work. That turkey's—"

" 'Big enough to stuff a pope.' I know," Mom said.

"Just buy wine," I said. "Plenty of it."

They turned to me.

"For Kenny?" Dad asked.

"Or you?" Mom said.

"Ha, ha." I stood, my stomach clenching and unclenching, hoping they'd let me through to the bathroom.

But Dad said, "No time for a shower, Luce. We're off to the mountains."

"Can I at least pee?"

Dad checked his watch. "Well," he said, drawing it out like it was this big decision.

So that's what we did. The three of us. Off to get our Christmas tree. A postcard family. Dad making up his own words to Christmas carols all day long. The traditional snowball fight, Mom ducking and yelling. Me blasting off Dad's hat. Eventually, Dad cranked up his monster chain saw and ripped through a tree trunk no thicker than my wrist. Zip! Made me flinch. Made me sick to my stomach. He was done that fast, but I was the one who staggered, on my way down.

As they dragged out the tree, me trudging along after them, falling behind, Dad started playing grab-ass with Mom. I could barely hear him sing, "Lainee with your rear so tight, won't you be my lay tonight." Slapping at his hand, Mom laughed.

CHAPTER TWENTY-TWO

I didn't see Kenny again till Monday morning. Before we took one step away from our front gate, he asked, "What happened? I can't even remember getting home."

We headed toward school, leaving Mom and Dad to whatever. I looked to see if Kenny could be kidding. "I carried you."

"I took a shower. I could smell it in the morning. The shampoo."

"Your mom. You puked all over yourself. She cleaned you up."

Kenny's eyes closed. Maybe he was seeing her giving his dad the same kind of shower. "You were there? You guys talked to each other?"

The chinook had torched off all the snow over the weekend, leaving everything gray and brown. "A little. You know. 'Hold his arm there.' 'Get his socks.' "

Kenny groaned. "How was Mom?"

"It was the middle of the night. You were hammered. How do you think she was?"

"Was she mad at you?"

"Me? I don't know. I guess."

"She was," he answered. "That's how it always went with Dad. Get mad at whoever he was with. Me if nobody else was around."

"She said we'd have a talk sometime."

"Don't do it. It'll all be crazy lies."

"She saw me. The other time. When I left that morning. She remembered me."

He shook his head. "Yeah, you definitely want to avoid that chat."

"You're coming over for Thanksgiving. How am I supposed to avoid that?"

"We're what?"

"She didn't tell you? She called the next morning. Dad invited her over."

Kenny whispered, "Fuck," which was something he never said. We walked another block before he said, "So, how was the party?"

I kind of laughed. "You really don't remember any of it?"

"Just how I drank Justin and Tim under the table."

"That was about it. After that the party pretty much fell apart."

After another block, Kenny asked, "What happened to my face?"

One cheek was scraped, his nose sort of swollen. "That bitch Jaimie pushed you off the front steps."

"I thought Justin might have popped me one."

"Justin? What for?"

Kenny puffed out a laugh. Or a sigh. "Just for being me. The pesky kernel. For being in the way with you."

"Once you set to outdrinking them, you weren't in the way long."

He shoved his hands deeper into his pockets.

"I mean, there wasn't much left to punch. Would've been like boxing with a jellyfish."

Kenny grinned helplessly.

I stopped. "Kenny, what were you thinking, anyway? What were you trying to prove?"

He shrugged, looking up at the brick face of Great Falls High. "I thought I could distract them from you."

"By getting shitfaced?"

He wouldn't meet my eyes, and I laughed, giving him a quick hug. I called him my knight in shining armor.

Which, when we got into school, Justin and Tim falling in beside us like they'd been doing it every day of the year, was not what they called him. They hooted, clapping Kenny on the back, calling him Animal and Beermeister, Justin so close to me he was like wallpaper. They never left us alone. Thank God it was a short week in school.

But Thanksgiving Day made school, even with Justin and Tim as our shadows, seem not so bad.

Working together all day in the kitchen, Mom and Dad couldn't keep from touching, from bumping "accidentally" as they moved around, cutting up vegetables for stuffing, looking for breadcrumbs. Dad peeled a bag of spuds, dropping them into a pot of water, reminiscing about KP duty in the army. He always said the same thing when he was home for a holiday's cooking. He'd never been in the army in his life.

Dad missed as many holidays as he made, as if he had to share the wealth, one with us, one with work, so when he was around, it was always a huge production. It was the one time Mom didn't mind cooking. Pretended that she could. Though inviting somebody else in was different. Somebody they had to share each other with. Besides me, I mean. I had to be there. They'd gotten used to that. I think. They'd been married five months when I was born. First math problem I ever did.

I tried to help cook, but Mom said the kitchen was too tight for all three of us anymore. She sent me out to vacuum. To dust. "Don't forget the bathroom. Put out fresh towels."

Maybe they hadn't gotten used to me. Maybe I was just getting too big to ignore.

I did what had to be done, then dropped down hard on the couch. To keep from gnawing off the stubs of my nails, I fiddled with the remote, turning on the football game, watching it as much as Kenny and I used to watch TV, what seemed like years ago. I kept wondering how I could escape.

Mom and Dad came into the living room together, still looking like the high-schoolers they'd been about the time I came along. Dad had bread crumbs clinging to his waist, caught in the rough wool of his shirt.

"We're going to clean up, Luce," Mom said.

"Company's coming," Dad said. "Get to meet your new man."

"You've met him plenty of times, Dad," I said. "And he is *not* my new man. He is not my old man. He's not even a man. He's a kid. So am I. I don't have a man. Why on earth would I want one?"

"Did I tell you she was smart?" Mom asked.

"My side of the family." He bumped his hip against Mom's. I clapped a hand over my eyes, dragged it down the length of my face.

"Why don't you get dressed, anyway," Mom said. "Even if, hope of hopes, you never do need a man."

"What do you mean get dressed? What are you making this?"

Mom smiled and shook her head. Dad studied the TV for the score. "This is what people do, Luce. When they invite somebody over. They cook. They clean. They get dressed up. They make it an occasion."

"*People?* Like who?"

"Real people. The rest of the world."

"How would we know one thing about what real people do?"

Mom said, "Turn off the TV, Luce. Come on up. Wear something nice. We're going to hit the shower."

So I tromped up after them. They knew I was there. When they

turned on the shower. When they started going at it in there. You could
hear by the rhythm of the water pounding down. The pulse of it. It was
like they were teaching me what dates were about, what it meant to be
an adult. They had to know I could hear. Even if they hadn't slipped,
if I hadn't heard the popping jingle of the shower-curtain rings as they
tore the curtain down, the staggering thumps of their bodies.

I jumped off the edge of my bed, bolting for their room. That kind
of crash didn't make you think; it made you rush for the remains. I
was all the way into their room when I heard what I always heard from
them. Laughing. Hysterical laughing. Both of them. Mom asking, in
gasps, "What on earth?"

Dad bellowed, "No chains can hold us!"

I stood there, and as the laughing died out, I heard something new.
A slick, plasticky rustle, gaining on itself, that heartbeat throbbing of
theirs. The other thing I always heard from them. I could imagine them
on the floor, the wet plastic of the shower curtain wrapped around them.
The pinkish-white glow wherever it stuck to their bodies. Still going at
it.

There was something wrong with them.

Turning away—thank God I hadn't barged in on that—I caught
myself in the long mirror on the open closet door. I'd only taken my
shirt off. I mean, what the hell was I going to wear to my own execu-
tion? I looked at myself in my jeans and bra. Then I slammed the door,
but it whooshed shut: nothing that, in their state, they stood a chance
of hearing.

After sitting in front of my closet forever, I just changed my jeans. Put
on a sweater. The baggiest I had. Trying to make myself, for Kenny's
mom, a harmless, shapeless blob. I saw my bike helmet in the bottom
of my closet, tangled up with my shoes and dust bunnies, and thought

about wearing it. The only protection I had. That and the Planned Parenthood condoms in the back of my underwear drawer. Wasn't much between me and my life.

Standing in the hallway bathroom, looking at my hair, I thought about asking Dad for the old shave. Get out the motorboat and turn me back into a boy. That ought to take the fight out of Mrs. Crauder.

But I just slicked it down, let it dry however. I did not want to look how people thought I looked. Not the way Justin saw me. Or Jaimie. Kenny. Not for her.

When Mom and Dad came down, Dad had a sport coat on. It had leather patches on the elbows and another on the shoulder, like he might decide to jump up during dinner and do some shooting. I'd never seen him in anything like it in my life.

Mom looked like she'd spent every second upstairs trying to look exactly how I was trying not to look. Her blouse had a nice cleavage "V" in it, the pleats of her black pants were pressed tight over her almost flat belly. I could smell the spray holding her every hair.

Of course I knew that wasn't how she'd spent every second.

My mouth hung open, seeing the two of them standing like that in our usual old house. When I could, I asked, "How's the shower?"

Dad grinned, but Mom looked right through me. "Is that what you're going to wear?"

"What? What do you want?"

"Well, I thought that this once—"

"What, Mom, what do you want me to look like?"

"Something a little more—"

"More like you? How about your thong bikini? Would that fit your plans? What are you, Mrs. Theodora? Trying to seal the bargain here tonight?"

If Mom's eyes had been lasers, I'd have been a smoldering ribbon on the couch.

Dad said, "What *is* it with the two of you?" but as Mom and I kept up our stare-down, he got this kind of far-off smile. "I forgot about that bikini."

Mom swatted him on the chest with the back of her hand. "Down, boy," she said.

"Who's Mrs. Theodora?" he asked.

"It's hormones, Chuck. Remember those days? She's not responsible for what she says." Mom gave him a push toward the kitchen. "Let's go check the turkey."

God, that pissed me off, getting swept under the rug that way. "Who the hell's got the hormone problem in this family?" I shouted.

Mom whirled around, a warning finger already leveled my way.

The doorbell rang.

Dad glanced at Mom. At me. "No, don't get up," he said. "I'll get it."

CHAPTER TWENTY-THREE

Dad ushered Mrs. Crauder into our hallway. He took her coat and passed it to Mom. Mrs. Crauder had on black jeans and a sweater kind of like mine. There was nothing she had that she wanted shown off. Kenny was dressed the same as any day. Jeans. Sweatshirt. He walked like his chin was glued to his chest.

"Come in, come in," Dad kept saying. "It's freezing out there."

The chinook wasn't finished with us yet. It was maybe fifty-five outside. Sixty. Kenny hadn't bothered with a coat.

His mom said hello, thanks for the invitation, her eyes flicking around, taking in the details. There wasn't much to see. We were not Jaimie Tilton. No knickknack cabinets, no oil paintings under their own lights. But maybe the lack of clutter caught her eye, the lack of dirt. When she saw me on the couch, her eyes locked on to mine for an instant, then went on roving.

Mom asked, "Could I get you anything? A glass of wine? Beer? Soda?"

Mrs. Crauder's eyes flicked back to me. "No, thank you. Nothing for me, please."

I clicked the remote. Instant crowd noise. "The game's on. Dad says you're a fan."

Kenny's mom seemed surprised. "I used to watch some. With Kenny's dad. He bet on it." Her expression said that was more than she'd meant to say, and we all caught it.

"Hope he had better luck than I ever did," Dad said.

"That man wouldn't know luck if it walked up and bit him."

Dad grinned. He would have been proud to have said that himself. "It's walked up and bit me plenty," he said. "I got Luck's teeth marks all over my—"

"Chuck."

I'd never once known Dad to gamble. To ever make a single mention of it. Dad the chameleon. I'd hardly ever gotten to watch him change colors right before my eyes. Not for anybody but us.

Mom brought out a plate of water chestnuts wrapped in blackened bacon, which explained the burned-fat smell. We all sat around the living room and the plate. Mom asked me to turn off the TV. I muted it. Mom gave me a look, but Dad kept sneaking peeks. Kenny studied the floor. Now and then I caught his mom's darting glances run aground on Mom's cleavage, her legs.

Mom said, "It's nice to finally meet you. Kenny and Lucy have been friends forever."

"We've met," Kenny's mom said. "When Kenny and I first moved here. I would never let him play with someone I didn't even know."

Mom blinked. "Of course not. I mean it's nice to get a chance to know each other better."

Dad picked up one of Mom's appetizers. The bacon was so hard you could hear the crunch of it in his mouth. "You grew up here, didn't you?" he asked.

Mrs. Crauder said, "How did you know that?"

"Not many people move here for the wind."

"We lived down near the park. The duck pond."

Dad smiled. "That must have been nice."

Mrs. Crauder opened her mouth but then didn't say anything. She did not look like "nice" was a word she'd ever thought of.

"So," Dad went on, "you're a Great Falls High survivor yourself. Funny we never ran into each other. Did you know the Tillmans? They lived down that way."

Before Dad could do anything else to point out exactly how much older Mrs. Crauder was Mom said, "I grew up right in this house. It's like I've never gone anywhere."

"I landed in St. Thomas's," Dad volunteered out of the blue.

"The orphanage?" Kenny's mom asked.

I spun away from the TV. This was not one I'd heard before.

Dad nodded. "A big vacant lot now. I came back from one of my first jobs and found the whole place razed. Every last brick. After me, I think, the sisters decided their good work was done."

I knew the lot. Four solid city blocks, the streets dead-ending at its curbs. A falling stone wall. Chunks of concrete. An old baseball diamond. All clogged with weeds. "You were *born* there?" I said.

Dad nodded. "Still lived there when your mom and I met."

"You're kidding."

Mom nodded. "He calls it his time in the army."

Peeling potatoes. I pictured him as a kid, hunkered over a huge pot, glistening white spuds piled high around him. "How come you never told me?"

"What's the difference? No matter the size of the litter, I'm still the pick."

"What about your parents?"

Dad raised his hands and shoulders in this way overdone shrug.

I sat looking from Mom to Dad, waiting for the punch line.

"Once I got free of John," Mrs. Crauder said into the silence, nodding at Kenny, "his father, this seemed like the place to come back to."

"Did you even know your parents?" I asked Dad.

A commercial came on, and leaning forward, Dad socked Kenny on top of the knee. "So, Kenny, you play any football yourself?"

"No sir, Mr. Diamond. My size, it wouldn't be fair to the other boys."

Dad grinned. "We don't want anyone getting hurt out there."

I stared at Kenny. It was like he'd studied tapes. That he'd boned up for this.

I felt like I was closed off in some bubble. Dad, the man with the vanishing parents, wouldn't quite look at me. Kenny didn't dare speak to me. What could we talk about with everybody listening, straining for clues?

Every now and then I caught Kenny's mom scoping me out, and I realized my shoulders ached from being hunched forward, keeping any trace of my boobs from pressing against my sweater. It was like she could see through my clothes anyway, see my mom leaking out of me, the body pulling Kenny away from her. I thought of the way she'd wrapped Kenny up in the shower, holding him tight.

He's already gone, I wanted to tell her. Whether I have anything to do with it or not. But she knew it. It was obvious in her darting, shifting eyes—the years she saw alone on her couch, his bedroom left empty, in case he someday came back. I could have told her that wasn't going to happen. But I smiled instead, leaned forward to offer her another stab at the chestnut-and-bacon char.

She shook her head, lips pressed tight as a clamp.

Mom disappeared to get things ready in the kitchen. Dad kept throwing out names of people Mrs. Crauder—whose name, I learned, was Elizabeth, or Libby—might know, but he and Mom were almost ten years younger, and Dad had never worked in town. They didn't come up with any hits.

Mom called Dad out to carve, and the three of us sat like statues without them. Mrs. Crauder a sphinx. A deadly piece of stone.

"Your parents are so young," she said to me, leaving plenty of blanks to fill in. She reached for a chestnut. "What a surprise you must have been," she added, whispery, like something she might deny saying altogether.

I looked at Kenny. "You don't play football because you're afraid you'll hurt somebody?"

He smiled, flexing a biceps that was mostly bone. "I'm wiry, but I'll pop you."

"Like you did the other night?" his mom asked.

Dad shouted, "Chow's on!" and I heard Mom moan, "Chuck!"

We used the dining room, something we did like maybe once a year. There was wine out, a glass already poured at each plate, which I wasn't the only one to notice.

Mrs. Crauder didn't wait to sit down. While Mom carried in bowls of food, Mrs. Crauder drained her glass and set it down, very empty. She reached over and picked up Kenny's. "I think you'll remember our conversation about Kenny's troubles with alcohol," she said, taking a gulp.

Mom and Dad stopped, Dad holding a platter of carved meat in his hand. He nodded. "Well, here's the start of things. There's plenty more, though."

"Bird's big enough to feed a whole orphanage," I said.

Dad didn't even blink.

Mom took one last peruse of the table and made us all sit. She sat last, like entertaining this way was something she did every day.

Mrs. Crauder poured herself another glass of wine.

"What did you do for Thanksgiving in the orphanage?" I asked Dad.

"Turkey," he said with a wink. There was no way to know if he'd made up every word.

He started passing things around. Clockwise. The way things go down the drain at the other end of the world.

Which, after dinner, is where I wished I was when Mrs. Crauder, surveying the picked-over plates, the half-empty bowls of food, helped herself to the last of the second bottle and said, "So, the two of you are all right with what our kids are doing?"

Dad had shoved back his chair, raised his hands to pat his stomach while drawing in a breath for his huge after-feast sigh. He interrupted his ritual long enough to lift an eyebrow at Mrs. Crauder.

"The sex, I mean."

Dad stopped. A purple smudge of cranberry sauce stained the edge of his lip like a bruise. Mom froze, too, her eyes sharpened icicles pointed at Mrs. Crauder's throat.

"What did you say?" Dad said.

Mrs. Crauder launched back the rest of her wine. "Our kids fuck-ing. No problem for you?"

"Mom," Kenny said, smaller than ever.

"Lucy?" Dad started, the shake in his voice making it obvious he had no idea what he was going to ask.

"Did you just say 'fucking' in my house?" Mom asked. "At my table? Did you just say that while asking about my daughter?"

Even if you couldn't have seen Mom—the grizzly-bear sow hackles of her raised, her charge only an instant off—the lethal-sharp edge of her voice alone would have told you to invent something, anything, to make it absolutely clear that was not what you'd said.

"Mom," Kenny said, just a shadow of him left. "Don't. Please."

"Watched your daughter traipse out of my place at six the other morning. Watched her carry Kenny straight to his bed the other night. No doubt about where it was. Watched her strip off his clothes for a shower." She turned to me. "What was it you said, sweetheart? 'Nothing I haven't seen already'?"

"You said that," I murmured. "Not me."

"That is enough!" Mom roared.

"Well, that's what I think, too," Mrs. Crauder said. "More than enough." She looked clam cool, but her face was flushed, and sweat stood in tiny beads on her lip, her hairline. "I don't want my son catching any diseases from your daughter."

She said "your daughter" like I was the disease myself.

Mom sprang out of her chair like she might go right over the table and sink her teeth into Mrs. Crauder's scrawny bird neck, claw her eyes free from their dark sockets. Dad was up, too, maybe to stop Mom, maybe to mop up the pieces.

"Get out!" Mom shouted. "You pathetic woman! Get out of my house!" She said it like she was banishing Mrs. Crauder from Eden— our house, which she'd only ever made fun of.

Kenny's mom stood: "Hiding your head in the sand won't stop anything," she said. We were all out of our chairs. "I won't have your daughter—"

Mom's finger lashed toward the door. "Out!"

I rushed for the stairs. I heard a chair fall over and hoped Dad hadn't kicked into action. Mom shouted, almost cackling, "*You* won't have my daughter? *You?* My daughter—"

I slammed my bedroom door behind me, cutting her off, but instead of banging shut, it banged on Kenny.

I whirled around to find him hanging on to his elbow.

"I'm sorry, Lucy. I didn't tell her anything. I begged her not to come here. I even went to Van's and bought a turkey to cook ourselves. I told her I was sick. I knew she—"

I pulled him the rest of the way into my room and held him as tight as I could, squeezed him hard enough to make my ears ring, but I could still hear them downstairs. Shouting. Dad now, too. I thought of the man at the fair, the blood etched between his teeth.

Twisting the lock of my door, I pulled Kenny onto my bed, the two of us sitting side by side, touching like on the top of the jungle gym. I shut my eyes, feeling the tears squeeze out. The run of one down my face. I flattened it dry. Downstairs, they were still shouting. I knew they hadn't noticed us gone.

"Your dad's whole orphanage thing," Kenny said. "Kind of sounds like a pretty good deal, doesn't it?"

I couldn't stop this tiny laugh. "You know, when you first moved here, I wanted us to adopt you. I had this whole big dream that we could be this great happy family."

"Me?"

It was almost too easy to please him. I didn't tell him it was only my plan to get Dad to stay. Kenny gave me a squeeze. A kiss down low on the neck. He called me sis.

But I'd started chewing my lip. "Maybe," I said, "maybe Dad's the one we should have adopted. Maybe that would make him feel like he has a real home here."

"Lucy, I'm not sure, but I kind of don't think you can adopt your father."

"You can pick your nose but not your parents."

"Yeah. Like that. I guess." He put his arm around me and said, "Happy Thanksgiving, Lucy."

"You know how my parents said that to each other? In the shower. Going at it like rabbits."

"Now, that'd be a *happy* Thanksgiving."

Things went quiet downstairs, and Kenny said, "I am so sorry, Lucy."

We listened to them come up the stairs, tap at my door. Dad said, "Luce?"

"Go away," I tried to say, but my voice cracked. I touched Kenny's face with the very tips of my fingers. "Go away."

Kenny sat beside me, his eyes wide, rolling to see his doom coming through the door. "I shouldn't be here," he said, his lips against my ear. I gave him a *no shit!* look.

"Lucy," Dad said.

"I'm okay, Dad. Okay?"

"She's crazy, Lucy," Dad said, and I saw Kenny close his eyes. "Crazy, and drunk, and rattlesnake-mean."

"Dad," I said, trying to stop him.

"Don't listen to a word she said. We didn't. She's crazier than a keg of nails."

"Wow, Dad. Hard to beat nails for crazy."

"That a boy," he said. He waited, probably hoping I'd let him in now that we'd had our joke. His constant hope. "Luce?" he said.

"I'll come down in a while, Dad. Okay?"

He stayed. "That woman," he said at last. "As if her son was some kind of prize."

"Kenny's all right," I said.

"I know. He can't help who his mother is."

"Nobody can," I said, meaning him, a woman who'd drop off a baby for nuns to raise.

"You can pick your friends but not your nose," Dad said.

Kenny's brows scrunched together, and I almost laughed. He smiled, and I looked away. All we needed was to start laughing.

"You sure you're okay, Luce?"

Mom told him, "It'd take more than that bitch to scratch our Luce."

"That's right, Mom," I said. "Diamond Girl."

Kenny raised his eyebrows, and I pointed my thumb at my heart.

They said they loved me then, and Kenny and I listened to them going down the stairs, which was a relief. It had been as likely, I figured, that they'd go down the hall to their room.

They hardly ever said they loved me. I mean, it seemed pretty obvious most of the time, but it wasn't something anybody in our family often said. I wondered why they didn't even say it to each other, with all they went after it.

One look at Kenny, and it was obvious it wasn't something he *ever* heard. Of all the stuff my parents had said about his mom, about him, even, that "We love you, Luce" seemed to be the one that really drove a spike through him.

Kenny didn't make a move to touch me or anything. He whispered, "I'm the one that really loves you."

I reached over and pulled him tight against me. "I don't even know what love is."

"You're looking at it," he said, but he turned toward the window and a moment later asked, "How am I going to get out of here?"

CHAPTER TWENTY-FOUR

A few hours later, leaving Kenny alone in my room, I made my appearance downstairs. They were on me right away, but I held them off, saying, "I know. She's crazier than a bedbug in a keg of nails."

"Luce—"

I held up my hand. "Dad, I don't want to talk about it. It makes me feel sick. Dirty, somehow. Like I really did something or something."

"But Luce—"

"Let her go, Chuck," Mom said.

I wondered how much she knew and how much she simply didn't want the subject of sex while he was away raised in connection with anyone, even me. No telling, where that might lead.

"I just came down to say good night." I stepped forward and gave Dad a hug, something we usually saved for his departures and arrivals. He hugged back, only an instant late.

Mom, when I moved to the door, stepped back so I could go through. No hugs there. " 'Night, Luce," she said. "You sleep tight."

At the doorway, I turned. "Dad? Was all that true? About being from the orphanage?"

He shrugged it off. "It was like having a hundred brothers and sisters."

"And no parents," I said. "Do you know who they were? Your parents?"

"They were kids, Luce. It was different in those days."

I didn't know what to say. Kids? Like what, Mom and him had been senior citizens?

Dad smiled. "And here you are griping about me being gone once in a while."

"Once in a while? *Once in a while?*"

Dad laughed like it was a joke, and Mom said, "Good night, Luce," again.

Upstairs, I found Kenny standing at the open window, ready to leap out, maybe, to a broken leg at best, rather than face my mom or dad.

"Close that," I hissed, locking the door behind me. "It's freezing in here."

"What am I supposed to do now?" he asked.

"We'll wait for them to go to sleep, then you sneak out. Like we already said."

"To where?"

I knew what he meant, but I didn't have an answer. "You could stay here," I mumbled. "But not now. Not like this." I gave him a little kiss, walking him over to my bed, letting him see he'd at least make it through the night. "They'll be up soon. We just have to be quiet."

I knew what would happen then. What we'd hear. I thought of Kenny an hour ago, promising that he was the only one who really loved me. "Remember," I asked, chewing at my lip, "that morning I came to your room?"

He smiled. "That's not something I'll probably forget."

I fiddled with the hem of my sweater, then lifted it up over my head. I worked quick, letting my jeans fall to the floor. "I told them I was going to bed," I said. Kenny, I could tell, wanted to look away, thought he should, but couldn't. I unhooked my bra, but then couldn't just stand there naked before him. Dodging under my covers, I said,

"I want to do it right this time, Kenny. Like it's supposed to be. Like it means something. Not like some stupid accident."

"Here? Now?"

I flicked off the light. "Come here," I said.

Kenny sat down on top of the covers. He petted my hair, gave me a few kisses.

Downstairs we heard the phone ring, and a few minutes later, Mom and Dad came up. We listened to their steps. Instead of going to their room, they stopped at my door.

"Luce?" Dad said. "Lucy? Are you awake?"

"What, Dad?" I answered, trying my best to sound asleep.

"Kenny's mom is on the phone," Mom said. "She's not making a lot of sense, but Kenny's not home, and she's frantic."

"Too bad," I said, but Kenny sat up straight, like he might bolt right out the door for her.

"She doesn't know where he is. We lost track of him when she was leaving."

"Do you know where he might go?" Dad asked. "Any idea where he might be?"

I sat up and rubbed Kenny's back, his shoulders. "I don't know. The park? The jungle gym?"

They were quiet. I heard steps go down the hall to their room.

"Dad?"

"She's still on the line, Luce," Mom answered. "He went to tell her."

"Oh."

"Any other ideas?" she asked.

I shook my head in the dark. "No."

"She thinks he's over here with you. She said she'd come haul him home if we didn't."

"Don't let her, Mom. Don't let her come back."

Mom snorted some kind of laugh. "I wouldn't worry about that. She didn't sound as if she could make the walk." She didn't say anything else, but I didn't hear her steps going away. Then, out of the quiet, she said, "I just hope Kenny's all right."

"Me, too," I answered.

She waited longer this time, until I wondered whether I hadn't heard her walk away.

"Chuck just hung up," she announced. "That's done with." I heard the knob twist. "You're not thinking about letting me in there, are you, Lucy?" She had her mouth right against the crack of the door. So Dad couldn't hear.

"I'm in bed, Mom. I don't have any clothes on."

She knew I didn't sleep naked. She knew we never locked doors.

"Naked?" she said. "Lucky boy."

She said it so quiet, I wasn't sure I'd heard what I heard. But I was. I knew.

We heard her steps fall away down the hall.

The two of us had, the whole time, been frozen tight. I didn't realize it until Mom left, the stiffness of every muscle in my body. I lay down flat, blew out this long breath.

Kenny finally lay down beside me. "She knows," he said.

I knew what was coming. I said, "Just wait a minute."

It was maybe twenty minutes before Mom and Dad started their bedtime ritual. I felt Kenny slowly turn to me in surprise. I hugged him, and said, "Would you get under the covers now?" I pulled his sweatshirt over his head. "Believe me, they won't hear a thing."

"This is suicide," he said, but he did as he was told. I got his pants off.

It wasn't long before I reached behind me, fumbling open my drawer, scrambling my fingers through the tangle of my underwear. I found one of the condoms, pulling the foil open with my teeth.

"Are you trying to get us killed? Me?"

"What did you tell me before?"

"What? That I love you? I do, Luce, more than—"

I put my mouth over his.

Kenny struggled in the dark with the condom and then, only seconds later, he was in me. I whispered, "Tell me again," and Kenny did, saying it over and over, as best he could between kisses. I listened for the rhythm of my parents, straining to match it. Kenny pulled away from me, up onto his elbows, my mouth no longer able to silence him. But we were moving against each other then, and I don't think he was saying anything.

We were too near the side of the bed; Kenny, I think, still that ready to run. One of his legs slipped off the mattress. He had to stand up on the floor. He held on to my rear, lifting me half off the bed. Something he couldn't stop. I started to hear our own rhythm, and I nodded to it. I opened my eyes, but Kenny's were shut tight, his face caught in what we were doing.

We were much closer than we had been before. Closer to what Mom and Dad did. I tried to make it closer still. I concentrated on Kenny's face, saw the cords of his neck standing out the way his mother's had down at our table, making her accusations.

He kept going, no way to stop now, no thoughts of running. He bit his lip, his hips twitching. Slowly his eyes opened. You could see he'd crossed some line, made some decision that this was how he'd chosen to die, and he was still, for a few more seconds anyway, surprised to find himself back here breathing.

"I love you, Lucy," he told me. "More than anyone else ever, as long as you live."

From down the hall, we could hear Mom and Dad still going.

Kenny lay panting beside me. Our sweat had dried and our breathing was normal before their rhythm went frantic and then stopped. A few minutes later, they were laughing.

"What in the heck?" Kenny said, inches from my ear.

"It's like that every night."

"Your parents?"

I pulled him tight to my side, held him there, his arms around me. Not like some kid stealing into another kid's house at five in the morning. Not like a couple of kids groping on a couch. Like real people do.

Kenny waited until two in the morning before sneaking out, his shoes in his hand. I watched him from my window, walking up the block, disappearing after the streetlight, then reappearing in the next. The three branches blocked him off before I could see him reach his house. His mother.

CHAPTER TWENTY-FIVE

The next Monday; no word from Kenny since the big dinner, I came downstairs for breakfast, anxious to see him, barely noticing the sound of Mom and Dad talking in the kitchen, the way they were talking.

I was at the last step when I heard Dad say, without a trace of laughter, "While I'm here? You'd actually do that?"

Mom didn't say anything.

"That's what you want? To leave while I'm here?" He grunted this kind of laugh. "Well, that's just grand. So you can go and call strangers. That, Mame, would be the gravy on the cake. Anything else'd be icing."

"It's not like I can choose to come and go when I want, Chuck. It's a job."

"I can sure as hell choose for you."

"No," Mom answered, her voice as flat as Dad's. "You can't."

I could feel them each waiting for the other to back down.

"I don't want you having a job. I never did."

"It doesn't make any difference what you want, Chuck. You know what you're like? The weather. A front blowing through now and then. You did that to yourself."

I heard Dad's chair scrape back. "Quit the job," he said, so low I almost missed it. "I am not sitting around this house like a dump on a log while you go to your minimum-wage hobby."

"What the hell do you think I'll be doing the second you leave but sitting around this house?"

"Raising Lucy."

"Fine. Then *you* raise her while *I'm* at work."

"But you're not going to work."

"Oh, yes I am. It's your turn, Chuck. Your turn to be this amazing parent you never had."

"You'll stay right here! We've been over this a million times. I didn't have her so she could grow up without parents. Look at her! She needs it now more than ever."

Mom drew in a breath. "You think you can fight biology, Chuck? Lucy isn't six years old anymore. She's a young woman. You can't build a compound tall enough, strong enough. What the hell am *I* supposed to do?"

"You make it your *job*!" Dad shouted. There was a bang, a rattle of silverware, Dad's fist, probably, on the table. Or Mom slamming the drawer. Then silence.

I put my hand on the banister, slowly turning the corner toward the kitchen.

They were glaring at each other, the kitchen table between them. "If it's of the slightest interest to either of you," I said, trying to keep my voice from shaking, "I'm perfectly capable of taking care of myself."

They didn't speak.

"I've been doing it for years. I mean, it's not exactly like I'm the number one priority around here."

"Lucy," Dad said.

I pulled a banana from the clump on the table, broke it open, and turned for the door.

"You've always been our—" Dad started.

"Don't even pretend," I interrupted. "Maybe next time you should try a *cold* shower."

"Lucy!"

I reminded myself so much of Mom, running out the door with her banana in her mouth, that I shouted, "To market, to market, to buy a fat pig!"

There was Kenny, waiting outside the gate like always, like everything would always be this way. I stormed out, and he fell in step right beside me, but I shook off his arm. "They might see."

"Who?"

"Mom. Dad. We can't ever let them know anything about us."

"Why?"

"We can't give them anything to go on." Dad could believe whatever he wanted, but if we waved it in his face like a red cape, he couldn't help but snort and charge. Kenny would be stomped to nothing. "So, how'd it go with your mom?" I asked.

"She's fucking nuts. She spent half the weekend on the phone. Screaming at my dad."

I was looking him over for bruises, scratches. Not that he said she was ever that way, but it was something you might expect. He seemed so defenseless, so breakable. But there was none of that.

He said, "She told him I was drinking. She told him that—that we were—you know."

"So he was screaming back?"

Kenny shrugged. "What about your mom?"

"She was cool. I think she was fishing, you know. I don't think she really knew anything." She knew, all right, but we had this sort of balance of power now. The whole mutual-assured-destruction thing we'd talked about in U.S. history. I thought of her and Dad, duking it out about her job. "She's got other things to worry about, anyway."

We were out of sight of the house, and Kenny put his arm around me again. I let it stay. "So what's your dad's deal about fixing up the jungle gym?" he asked.

I glanced over, ready to laugh. "What?"

"He called last night about—"

"*My* dad called *you*?"

He nodded.

"About the jungle gym?"

"He said he wants to fix it up for us. Said he wanted to talk to some of the other people around who use it, get them to chip in."

"He always said they only left it standing because they forgot about it. That it was so high, it was a happening waiting for an accident." I looked at Kenny. "How can you fix a jungle gym? What did you tell him?"

"That we hadn't played on it in a long time. He said it didn't matter. Who did we *used* to play on it with?"

"And?"

"It was always just you and me."

"You didn't tell him that, did you? Kenny, I'm trying to make him think you're nobody. I'm trying to save your life."

"I told him Rabia used to be there. A long time ago. Scott some-times."

We reached school, Kenny dropping his arm before anybody could see. He followed me to my room, and since we'd managed to give Justin and Tim the slip, I gave him a kiss that I broke off before it could really get going.

He smiled, all chagrined. "Used to be we could only do that at your house. Now only at school."

I gave his arm a squeeze. "We're laying low for a while, Kenny. Just till we get Dad off his warpath. It's not safe for you."

"I don't need no stinking safety," he said, dodging in for another kiss, just a peck. He smiled, but I knew he meant it, that he'd take death for another kiss.

It was pathetic really, but there were worse things to know.

CHAPTER TWENTY-SIX

Even with the no-kiss rule in place, Kenny was there at the end of the day, patient as a buzzard. As we walked home, I got a feeling that he'd always be there waiting for me, no matter what I did. He paused at our gate, hopeful, but I tipped my head toward our windows. "We'll find a time, Kenny. Dad won't be here forever. He's already stretching records."

As usual, that—wishing for Dad to be gone—left me feeling about two inches tall.

I walked up the steps and shoved a shoulder against the door,

falling inside and starting to shout "Home again, home again" before
I realized that I was hearing Mom shouting, that I'd sort of heard it
even as I came up the steps, watching Kenny walk on alone to his
house.

"What is wrong with you?" she yelled. "Chuck?"

She was using the same voice she flailed me with whenever I
pulled something particularly boneheaded. Not weeks ago, I'd thought
my parents never fought. Now I wondered if they'd ever stopped. If
they'd been at it all day.

"Just wait. You'll see," Dad answered. "Here she is now."

I pushed the door shut behind me, wondering if I shouldn't back
straight through it. Run and hide in Kenny's house. Maybe we could
flee between our houses, back and forth, depending which was worse
at any given second. The fire and the frying pan.

"Lucy," Dad called. "Come in here, please."

"Chuck," Mom said, sounding desperate, less angry. Almost
scared. "Does the word 'kidnapping' mean anything to you?"

"Lucy!" Dad shouted. "Lucy!"

His voice jerked me forward. I'd never heard anything like it. He
was not kidding. I peeked around the corner into the living room. "Holy
shit," I whispered.

Dad had Scott Booker by the throat of his jacket, twisted up tight
in his fist. Scott's eyes were wide and wild, latching on to me like I
was his only hope.

Mom's mouth was open, looking for the next words, something that
would shock Dad into letting go. She was dressed for work, her makeup
in place, but her hair flew around her head like she might have been
wrestling with Dad, trying to break his hold.

Dad had this victorious grin slashed across his face. "Uh-huh! Now
you'll see!" He turned to me. "This is him, isn't it, Luce? The creep!
Right here in the flesh!"

"Dad? What are you—"

"It's him," he shouted, his voice a slap. "Isn't it?"

I nodded. "But Dad, it was nothing. It wasn't even his—"

"Nothing! Nothing?" He shook Scott like a rag doll. "This wasted sperm forces you to kiss him, and you say—"

Mom slapped her hands against her sides. "What in the hell are you talking about? Have you completely lost your mind?"

Tears were leaking out of Scott's eyes. His skin looked like candle wax. He was yanked up to his tiptoes, his coat and shirt pulled off his waist, exposing the roll of flab that always made him seem so repulsive. Now it just made him look like a chubby little kid.

"Dad," I said, my voice small and shaky. "That was like a hundred years ago. We were kids, we—"

"You are an untouched vessel!" Dad bellowed.

I blinked. *"What?"*

"Let him go, Chuck. Let him go home."

"Yeah, Dad. He didn't do anything. He's nothing."

"Nothing! After what he made you do?"

"It was my idea, Dad. He wouldn't have thought of it in a million years."

Dad's arm drooped a bit. Enough to let Scott stand flat on his feet. "What?"

"It was, Dad. I did it for Kenny. The kiss was nothing. I haven't even seen Scott since last summer."

Dad stared at me.

"It wasn't some big deal, Dad. Really. It was kid stuff. He—him— he's just a big loser." I felt bad saying that right in front of Scott, but it was for his own good.

Dad gave him a halfhearted shake. "He agreed," he said, the fight going out of him.

"Well, who wouldn't?" Mom asked, sounding disgusted again, less scared. I gaped at Mom. What was it with her?

Dad looked between the two of us, then down at Scott. "Apologize," he said.

Immediately, Scott said, "I'm sorry, Luce. I'm sorry."

"Her name is Lucy."

"Lucy. I'm sorry. Really."

"And you'll never do it again."

"Dad! Of course he never will! Do you think I'd ever give him the chance?"

"I never will. Not ever," Scott pleaded.

"You should be the one apologizing," Mom said.

Dad snapped her a look. He let go of Scott's coat, gave him a shove toward the door. "Leave my daughter alone."

Scott shot to the door, hurrying too much to straighten up, to pull his jacket and shirt back down. I watched him fumble at the latch, fling the door open and run. The door bounced back hard enough it nearly closed itself.

I walked down the hall and pushed it shut tight.

They were silent in the living room, no one moving, until I heard Mom say, "It's good to see you've got the whole jealousy thing under control."

"Quiet," Dad said.

"Well, for crying out loud, Chuck! You'll be lucky if his parents don't press charges. Dragging a fifteen-year-old across town because he kissed your daughter?"

"Forced her."

"What is it, Chuck? I'm not enough to get jealous about anymore? You have to throw Lucy in now, too?"

I walked back down the hall, saw the two of them standing exactly where I'd left them. Dad's hands, without Scott to hold, looked big and empty.

"Is there something I should be jealous about here, Mame? About you?"

"If you could see how ridiculous you look." She shook her head. "I can't believe you. Can't believe you called me home from work for that stunt." She kept shaking her head. "They'll fire me now for sure. Gone for a week and can't make a day before a 'family emergency.' Is that what this was really all about?"

Mom looked over to me. She was still shaking her head, but now she smiled, almost a can-you-believe-the-shit-I-have-to-put-up-with smile. Then she started talking as if Dad weren't there. As if she'd admitted that was what she hoped for. "How was school, Luce?" she asked, like any other day. "Maybe we should start thinking about what's for dinner."

She started over to me, the kitchen, and I was backing out of the doorway to let her through, when Dad snapped out and snagged her arm above the elbow, spinning her around to him. "*Is* there something?" he asked, his faces inches from hers. "Something I should be jealous about?"

Mom glared at him. Then down at his arm, his hand.

He let go.

"Take a shower, champ," she said. "Go cool off before you do something *really* stupid."

Then she came past me on her way to the kitchen. She was rubbing at her arm, and though she seemed cucumber-cool, I could hear, as she passed, how fast and light her breathing was.

CHAPTER TWENTY-SEVEN

I followed Mom into the kitchen, but instead of opening a cabinet or the refrigerator, pulling out any pot or pan, she gripped the edge of the stove and stood there. If it wasn't for the trembling of the few flyaway hairs, you wouldn't have known she was shaking. She was working on her breathing. Trying to get it back to where it brought her air.

Behind us, I heard Dad climb the stairs.

The phone rang. I was standing right next to it. "Hello?"

"Hey, how's the sexiest chick at Great Falls High?"

Justin Haven. I couldn't stop a smile. But I said, *"Chick?"* and slammed the phone back into its cradle.

Mom leaned back against the stove, watching me. Her mascara was smudged, not quite raccoon eyes but heading in that direction. "Boy troubles?" she asked.

I rolled my eyes. "That idiot won't leave me alone."

Mom nodded, kind of smiling. "Get used to it."

"No way."

"There's no calling them off, Lucy. I know. All you can do is get used to it."

"I can *not* like it. Not as much as you."

I could see that stung, that she'd thought we were about to have this mother-daughter bonding experience like they write about in doctor-office women's magazines. I didn't even know why I'd said it. I wasn't mad at her. I was mad at myself, at smiling over Justin Haven calling me a sexy chick.

To get out from under her gaze, I turned to the phone. Scrabbling for its plug, the clip you have to squeeze shut to get out, I yanked it clear. "There," I said. "I don't have to take it after all."

"There are other phones, Luce."

"And they've all got plugs."

I unplugged the one in the living room, then headed upstairs for the one in their bedroom. I really thought, desperate as I was, that I was accomplishing something.

Sexiest chick at Great Falls High. God! I should have felt like I needed a shower.

I walked into their room and almost ran over Dad. "Hey," I said.

"What are you doing?"

I dodged around him, intent on the phone, the one link between me and the world of boys. "Operation Incommunicado," I said, yanking out the plug and holding it up for him to see.

He stood waiting for a punch line, maybe, and that's when I saw he had his duffel.

I dropped the phone cord. "Maybe the question is what are *you* doing?"

"You're too late." He nodded toward the phone line.

"What?"

"Work called. I got to go."

I watched him. "Called when?"

"A minute ago."

I started to say, "I answered the phone," calling bullshit on him once and for all, but all I got out was one tiny "I." He didn't care one way or the other if I believed him. He had a story now, something he'd stick to. Same as the orphanage.

"Where to this time?" I asked.

"Same old, same old."

"Chopping down gold?" I asked, making it too easy for him.

He smiled. "Putting the bacon in the bank."

"Sure beats sitting here with the two of us, doesn't it?"

He looked around me. "There's nothing I'd like better—"

"Oh, give it a rest, Dad. I'm not retarded."

"You might not understand all that you think."

"I think I understand enough."

He shrugged. "Maybe yes, maybe no, but I still gots to go." He said it singsongy, a rhyme he'd stumbled across.

"When I was six, Dad. And it barely worked then, okay?"

He sucked his lower lip into the corner of his mouth. "Maybe I better head on out."

"Before dinner?" I asked. "At five o'clock at night? They've got night logging now?" I halfway didn't believe he was logging anymore. Or maybe he never had. Who knew what he did? Drug smuggler, maybe. High-seas pirate. International spy.

"It's a long drive, Luce."

"Drive all night, work all day. Sounds like a recipe for disaster. Saw off your leg. Drop a tree on some guy's head."

"We're used to it."

"To trees dropping on your heads?"

"The hours, Luce." He turned and walked down the hallway. I followed, nearly walking over him again when he stopped outside my room.

He looked in at my unmade bed, my clothes on the floor. There was underwear there that suddenly looked pretty skimpy; a bra on the edge of my bed. I stepped around him and closed the door. "I'll get that cleaned up. Things been a little wild around here."

"A little," Dad agreed. Then he looked at me for real, not waiting for a reaction or a laugh. "Mom's right," he said. "You are a woman now. Didn't even realize it myself. Driving back this time, I was still picturing how I'd give you a haircut." He smiled. "Remember those?"

"For Christ's sake, Dad, it was my hair."

"How we'd get laughing? Making those motorboat sounds?"

"That's not exactly what stuck with me most."

He reached out, rumpled the length of my hair. He was looking at my door like he could still see the evidence of all the changes scattered across the floor. He was chewing on his lip again, something I'd never noticed him do before. "Has Mom talked to you?" he asked.

He wouldn't quite meet my eye, and it was second before I realized what he meant. "God, Dad! Like the birds and the bees? Come on!"

He smiled. "Never did get the whole bird-and-bee thing. Which is which? Either way, somebody's coming away from that less than satisfied. Or injured."

"Dad! Yuck!"

"What I mean, Luce. Is. Well, what I mean. The shower the other day. What goes on between your mom and me. Luce, that's taken years."

Years? Like I was what, immaculate conception?

"It's different from anything you'll know for a long time yet."

"At least there's that hope."

Dad tried to smile. "I mean, that's not where you start. That's not how you should begin."

"I've got no interest in starting anything, okay, Dad? Rest easy about that."

He smiled for real, relief pouring off him. "Well, when you do, remember. We're not your example, all right?"

He was standing there holding his duffel bag, imparting this wisdom to keep me—what did he call it—an untouched vessel until he made it back to protect me for another couple of weeks, drag in some other poor lope like Scott Booker.

Don't bother with the door, I wanted to say, *the barn's already empty.* Instead, I said, "You're not my example. Got it."

"Luce?" he insisted.

"Yeah, Dad, whatever. The whole thing grosses me out, okay? Why do you think I say no to the parties? Why do you think I hang around with Kenny all the time?" That to keep Kenny out of Dad's clutches a while longer.

Dad grinned. "What? Is he some kind of homo or something?"

"What? No! God! But he's Kenny. It'd be like dating your kid brother."

"I don't have a kid brother."

I shook my head. Like talking to your own wooden puppet.

"Poor Kenny," he said, starting down the stairs.

Why did everybody keep saying "Poor Kenny"? But really, I knew. Hell, I said it myself sometimes.

When we came around the landing, we saw Mom standing at the bottom, leaning against the banister, looking up. She watched us come down, Dad with his duffel. As soon as he opened his mouth, she held up a hand. "Not one word," she said. "I think if I hear another lie right now, I'll go straight out of my mind."

Dad hesitated but couldn't help himself. "It's just work, Mame."

"Oh, for Christ's sake, will you stop?"

"Mame."

"Leaving me holding this bag of shit?" she asked, sounding exhausted. "You gutless fucking coward."

Dad took a step back, almost on top of me. I peeked over his shoulder, making sure this was my mom, not Kenny's somehow sneaked into her place.

"Mame," Dad said soothingly. "Mame."

"What is it that you do, anyway? What have you told her?"

"You know what I do."

"But where this time?" Mom snapped. "Who?"

"Who?"

"Don't play me for a fool, Chuck. I am so sick of that game."

"Easy now, Mame."

"Easy?"

He looked at her a long, long time. "Glass houses," he whispered, adding, so low it sounded almost like another breath, "Lola."

Mom stared back. Her lips worked, but no actual words came out. He reached a hand out and put it behind her head, on her neck, gave her a rub while he pulled her in to his chest. I could see the muscles in her neck as she tried to hold back, but then she was against him, and I couldn't see her anymore.

"Just go, Chuck," I heard her say. "If you can't handle it here, just go."

I backed up the stairs, giving them what privacy I could.

"I can handle anything you throw past me," Dad said, all soft and buttery.

"Lucy? Threatening to kill some fat high school kid? How'd you say you handled that?"

Dad didn't answer, and Mom gave this kind of laugh. "It's called growing up, Chuck. You should try it sometime."

CHAPTER TWENTY-EIGHT

I backed up the stairs, watching the two of them holding on to each other, at last looking like people saying good-bye, sad and knowing something's going away, instead of how they always said good-bye before, as if they could barely keep their clothes on long enough to get him into his truck.

When I heard Mom ask how he was handling me, I turned away. I almost went into my room but was stopped by the scatter of those Victoria's Secret undies. I didn't want anything to do with them. I walked down the hall to the bathroom, locking myself in for no reason except I didn't want to face Mom right away, the two of us alone again.

I remembered once, when I was a kid, following Mom up to her room after one of the long good-byes. Reaching her bed, she dropped down on the edge like a half-empty sack. I sat next to her, our arms touching, and watched her strip out of her nylons, rolling them down her legs one at a time. It was six o'clock in the morning. She'd only had them on a few minutes.

I asked, "Are you going back to bed, Mom?" I was afraid she would. She looked like that was all she wanted, to crawl in and pull the blankets up over her head.

But she said, "No. These were just something for him to keep me in mind."

I leaned against her. "He couldn't ever forget you. Not the way you two say good-bye."

She stood up, wriggling out of her slip, letting it crumple around her ankles. "It's what we do best," she agreed.

"Practice makes perfect."

She rubbed the top of my head. "You sound exactly like him. As little as you see him, you sound just the same."

For years, that had made me kind of proud and sad both. Now it seemed like this glowing time from our paradise days. Something Hallmark would do.

I sat down on the edge of the bathtub and held my head in my hands so I wouldn't have to see myself in the mirror. I had wished for this. That he'd leave. So Kenny and I could get back to our boinking. And now he was gone.

The ghost of Lola was here with us, too. Whoever she was, there was sex involved, you could count on that. Dad warning me it would take years to get to their level. Mom telling me I'd have to get used to it. Kenny hovering. Justin snorting. How could something that felt so good mess everything up so much? No wonder they called it screwing.

Slowly, I lifted my head, forcing myself to see what the mirror had to say. The sexiest chick in Great Falls High.

Just sitting there in my T-shirt, my boobs jutted out at the world. I hunched my shoulders, but that made the neck of my shirt gape, a shadowy void the boys would sweat over, wondering how much they could see.

I shook my head, running my fingers through my hair. I'd give anything to be built like a stick again. To be able to sit next to Kenny at the very top of the jungle gym, sweating over nothing more than the climb, do the supersonic death spiral, my T-shirt caught up around my head, my chest as tan and skinny and uneventful as his.

Maybe it just all had to stop.

I pulled open the big bottom drawer, the catchall, started rummaging through old spray bottles, a broken box scattering Buff Puffs. At the bottom, I found it, under the tangled cord of Mom's old hair dryer that Dad said he'd fix for me.

The motorboat.

It was in its clear floppy plastic case, a rubber band holding it in with its comb and grease, the black plastic forks of its attachments. The rubber band broke as I worked it off, its stretch used up. A bunch of the attachments slipped onto the floor, tiny plastic clatters. I would have known the one he used, the quarter-incher, even if it hadn't been speckled with bits of my blond stubble. Leaving the others on the floor, I snapped it over the metal teeth. My hand shook enough I had to steady it with the other to get the plug into the socket.

Outside I heard the roar of Dad's pickup; his first hard, starting stomp. The engine settled into an idle. I wondered if he'd come back in for another kiss, if they'd managed to salvage that much.

I pushed the clipper's switch forward, and it vibrated in my hand with its nasty, high-pitched whine. Sometimes Dad would pull at the clipper, like he had a cord start wrapped around a tiny outboard. He'd click the clipper on then off, shake his head, and wrap the cord again—a reluctant motor on a still, cold morning. I could hear the way he'd laugh.

When I faced myself in the mirror to start cutting, everything blurred over. I wiped hard at my eyes, then put the tickling, tingling blades down flat on my forehead. "Vroom," I whispered.

Hand still shaking, I ran the clipper up over the top of my head, all the way down to the base of my neck, where the shiver made my shoulders jump, just like always.

My hair fell away in a clump I could feel hit the swell of my rear.

I made the rest of the runs. Complete with jumps.

There was hair all over me. Except on my head. I almost couldn't help a smile at the old silvery stubble. Like a friend you hadn't expected to ever see again.

I pulled my shirt off, shook it out over the sink, scratched at where it had pinched the hair against my neck. I finger-combed as much of the hair out of the sink as I could, threw it into the pail underneath. Even so, when I ran the water around to wash the last of the hair away, it swirled around in a puddle that barely drained out.

I unhooked my bra and threw it on the floor. There was more hair stuck against my chest. I unbuttoned my jeans, shucked them down next to my shirt. My panties last.

Then I studied myself, my boobs, standing up just as straight without the bra, my waist curving in and then out, my stomach flat, the clean-looking patch of soft blond hair between my legs. Here and there, from my neck on down, cut hairs glinted, catching the light.

I hadn't changed a thing.

I still had everything they wanted. Except hair, maybe. But looking at myself, I knew that wouldn't really matter to any of them.

Kenny would say he liked it. That he'd missed it.

Justin would step back, but it wouldn't be a second before he'd get something out like "Whoa, kinky." Tim would whistle and laugh.

Dad would rub it for luck. At least I wished he would, that I could feel his hand, warm, covering my whole head, moving me gently back and forth before tipping me safely in to his side.

I pushed aside the shower curtain. Maybe the water would last long enough I'd drown. Or melt and run down the drain. Before stepping in, I flicked off the lights. Standing in the darkness under the gush, almost hot enough to burn, was just right, right then.

It was a long while before I dared to lift my hands, to feel the stiff, bristly armor of my head, remembering the way it tickled my palms, made me feel like a kid again. A boy. A born again virgin.

In the darkness, my hands on top of my stubbly head, there was no way to tell any different.

CHAPTER TWENTY-NINE

When I crawled out of the shower, feeling for a towel, the first thing I realized was that I couldn't hear Dad's truck. He was gone. Or maybe Mom had talked some sense into him, made him see at last what all his leaving had done, would do now.

I didn't want to know which. Not yet. I stood naked and dripping, my ear against the door. Everything quiet. I cracked open the door, then cut down the hall to my room. I buried myself in my bed in the dark, no way to see anything around me, none of my own mess, my own life. But I listened. For hours.

All through dinnertime, into the night, I heard not one sound. With none of their night noises, I knew Dad wasn't here anymore. He couldn't be. I began wondering if Mom had left with him. It was almost enough to tempt me out.

But I couldn't really believe that of them. That they'd leave me for each other. Even if they wanted to. Even if I wanted them to.

I woke up in the morning, still naked, my tangled towel damp and cold on the other side of the bed. I heard something. Somebody in the kitchen. Mom. Getting ready for work.

I headed to the bathroom dressed slowly, keeping away from mirrors, peeing in the dark with my head down.

Then I eased down the steps, hearing the splash of coffee as Mom poured her out-the-door cup. I stepped into the kitchen, saw her looking around for her keys.

"Is he gone?" I asked.

"As a goose," she said, scanning the countertops, careful not to make eye contact, well into the everything-is-normal-if-we-pretend-it-is act. "Now I get to go see if I can talk Tato into letting me keep my job."

That explained the dress. Her black one, V-necked halfway to her navel. Tight around her hips, her rear. She looked like she was off to a party.

"That dress, he'll probably give you a raise."

She glanced over, proud, but her smile died as soon as she saw me.

"Luce," she started, not quite getting out the whole word. Her hand went to her own hair, still damp from the shower but on its way to its carefully carefree tumble.

"It's late," I said, moving in for the coffee. "I got to get moving." I poured a cup and took a sip, walking out to the front hall, shrugging into my coat.

"Why?" Mom asked.

I stopped in front of the door. "I was sick of it."

"Of what?" she asked, her sixth sense honing in on me, knowing it wasn't my hair.

"Everything," I said.

"Everything what?"

I pushed aside the lacy curtain over the front-door window. "That," I said.

Mom went up on her toes. "You're sick of Kenny? How does cutting . . ." She let it trail off, seeing what I meant.

"I'm sick of him. Of Justin. Of Dad. Of you. Of everybody *looking* at me." I slapped my hand down across my boobs. "Like this is something I asked for."

"Lucy, you're just growing up."

"I'd trade these in for a pair of nuts in a second."

"You think boys have it easier?"

"Yes!"

Mom smiled. "You may be right." She found her keys on the edge of the stairs, right at eye level, where she always left them. Turning to me, she said, "But God, Luce, would you really want to be a boy? Locked in to that blindered tough-guy life? 'Hey, great game, huh?' 'Uh-huh, you want another beer?' 'Fuck, yeah, then let's go huntin'.' 'Yeah. Kill something. That'll be great.' " She lifted her leg and, screwing up her face with effort, did this big fart imitation.

I couldn't quite stop a smile, but I insisted, "It'd beat being treated like some freak of nature every time anybody looks at me."

"Your haircut ought to stop that dead."

"Worth a try anyway."

Mom shook her head doubtfully.

"Come on," she said, waving her keys at me. "I'll give you a lift."

I nodded at the door, at Kenny out on the sidewalk.

"He can squeeze in, too."

"No. I got news for him. Something I better tell him now." I wasn't looking forward to discussing my newfound virginity with him.

"The sooner the better?"

"Yeah."

"Breaking it off?"

I looked at her. "I know what you think, Mom. But there really wasn't ever that much to break off."

"Okay," she said. But she still stood there. "You look so young again," she said. "Like it was years and years ago."

"That was the plan."

"Doesn't work, though, Luce. No more than a corner-of-the-eye thing, a 'Wait is that my little girl?' second."

I shook my head.

"It's too bad, in a way," she said. "But you've got loads of good stuff ahead of you. You don't want to be going backward yet."

"Doesn't matter what I want."

"True," she said, checking her watch. "God. Now I'm late on top of everything. Come on, maybe I can still get you there on time. I'm sure Kenny's long gone."

"Mom, Kenny would wait out there till glaciers carried him off."

She shooed me out. "Go get him before he freezes, then. Poor Kenny. And run. You're late, too."

"Good luck at work." I said.

"To market, to market," she answered, heading out the back.

"To buy a fat pig," I shouted.

Kenny looked up from the gate, his brows already scrunched together in a question.

"What's with the pig?" he said, but then he saw my hair. His smile was immediate, growing into a full-fledged grin before I took one step. "Yes!" he cried. "You look great!"

I ducked back inside and snagged one of Dad's caps from the coat rack, a black one with the Stihl logo on it. I pulled it down tight, feeling my ears press out Dopey-style. I stomped past Kenny.

"I thought I'd never see you that way again," he said.

"Don't worry," I said. "There's other ways you're never going to see me again."

"What?"

I shook my head, breaking into a trot. "We're late."

Kenny jogged beside me. The way he stared at me, if I'd veered off the sidewalk, I could've driven him straight into a tree, a signpost, a fire hydrant. "Quit already," I said.

"What made your dad decide to do it?"

"I did it myself. Dad's gone."

His step faltered, then he was right back up with me. "My mom's gone, too."

I had to look at him. "Gone?"

"She went to Kalispell. Some final legal stuff they had to do."

"They've been divorced for years. What's more final than that?"

"Something about custody. Mom said it was lawyer crap. The way they squeeze the last drops of money out of you."

I wondered if I'd be going through that soon. Or if Dad would just stay away. Not bother any lawyers.

We ran up the school's deserted front steps. We really were late. I swooshed back the door.

"You know what this means, don't you, Lucy?"

I glanced at him.

"We've got both our houses to ourselves."

Kenny was heading toward the attendance office like a good kid, but I was cutting off toward my class. I knew my head, my new look, would make Mrs. Dubrow afraid to ask me about anything.

I slowed, walking backward. "That doesn't mean what you think it does."

He gave me his puzzled-dog look.

"Kenny," I said. "We're going back to the old days."

He didn't have a clue what I was talking about. And letting myself imagine us tearing back to our empty houses, clothes flying as soon as we blew through the door—the feel of him first inside of me—I had to admit that being a boy again didn't seem like such a hot idea.

Living so long with Mom and Dad hadn't left me unscratched.

CHAPTER THIRTY

Between every class, and on the way home, I tried to explain to Kenny how it was going to be from now on. The way it had always been. Before. It hardly made sense to me anymore, not the way it had when I was mowing myself bald; and Kenny was way too wired about having me to himself again to hear anything I was trying to tell him. He didn't even slow down at our gate. Just followed me up the walk, through the door. "Um?" I asked. "Isn't your house down thataway?"

He laughed and slipped past me to the living room. I stood there, mouth open, heard the TV come on. "Lucy," he called.

I could still smell Dad here.

Kenny was on the couch, so fired up to watch a movie that he couldn't sit still. He kind of bounced. His smile looked like it had to hurt.

"Kenny," I said. It felt almost like crying.

I stepped into the kitchen. I knew if I looked at him like that one second longer, I would cry. I went straight to the phone. Dialed Mom's emergency number.

She picked it up on the first ring. "Lucy?"

"Hi, Mom."

"Are you all right? Everything okay?"

I took a deep, quavery breath. "It's so empty, Mom."

She didn't answer right away. I knew she knew the feeling. That she'd probably been feeling it all day, even there.

Kenny came up behind me. I closed my eyes and leaned my forehead against the cool wall. "So they let you keep your job," I said. "Tato's a good spud."

"Yeah, Tato's okay," she said. Then, "Is Kenny there?"

"Uh-huh." It hardly even surprised me anymore, how she knew these things.

I had to wipe my nose, but the Kleenex box was on the other side of the room. I used the back of my hand. I wanted to be a kid again, but this was too much.

"How'd he take your news?" she asked.

"Ha."

Mom laughed a little. "It takes a two-by-four, Luce. A brick. Some kind of blunt object. Maybe even a sharp one, if you're telling them things they don't want to hear."

Kenny touched my back, started to rub my shoulders. He was trying to help.

"Maybe a bazooka, Mom. Some limited thermonuclear device."

"We'll be okay, Luce. We'll skate through this. The readjustment days."

"I know."

"We always do. We're experts."

"It's what we do best," I answered, recognizing that Mom and I had our own lingo, our own traditions. They'd only been overshadowed by Dad's.

"Speaking of Tato," she said, "here he comes."

I nodded, clinging to the phone. "I'll make us some kind of treat tonight. For dinner."

"Want to hit Tracy's? We missed it this morning."

"No. It'll be all right here. Once you're back."

"Okay, Luce. I'll see you then. Not long now. You'll be fine."

"I know," I answered, and she clicked off. Back to talking to strangers.

Behind me, Kenny kept rubbing my shoulders. They were like knots beneath his hands. Something he'd break his fingers on.

"Kenny," I started.

"You get used to it," he whispered. "Having him gone. Even if he never came back, you'd get used to that, too."

"He always comes back."

"Some don't."

"Maybe some. But not him."

I turned away from the wall, not to face him, but that's not what he thought. His hands still on my back, he pulled me to him. "God, Lucy, you don't know how I missed you."

"I think I know," I said.

He kissed me and really, I kissed him back just as hard.

As soon as we came up for air, he moved in for another round. I twisted away. "Please," I said.

"What, Lucy?"

"Just, just—" I stomped my foot, for Christ's sake. "Just don't you *remember* when you were my *friend?*" I felt the tears coming, hot and stinging. "Just, I'm sorry, Kenny. I'm a fucking mess. Go home, okay? Just go. I'll come over later. But now, just, you have to go. Please?"

"Lucy," he pleaded. "This always happens when he leaves. You get all lonely for a couple of days. Sad. But then you're okay. You'll be fine."

"Is that what always happens?"

"Well, yeah."

"You don't get anything, do you? This isn't always going to keep happening." I swiped at my cheeks. "They're finished. I don't think they even know it themselves, but he isn't going to keep coming back."

"Lucy."

"Go home, Kenny." I wiped at my tears again. "You think I want you seeing me like this? Anybody?"

"I don't mind."

"That's great. You don't mind seeing me cry. That's a comfort." I started up the steps. "Don't follow me, Kenny."

I banged my door shut and threw myself onto my bed. Then I spun around, knowing he'd come up, that I'd be in some sort of wrestling match trying to keep my best friend. I tried to look scary, mean, determined. Trying to keep what I'd already lost. If he did come in, I wasn't sure we wouldn't in seconds be filling the house with the pulse of our own rhythm. That that wasn't what I wanted most in the world.

But it wasn't long before I heard the hinge scrape of the front door. Kenny leaving.

CHAPTER THIRTY-ONE

After telling Mom I'd fix some kind of treat for us, I wound up sitting on my bed, staring at the door, wondering who, what next, until it was so late I didn't even have time for macaroni and cheese. I barely got the water into a pot before Mom opened the door. "Home again, home again!" she called, the start of our cheerful phase.

I dumped the brittle macaroni into the cold water and threw the box into the garbage. "Riggedy jig," I answered, cranking on the burner.

She walked right up to the stove and hugged me. This was not a normal part of our cheerful phase. Or any other phase. But the hug was for real, not just some dumb comforting thing. "It gets harder every time, doesn't it," she said against my shorn head.

I nodded. "Even when the visit wasn't the best."

Mom gave me one more squeeze. "You know, at your age, I thought I'd go through this rough spot,"—she let her voice go all horror-movie—"*adolescence*, and then I'd be out the other side, in the clear, and things would be coasting from there on out. Till I was old, anyway. Tottering around. Cancer or that kind of thing coming up to ruin an otherwise decent enough day."

"Cancer," I said. "What a pain."

"But you know what, Luce? It doesn't get easier. You move from one thing to the next, each one complicating what came before, what comes after."

"Like having a kid?"

"Yeah, like that," she said, not trying to dodge. "And then raising her yourself. Having your husband decide who he was at eighteen is not who he's going to be for the rest of his life. Having to wait fifteen years or so before you can even think about deciding any such thing for yourself. Deciding *anything* for yourself. Even being able to think about yourself."

"Because of me."

"Not you, Luce. Life. Don't get thinking you're some ball and chain. I wouldn't trade a second with you for anything."

Not a second, no, I thought, but years? The rest of your life? "So, is that what you're thinking, Mom? About who you want to be now?"

"Starting to, Luce. Just starting to. You and me both. We got our whole lives ahead of us yet."

She said it like we were going to be partners forever, like Batman and Robin or something, but really, I couldn't see myself fitting into whatever plans she came up with.

Kenny wasn't there waiting for me the next morning. I ducked back inside to check the clock, but it was time. I blew out this big breath of relief and started off for school. I hadn't gone more than a couple of blocks though before I began feeling like I'd left something behind. My books, maybe. An arm. I kept checking over my shoulder. The sidewalk was too wide.

After each class, I looked for him. I thought, with his mom gone, maybe he'd overslept or slept in on purpose. I poked my head out after each hour, thinking I'd see him there with his stupid, sheepish grin, his hair not even combed flat from the sheets.

But Kenny wasn't there at the end of any of my classes. I saw Justin and Tim in the nick of time and dodged around them to walk home myself, thinking maybe Kenny had decided that without his mom there to know, he could start skipping whole days. As if she wouldn't find out as soon as she got back. Or maybe he was into the pout of all pouts after figuring out we were on a screwing sabbatical.

I walked through our gate and into our house, but the echoes off the empty rooms were too much. I walked back outside and took these gasping breaths, like I'd nearly suffocated in there. I looked up the block toward Kenny's. A friend would go see, wouldn't she? To make sure he was all right. Not in there sick and alone.

I walked slowly up to Kenny's house. The porch chair was empty, but a curtain fluttered in Mrs. Bahnmiller's window. I wondered if she kept a log, if she was marking my appearance in some book. I waved. "Hello, Mrs. B."

I stepped onto Kenny's porch and tapped on the door. Pushing it open, I walked into the front hall. "Kenny?" Moving down the hall, I got the spinal shivers, expecting Mrs. Crauder to leap out from behind the piles of stuff, a kitchen knife in her hand or something, cackling and all.

"Kenny?"

Maybe she'd come back. He hadn't said how long she'd be gone. How long could final details take?

I peered into the living room, and there he sat on the couch, in her spot, staring at the TV the same way she did. Only the TV wasn't on. I checked the end table for a glass, but it was empty except for the phone base, with its cord trailing down to the floor, the headset lying there.

"Kenny?"

"Hey, Lucy," he answered at last, just when I was starting to think I'd find that kitchen knife in his chest, hear the door slam behind me, more cackling.

"Are you okay?"

He kept looking straight ahead. At the TV.

"I missed you at school. I came to see if you're okay."

"I'm okay."

I stepped farther into the room. "You don't seem that okay." I bent low, eye to eye, then sat down next to him. The worn-out couch springs sagged us together, but he didn't reach to put an arm around me.

I pointed at the phone lying on the floor. "Expecting a call?"

"Got one already."

"Tired of being bothered?" I said, thinking of Mom, bothering people her job.

Kenny just sat there.

"So," I said, "who was it?" Then a bad thought struck. His mom drinking, the pass over the mountains between here and Kalispell. "Is your mom all right? Did something happen?"

"Something happened," he agreed.

"Is she all right, Kenny? Is she going to be okay?"

"*She'll* be fine."

"What then? Your dad?"

"She lost custody."

I patted the hair flat on the back of his head, kept my hand on his neck. "What do you mean?"

" 'The last details.' I'm Dad's detail now. I have to go live with him."

"What?"

"I don't know what happened. Maybe she went to court or whatever shitfaced. She said Dad made them think he's sober. He had these guys from A.A. with him."

I gave Kenny a hug, trying to make it like the one Mom had given me last night. "It'll work out," I said, the words sounding so stupid that I rushed on, "They can't really make you move to Kalispell."

"We're kids, Lucy. They can make us do anything."

I saw that he might be the one fighting not to cry this time. I kissed him at the corner of his eye, where I knew the sting would be. I rested my forehead against his temple. "Just wait. Just wait till we know more."

"It's done, Lucy. Mom called to tell me about it. There's no 'more' about it."

"Was she—"

"Totally. Absolutely shitfaced."

"When is she coming back?"

He shrugged. He was like this block of ice beside me, hard and cold and unmeltable.

"When are they making you move?"

He shrugged again. "I threw the phone down before she got that far." He gave this funny smile. "It was kind of neat, listening to her screaming and crying, this tiny voice down there on the floor, so mad but so far away. All I had to do was push the button and she was gone."

"They'll have to wait until the school year's over."

"Lucy. They don't *have* to do shit."

I kissed him once more, seeing if there might not be some chance of warming him. "I looked for you after every class today. It was weird without you. I was like some pirate who'd lost her wooden leg."

"I'm your crutch?"

"No, I mean that . . . You know that's not what I mean."

Kenny nodded. A reaction at last. "I know," he said. "But it's a feeling you're going to have to get used to, Captain Hook."

"We'll see, Kenny. Like you said, she was drunk, and—"

"You think she made it up? That's not how it works. She gets mean, but she couldn't invent something like this."

"It'll be all right, Kenny. We'll think of something." I kissed him. On the mouth this time.

And that, at last, got a response.

We got pretty wound up right there on the couch, his mom's bed, and when most of our clothes were barely half on, I managed to whisper, "Are you sure she won't be home soon?"

"It'll be a day or so before she can find her car."

I stood up, took his hand. "Even so," I said, gathering my clothes. There was a moment of panic in his face, one I covered as fast as I could with a kiss. "I'm not leaving," I promised. "But let's go to your room. At least I'll be able to bail out your window."

He moved with me; my abstinence plan, not quite two days old, in shambles.

We did it twice that afternoon. We were getting way better at it, even the afterward part that was always the worst. After being practically hypnotized, your body taking over and driving and driving until, wham, you fell back to earth, found yourself sitting next to your goofy old friend, all sweaty and sticky. We'd look around each other, the very idea of kissing too weird to think about, when a minute before, licking him wasn't out of the question; when I'd been grinding my head into the pillow for the feel of the stubble, the bristly, over-alive tingle of every inch of my body. This time we wore ourselves out so much that we fell asleep next to each other for a little while, Kenny's head nestled into the hollow of my shoulder. That, more than everything else we did, made me feel like we might actually be getting to be bona fide adults.

The next thing I knew, the room was dark. I jerked up, dropping Kenny down to the mattress. I was looking for a clock, wondering about Mom.

Even just bounced awake, Kenny automatically began sliding his fingers up and down my back. He whispered my name, as if we always woke up like this.

"What time is it?" I asked, still confused, sleep-groggy. I wiped at a wet spot on my collarbone. Kenny's drool. "Holy shit! Six-thirty! Mom's home waiting for dinner."

I started crawling across him, but he stopped me halfway, one of my legs over him. His hands drew gentle circles around my boobs, bumping over my nipples. He said, "I'm the luckiest guy in the history of the world."

Getting yanked out of his house to live with his dad, who he hadn't seen in years. Luckiest guy in the world.

"Kenny, my mom's home!"

"Stay here, Lucy. Nothing bad can happen while you're here."

"Oh, yes it can." I thought of his mom showing up. And of fifteen years ago, Dad saying something like that to Mom, their lives rerouting in the next few instants. "Kenny, this can make a whole world of bad."

He slid a hand down my side, over my hip, grazing my rear but then sliding over my thigh, knuckling my hair. He smiled at me.

"Kenny. Don't."

"Lucy."

"Ah, shit, Kenny. I've been trying to tell you that we're done with this. I don't want to do this anymore. I just felt so bad for you that I—I don't know, but this, I don't—"

"All afternoon was because you felt bad for me?" He waited, but I didn't know what to say. "That didn't seem like the only reason."

"No, Kenny. That's not what I meant. But—"

I felt this thing hard beneath me. He rocked his hips. I shifted away. "It's not that I don't want to. But Jesus, Kenny, don't you remember before? Why can't we do something like we used to do? Remember when we did things? Remember going fishing?"

"The river's frozen."

"Skating, then."

"Ice isn't thick enough. We'd crack right through."

His hips kept rocking. It was like being on a boat. "For Christ's sake, how about a walk? We used to walk all over."

"Chinook. Too windy."

"Goddamn it, Kenny. Then let's steal my mom's car. Let's go for a drive."

The head of his thing pushed against me, searching. "That sounds pretty good. Just running away together." It almost got inside me. "But if we got caught, Lucy." He was hardly breathing. "We couldn't do this in the detention center."

He pushed in.

I closed my eyes, drew in my breath, but then got strong. I jerked away, sitting down on him, pinning his deal against his stomach.

Kenny stared at me. "I know what this is about."

"Would you please tell me?"

"This is so you can go fuck that fucking Justin Haven."

My jaw dropped. Here I was sitting naked on top of him, after this whole afternoon. "Boy, you nailed it there," I said. "This was practice. Shaving my head, that—that was—that was just to drive him over the edge, to make myself that much more the sexiest chick in Great Falls High." I could feel tears starting up. Looking down at his face gone all flat and mad, I wanted to punch him. Goddamn it, I never cried.

"Fuck!" I shouted, waving an arm around. "I'll be able to fuck them all now! They'll be screaming up in droves to do the bald bitch."

"Lucy, stop."

"Fuck you, Kenny! How fucking stupid can you be?"

"I'm sorry, Lucy."

"Sorry?" I laughed. "You're fucking sorry? No, Kenny, I'm sorry. I'm sorry—"

He grabbed my hands, stopping me. "You want to go back to the jungle gym, Lucy? Is that what you want?"

"No. Well, I don't know. Yes. That is what I want. Remember how it was? Don't you see, Kenny, that's how I always want it to be for us." Pulling my hands away from him, I flattened my boobs down, hid them away, made them disappear. "Don't you remember how good it was then?"

"But Lucy—"

I put my finger down over his lips. "The rest of this is messing everything up, Kenny. I mean, look at us. Shouting. At each other."

He shook his head. "You don't get it, do you?"

"I want to get it, Kenny. I want you to be my best friend again."

"There is no more everything else. Can't you see that? They're taking me away. Away from you."

"But that hasn't happened yet."

"It's going to!" He turned his head away, his hair snarly against the pillow. "Mom said, 'He's stealing you,' but I know what happened. She went over there to make him take me. To get rid of me."

I chewed my lip. "Because of me? Because of us?"

He shrugged.

"Well, don't you see, that's one more thing we messed up with all of this." I slid my other leg over him and sat on the edge of his bed. I pulled my pants off the floor and stepped into them without bothering to search for my panties. I was a sticky mess, already wondering how I was going to get home, and up to the shower before having to see Mom, before giving her a chance to see me, to know.

"I think maybe she was sick of always having me around," Kenny answered. "Of always having to worry about me."

"She didn't seem to spend much time doing that."

He shook his head. "You really don't know much about it."

"You could tell me."

"Is that what we get to do together now? Talk about my fucked-up life?"

I pulled my shirt on and tucked it in quick. My jacket was out by the couch. I hadn't exactly covered my tracks if I'd had to jump out the window. "We can't even be friends anymore, is that it?"

He thumped his head back down against the pillow. "God!" he shouted.

I found a sock and tugged it on. The other one. My panties were tangled into a knot, almost under the bed. I stuffed them into my rear pocket. I flipped back blankets, looking for my bra. Bent over that way, a tear fell from the corner of my eye, straight off the bridge of my nose. It tickled, and I rubbed at it. "Where in the hell is my goddamn bra?" I didn't want to leave any souvenirs, sure didn't want Mrs. Crauder showing up at our doorstep dangling my underwear from her talons.

Then I found it under a pillow on the floor. I snatched it up. "Never mind. Don't get up. Found it myself."

"How did you get so fucked up?" Kenny asked.

"Try a mirror," I said.

I snagged my coat, my shoes, from out by the couch, and tore out of there. I was halfway home before I realized I was still carrying my bra in my fist. I stuffed it up the sleeve of my coat. That would have been quite the conversation starter with Mom.

CHAPTER THIRTY-TWO

As soon as I got the front door open, Mom called, "Luce?" I heard her chair push back in the kitchen. There was no smell of food. She was just waiting.

She made it to the kitchen door as I leaped up the steps, three at a time. "Luce? What is it, honey?"

"Kenny," I shouted.

I heard her say, "So you let him down easy," and then I was upstairs and in the bathroom. I had the water started, my clothes scattered on the floor, my underwear pulled from my pocket, my sleeve, before she tapped on the door.

I yanked back the shower curtain. I hadn't ever realized there was such a reek about sex. I grabbed the soap, started scrubbing at myself before I was even wet. This was the smell of Dad, I realized. I always thought it was his smell, something he brought into the house with him. I'd never connected it to something they made together.

Mom was leaning up against the wall in the hallway when I stepped out. Steam rolled out with me, the pungent fake scents of Ivory soap, my shampoo.

I shook my head. "He took that like a gunshot to the gut."

"But there wasn't all that much to break off?"

"Depended on your point of view, I guess."

She studied me, hiding behind my towel, and pushed herself off the wall. "All these things are hardest the first time."

"You mean he'll get to like being dumped?"

"For you, I meant. Dump*ing*. Dump*ee* is never much fun."

"Oh yeah, Mom. Like you've got a lot of experience there."

She smiled.

I wrapped my towel more tightly around me. "That's what made this so bad, Mom. I wasn't trying to get rid of him. Just to—I don't know." I made it to my room and threw my clothes into the corner, started pulling sweats out of my drawer.

Mom followed me right in. "Just trying to get him to keep his hands to himself?"

I nodded. His hands were the least of my worries. I stood there holding my sweats. More than ever, I did not want to be naked in front of her.

"Wanted him just to be friends?"

"Yeah."

"It's the 'just,' Lucy. Says it all right there. Nobody wants to be 'just' anything."

She looked at me until I mumbled, "I guess." But she wouldn't leave. Finally, I held up my sweats. Kind of shook them.

"Right," Mom said. She started for the door, but before going through, she turned back. "You're still on your no makeup kick, correct?"

"It looks dumb, Mom. Half the girls at school look like scarecrows." And the other half, I thought, like prostitutes.

"Amateurs," Mom said, but that was knee-jerk. All nonchalance, she said, "When you're dressed, come to my room. I'll give you some pointers. Show you how to cover those up."

"What?" My hand went to my face, wondering if some new zit had popped up.

"Your love bites, Luce. I'd say it looks like you let him down pretty easy."

She was gone then, and I whirled around to my mirror, my face already fire-engine red. Three of them, in a line, on my neck. Big oval bruises. Hickeys. Love bites.

"You son of a bitch," I whispered.

Staking out his territory. *Kenny was here.* I guess I was lucky he didn't piss on me. Like any dog.

I planned on killing him for the hickeys, but Kenny wasn't waiting for me out front the next day. He wasn't at school either. Me in my turtleneck, searching. He still wasn't there the day after that, and instead of staying mad, I got scared. I called his house as soon as I got home, to ask what was going on, was he really leaving, would it be after Christmas or not till spring. But I'd already guessed that wouldn't happen. If the courts had yanked him, they'd get him away from his mom pronto.

The phone rang and rang until finally his mom answered. I hung up, my breathing fast. For some reason, I hadn't expected her, had had this vision of Kenny still sitting there on his couch, alone, watching the blank TV.

I called again from school, when she'd have to be at work, but the phone rang on and on. I stood in the hallway listening to that empty sound, kids streaming past me, shouting, laughing. I put my head against the cold metal of the phone box. "Answer the fucking phone," I whispered.

I hung up and called information.

Mrs. Bahnmiller was confused at first, but obviously excited to get a call from anybody, even me. I wondered if this was what Mom did all day, chat with people so lonely they'd buy whatever she had to sell just to keep her on the line.

"Yes, I think he's still here," she told me. "Though I hardly see him anymore."

"Have you seen him at all?"

"Are you two fighting?"

"We're pretty much past that. Listen, Mrs. B., if you do see him, tell him I'm looking."

"You know right where he is. You could always come over."

"I don't really think I can." I thanked her, then hung up.

"Wrong number?" somebody said behind me.

I spun around. Justin. Tim. "Remind me how that would be any of your business," I said, but my voice shook like I'd been caught at something. I started for my locker, and they fell in with me, one on each shoulder.

Justin made this big show of looking around, twirling through an entire circle. "Where's your shadow? Lose him for good?"

"I think so."

Justin flashed a grin at Tim. "So, Friday? Party at Roehmer's."

I rolled my eyes. "You've got a dream life that should be in movies."

"We'll pick you up."

"Where do you live?" Tim asked.

"In hell," I muttered.

Tim nodded. "What's that address again?"

"You want me to go to some party with you, and you're both going to pick me up? What is it with the two of you?"

Justin threw an arm around Tim's shoulders. "Friends to the end," he said, like some chant they did.

"Uh-huh. Seems pretty gay to me."

Justin jerked his arm off of Tim like he'd been scalded.

By Friday I couldn't stand it anymore. Maybe—probably, even—Kenny was leaving, and he still wouldn't answer the phone. I must have hung up on his mom twenty times, hoping to catch Kenny walking past. I pictured her perched at the corner of the couch, hovering over her phone. Kenny couldn't get it if he'd wanted to. If.

As soon as I got home from school, I called and listened to the endless ringing. Later, as I started digging through the cupboards for something to make for dinner, I tried again. I'd just hung up when the phone rang. My hand was still on it. For some stupid reason, I said, "Kenny?"

There was a moment of nothing, then Mom said, "Still letting him down easy?"

"I just called him. To see when he's leaving." I'd explained that much. She'd shaken her head, saying it would be for his own good, "What with that woman."

She waited until I said, "No answer. Haven't gotten an answer all week."

"Maybe they're—"

"She's there. I hang up when she answers."

There was another moment when neither of us said anything. "Well, listen, Luce, I only got a second here. We're swamped. I'm going to be late. Don't plan dinner for me."

"Overtime," I said, letting myself fall back against the wall, thump my head against it.

"Just a couple of hours."

"Friday-night overtime."

"Come on, Luce. Don't go getting your panties all in a bundle."

"How long has Dad been gone?"

"The better part of fifteen years. Give or take the odd week."

I didn't say anything.

"Lucy, it happens. I can't help it."

I bet you can't, I thought. "Okay. Fine. Whatever."

"Thanks for understanding," she snapped, and we hung up on each other.

Since I was standing there, I tried Kenny again. His mom answered. I hung up. Alone in my kitchen, the phone still warm from my mouth, my ear, I screamed, "You fucking bitch!"

I was pretty sure I meant Mrs. Crauder.

After standing there a second more, I charged to the front door, snagged my coat, and kept right on going. I couldn't just do nothing. Not for one more second. What was his mom going to do? The whole horror-movie kitchen-knife thing? Even I didn't believe that.

I leaped up their porch, running to keep myself from stopping, from turning around. I pounded on the door for the same reason. I could hear a hollow booming trail into the cold air down the empty street. "Kenny!" I shouted.

The front door flew open. Mrs. Crauder standing there just like I'd imagined, not even opening her mouth to speak.

"I—Is he, Kenny . . ." I had to start all over. "Did you send him away? Really?"

"You quit calling me. I'll get the police."

"I'm not calling you. I'm calling Kenny."

"He doesn't want to talk to you."

I looked at her. "Really? Kenny!" I shouted over her shoulder. "Kenny!"

She closed the door in my face.

"Is he even there?" I yelled. I kicked the door. "Goddamn it! Is he?"

"I'm calling the police," came her voice, muffled but still menacing.

I stepped off the porch, out of the light drifting down from Mrs. Bahnmiller's side, the one she always left on, like company might arrive any second. I walked into the darkness, started shuffling home. Our house as dark as Kenny's.

I didn't even notice them pull up, idle alongside me. Didn't know they were there until I heard Tim say, "See, I told you she'd be waiting."

When I looked over and saw Justin's primer-spotted Camaro, Tim was already out the door, flipping the seat forward, sliding into the back. Justin slapped the seat. "Come on. It was only Tim. His cooties wash off."

Behind me was Mrs. B.'s porch light. I imagined Kenny's mom still standing at her door, all harpy, keeping her boy safe till she could ship him over the mountains. If she hadn't already.

I glanced up to our own dark porch. "Fuck it," I said, and climbed in.

Justin gave this cowboy whoop and squealed rubber for the rest of the block, not slowing or even looking at the corner; just barreling ahead, knowing he was charmed.

I shook my head. "Nice car." I had to admit, it felt nice to be able to just leave. "Is this as fast as it goes?"

CHAPTER THIRTY-THREE

Justin's car, it turned out, went a hell of a lot faster. He shot out toward the base, then hooked south for the highway to Belt. On the four-lane stretch, it wasn't that scary: there was room to pass, and the cone of the headlights seemed to give us time to dodge around the other cars. Tim pushed a clear bottle up from the backseat, his wrist resting on my shoulder, the bottle wagging in my face. I tried to study it in the shaky glow from the headlights. For some reason, there were no dashboard lights—no way to see how fast, exactly, we were going.

I took the bottle. "What is this? More of your toothpaste stuff?"

"Mouthwash," Tim said. "Guaranteed to turn you into the world's best kisser."

I took a swallow. "What if I already am?"

"Am what?"

"The world's best."

Justin did his cowboy yell again and pulled the bottle from my hand. "We got us a live one, Shaughnessy!"

We shot through the railroad underpass, and the four lanes cut down to two, the reflectors the only thing showing the road, and those just tiny, blurry dots flashing past. With the bottle up to his lips, Justin swerved around a cattle truck, the two yellow lines curving sharp with us, the truck's horn blaring. Justin launched us back into our lane in front of the truck, the body of the car lurching right, then left, the tires clinging to the pavement. There was nobody coming at us, he was just showing off. I rocked with it, and Justin, wiping his chin with his sleeve, held the bottle back to me. I took a swig and passed it back to Tim.

"Where the hell is this party?" I asked. "Lewistown?"

"We're the party! Right, Tim? Wherever we go." Justin was going so fast he couldn't take his eyes off the road for more than a blink, but he did then, his smile glinting in what light there was. He reached his arm out and rubbed my bristly head.

I knocked it away. "Don't do that!"

They both went quiet.

"It's something my dad does," I said, not wanting anything to slow down. "Rubs my head for luck. I can't stand it."

Eyes back on the road, Justin said, "Definitely don't want anybody thinking about their dad here, do we, Tim?"

Tim didn't answer, just held his hand out with the bottle.

We didn't get even close to Lewistown. At the Belt turnoff, Justin stood on the brakes, about putting me through the windshield. Even in the cold, with the windows all rolled up, the car filled with the sharp reek of burned rubber. Then Justin swung down the cut leading into town, slapping me up against the side window. The tires did all they could, but we slid on the tight curves, more squealing.

"Justin," I said, and we shot underneath the one-lane stone railroad bridge, no way of knowing if anybody was coming at us or not.

Then down the main street, one block long, slinging through the turn, over the Belt Creek bridge and out, back to the highway. Don't think we went under fifty the whole time, except maybe on some of the turns.

We'd been out maybe fifteen minutes, and I was breathing like I'd run the whole way. If one person had stepped in front of us or a car had shown up driving normal. I held my hand out for the bottle. "I think you've had enough of this," I said to Justin, wondering if I should drink it all to keep him from getting any more.

"More is better!" Justin yelled, laughing like it was the world's greatest line.

He drove even faster on the way back to the falls, and when the schnapps was gone, he handed the bottle back to Tim and lowered my window, shouting, "Fire in the hole!" Tim leaned over me from the backseat, smashing me flat, the wind biting wherever he wasn't covering me. He whipped the bottle out at some sign I couldn't see, and Justin shouted, "He shoots! He *scores!*"

I couldn't see any of it.

Tim kept yahooing, pumping his fist. I had to shove him off of me. "Jesus," I gasped. "Why don't you just crawl up here and sit in my lap?"

Tim started to. Justin shoved him back. They were both laughing like crazy, and I could have sworn Tim gave my shoulder a squeeze.

At the edge of town, Justin did his brake-standing stunt again, the car filling with that awful stench.

"Is there really a party tonight?" I asked.

"Yeah. Roehmer's."

Roehmer, whoever the hell he was, or she, wasn't that far from my house. Six blocks, maybe. Seven. When we pulled in, it was already in full swing, the other football players already there, not having taken time off to shoot through the Belt run.

Tim and Justin were in such a hurry to get in that I had to hop not to get left behind, not to have to come in alone like I had with Kenny. But at the door, they hung back, waiting, and when I stepped up, Justin threw his arm over my shoulder, hugging me to him so we could squeeze through the door together. Tim, trying to get in at the same time, got popped through ahead of us. He turned and shrugged an "Oops," but it seemed he was looking at me, mostly, apologizing or regretting something that had happened.

I tried to step out from under Justin's arm, but he stepped with me, jostling me back and forth. "You're a quick one," he said. Then he pulled me around to face the girls. Jaimie Tilton and her gang. Tim was already off to get beers. It was like they did the same thing, with the same people, every week.

"Jaimie, baby," Justin called. "You know Lucy. And Luce, this is Britt, and—"

"We know who she is," Jaimie said. "Kind of hard to miss with that hair. Justin, baby."

They turned and left as one, nearly dumping Tim's beer as he swerved out of their way. "What happened to them?" he asked.

"I did," I said. I wasn't proud, exactly, but it was kind of cool, discovering there *was* something in me, some dangerous superpower. Like there was something to that Supergirl shirt I slept in every night. Diamond Girl.

Tim lifted his beer cup. "To the face!" he shouted.

Justin downed his automatically. I followed suit, not automatically, but because I could feel the eyes on me. Everyone's. As I tilted my cup farther back, squinting when the beer stung my throat, I saw the girls all lined up together, glaring at me. I wished I'd had time to get dressed for this. One of Mom's drop-dead outfits. Not my skanky old sweatshirt.

Justin tipped his head forward, his cup empty. Sucking in some air, he smashed his empty cup against his forehead.

That, for some reason, struck me as the funniest, stupidest thing I'd ever seen. Somebody busting a flimsy plastic cup against his head to show how tough he was. I burst out laughing. Justin turned to look. The girls were on me like stink.

I reached a hand up behind Justin's head and pulled his face down to mine. I tongued his tonsils. There was beer dripping off his forehead. It got in my eye, burning. I couldn't stop laughing. I had to break it off.

"Whooee!" I cried.

" 'Whooee' is right," Justin said. His arm went back around my shoulders. He wasn't letting me go anywhere.

Tim stood before us, looking as dumbstruck as the girls. I grinned at him. "To the face!"

"Right," he said, and held his hand out for my cup.

Justin and I walked around some, Justin yucking it up with his buddies now and then. He didn't introduce me to anyone after Jaimie, and I wondered how long ago they'd been together—or if they still were—if I was going to end up with a knife in my back. He kept his arm around my neck, hugging me in tight every few minutes, as if to make sure I was still there, that I hadn't slipped away while he attended to his social duties.

Tim found us with another round, and they yelled, "To the face!" at the same time.

The third round I got it out first, and they smiled in surprise. They lifted their cups, saying "To the face" without shouting it, welcoming me into their camp.

We threw back our beers. My stomach churned with it, but I smashed the cup against the top of my head, feeling the cold trickles wind through the maze of my stubble.

Tim wandered away with the surviving cups, and I wondered how long this would go on. Could go on. I pictured Jaimie Tilton heaving me out the door this time. Her and her friends putting the boots to me out there in the cold. Kenny would be so proud.

I watched Tim go, thinking he was one of the nicest guys I'd ever met. For no particular reason. Just a good guy. Funny. But when I saw somebody start talking to him, I hoped he'd stay there all night instead of making it back with another round for the face.

Leaning against a doorway, I shook my head, trying to clear it. I rubbed at the beer in my hair. The Jaimie girls still glared at me from across the room, trying to shred me with their laser vision. Get me to burst into flames.

I looked around for Tim but couldn't see him anywhere. Making sure Jaimie was watching, I stuck out my tongue and licked the rim of Justin's ear. Over his shoulder, I mouthed, "Take a picture, it lasts longer," and blew the girls a kiss.

Justin pushed me into the doorway. He bent down and started kissing me hard. Jaimie looked like she might cry or throw up. Maybe both.

Keeping one eye on her, I slid my hand down onto Justin's ass, spread my fingers, and pulled him tight to me. Not that he needed any pulling. He was already trying to split me in half against the corner of the door jamb.

"Easy there, T. Rex," I murmured. "You're breaking my back."

He eased up the tiniest bit. His hand was inside my coat, grabbing and kneading.

"Everybody's watching us," I said.

"Let her watch."

"Her?"

"You know who I mean."

"Well, hell," I said. "Then let's give her a show."

I popped the top button of Justin's pants before he'd quite heard what I said, shot the zipper down. He pushed against me, but not like before: this time just to keep himself from mooning the whole party. "Whoa, Lucy!"

"This isn't what you wanted?" I reached like I was going to grab his thing.

"Let's find someplace," Justin breathed.

Jaimie ran from the room, her girls flocking after her.

I got my hand away from his pants. It was like this kind of joke.

"Lucy, um, let's." He pushed away from me, trying to hunch, to keep his letter jacket covering him while he rezipped. People were smiling. Justin propelled me down the hallway. I let him. I looked back, checking once for Tim, hoping he hadn't seen any of this.

Justin found a bedroom. Pushed open a door and charged in. He was that kind of guy, that kind of luck falling all around him. If he needed a bedroom, believe me, there'd be one right there.

He drove me backward across the room until we hit a bed, me going down, smacking my head against the headboard. Hard enough I saw stars. Him on top of me.

"Goddamn," I said.

Maybe he hadn't rezipped. Maybe he'd been holding his pants together. Otherwise, I don't know how he could have gotten them open again so quick. "And you said I was fast," I tried, but he wasn't up for much more in the way of jokes. He was all over me, all hands, all hot, beery breath, whisker scratches, all this weight driving me down.

"Easy there," I said. "I still have my coat on."

He started shoving my coat down off my shoulders. Got it around my elbows before it snagged, more straitjacket than coat. He tried again, but he would have had to start over at the cuffs. I mean, think of the time that would have taken.

Instead, he shoved my sweatshirt up. Unlike Kenny, he knew his way around women's underwear. He had my bra open before I could wriggle the sweatshirt off my face.

And then. You'd think I was a cow. That he was after some speed-milking record.

"Justin," I said.

"Man," he breathed. "You've got the greatest tits."

"Wow. Gee. Thanks."

He never stopped. With his unoccupied hand, he lifted me up at the waist and peeled my jeans and panties down to my ankles in a single swipe. If they hadn't been mine, it would have been a move to marvel over.

His tongue jammed down my throat at the same time his finger shoved into me. I tried to spit out the one and squirm away from the other. I started to bite down to let him know I was still there, that I was part of this, too.

He pulled back.

"For Christ's sake," I said. "I can't even move my arms."

He waited a second. For me to explain the problem, I guess.

"I mean, where's the fire, Justin?" I tried to laugh, but my throat was burning, dry and tight. "My hands are going numb."

He started pumping away with his finger again. I'd won ten seconds.

"That is pretty sexy," I said, trying to close my legs, to reach down and stop his hand.

He shoved his finger as far as he could.

"Quit," I said. "That hurts."

He shifted his position. His weight. He was straddling me, but up above my legs, making me think I might have a chance.

"Justin," I said.

"If you put this in your mouth, maybe you won't have to talk so much."

He was waving it at me. His magic wand.

"Put it in your own damn mouth," I said. Brilliant.

"Suit yourself," he answered.

He slipped down, getting his knees between mine, opening me up like a clam. Then he drove into me like there was something down there that had to be killed, stomped and beaten to death. Some terrific evil he was sworn to destroy. It was like falling under a pile driver.

I kept hearing that "Suit yourself." Like I'd made some kind of choice.

I closed my eyes, tried to think of Kenny, of our supersonic death spin at the top of the jungle gym. The room spun. That was about as close as I could get. I had to open my eyes before I threw up.

Justin started this groaning moan, "Uh-huh, uh-huh, uh-huh," keeping time with his awful thrusting. I couldn't help thinking of Dad. Mom.

Then Justin went all spastic, his hips jerking and quivering, shooting into me. I closed my eyes, listened to my molars grind.

He lay down on top of me. Squishing me. Like we might whisper things to each other now. Nice things.

Still pinned inside my coat, my elbows burned. My hands tingled, asleep. He lay there catching his breath. His hand went to my chest.

I think if I'd had a sword, been able to cut off his whole arm, his hand still would have crawled toward my boobs.

"Wow," I gasped. It sounded too real, too impressed, but I had to swallow to get it out. I swallowed again. "Don't feel bad," I said. "Nobody's any good their first time."

Justin gave a tiny, unbelieving laugh. "What?" he asked.

"I mean, it's not like you'll never get any better."

He sat up with a grunt. A fuck-you, a laugh, I couldn't tell which. "My first time tonight. Is that what you mean?"

"I don't know where you're going to get any seconds."

He waved his arm, barely visible in the dark. The whole party, he meant, his whole world. At least he didn't point at me.

He stood, pulling up his pants, gingerly tucking in his limp, wet thing.

Even before I saw that, I was afraid I was going to throw up. I'd been afraid ever since he'd been pile-driving into me, sloshing all that beer back and forth.

"Do you know where the bathroom is?" I asked, sitting up, wrestling my jacket up to my shoulders, flexing my fists, trying to get the blood back into them. "That was so romantic I have to puke."

He cracked open the door and shrugged. I could see by the light seeping in behind him. He hesitated, then closed the door. The light winked out. I thought he was gone.

Then, out of the darkness, he said, "You tell anyone, I'll kill you." He was invisible after the moment of light. Dangerous.

"*Tell on you?* Fuck, Justin, you didn't steal my homework."

"Nobody'd believe you, anyway. They won't even care. They—"

"One word to my dad, your life span'll be measured in seconds."

"Everybody saw you out there. They . . ."

I stared into the darkness, having at least that quaver of fear in his voice. "Really," I said. "I have to puke. Do you know where—"

He opened the door, slipping back out into the sound and the light.

Seeing him in the light made the bile surge into my throat. I stood up fast, but my jeans were bunched around my ankles. My bra scratched in my armpits.

"You fucker," I moaned, trying to pull up my pants, knowing I was going to throw up right then, before I had a chance of getting anywhere.

I did. Right beside the bed. It came out like I'd turned a spigot. All at once. Everything.

I straightened shakily, wondering if there was more to come, but knowing that I'd emptied myself. I pulled up my pants. Rehooked my bra beneath my sweatshirt.

Creeping to the door, making sure he'd shut it, I felt for a light switch. I'd have to try to clean this up as best I could.

The light blinded me at first. When I could see, I wished it had been permanent. There was a huge Spider-Man poster on the ceiling. A Buzz Lightyear bedspread, with Justin's stain darkening Buzz's white elbow.

My puke was puddled around a pair of slippers. Power Rangers.

That's when I started to cry, which, with everything, was a total surprise, something I hadn't been even close to before.

Where was this kid? Who were these people? What on earth was I doing here?

I flipped the light off and ran out the door into Tim.

He stopped me, holding me by the arm. "Hey, Luce. You okay?"

I shook my head. "Got a little too funny for my own good. Joke gone bad."

"What?"

I looked up at him. "I got to go, Tim. Your friend Justin. He is a world-class prick."

It seemed like maybe that wasn't the first time he'd heard something along those lines.

"I don't mean that in the good way," I said, pulling my arm away from him.

"Wait, Lucy."

I searched frantically for the door. "Who in the world lives here, Tim? Where are they?"

"I don't know. Some sophomore. His parents are gone."

I made it out the door, Tim still standing there, raising his voice, asking again if I was okay.

CHAPTER THIRTY-FOUR

I tried to run home, but it was more of a stagger. Some stretches it was hard just staying on the sidewalk. I didn't want to open my eyes, see anything around me. I switched to alleys after the first block, embarrassed by the streetlights.

I went in through our back door. No lights left on. Either Mom had forgotten, or she wasn't home yet herself. All that emergency overtime.

I picked up the phone and, for the first time in years, had to fight to remember Kenny's number. I didn't know what time it was. Midnight, maybe. She didn't sound asleep, though.

"Please," I said right off. "Please let me talk to him."

There was a long silence. A collecting of breath or patience. "He's not here."

"Please. I need to talk to him."

"He's not—"

"I really need to, Mrs. Crauder, you don't—"

"Lucy, he's not here."

The way she said my name, like there was no reason to be my enemy anymore, I was all of a sudden crying all over the place. "Please let me talk to him. Please. Please."

"I can't."

I screamed. No words, just a scream. Then, "God, you fucking bitch! Let me talk to him!"

She'd hung up. Maybe during the scream.

I still had my coat on, my shoes. I stormed out the door for Kenny's.

Their front window was almost dark, the light shifting with the TV's flash. I couldn't fight my way through her. Instead, I walked to the back of the house, around Mrs. Bahnmiller's black windows. I tried to picture the inside of the house, the kitchen. Kenny's bedroom. I tapped at a window, whispered, "Kenny." He'd told me he'd crawled through here before.

I pushed up on the wood around the glass. It opened, though it wasn't very quiet.

I whispered his name again, but still no answer.

I pulled myself over the sill, kicking the wall, wondering if the light would flash on, Mrs. Crauder slamming down the window, slicing me in half.

I fell in on top of Kenny's bed. But Kenny wasn't in it. I felt around. It wasn't made. It didn't have any blankets. Any sheets. Only the rough, buttony mattress. I felt on the floor, my hands running over bare, cold wood. No clothes, no pile of blankets. The room was empty.

She was still sleeping on the couch in an empty one-bedroom apartment. Exactly like I'd known she would.

Kenny's pillow was there, without a pillowcase, and I curled around it. The door was closed, but I could hear the murmur of the TV voices not far away. It was more than my house had to offer.

I guess I cried some. I mean, this was my life now. Getting fucked by Justin Haven. Sneaking into an empty room where I used to have a friend. Listening to voices that weren't even real.

Why, I wondered, hadn't I let Kenny do what he wanted, had sex with him one more time, since now he was gone anyway? I couldn't remember what I'd been thinking. I hurt down there, Justin rasping away at me dry. I curled up in a ball, tight, unable to believe how I'd screwed up my life, taking Kenny down with me.

He hadn't called to let me know he was going.

He hadn't even called.

I didn't hear Mrs. Crauder until the door cracked open. I froze, still wrapped around Kenny's pillow. I could feel her watching me, then leave the doorway. I thought about throwing myself straight through the glass, but before I moved a muscle, she was back. I closed my eyes and listened to her walk into the room, right up to the bed.

I clenched my teeth together, waiting for a blow, shouting, the police. Anything but what she did. Very carefully, Mrs. Crauder draped a blanket over me. I felt the draft of it as it settled down, then her touch as she pulled the blanket up to my neck, tucking me in. I heard her slide the window shut. Then she was gone.

I didn't move for what felt like hours. I kept my eyes closed but didn't get anywhere near sleep. Me and Mrs. Crauder, partners now. Was she so lonely without him that she'd be nice to me just because I knew him too? When I tried to sit up, the rough wool blanket scratchy against my neck, my head throbbed, my stomach ached, my crotch burned. I pushed myself up the rest of the way, my hand scraping across the coarse, bare mattress.

Facing the door, I clutched the blanket to my chest like a shield. I fumbled behind me, sliding the window up, wincing at the noise. Never taking my eyes from the door, I slid outside and dropped to the ground. It wasn't quite light yet, just a pale over the Highwoods.

I ran around Mrs. Bahnmiller's side and crossed the street, through the Tuckers' yard and into our alley. As quick as I could get away from the open eyes of Kenny's front windows.

I rubbed at my face, trying to feel something other than the creeping panic that somebody was gaining on me from behind. I had enough to worry about ahead. There wasn't going to be anything pretty at my house. I vaguely remembered calling Kenny's, screaming into the phone.

What if Mom had been home for that? What if she'd been coming down the stairs for me right as I blasted out the front door? Sitting up for me ever since?

I edged open our back door. Stuck my head in. There were no lights on. The kitchen was empty.

I checked the couch, seeing if she might have fallen asleep waiting for me. Empty.

I walked up the stairs, not so sneaky anymore. My door was open. Mom's was open. She wasn't home.

I stood at the foot of her bed, trying to get my tongue loosened up enough to swallow. The machine's message light was blinking, and I walked around the bed, afraid to push the button.

Mom saying she'd scrammed?

Dad saying she was with him?

The police? The hospital?

I pushed.

It was a woman's voice. All whispery. "This is Libby Crauder, Kenny's mother. I'm calling to let you know that, um, that your kid is over here. She's safe. You got nothing to worry about. She's—she just—"

I hammered at the delete, cutting off her voice, my heart going a hundred miles an hour.

One shaky step after another, I made it down the hallway to my own bed and pulled the blankets over me. I'd heard kids talk about passing out, or, even better, blacking out. Whole nights forgotten. I couldn't even close my eyes. I got up and turned on the light in the hall. A night light.

A long time later, I heard Mom come in, start immediately with her kitchen noises. The smell of coffee.

I glanced at the clock. Eleven thirty-five in the morning. My head thundered.

My door was wide open. I still had my coat on. My shoes. I hadn't slept one second, just lay there staring at the ceiling, tracing the cracks in the plaster, watching the night fade, then the day getting brighter and brighter. Every time I came close to shutting my eyes, there was Justin: "Suit yourself." Mrs. Crauder tucking me in, like I was an orphan now, too.

Forcing myself up, I made it to the bathroom and stripped down, throwing my panties in the trash under the sink. In the shower, I gave myself a once-over. Despite everything, all Justin could do to me, my slumber party with Mrs. Crauder, there were no missing body parts, no gross deformities. At least until the lab results came back, I was still somehow just fuzzy-headed Lucy Diamond. The coolest thing going.

CHAPTER THIRTY-FIVE

Coming down the stairs, I tried to remember what the old me would have done with Mom failing to come home, Dad gone all of a week. I knew I'd have to act furious, but I couldn't bring anything up in me at all. If Planned Parenthood had been open on Saturdays, I would have headed straight out the door, get myself poked at once more, checked for whatever else Justin might have done to me.

I didn't bother with Mom in the kitchen. I walked into the living room and pulled the curtain shut and sat on the couch in the gloom.

It was quite a while before she ventured in. "Hey, Luce," she said, all quiet. She stood in the doorway. "Were you late?"

"Late where?" She didn't have the foggiest idea where I'd been last night.

"What did you do?" she asked.

"Nothing."

She walked into the room and sat down in the chair opposite the couch. Dad's chair. She bent low to look at me, and I turned to the window, blocked by curtains.

"What's with the dark?" she asked. "Looks like a funeral parlor in here."

I shrugged.

"We had a Christmas party at the office last night."

She sat waiting until I had to say, "And you worked right through it. The overtime queen of—"

"I didn't know about it. It was kind of impromptu."

How many people make up an impromptu party? I wondered. Two? I had a kind of impromptu party last night myself.

"I had too much to drink," Mom said. "I didn't have any dinner. Don't ever drink on an empty stomach."

"I don't drink," I said.

"Don't start," she said, trying to make me smile. "Anyway, what I'm saying is, I got drunk. I'm not proud of it. But I wasn't in any condition to drive. There's a cot down there, and that's where I slept." She paused. "By myself."

"You don't drink, either," I said.

"Not usually. And I'm remembering why, believe me."

I looked away from the curtains, over toward her. "I didn't ask you one single question. You don't have to explain anything to me."

"I want you to know."

"Maybe I don't want to know. You ever think of that?"

"There's nothing *to* know, Lucy. That's what I'm telling you."

I got to my feet, my head lighter than air. I snorted. "Come on, Mom."

She waited.

"You stretched out a cot in the middle of a party and took a little snooze? You think I don't know that it doesn't quite work that way? That I don't know what they all want, the price they'll make you pay for something like that?"

"What are you talking about, Lucy?" She was up on her feet, too.

My eyes were starting to burn, tears surging up. I'd become a regular faucet. I strangled out, "I know, all right," and started for my room.

"Lucy!" Mom shouted.

I turned, holding on to the banister.

"Lucy, we live here together." It was Saturday. She didn't have to go to work. There was no escaping each other. "We can't make it work if we pretend we don't."

"Pretend? Mom, who's pretending? It's like twenty blocks! At the most. You could have walked! You didn't have to sleep with—what did you call it—'sleeping on a cot'!"

"Lucy."

"Well, shit, Mom! What would you be doing right now if I hadn't come home? If I was the one slipping in, lying about being drunk, deciding to sack out at a party?"

She eyed me. "There's a difference, Lucy. I'm not fifteen years old."

"And I'm not married!"

She let me go up the stairs without saying another word.

I didn't see her the rest of that weekend. Saturday I never came down again. I couldn't have eaten a thing, anyway. I ducked into the bathroom now and then for a drink of water. I threw up the first one, the water coming up as cold as it had gone down. Later it stayed down and started to feel as if it might save my life.

Sunday I ate a bowl of cereal at five in the morning. I was back upstairs before she came down. I left my milk-rimed bowl on the table for her to see.

Thing was, I wasn't really mad. Just acting the way I thought I should. I couldn't make myself care. Who she was with. Why. What they did. Big difference.

I lay on my bed, Justin still waving his thing in my face: "Suit yourself."

That night I listened to Mom answer the phone and trudge up the stairs to my door.

"Lucy?" she said from the hallway. "It's for you."

Mrs. Crauder? Sweat popped out on my forehead. I didn't answer.

"Kenny?" I finally asked.

"No. Tim somebody."

I closed my eyes. At least there was Christmas, no school for a couple of weeks.

"Lucy?"

"Tell Tim to go fuck himself."

She paused, then said, " 'Go fuck himself,' " like she was taking notes. "Got it. Those words exactly?"

I sort of smiled. "Whatever. You'll do fine."

She was gone less than a minute before I heard the creak and twist of my doorknob. She poked her head through, hesitated, then came straight in, perching on the edge of my bed.

"Doesn't anybody knock anymore?"

"What happened, Lucy?" she asked.

"I grew up. Remember?"

She let that slide. "Friday night, Luce. You haven't talked to me since. You—"

"Since you didn't come home."

"You're asking me to tell your friends to fuck off," she went on.

"Fuck *themselves*," I corrected. I could hardly believe we were saying that to each other. Like we were just talking. "And he's not my friend."

"Why, Lucy?"

"I don't want to talk to him, okay? I don't want to talk to anybody."

Mom took a deep breath. "Lucy, God's own truth, nothing happened."

I was lying on my back, and she was sitting beside me, kind of pinning my wrist against my hip. I looked up at the ceiling. "Mom," I said slowly, "it's not always about you."

Her lips, always full and perfectly painted, narrowed into a thin line. She patted my hip with her hand, counting to ten.

I rolled over to face the wall. Mom kept her hand on my hip. "Kenny's gone," I whispered. "She wouldn't even let me talk to him before he left."

Mom sat there a long time, patting my hip, running her hand up now and then to my shoulder, stroking down my side to my leg. She didn't say anything else.

After a while I said, "When you leave, would you get the light?"

I had my eyes closed as hard as they'd go, but I could see when the room went dark.

She still hadn't said anything.

CHAPTER THIRTY-SIX

On Monday, as soon as Mom left for work, I trudged down to Planned Parenthood to treat myself to my first pelvic exam. RELAX! But after they took my blood, I got the great news that I had to wait two weeks before they could test for STDs, and it would be almost that long before they'd know about HIV. When I said it hadn't been exactly consensual, they pushed me to go the police and they asked about another round of emergency contraception. But I'd checked, and I'd been keeping on schedule with the pill. Feeling that shitty was the one thing I figured I could do without. The last thing I had any control over.

So I spent the whole Christmas break waiting to see if he'd killed me besides. I dodged Mom, slumping around in the mornings after she left, pulling the curtains shut behind her. If the phone rang, I let it go, then deleted the message as soon as I found out it wasn't Kenny or the clinic. Twice it was Tim's voice, which I chopped off as quick as I could. Two other times somebody knocked on the door, and I hid against the wall in the kitchen. Like it might be Justin, searching me out, his big, hard thing jutting before him like a divining rod. Once it was the UPS woman—Dad remembering to send a package this time, and the other time I don't know, though I heard the slam of a car door, some throaty, mufflerless roar shooting away down the street, leaving my breath racing.

Back in April I'd gotten Mom a necklace and earring set I saw, so I didn't have to do any shopping. I guessed Mom had sent a package to Dad, if she knew where he was, but she didn't ask if I had anything to add. She been putting my name on presents my whole life.

I ventured out once, stealing through the evening-dark streets to Spencer's to poke through their postcard collection; some night views of the river, the dams, one of the oil refinery, a couple of the old smelter stack they'd blown up before I was born. I got them all, my favorite a picture of the dams lit up, with big yellow letters yelling, GREAT FALLS, A GREAT PLACE TO BE!

At home I addressed every postcard to me, licked and smashed on the last of our old stamps until my tongue tasted like dried horse bones. Then I found a box, some of the wrapping paper Mom saved. When I had it all ready, I wrote Kenny's name on it, but I didn't know his address. Information, when I called, wouldn't give it to me. They did have a phone number for a Crauder, though, and I wrote that down on the inside of my wrist. When I tried it, it was a machine: "Leave a message." I didn't.

I'd have to get his mom to send it. So, in the sender spot, I wrote "Scott Booker," hoping it would be a name she'd remember as one of Kenny's friends. That night I sneaked over and dropped it between the doors, dashing back home like the hounds of hell themselves were snapping at my heels.

Christmas afternoon Mom and I opened our presents. She liked hers, put the necklace on right away. Mine was two packages she'd wrapped the same, tying them together with ribbon. One big, one small. "What are they?" I asked, already opening the small one. But then I could only hold it in my lap, looking at it. A pair of earrings, tiny golden hoops.

"Mom," I said, "I don't have holes in my ears."

"Does seem that way sometimes," she murmured, but before I got it, she said, "There's a coupon in the card for a piercing."

I pulled one of the hoops from its piece of cardboard. It weighed absolutely nothing. I held it up to my eyebrow. "How does it look?"

She smiled. "Your father would poop himself."

I opened the bigger box. An entire makeup set. The works. All this Maybelline stuff, mascara and eyeliner, nail polish and lipsticks, tubes and jars of who knows what, glosses and blushes, brushes and tweezers. I picked up a mirror that made my face twice as big. I sucked my lower lip between my teeth. Really scary stuff.

I traded the mirror for a scissors-type thing with curved tong ends. Something to pull eyeballs out with? I snapped it at Mom. "Are you trying to tell me something?"

"I thought maybe it was time. That that's what you were deciding."

I hadn't decided anything. I hadn't had a say in it ever. I stared down at the eye shadow, shade after shade in their little squares, like a kindergartner's watercolors. It was all so Barbie, I couldn't help laughing. I managed to squeak out a thanks.

Mom smiled, unsure. She did this reluctant sigh. "Well," she said. "Are you ready? Shall we see what he sent this time?"

"If you are."

She got a pair of scissors and started on the tape of Dad's box. She rummaged through the crumpled newspapers. Canadian. British Columbia.

She hit something, and her eyebrows scrunched down. Then she pulled the gifts out. One after the other.

Two stuffed jackrabbit heads, mounted on unvarnished pine boards, short deer antlers sticking out beside their ears. A matched pair, one for each of us. I could hear him laughing over it. Whoever he was with.

Jackalopes. The mythical creature of the plains. "They're not just mystological," I could hear him insisting. "I've seen them!"

"Won't these look lovely above the fireplace?" Mom said.

"Or in it," I said. We didn't have a fireplace.

Mom put hers back in the box, shaking her head. "You know, there are days when I can't believe I married that man."

"*Days?*" I set my jackalope alongside my earrings and makeup.

Dad usually called on Christmas Day, his one break of the incommunicado tradition. But he hadn't yet. Without admitting it to each other, we'd been waiting for it all day, trying not to talk about it. Or him.

Mom and I'd made cookies that morning, our one homey touch, something we used to do before Christmas Day was actually upon us. The whole time I don't think we said more than five or six words, and those things like me telling Mom where things were, her asking.

But now she got up and stretched like we'd been busting our butts all day. "Wow," she said. "I feel like I did when you were small, coming in at five in the morning, dying to see what Santa had left."

I looked over the haul. Santa must have been busy elsewhere.

"I'm going to hit the shower, Luce."

Something was up. No doubt about it.

She never said a word about dinner, and at five o'clock, when she was still upstairs showering and what all, I stuck a chicken in the oven to roast with a few potatoes and onions, some carrots. Not exactly turkey or ham, but.

When she came down, it was practically ready. She said, "Something smells good."

All I could smell was her perfume. She was dished out like I'd never seen her. Classy. Leaving everything to wonder, instead of hanging it out there for anyone to see.

"It's chicken," I managed.

She nodded, not quite meeting my eye. "I've got to go to a dinner, Luce. I'm sorry. I didn't know you were fixing anything." She really did look sorry.

"I didn't have any plans," I said.

She smiled. "I'll sit with you, Luce. While you eat." She checked the tiny wristwatch clinging to her white wrist on its black string bands. "I've got time."

"You don't have to, Mom."

She followed me into the kitchen. I banged down the oven door and opened the pot. Still wearing the hot pad, I grabbed the end of a drumstick and tried to twist it off, but the bone came up empty, the meat still clinging to the thigh. I held the bone up for Mom to see. "Must be one of those free-range chickens."

"Is a bit on the scrawny side."

I pulled a knife from the block and sawed off a leg. I tossed it on a plate, kicked the oven door shut, and turned it off. Sliding the plate onto the empty table, I said, "Really, Mom. Why don't you just go?"

She was pulling up a chair across from mine. "I'm sorry, Luce," she said, sitting down. "This was one I couldn't turn down."

"One what, exactly?"

"I know where you'll go, so I don't even want to start."

"Totally harmless, eh?"

"Yes, as a matter of fact."

"Something completely inconsequential that you couldn't turn down."

"I didn't say that."

"Worth leaving me alone on Christmas night for?" I was stunned to find myself nearly choking on the bite I'd torn off the chicken leg. Picking up my napkin, I hid my face in it, coughing. I spat the chicken out. "Fuck this, Mom. Okay? Just fuck everything." My chair tipped over, and I think if she'd been quicker, she'd have tackled me.

I dashed upstairs and got my door locked, and like she had the other morning, Mom tried to walk in. "Go have your fucking life!" I shouted as she twisted and pushed.

"I'll stay, Lucy. I don't know what I was thinking."

"They're called hormones, Mom! You *weren't* thinking!"

"I'll stay!"

"Don't. Don't you see that'll make it worse?"

She stopped banging away. "What?"

"Oh, God Mom, like you don't think I don't know how much I've fucked up your life?"

"Lucy," she said, "please let me in."

"Not in a million years."

She tried the door again, as if it might have become magically unlocked. There was a sharper tap: a kick from her high heel. "Why do you have to be like this?" she shouted.

"Go! Have a great time! Write when you find work. Don't be any stranger. After a while, alligator. See you later, crocodile."

"Don't you dare start that!"

I kept shouting. "Adios, amoebas! See ya, see ya, wouldn't want to be ya. See you soon, my sweet baboon." All of Dad's hundreds of ways of saying good-bye.

I pictured her in the hall, hands clasped over her ears so she wouldn't have to hear any of them one more time.

"Hit the road before it hits back. Don't let the door smack you last!"

When I stopped, she was gone. I sat on my bed, my ears ringing with the silence.

I unlocked my door and peered out. I went through the whole house like she might be hiding, playing a trick. The whole thing some elaborate game, like Dad used to pull when I was a kid. When we used to play here.

CHAPTER THIRTY-SEVEN

That night I was making the tour downstairs, locking the doors, turning off the lights—only leaving the Christmas-tree lights on for Mom, more hoping to twist the knife than out of any sort of kindness—when Dad called.

Maybe it was planned, calling late enough that if one of us wasn't home, it would be hard to explain. I stood in the dark in the kitchen, looking out at the tiny sparkling tree lights as he went through his usual holiday routine, about how he hated to be away, how much he missed us, did we get the jackalopes, weren't they the best. And then, finally he cut to the chase. "What did your mom think of them? Did she get a kick out of them? What did she say?" Before I could answer, he said, "Put her on, let me hear it straight from the horse's face."

I glanced down at my makeup and jackalope. "She got me makeup. Can you believe it?"

"Let me talk to her, Luce."

"She's in the bathroom. I made my special roast chicken for dinner, and she hasn't been feeling so good ever since."

Dad hummed something sympathetic and asked about my makeup, but he was only biding time.

"It's incredible. I've been practicing with it all night. For a while there I was closing in on Britney, but right now I'm more Bride of Frankenstein."

"Uh-huh," Dad said. "Is she there yet?"

"I shaved my head again, Dad. Right after you left. The old buzz."

"Lucy, where is she?"

"Got the motorboat out and went water-skiing all by myself."

Nothing.

"I'm pregnant with triplets," I said.

"Lucy, go get her."

"The father's an Indian. The youngest fifty-year-old you'll ever meet."

"Is she in the bathroom or what?"

"They say with teeth, he'd be handsome, in a rugged kind of a way."

More nothing.

"Just a second, Dad. I'll go see."

I dropped the phone on the counter and hauled myself upstairs into their room. I poked my head into their bathroom, Mom's own makeup scattered across the counter. Sitting on the edge of their bed, I picked up the other phone. I could hear him waiting, hear our empty house through the phone down in the kitchen.

"She's asleep," I whispered.

"What? It's ten o'clock."

"Eleven here. Dad, I think I might have given her food poisoning."

"Why aren't you sick, then?"

"Tell the truth, I'm not feeling so hot."

"Go ahead and wake her up, Luce. She won't mind. For Christ's sake, it's Christmas."

"I know what day it is."

"Go on."

"No, Dad. I'm not going to wake her. She's really sick. She's needs to sleep."

"Lucy." He was all but shouting.

"Dad, give me your phone number. I'll have her call you as soon as she's awake. No matter what time."

He snorted. "Awake."

"I've got a pencil, Dad."

"I'm at some bar, Luce. I'm thirty miles from where we're staying."

"I don't hear anything. Pretty dead bar."

"What do you know about bars?"

"That they're supposed to be noisy. People drinking and laughing and stuff."

"I'm outside. I don't like bars."

"Outside? Aren't you freezing?"

"Yes. Please wake her up, Luce."

"You don't have a phone at your camp or wherever? Where you're staying?"

"It's in the middle of nowhere."

What a perfect place to be, I thought. "How about an address?"

"Lucy."

"I still need to send you my Christmas present. I got you a cell phone. You'll be able to call every day."

"There's no reception up here, Lucy. Too much iron in the ground or something."

"You're kidding."

"Nope. The guys that have them leave them in their trucks."

"Where on earth are you? Lower Slobovia?"

"Practically. Canada."

"You know how to spell Canada, Dad? C, ay? N, ay? D, ay?"

He waited. "You really aren't going to put her on, are you?"

"I can't, Dad."

"Won't or can't?"

"She needs to sleep, Dad. You should have heard her ralphing. Thought she was going to hurl up a lung."

"I thought you said she just wasn't feeling so good."

"I didn't want to scare you."

"I don't scare," he said.

"How come you never call when you're gone?"

"I told you, Luce. It's not an easy thing."

"The iron in the ground."

"That's right."

"Bet it plays hell with a compass, too. No wonder you can't find your way home."

"What?"

I heard something downstairs. "Hang on, Dad," I said. "I think maybe I hear her getting up."

I was already bolting out of their room, down the hall. To the stairs. Mom looked up from the banister post, where she was hanging her coat. She smiled, her mouth opening to say something—"Home again, home again," "Hey, Luce"—who knew what? I shook my head as fast as I could, slapping my finger across my lips, mouthing, "Shh, shh."

She waited, wondering. I raced down the stairs on tiptoe. "Don't make a sound," I whispered. Her perfume scented the air around her, breezed after me down the hallway.

I got into the kitchen and picked up the phone. "She's up," I said. "Sounds like she's throwing up again."

"Really?"

"You want to talk to her when she gets done?"

"Only for a second, Luce. I want to tell her merry Christmas."

"Okay, hang on."

I hung up the kitchen phone, slip-footing it back out to Mom. Touching my finger to her lips, I took her by the arm and started her up the stairs. She'd heard me on the kitchen phone. She wasn't going to do anything stupid.

I herded her into my room. "He's been on almost half an hour. I told him you've been throwing up all night. After eating my chicken. I wouldn't let him wake you, but now you're puking again. The phone's on your bed."

I shoved her into the hallway, down to her room.

The way she fell across the bed, she did look sick. She pulled the blankets over herself, fumbled with the phone. "Hey, Chuck," she murmured. "Some Christmas, huh?"

She was a pro. I could practically smell the vomit. I closed the door. As good as she was, it wasn't something I wanted to see.

Even though I'd closed the door, I couldn't make myself go away. It wasn't more than a minute before I heard Mom's fake sick talk give way to this kind of weak, wispy laugh.

"You should have seen her face when she opened the makeup. Like she was holding a dead fish. How she laughed trying to get out 'Thanks.' " Then, "She's still a kid some ways. She'll get used to it." Not until a moment later did she say, "The jackalopes were great. Luce loved hers."

They talked a long time. They laughed a lot.

After a while I walked back down to my room. Slipped under the covers. I was frozen, my skin chickened. I curled up and rubbed at myself. The blanket rustle masked her approach. I didn't hear her till she opened my door.

"Don't ever make me do that again," I said.

"Lucy."

"You do your own lying from now on. You're way better at it than I am."

"Am I?"

I stared at her silhouette outlined in the door, same as Justin's had been right before I threw up. "I did not love my jackalope."

She chuckled and said, "Don't let the bedbugs bite," easing the door shut between us.

On the phone, they had sounded normal, like he'd never left. Like she hadn't just slipped in from some date. I wondered why he didn't call all the time.

Iron in the ground. Give me a break.

Maybe we were all hopeless liars. Maybe everything we'd ever said was lies.

CHAPTER THIRTY-EIGHT

The first day after the break, walking to school alone, the black hole of Kenny's being gone nearly swallowed me whole. It made it hard to think. To breathe.

It was about a hundred degrees below again; the kids a bunch of blobby dark shapes shuffling beneath the white clouds of their breath.

I tromped up the stairs, caught in the crowd, completely alone, letting myself get jostled down toward my locker. This, I figured, was what it was to be Rabia Theodora.

But I wasn't completely alone or ignored. Before I reached my locker, I could feel the hubbub—kids turning to look at me, some smiling, some looking sorry.

I studied the floors, polished hard over the break. There was some kind of sick reek in the air, something way past Pine-Sol. Kids made retching sounds. Kids laughed.

The smell. I surprised myself by recognizing it as Tinkerbell, the world's cheapest perfume. What third-graders wore. That's what had made me think of Rabia Theodora.

A gap opened around my locker, a gap I wasn't aware of until I broke through the kids and fell into it. I looked up, saw everyone watching me.

"WHORE!" was scribbled across my locker in wide red letters. "Look like one, smell like one" was in smaller letters, an afterthought. Like somebody might not get it otherwise.

I stepped up close, burying my face against the gray metal door, starting on the combination. The letters were thick, peeling back at the edges like wax. Lipstick. Pulled straight out of Jaimie Tilton's purse. But the Tinkerbell, that required planning. Jaimie Tilton wouldn't have used Tinkerbell since slicking it across her Barbies.

I swung back the door. The reek was gagging. Somehow they'd gotten inside my locker. There were pictures taped everywhere, huge lurid penises, women sucking, gagging, their eyeballs wide, women impaled from every angle.

I tore at them, crumpling them up before I could really see, before anyone else could. All this stiff glossy paper. The same word was lip-sticked across the cover of every one of my books. There were more pictures folded between their pages. The stench made my eyes water.

I slid down to the floor, opening my books, shaking them upside down, wadding up whatever fell out, adding it to my pile.

The kids weren't laughing anymore. Everybody had gotten awful quiet.

I didn't see Mr. Sledden until he came through the crowd, saying, "Break it up, now. Everyone off to your classes." I looked at his shiny black oxfords.

"I'll get John to clean this up," he said. "Right away."

I shrugged. "Doesn't bother me."

He reached down, and though I tried to block him, he got a handful of the pictures. I listened to the crinkle of paper as he smoothed one out flat. He crumpled it again quick. "Do you know who did this?"

I shook my head.

"Come on," he said, holding a hand down for me to pull myself up with.

I stood without it.

"Let's go to my office. You can get yourself cleaned up there. Wash your hands, at least. Leave your books here. John will have this taken care of by the time you get back."

The kids hadn't listened to Mr. Sledden about going to class. He saw them still clustered around, like drivers around a wreck, and he bellowed, "Go!"

They went, Jaimie Tilton and her gang lingering long enough to etch their smiles into me. Jaimie reached her hand to her mouth and blew my old kiss back to me. I had that one coming.

I smiled, caught her kiss, and touched it carefully to my ass.

No Justin to be seen. No Tim.

The rest of that day, the Tinkerbell stench wafted around me like a cloud of plague. Kids left me a wide berth, but they didn't stop looking, they didn't stop whispering.

Before, I'd only thought I knew what it was to be Rabia.

I skipped out early, not so much driven away but sick of them all. Being cooped up with such a bunch of children.

On my way home, the feeling of being alone, what had seemed so hard in the morning, was like being handed a get-out-of-jail-free card. I sucked the air into my lungs, the cold making my nose stick shut, then rushed it back out in a white fog laced with stale Tinkerbell.

When I swung open our door, I stepped in on the day's mail, and the first thing I saw was a postcard sticking out. Not one of the ones I'd sent Kenny. I barely had the heart to see what Dad said this time. I pulled it out slow, studying the picture before daring any of the words.

Instead of one of his usual, it was a painting, that one of the girl sitting in the grass with the wind blowing, looking up a long hill to a big old house. You can't see her face, but you know there's something not quite right with her, like that house is a place she'll never be able to reach, though it's where she belongs.

I turned it over. Kenny's writing. "Since these cards are what pass for love at your house, I thought I'd better get started."

Not signed. He must have studied Dad's style.

I carried it into the kitchen. Digging the tape out of the drawer, I stuck it on the fridge. Kenny 1, Dad 0.

Putting a couple of potatoes on to boil, I started throwing things together for dinner. Hamburger and oatmeal. Meat loaf. Dad called it mate loaf, saying nobody would cook it for someone unless they were already married. I kept looking over at Kenny's card. Love. After nothing for weeks. After leaving without a word.

I glanced down at my arm, where I'd written the Kalispell Crauder number. But that had been weeks ago. I called information. This time I wrote it on the wall alongside Dad's mess of numbers, where he'd write anything if the notepad was empty, like it always was.

When I lifted the phone to call, steeling up my nerve, there was already somebody on the line. "Hello?" I asked.

"Lucy, it's me, Tim. It didn't even ring yet, you just—"

"What?"

"I called you over Christmas, but—"

"What the hell?"

"I heard about today," he said. "I'm sorry, Lucy."

"Those are some pretty cool chicks you hang with."

"I didn't have anything to do with that. I—"

"You can pick your friends," I said, "but not your nose." That stopped him, and I shouted, "Look. Don't ever call me again. I don't want anything to do with you or your fucking friends. Okay? Leave me alone!"

"It's not my fault, Lucy," he begged. "I didn't want it to happen."

"Well, that's great. Almost the same as it never happening, huh?" I slammed the phone down. The potatoes were boiling, water splashing over the burner.

I dialed the Crauder number. Got the machine. "Hey, Kenny," I said. "If this is actually the real Kenny, the co–undisputed universal master of the jungle gym, give a call. I'm in the same old place as always." I called back right away. At the beep, I added, "Postcards aren't the only thing that pass for love here."

I pulled the potatoes off the burner and stuck a fork into one. They were done, about an hour early. And there sat the mate loaf in its pan on top of the stove. The stove still cold.

What if his dad got the messages first? Did I still have a brain in my head?

I drained the water off the spuds, dumping them onto a plate on the table. Pulling up a chair, I watched the steam rise up and reached for the pepper. I ate them without thinking, waiting for the phone to ring, looking at Kenny's card where Dad's should have been.

Mom found me still sitting there, the mate loaf still on top of the stove.

I glanced down at my pepper-flecked plate. "Sorry," I said. "I ate already."

She tipped her head to the side, then wrinkled her nose, taking a sniff. "What is that smell?"

"Like it?" I asked. "Some girls at school were nice enough to share it with me."

She coughed, stalling.

"I think, with my makeup, it might make the complete package."

"Exactly what kind of package is what worries me." She sniffed again. "What is that stuff? Tart's Revenge?"

I smiled. "That would be about perfect."

Slowly, while I nuked a potato for her, she drew the day's story out of me. I left out the part about the pictures. I mean, how could you describe those to your mother? But I did tell her what they'd written on my locker.

"Pretty upper-class," she said. "In my day it was 'slut.' "

"Did they have Tinkerbell for your locker?"

"No, that's a new twist."

She said thanks as I slid her potato in front of her and passed the salt and pepper. She pushed the butter away. "Tinkerbell. Is that really the name? What kind of sick bastard came up with that? Little girls pretending they're all grown up. Isn't that the opposite of everything Peter Pan stands for?"

"Anybody who could come up with that smell, the name part would be like falling off a dog."

"If they made a Peter Pan, you'd wear that, wouldn't you?"

I smiled. "Take baths in it."

Mom slipped a bite between her lips. "So," she said, chewing, toying with her fork. "You've told me all except why."

I shook my head. "The quarterback kid developed this thing for me." I bounced my boobs once. "For these. The cool girls aren't too happy about the competition."

"And?"

"He's a rancid piece of shit scum."

"Ah," she sighed. "Young love."

It wasn't until she stood up, setting her plate on the counter, that she saw the postcard taped on the fridge. "Well, that's a change of pace for him. Nobody naked. No rock-hard derrieres."

"It's from Kenny."

She turned and gave me this glance. "Really?" She reached out to flip it over.

"I'll let you know when there's one for you."

Her hand stopped inches shy of the card. "Right," she said. "So you've got your own long-distance deal. Haven't you learned any better than that?"

"I know better."

"But can't help yourself. I know the feeling."

I watched her dying to read that card. "Are you two going to stay together?"

Mom's hand dropped down to her side. "Luce, how the hell would we know what 'together' is?"

I studied the tabletop. "We're together, Mom."

She brushed her hand across the top of my bristly head, something I didn't think she'd ever done before. She left it there, barely rubbing back and forth. "You got that right," she said. "Snug as a couple of jackalopes in a box."

I snorted out some air, a laugh, I guess.

"Luce," Mom said. "Do me one favor, okay? Let's leave the hair clipper back in childhood. Okay? It's time to let this grow out."

"And you keep the uncles away. You've got a life here already."

She looked at me but didn't say anything. Just stood there rubbing my head.

CHAPTER THIRTY-NINE

A couple of weeks later, the phone rang at precisely seven-fifty in the morning, Mom out the door one minute before, me getting my coat on. I grinned, running down the hall to the kitchen. Timing like that, our lives mapped out to the second, it had to be Kenny. He didn't even get out "Hey Lucy" before I said, "I knew it had to be you! God, it's about time!"

And then we just listened to each other breathe. Kenny recovered first and stumbled on about Kalispell being okay. His dad really was dry so far. He still didn't have any friends.

"Except for me," I said, and he answered, "Of course."

When he asked how I was doing, the first thing I wanted to tell him was about the clinic, their call the week before with my clean bill of health, how it was like I'd been floating ever since, but of course I couldn't say that. Instead, I said, "Remember your old pal Jaimie? A few weeks ago, she and her buds douched my locker with this skanky perfume and wrote 'whore' all over my books. And Justin's buddy Tim keeps calling me."

"Why?"

"How the hell should I know? Probably wants to know why I won't talk to them."

"You won't?"

"Please! I wouldn't talk to them with *your* tongue."

I could practically hear him smiling.

"How about you? Girls falling all over you?"

"I need police protection to get to class."

"Hey, you know what I got in the mail the other day?"

"Postcard?"

He'd been sending me a postcard every day. There was a double line of them on the fridge. Dad's side was still empty.

"Besides that," I said. "A wedding invitation. To Rabia Theodora's wedding."

"You're kidding?"

"Next month. The day she turns sixteen, I guess. She wrote it herself. In ballpoint."

"Are you going?"

"I don't know. I suppose I'll be the only one there. I mean, if she's asking me, she must not have any friends. Says I can bring somebody else. What are you doing March third?"

"Hanging here without a driver's license."

We talked a few minutes more before he said, "Lucy, I'm late," all apology.

"Kenny," I whispered. "I love your postcards."

"I love you," he answered, even softer.

Though I knew better, I accidentally left Rabia's invitation where Mom could find it. She made fun of it endlessly, but then the day of the wedding, she asked what I was planning to wear.

I looked up from my Special K. "Wear?"

"It's a big deal, Luce. The first wedding of any of your friends."

" 'Any of my friends'? Mom, the only reason Rabia asked me is because she doesn't have any friends, either."

She waved her hand like I was talking utter nonsense. Like I had droves of friends out there, and they were all going to be at this wedding, the social event of the season. I was too surprised to keep her from dragging me up to her room. I sat on her bed as she rifled through the hangers in her closet, inspecting and rejecting. She'd eyeball me now and then, pursing her lips, shaking her head. Finally, she pulled out this red sheath, held it up in the air at me, and said, "Let's try this."

"Mom, I'm not going. I can't. It would be too pathetic."

"Up," Mom said, flicking her fingers impatiently. "Off with it. Come on."

We hadn't done this kind of thing since I was six. Mom trying clothes out on me, playing dress-up.

She harrumphed out this sigh and tossed the dress onto the bed. Then, from behind, she yanked up my T-shirt. I either had to let her or end up in a wrestling match.

With my T-shirt dangling from her hand, Mom studied me. Slowly, she smiled, shaking her head. "You, child, are going to blow their socks off." She slipped the dress over my head, slinking it down, tugging here and there, smoothing till it clung to me like paint. Leaning back, she eyed me like an artist does a canvas. "Lose the jeans, and we're on to something here," she said. Stepping back in, she cupped my boobs with both hands, pushing them up and in. She whistled. "The right bra, and this might not even be legal."

I knocked her hands away. "I am not wearing one of your bras."

She nodded. "You don't need to." As fast as she tugged it on, Mom peeled the dress back off. "Jump in the shower," she said. "When you're done, we'll see what we can do with your hair. Your face."

"I'm not wearing makeup, Mom."

"Just a touch, Luce. Just a touch."

I shook my head. "I'm not your long-lost Barbie."

She pointed. "Shower."

She was sitting beside the sink when I pulled back the curtain.

She held out a towel for me and, after I'd dried off, went straight to work on my face, "To make your eyes stand out," then my hair, slathering on the gel. She even made it kind of fun, like the motorboat days, only this time going in the other direction, trying to make me beautiful instead of a weirdo. Through the steam on the mirror, I could see she'd shocked my hair into this punk-rock thing. I kind of liked it. Made me look wild.

She marched me down to her room, still in my towel. She had my underwear on her bed, the dress. She wouldn't leave for me, but just said, "For God's sake, Luce, I changed your diaper!" Then after that, she whistled when I took the towel off. I threw it at her, and we both laughed. I've never gotten dressed so fast in my life.

Mom touched up my hair, then threw back the closet door, this big voilà move. There I stood, this total stranger. A knockout, I had to admit. Except for the hair, I could have starred in a beer commercial. I couldn't help smiling in this sick kind of way. Behind me, Mom grinned. "See?"

"I can see just about everything."

Mom touched my shoulder, twisting me around. "Get a load of your locomotion."

"My *what*?" We were both laughing. She closed the door too soon.

By the time she loaded me into the Corvair, I felt like I was riding next to this other girl. I glanced down at my legs—in nylons, no less— my boobs out there for everybody's appraisal. But as we approached the courthouse, as I could first make out the tiny wedding party standing there, I stopped feeling anything close to wild. When the light changed and Mom crossed the last street, Justice standing all green on top of the dome, a brace of cannon bracketing the long front walk to the door, I said, "This isn't right, Mom."

We could see Rabia in a light-colored dress that was more than a little tight for her. She had boobs herself now, her dress cut as low as mine, showing them off. With the pregnant belly underneath, I wasn't sure it was the effect she should have gone for.

Even so, she looked nice, happy, and her soldier didn't seem so bad. Almost as scrawny as Kenny, his head shaved closer than mine. There were two of them, clones of each other, and I realized I didn't know which one was Rabia's, which the best man.

Beside them, Mrs. Theodora stood checking her watch like some kind of dark, nervous hen. I said, "Don't pull over, Mom." I slunk down low in the seat. "Just keep going."

"Honey—" Mom started.

"Look at me, Mom!"

"You look great, Lucy."

"The bride, Mom. Not me. It's about the bride."

"But she won't have any friends there."

I put my hand on the shift, keeping her from taking it out of gear. "Please, Mom. She already doesn't have any friends."

Mom studied me a second, then the wedding party, then slowly eased back out into traffic. I didn't have the heart to look, but I knew Rabia recognized our car, could plain as day see us driving away. I slid all the way down below the window.

It occurred to me that Mom hadn't noticed them till then. That up until that last second, she was seeing only her own wedding, their gang of friends wishing them bon voyage as they sailed into their lives as adults. Thinking of that, it seemed a miracle she'd gotten so close to the courthouse at all.

By spring, Kenny's line of postcards stretched down the refrigerator four wide, the first two rows doubled up, but it wasn't like having him around. Wasn't any side-by-side supersonic death spiral, if you know what I mean. Dad had four postcards in his row.

Rabia Theodore dropped out of school the day she got married. Poof. Vanished off the face of the earth. Swept under the rug of base housing. Into the world of motherhood. Diapers, drool, desperation.

My transformation from coolest kid alive to Tinkerbell whore, then back to my old absolutely invisible nobody self, was amazing. It was like the storm fronts that came screaming out of the mountains. Sunny and calm one second, then tearing black clouds and snow. Wind blasts that could thaw or freeze. It was like back when I was a boy.

Jaimie and her girls weren't perfect at it. They glazed over whenever we were forced close together; made certain not to make eye contact. You could see the effort it took to make me invisible. Justin, on the other hand, had practice on his side. I wondered if he'd attacked every girl in the school. He could cruise past me without skipping a beat, laughing with whoever he was with, his white teeth glistening inside his grin. He had a mustache now.

Tim couldn't ignore me at all. Watching them bowling down the hall shoulder to shoulder, right down the middle like a snowplow, kids piling out of their way, I'd see him glance at me, then quick away, then back. With Justin, he'd get bindered up. Sometimes he'd smile at me. A few times he saw me when he was alone, and he'd try talking to me. That's when he learned what being invisible was all about.

CHAPTER FORTY

Mom celebrated the start of spring break by having a date. She called from work. Instead of saying something about overtime, giving me that much credit, she just told me she wouldn't be home for dinner. "Don't wait up, Luce."

"Whatever," I answered.

It wasn't much fun going to bed alone in the house. In fact, it was half spooky. But I fell asleep still not waiting up. She woke me at nearly two, cracking open my door to check on me. I heard her whisper, "Sweet dreams."

When I got downstairs the next morning, I found a cigarette butt sitting in a saucer on the kitchen table. There were two coffee cups out, one stained with Mom's lipstick. The other held the butt. I picked it up with the very tips of my fingers, by the ash end, rather than touching where whoever's mouth had sucked on it.

She'd had somebody over while I slept. Sneaked an uncle right into the house.

I didn't pitch it in the trash. I walked upstairs, holding it in front of me like a rat by the tail. I walked straight into Mom's room, at the last second having this spasm of fear. What if she wasn't alone? What if I saw some big fat hairy uncle back rising up over her? The very idea made me feel I could puke, but by then I was already in.

Mom was by herself. Out like a light.

In relief and anger after being so grossed out, I kicked the foot of her bed.

She jerked but started to settle.

"Hello?" I said. Loud.

She sat up, blinking, rubbing her eyes. "Lucy, what is it, honey?"

"Just what I wanted to ask you."

"What?"

I wagged the butt in front of her face.

"It's a cigarette," she said. She shook her head. "God, I knew I was keeping you too sheltered."

"I know what it is. I found it on the kitchen table."

She was awake now.

"The least you could do is cover your tracks," I said. "Nobody here smokes."

She watched me as if I were some total stranger. "I might have a smoke now and then," she said. "I might just take it up. You never know what I might do."

"And two cups of coffee?"

She gave this flourishy shrug. "Hell, Lucy, I might even have three. Caution to the wind. Damn the caffeine, full speed ahead."

"That's not what I—" I started. "Out of two cups. You know exactly what I mean."

"What good's all the china if you can't use it?"

I sucked the corner of my lip into my mouth. "You can't leave stuff like this lying around, Mom. What if Dad had come home last night?"

She looked at me evenly for a long time. "Come on, Luce," she said at last. "What do you figure are the odds of that? No more than a snowball's in a blizzard."

"But what if?"

"So I had a girlfriend over for coffee. Big deal."

"You don't have any girlfriends! 'I'm too pretty for *girl*friends.' Remember that?"

"I was younger then."

"And what, you're some kind of hag now?"

She shook her head.

"Only one cup had lipstick on it."

"There are women who don't wear lipstick. Take yourself, for example."

"Maybe it was the two of us having a cup together in the middle of the night?"

"Why not?"

"Which one of us was smoking?"

"Take your pick."

"You can't even make me believe you. You think he will? You want him dragging your date in here by the scruff of his neck?"

She lay back down, plumping her pillow. "It is Saturday, isn't it? Can't you let me sleep in one day a week?"

I watched her close her eyes, the hills and valleys of her under the blankets. The spill of hair across the pillow. "Want me to go watch cartoons?"

"It's a free world." She gave me a wave with the fingers curled over the edge of her blanket, under her chin. "Take your cigarette with you, please. The smell is disgusting."

"It's all pretty disgusting, if you ask me."

"I'll make a point not to."

I slammed her door, storming downstairs, but then couldn't sit still. I shoved the coffee cups into the sink, jerked the faucet to full hot, and scrubbed at the smudge of ash in the saucer. I swiped hard at the table with a sponge, leaving the water gushing, filling a mop bucket. I threw in the ammonia. Mopped like my life depended on it.

Mopping, for Christ's sake.

That's what our weekends had disintegrated to, household chores—vacuuming, scrubbing, mopping—all keeping Mom and me from having to do anything together. Even speak to each other. The place got looking supernaturally clean, Martha Stewart a pig farmer next to us. You could have done surgery on our floors.

That Sunday night Mom even tried cooking. Never a pretty sight. I asked her why she wouldn't let me crank something out.

"Do you think you'll always be here, Luce?" she answered. "God, I can only pray we haven't done you so wrong."

"You've already set your sights on me leaving?"

"Preparing for the inevitable. Kids, soon as you get 'em trained up, they leave."

"I'm not making any plans, Mom."

"Well, don't think of sticking around for my sake. You think I'm not used to being left? God, even a rat would've learned this trick by now."

"Okay, Mom. Settle down. Jeez."

"Don't 'jeez' me. And don't you dare get comfortable with life here in Great Falls. Christ, this isn't life. This is—I don't know what. Suspended animation. I've got no plans of sticking around here forever myself." She banged her pans around, then slammed one down on the burner, hard, like there was something there in desperate need of flattening. "Where in hell is the flour?"

"Right here, Mom." I reached into the big drawer with the baking stuff. "It's right here."

Jerking back and forth across the kitchen, not asking me for a single thing though I would have helped, she whipped up something reddish gray and kind of flat. I set the table, then sat watching mine on my plate, not meeting Mom's eye. It used to be a pork chop. I'd seen it. Mom ate hers with gusto, which only made it that much more disgusting. Hearing her chew. I didn't have those kind of nerves. That kind of stomach.

"If you don't try anything new, you'll never know what you like," she told me.

"I'll go with instinct on some things."

"Oh, you will, will you?"

She pushed back her chair as soon as she'd made a point of eating every last bite.

I poked at mine with a fork.

"Quit that," she said. Then she muttered, "I don't know why I even try," and she snapped off up the stairs. I heard her bath filling. Definitely a sulk tub.

The next morning she hightailed it for work, like every morning, leaving me with nothing to do and no one to do it with. Not that the two of us would have done remarkable things together.

I poked around. Looked through a few of her catalogs. Watched a couple minutes of *Sally Jesse*. People watched that, I figured, so their own pathetic lives wouldn't look so miserable. It was the only possible reason. I snapped it off.

I checked the mail, but it was too early. No postcards.

When the doorbell rang, middle of the morning, it gave me a spook. I looked out, but there was no UPS truck, no brown-jeaned guy dragging up huge crates of Dad's lost postcards, a whole new childhood for me to read through. There were no low-slung, low-rumbling cars, either.

I stopped in front of the door. I bent low to shout through the mail slot. "Who is it?" I'd never felt more like a girl. The door wasn't even locked.

"Open up, or I'll huff and I'll puff!"

I flung the door open. Kenny stood there, his grin splitting his face. "What are you doing here!" I shrieked. I sounded like Jaimie or one of her crew. Disgusting.

I threw my arms around him, pulling him inside. He seemed tinier than ever, but I tripped on the threshold, and we went down together on the floor of the front hall. I squeezed until I could feel the give of his bones, the accordion of his ribs. I kicked the door shut behind us, felt the rush of cold air cut off.

It wasn't ten minutes before another bold five-year plan of abstinence lay in shambles. We did it on the living room floor, sort of in the entryway, and as soon as he was in me, it was so not Justin Haven that I couldn't help crying. Just tears, mainly, no sobbing or anything, but Kenny stopped, begging to know what was wrong, was he hurting me, was he . . .

I shook my head, straining to bury my face in his shoulder, rocking my hips up and down until we got it going again. "I'm just happy," I whispered, surprising myself by realizing it was true, that I hadn't felt that way in a long time. He whispered that he loved me, and I nodded into his shoulder, my hair scraping against his pale skin.

After a few more strokes, he sort of laughed. "I can't believe we're doing this!" He was so amazed, you could tell it was something he'd thought about, some kind of wild boink-around-the-house fantasy probably all boys had. I'm sure he wished he had pictures.

I looked at Kenny, listened to his breath straining in and out. We were totally quieter than Mom and Dad ever thought of being, but that was about the only difference. He drops out of the sky, and we're fucking like rabbits. If you put Mom's head on me and Dad's on Kenny—that and about a hundred pounds of muscle and bone—we'd be exactly the same people.

I kept countering his every move, but after seeing us the same as them, I knew nothing was coming my way this time. I clutched at Kenny, feeling again like I might cry.

God, I hate to cry.

When he finished, our clothes in rumples around us, our sweat drying, both of us starting to shiver, Kenny, still catching his breath, said, "I don't suppose there's any chance of your mom coming home?"

"About the same as my dad walking in."

He shivered. "Good God."

Right then a car door slammed across the street. I thought I'd have to call the firemen to come get Kenny off the ceiling. We laughed till we cried, deciding we better find our clothes, either get into them or get up to my room behind some door with a lock.

Kissing him, I told Kenny I had to use the bathroom, that I'd be right back. "Let's get out of here, then. Let's go somewhere. For coffee or something. I don't care."

"Coffee?"

"Whatever. Something." I dashed up to my bathroom and slipped my pill container out of its hiding place in my tampon box counted up the days on the ring. I was all right, remembering every night when I flossed.

Straightening myself up, doing a quick once-over in the mirror, I saw the shower curtain behind me, the shiny clear plastic, all its swimming, bubble-blowing angelfish. Maybe I should invite him up to shower with me. That was bound to be a major stop in the around-the-house fantasy.

But we could just wash. Hold each other. No moaning. No laughing. Then we could go out somewhere. Be like our own adults for a while. Not Mom and Dad. Not ripping down shower curtains.

I went to tell him my plan, but he was standing at the door with this weird look on his face. "There was somebody here," he said.

"You answered the door?"

He shook his head. "I froze like a jacklighted deer."

"Are they gone?"

He nodded. "I heard him walk off the porch. I peeked out the window."

"And?"

He wouldn't meet my eye. "That asshole friend of Haven's. The big redheaded one."

Tim. "I told you," I said, thanking God I had, "he won't leave me alone."

Even watching him for whatever reaction there might be, I smelled the house. It smelled like Dad was back. I said, "We've got to open some windows."

"The windows? Why?"

"It reeks of sex in here."

He smiled. Proud of himself.

Boys.

CHAPTER FORTY-ONE

Kenny, it turned out, had taken the bus over for spring break. When he told me he'd come straight to my house from the bus station, walking all those miles instead of letting his mom know he was here, I couldn't hide my smile.

Of course he told his mom he was there later that day, but all week long, I never told mine. Five days. Both our moms at work all day, both of us hanging with them at night, no uncles sneaking through. I cooked for Mom, complaining about how boring the days were. Kenny did whatever he and his mom did.

It was the best spring break in the history of the world.

His last afternoon, after making love, we took a shower together the way I'd planned. Holding. Soapy. Quiet. A whole tankful of hot water. Both of us coming out squeaky clean but already getting quiet.

I'd lifted Mom's spare set of keys. We walked downtown to her office and stole the car so I could give him a lift to the bus station. It worked like we were master thieves. The car was there, and, as dad would say, it started on a dime. "Buckle up," I said.

We had a lot of time, so rather than heading straight up airport hill, we eased out the Sun River. I drove slow, the sun warm on us, as different a trip from my death ride to Belt as it was possible to get.

Kenny looked around, out the windows, at me. "I could do this all the time," he said.

"We'd run out of gas."

He smiled only because he was supposed to. "You know what I mean. This week. Being together like this."

"Till I had to leave for work."

"Leave?"

"Gone months at a time. Like when you're in Kalispell." Instead of curving with the trees of the river, I followed the narrow road that led up to the buffalo jump.

"You know," he said, "not everybody's like your parents."

I smiled. "We've done a pretty good imitation all week." Once we'd tried groaning and wailing the way they did. We got laughing so hard he fell out of me.

"Lucy, normal people—"

"Normal?"

"Other. *Other* people live together. All the time."

"Like your mom and dad?" I took the last turn, the Corvair bucking up the rutted dirt, tires chittering over gravel, rocks pinging in the wheel wells.

"It can happen, Lucy. It can actually work out between people."

I bounced over the cattle guard. "Like Rabia and Keith?"

"Maybe they're doing fine."

"Maybe she's hanging in a bag in his closet. You think that's a life, vanishing off the face of the earth?"

"She moved, Lucy. People do it all the time."

"She moved like thirty blocks."

"What does she have to come back for? Who? You wouldn't even go to her wedding."

"Her mom lives a block away." I stopped the car. The only sound was the wind, keening through the bumpers, the antenna. "Have you ever been up here?" I asked.

Kenny shook his head.

I told him about the jump. How the Indians, before they had horses or guns, used to stampede whole herds off the cliff in front of us, using their stone knives on any survivors thrashing in the heap of carcasses below. Whittling the whole pile down to nothing but bones.

"There'd be one guy, the fastest runner, I guess—or maybe the slowest thinker—who'd put on a buffalo robe and lead the herd, get them to follow him once they got running. He'd dash out and take them over the cliff."

"What about him?"

"He'd have to jump over, too. Find some spot protected by an overhang or something. Hide there as the buffalo came waterfalling over."

"Or?"

"Fast-guy pâté."

Kenny rubbed a finger through the dust on the dashboard. "Great work if you can get it."

"That's Rabia. She took the mad-dash approach. The rest of us are charging behind."

"And you think she got pâtéd?"

"Flatter than North Dakota."

I opened my door, the wind trying to rip it out of my hand. Together we walked to the edge of the cliff. Nothing spectacular but enough to be the end of a buffalo. They weren't made for jumping. "They say the cliff used to be higher, but that there's hundreds of feet of buffalo bones down there under the grass."

West of us, the mountains stretched white and cold clear to Canada. South, more mountains hemmed in the river's path. The Highwoods stood up out of the plains in the east. The Belts. It was like we were surrounded, trapped forever in Great Falls. No wonder Mom hated coming up here. Dad had taken us a couple of times, but she refused to get out of the car. "Too many snakes," she'd say, which was true, you always saw rattlers; but seeing these mountains, I doubted that was the reason. At least not the only one.

Kenny put his arm around me. "Lucy, I'm going to miss my bus."

I turned away from the cliff edge. "Got to hit the trail before it hits back."

Kenny scrunched over next to me as we drove down off the top, took the other road to Ulm and the interstate. We didn't talk much.

At the bus station, people were already climbing on board. "Well," Kenny said.

"Yeah. See you in the summer, maybe. Christmas break. Don't be any stranger."

"Lucy."

"You know," I said, to keep him from saying whatever he was going to, "up there, talking about Rabia, about how people can stay together, *normal* people, it sounded like you were going to ask me to marry you or something."

"I was just thinking how—"

"Do me one favor, Kenny. Okay? Promise me you'll never do that. I mean, we've been best friends our whole lives. I think I deserve that much."

"Deserve? But—"

"Look," I said. "They're not getting on the bus anymore. It's about to pull out."

Kenny swore, "Lucy—"

I planted a big one on him. "You better go."

"I love you so much, Lucy."

"Adios, amoebas," I said. I watched him walk to the bus, keeping his gaze on me. "After a while, alligator," I whispered.

He walked into the bus, bumping his head. He rubbed at it, giving me a dopey grin.

"See you later, crocodile."

Going up the steps, he dug in his pack for his ticket. He got the front seat, waving at me through the smoked glass, just this smudge of hand you could barely see.

Coming off the airport hill, Great Falls lay spread out below me, the Missouri arcing through, big and wide and blue, the Sun muddy-looking, angling in from the mountains. I always thought it looked kind of pretty from up there—lots of trees, even without the elms—but today it looked empty, tiny, smothering. I hardly managed to get off the highway at Central. Could have as easily wound up in Shelby. Alberta. Dad.

The closer I got to telemarketing HQ, the more I worried about Mom's parking spot being taken. It wasn't like she had an executive slot, her name painted on the wall. And I'd cut it awful fine. The plan had been to drop Kenny off, not wait for his bus to leave.

No need to worry about somebody stealing my spot, though. As I drove up, I saw Mom standing out on the sidewalk, watching her car coming up the street. I pulled in to the curb. Buffalo raining down on top of me. I started to get out, but Mom said, "No, I'll ride."

I sat back down. Closed my door. She got in and closed hers.

"Well," she said. "Isn't this a pleasant surprise?"

I stared straight ahead.

She asked, "Are we going straight home?"

She let me drive almost all the way there before, just as we were passing the playground, like the jungle gym had reminded her, she asked, "You get Kenny off okay?"

I chewed on my lip. She had X-ray vision. Spy cameras. ESP. Everything. I pulled into our driveway, pointing at the dark, narrow slash of our garage door.

"You want to give it a shot?" she asked.

I rolled forward, never touching the brake. Slid into our tiny garage like I'd been doing it my whole life. An inch to spare on each side.

"Beautiful," Mom said. "Driving like that, sneaking boyfriends in and out, appropriating a car when necessary, you'd think you were the one pushing thirty."

"You're thirty-three, Mom," I said.

She slipped a hand into her coat pocket. "This morning, while you slept in, I ran around like a chicken. Same old, same old. To market, to market. You know. And topping it all off, it's that time of the month, and what do you think? Completely out of corks. Looked everywhere, even my emergency ditty bag. Zip. Zero. Nada. So I checked your stash, hoping you had one I might snitch." She took her hand out of her pocket and gave this backhand flip. My birth-control pills landed flat on my lap.

I let them sit there. So busted.

"You're thirty-three," I said again. Like a giggling little kid in trouble, knowing giggling is the worst thing to do.

"Oh, but you're gaining on me in a hurry, aren't you?"

"About the same speed you're trying to come back my way."

You could feel the heat rise off her. "Kenny?" she asked.

"No. They're mine."

If I could have, I would have bolted. But the damn garage was so tight, you had to ooze out like a snake. Less than a dramatic exit. Maybe, if she ever got out, I'd back out of here and take off. Pass the bus on its way to Kenny's. Be there waiting for him.

"Get inside, Luce," Mom said at last.

"They're for my complexion, Mom."

"Mmm-hmm. That's always been such a priority of yours. Your looks."

"Never too late."

"No," she said, at once serious and loud. "But it is too early. Way too goddamn early!"

"I should wait the way you did, Mom? What? Another month? A few weeks?"

I could feel the voltage between us, the currents of sparking fire. I thought she might hit me. But she waved her hand toward my pill pack, something it seemed she couldn't quite bring herself to look at. "That—that is one thing. It's inevitable. It's biology. At least you're smart enough to use them. At least I taught you that much."

"*You?*"

She ignored me. "But the lying, Luce, that's what I can't bear. That's what really pisses me off. You thinking you have to keep secrets from me."

"Lying bugs you? You taught me about the pill but not about *that*? A chip off the old blockhead, I'd say."

"Get inside, Luce. It's where you're going to be for a long, long time."

"Like that'll be a change."

She reached across me and popped open my door, banging it into the wall. "Go!"

CHAPTER FORTY-TWO

Being grounded was nothing. Less than nothing. I mean, it didn't even scratch my lifestyle. All I did was come home from school, anyway. Make dinner. Mom poked and pried about Kenny, but I didn't give an inch. Name, rank, and serial number would have been a major break-through for her. "He's gone, Mom. All right? Okay? You win."

"*I* didn't send him away."

"But you wish you could, don't you? Wish you could send *me* away."

She stamped down on the vacuum cleaner's switch, drowning us out with its roar.

What turned the house into a cell, Great Falls a prison, was Kenny leaving. That made everything look the way Mom talked—being stuck here, trapped, nothing to do but escape, get a life, change. And Kenny had only been gone a few weeks. Mom had spent her whole life stuck here, Dad leaving. No wonder she acted the way she did.

If our house was clean before, now it got looking like some kind of lab. Where people wear those white suits. Not touching anything except through those walls with the gloves sticking out of them. Mom dusted the ceilings. My room became my lair, stuff thrown everywhere, a comfortable pigpen in the sterilization suite. Mom learned to not even think about looking inside.

One Saturday, me running the vacuum this time, Mom tapped me on the shoulder. I flicked off the vacuum, wondering what could have caused her to break the silence. "There's someone at the door," she told me.

"So answer it," I said, reaching to turn the vacuum back on.

"I did. He's not here for me."

"Who is it?"

"Exactly what I was wondering."

I took the two steps, and saw Tim standing just inside the door. Our eyes met. I ducked back. "Tell him I'm not here," I said, loud enough that he'd hear.

"He knows you're here."

"Tell him I can't come to the door. Tell him I'm busy shaving my head."

"Get out there."

I rolled my eyes and trudged out to the hall. "Hey, Tim!" I called, all excited-sounding. "I'm glad you're here. I was just wondering if it's possible to flunk an IQ test. I mean, I figure it's something you'd know."

He blushed, which I almost couldn't help liking him for. "I've been coming by sometimes," he said, like it was something he'd rehearsed. "But you're never home."

I waited until it dawned on him.

"You never come to the door."

I gave him a big bright smile, like you would to the slow kid in class, finally nailing an answer.

"I was going fishing," he said. "I thought you might want to come along."

"Fishing," I said. This, in Great Falls, I guessed was a date. "What does your buddy Justin have to say about this?"

"He's not my buddy, Lucy."

"Give me a break. You guys are Tweedle and Dum. Dumb and Dumber."

"Not anymore."

I grinned. "Really?"

"I told him I wasn't going to spend the rest of my senior year hanging around with an asshole."

"What did he say?" God, please tell me you killed him.

Tim kind of smiled. "He didn't exactly see my point of view."

Not exactly death, but I'd take it. "Great. And you know what? Even though I'm just a freshman? I've made the same resolution. So have a good life."

"Lucy, I'm not an asshole. I'm not Justin."

"That's your résumé?"

He stood there.

"I mean, it's a big thing, but it still makes for a kind of thin list of achievements." I craned up on tiptoe to see past him. He had a car like Justin's, long and low and loud. He'd left it idling at the curb: at least he'd had that much sense.

"You're not an asshole?" I said. "Prove it."

"How?"

"Go away." Stepping around him, I held the screen door open for him.

He followed me out but stopped on the top step. "If that's what you want, I will, but—"

"It is."

He took a step down. "We don't have to go fishing. We could go for a ride. Go to a movie. We could do anything you want. Go to Four B's and have coffee."

"I've been for a ride," I said, swinging the screen door back and forth. "I hate movies. Coffee makes me gag."

"Okay," he said. "I'm going, Lucy. But I don't think I'm going to stay away. Okay?"

"Free world," I said. Not exactly setting my position in stone. But he was going away. Doing what I asked. Compared to his old buddy, that made him practically heroic.

A breeze eddied across the porch, making me realize the day was gorgeous, sun everywhere, the new leaves starting to flutter. The grass already needed mowing. A trip down the river sounded perfect. "You got two rods loaded and everything?"

He smiled a little. "No hurt in hoping."

"There can be a world of hurt in hoping." I waved to him. "Good luck. I have to go dust under the floorboards. Scrub inside the toilet tanks."

"I'll try you again. When you guys are finished with your spring cleaning."

"It's year-round."

He shook his head but kept smiling. "Maybe someday you'll run out of cleaner. Rags."

"Not likely. We clean every weekend. It's what we do. Our quality time."

He flashed me the thumbs-up. He'd seen the opening before I did. Five days a week we didn't clean.

He climbed into his car and eased off, the engine rumbling, not roaring. Relaxed.

When I turned inside, Mom was standing right behind me. "Is he next?"

"God, you've got a filthy mind."

"Is he?"

"I'm sure you heard every word. Here at the privacy palace. I wouldn't even go fishing with him."

"Fishing is not what I'm worried about."

I looked all blond at her. "Jeez, what is?"

She stomped off down the hall. I took the time to slide the storm window up on the screen door. It was practically summer, and I hadn't even noticed.

The first week of May, we had an early out from school, the day over at one o'clock. I walked home slow, the weather still too beautiful to be believed. I felt like a bear stumbling out of hibernation, and by the time I made it home, Tim was already parked out front. He was on the porch, pushing at the bell. I stood and watched. Dividing him and Justin would be like splitting the atom, but . . .

"Place is vacant," I called. They wouldn't stand a chance against the Amazing Diamond Girl.

Tim turned. "Not cleaning yet?"

"Only Saturdays, Sundays."

"So? Fishing?"

I looked at his car, then up to the blue sky. "Only the two of us? No Justin?"

"I told you. I don't hang out with him anymore."

"Because of me?"

He opened his car door. "They're getting away out there."

Just the idea of getting out of Great Falls seemed too good to be true. And this would be the last straw in the coffin lid for Justin and Tim. I told myself I'd tell Kenny all about it.

Tim took the frontage road the whole way. Said he didn't like interstates. I'd never heard of anything like that, but the narrow, curving roads were fun, and though the weather wasn't quite warm enough, we drove with the windows down. The smell, all muddy and grassy and new, made me close my eyes, put my head back, and breathe deep through my nose, filling myself up. The rush of air and sound made talking impossible even if he'd wanted to.

We caught a few fish. I mainly kept an eye on Tim, but he never tried a thing, not even wrapping his arms around me to teach me how to cast a fly rod—which Dad had done years and years ago anyway, didn't move too close when we sat down for a break, him pulling out a couple of Cokes. He didn't bring out any schnapps. Any beer.

It got dusk way faster than I expected. As we headed back to town, the river bugs ticking against the windshield like rain, I asked him to pull over at Osterman's so I could call Mom.

"You can use my cell phone," he said, flipping open the glove box.

I punched in the number, but only the machine answered. Overtime again?

"Hey, Mom. I went fishing and I'm on my way home. I'll make some dinner when I get there. About half an hour. I'll see you—" I stopped. "Shit. I forgot I was grounded. My only hope now is to beat her back."

Tim launched up the next ramp onto the highway. We were flying. We had to roll up the windows. Ninety miles an hour. Ninety-five.

"How many speeding tickets do you have?"

He grinned, driving one-handed, like we were still cruising back roads, and for a second I could see the attraction between him and Justin. "What are you grounded for?" he asked.

I thought it over, then said, "My mom found my birth-control pills."

Tim didn't answer. Not even a nod. His eyes were fixed straight ahead, like suddenly driving was the hardest thing he'd ever done. I turned my smile to the door.

He didn't say another word until we were easing up to the curb in front of my house. The garage door was closed. Mom home.

"I am dead meat," I said, popping my door before he'd quite stopped.

"I'm sorry, Lucy. I—"

"You didn't know." I was out of his car, standing there. I thought of watching Horse Teeth dropping Mom off. Of her watching the same thing now. "I got to run."

"Want to go again sometime?"

"Yeah, soon as I get ungrounded. I'll only be forty."

I was through the leaning gate, halfway up the walk, when I heard him say, "I'll wait," and pull my door shut. He drove off as soon as I opened the front door, not wanting to be caught in whatever mushroom cloud was going to come boiling out of my house.

But Mom was sitting there watching TV. She glanced up when I came in. "Thanks for calling," she said. "I would have been worried."

"It was just fishing, Mom," I said, braced for battle. "Remember, fishing's not what you're worried about?"

She nodded. "With that guy who came over the other week? What's his name?"

"Tim."

She looked at whatever she was watching. Not a word about being grounded.

"Nothing happened, Mom."

She turned back to me. "Did I say anything?"

I tried letting the fight drain out of me. "I only wanted you to know."

"Good. I'm glad. I'm glad you're doing things with other people, as a matter of fact. There's a whole world out there besides Kenny."

I missed a couple of breaths. Is that what she thought? That I was forgetting about Kenny? Instead of yelling anything at her, I managed to ask, "What do you want for dinner?"

"Some of us went for burgers after work. I called but got your message."

"Great," I said. "I'm glad you're doing things with other people, too." But that didn't make any sense. As far as I knew, all the uncles were from work. I headed into the kitchen.

Beside my place at the table was the day's postcard from Kenny. A picture of some river. "Like this river, I'm always running to you!" written across the back.

Good Lord. "Only because you got so far to go," I muttered. I was not letting Kenny go. Hell, all I did was go fishing. It was beautiful out there. I was splitting the atom. Did he expect me to spend the rest of my life cleaning this dump, only ever smelling Pine-Sol?

Did he expect me to be Mom?

I picked up his card, stabbed a piece of tape across it, and stuck it on the bottom of row six. "Like a river," I whispered. "For Christ's sake, Kenny, you're on the wrong side of the divide. We'll end up in whole different oceans."

I wasn't hungry anymore.

I poked my head into the front room long enough to tell Mom I was taking a shower.

"Use some lotion," she told me. "Our skin was never meant for the sun."

I tanned way better than she did. Blond hair or not. I started up the stairs.

It was fishing. He never tried to touch me. Even dropping me off, he never even leaned over. It was just fishing.

CHAPTER FORTY-THREE

A couple of weeks later, the end of school something everybody could taste, Tim found me coming out of the cafeteria, starting back to afternoon classes. He fell in next to me, asking when we could go fishing again. I said, "Hey, you know, whenever."

Somebody called out, "Hey, the lovebirds! Carrot Juice and Juicy Lucy!"

Justin.

"What about now, Lucy?" Tim said. "Let's get the hell out of here."

I couldn't quite stop a smile. "Sounds good to me."

Tim put his arm around my shoulder and steered me toward the closest door. I picked his arm off and put it down at his side. Then I took his hand and led him through the door. I had achieved fission.

After that, it got to where I didn't make a lot of afternoon classes. Fish learned to fear me. Almost as much as Tim did.

He never once tried anything. It was like fishing was our jungle gym. He talked a lot about going to college in Missoula. His football scholarship. Once, planning for a future he didn't know he didn't have, he said how it would be cool for us to try out a few of those west-side rivers. I didn't say anything back, and he let it drop. If I tried out any west-side rivers, it'd be around Kalispell. With Kenny.

He made these big plans for Memorial Day. Borrowed somebody's raft. Set up a buddy to run a shuttle so we could float the Dearborn all the way down to the Missouri. He'd done it before. By the time he told me about it, it was all set up.

Uncle Guy was throwing a bash up at his cabin—Mom even asking me this time—but I could see her relief when I said I had fishing plans. I told her every time I went fishing, but in a way that made it sound like there was always a crowd. That it was after school, not during. Maybe she told me about Mr. Ed's cabin in the same kind of way.

So Tim and I fished all day, floating along in a rubber raft, baking in the sun. It got scorching, the water glare like needles in our eyes, and when Tim peeled his T-shirt over his head, I could hardly believe it. He and Kenny couldn't be in the same species. Tim was taller than Dad, at least half a foot taller than me, and though Dad was heavier-looking, I knew he wasn't carved out this way. Tim was built like a piece of marble. Something they'd chip out of Italy.

We put lotion on each other. It was, I admit, my idea. I just wanted to touch something that looked like that. But that was as far as anything got. Until the ride home, when Tim started talking about Missoula again. About not wanting to go.

"You'd rather look forward to being in my shoes? Being a sopho-more?" I should have said in my pants, not shoes. He would have died blushing.

He just kept on, earnest as ever. "They're going to find out I'm not as fast as they think I am."

Football, for Christ's sake. Here I was remembering the warm-rock feel of him under my lotion-slippery hands, and he was thinking about football. "You're as fast as they think you are. Faster than you think you are."

"How do you know? I've never had great acceleration."

"They've watched you. They know what they're getting."

"Do you?" he asked, his voice so serious.

This was not where I wanted this to go.

We were almost back to town, the lights of the airport in sight, when he asked, "You want to know why I don't want to go to Missoula?"

"No. I definitely do not."

"You," he said.

I pushed the heel of my palm against my forehead. Started thumping it there.

"I don't want to move away from you."

"I didn't ask for this, you know. I didn't ask you for anything."

"I know."

"I didn't ask for you to start talking about missing me. I didn't ask you to miss me."

"I didn't ask for it, either," he said. "Some things happen. It's like shit, you know. Just happens."

We were off the interstate, coming down the strip.

"Wow. Now, that is the way to a person's heart. They are shit. They just happen. Did you stay awake thinking that up? Did you stop to think and then forget to start again?"

"I didn't mean anything like that," he said, steering. "You know that. I meant—"

"You know what I know? I know I don't want anyone else leaving me, telling me how much he doesn't want to leave me. Is that so much to ask for?"

"But—"

"Just go. It's not like we have this big thing. Like we're anything I'll have to get over."

Tim turned north, toward my house. "You're not big on listening, are you?" he said. "Not a word-in-edgewise kind of person."

I smiled. Then laughed. I couldn't help it. "Go piss up a rope." It was something Dad said. I didn't have a clue what it meant.

"Be a cool trick," he murmured.

When Tim pulled up in front of our house, the porch light was on, and maybe the kitchen light, it was hard to tell. The place looked quiet, no one waiting.

We were just sitting there. I had my hand on the door handle. "Well, thanks," I said.

He reached out, at last, grazing the back of my thumb. "Thanks for coming."

Then, I guess because I'd jumped down his throat for liking me, I leaned over and kissed him. Quick.

He kissed back, every bit as quick. Mouth closed. "I didn't ask for that," he said.

"I didn't ask you, either."

He scratched his head, looking so puzzled that I couldn't help laughing. He started laughing too, real soft. I leaned in and gave him another kiss. We were both laughing. Our mouths were open. The kiss lasted long enough that I reached up to hold the back of his neck. His arms came around me, his hands on my shoulder blades, not moving, trying nothing.

I eased back against my door. "If you want—I don't know, there's not a whole lot else I got going this weekend."

"No cleaning?"

"Well, yeah, besides that." I opened the door, got out slow.

"I'll call."

"They're getting away out there."

"See you, Lucy."

I nodded, going up the front walk. "See ya, see ya, wouldn't want to be ya."

He stayed until I opened the door and turned to wave, like I had this whole history of boys watching me safely to my door.

I picked up the mail off the floor, knowing Mom hadn't been home.

With the bills was Kenny's latest: "Time to start planning for my summer vacation!"

I looked back out the front door, Tim's taillights going away, his kiss something I could still taste. I tossed the card down on the table. "Shit," I said.

CHAPTER FORTY-FOUR

I didn't get much sleep that night, wondering about kissing Tim—God just remembering the way he felt—then about Kenny's summer vacation, what would happen if he decided to bus over for the long weekend. Try to surprise me again.

Mom crept in at two-thirty, straight to her room, not bothering with any 'sleep tights' as she passed. Listening to how quiet she tried to be, I had this horrible realization. My life had turned into hers. Lainee and Lucy, the Astounding Jugglers of Men!

Long before dawn, I gave up and went down in the dark to fix coffee, pretending it was Dad I heard sneaking in last night instead of Mom, that I'd beaten him downstairs for the first time ever.

I sat at the table, wondering what to do about Kenny.

Then I heard Mom coming down. It wasn't yet six in the morning. Maybe it had been Dad. I leaned over to see.

But though it was a man turning the corner at the banister, it was not Dad. Not even Horse Teeth. He stooped to slip on his shoes, then headed for the door.

"Late for church?" I said, my voice jarring in the quiet.

He turned, guilty but smiling. His shirt tails hung out. I didn't know him. A brand-new uncle.

"Who the hell are you?" I said.

He put his finger up to his lips and winked. "The Tooth Fairy." He couldn't hide the way his eyes dropped, the quick checkout look. I crossed my arms over my Supergirl chest, and he waved, slipping out the front door.

It was minutes before I could think enough to breathe. I kept seeing that wink, that wave, that finger up for keeping secrets. It was as if I'd watched the curl of breeze that would at last bring down our house of cards.

I was still sitting there, hours later, when Mom came shuffling down. "Morning, Luce," she said.

She was barefoot, wearing her buffalo robe. She stopped in front of the table, reading Kenny's postcard. "That should be interesting," she said.

I watched her like she was a bomb ticking.

"What?" she said. "Oh, right. Sorry. Shouldn't have read your private postcard."

I just stared.

"What time did you get in? Did something happen, did . . ." She stopped, sniffing at the coffee's scorch. "Oh, God. How long have you been up?" Her eyes darted around the kitchen, trying to fill in the space I took up, trying to make me disappear. Finally, she said. "I'm sorry, Lucy."

I shook my head the tiniest bit.

"It couldn't be helped," she said. "He's got kids. We couldn't go there."

"You don't? Have a kid?"

She did this grimace. "His are young."

"How much younger could they *be*?"

Mom ran her hand up through her hair. She looked like shit, smeared mascara making her look like she'd lost a prizefight, her hair destroyed by the pillow. She banged open the cabinet getting out a coffee cup. "Don't think I'm proud of any of this, Luce. Or that I'm happy this is how things worked out. Don't let yourself think that."

"It's not exactly like you don't have any say."

"You don't have any idea what it's *exactly* like." She poured herself the last of the coffee and started out of the room with it. "Not one clue." Then she turned back. "And what about you?" She pointed at Kenny's postcard. "Are you going to welcome him with open arms? Tell your fishing buddy to lay low for a while?"

"No," I shot back. "I have a say. What I'll tell Kenny is that he isn't going to start doing that to me. Dropping in whenever. Pulling a Dad. I'll tell him there is no way I'm going to let him turn me into you."

Mom looked into her coffee, then up. "And that'll make you feel good, I bet. Almost as good as it did saying it to my face."

"Well, God, Mom, look at your life."

She walked away. "Look at it? I don't even want it."

I followed her up the stairs. "Mom," I said. "Mom!"

She didn't hesitate or flinch. Just kept on. I stood at the head of the stairs, watching her go into her room. She pushed the door behind her, but it didn't close all the way.

I tapped on it, nudging it open. "Mom?"

The buffalo robe was on the floor. I caught a glimpse of her bare backside as she slipped into her bathroom. She'd been naked under the robe, naked last night. It wasn't some huge surprise, but it stopped me cold. I had to put a hand up against the doorjamb.

I heard the water start. I gave her a minute to get the temperature right. It wouldn't be as hard, talking to her behind a shower curtain. I crossed the room but made the mistake of looking at her bed, the clot and snarl of it. Closing my eyes, holding my breath, I dove in, stripping the sheets off in one tugging swipe. I swept her clothes, in, too, knotting them into the tangle I threw out into the hallway. I got fresh sheets, did my military corners. When she came out, it would be a new room. Not a place where anything had happened.

Gathering myself, I tapped on the bathroom door. Eased it open. "Mom."

She wasn't in the shower. She was just sitting there on the closed toilet. She turned away from me, but not before I could see that she was crying. Her mascara drained down her cheeks, skinny black waterways. Naked, she held her hands to her face, shielding her boobs with the crook of her arms.

"Mom?" I whispered. "Look. I'm sorry."

"Go away, Luce."

I'd never seen my mom cry in her life. Never even considered it possible. "Are you okay?"

"Not even close."

The shower drummed, the air hot and thick, tropical. I walked across and knelt beside her. I put a hand on her naked thigh.

She gave this odd sob and brushed the top of my head.

"I didn't mean that, Mom. About not wanting to be like you."

"You better have." Her face still away from me, she yanked at the toilet paper, unwinding a long piece, wiping her cheeks with it. "You better mean it. You know how long I'd known that guy? About six hours. Never laid eyes on him before that. He's married, for Christ's sake!"

Trying to make her laugh, I said, "At least you got that in common. Something to talk about."

Sucking in a stuttering breath, definitely not a laugh, she said, "I am not this way, Luce. I'm not."

I swallowed. "It's okay, Mom."

"And now that's on your shoulders. You got that to carry around for me, too."

It was a second before I realized what she meant. Dad. That we were partners in the lying, more secrets.

"I can do it, Mom. It's not a problem."

"It should be."

I rested my cheek against her leg. It was cool and hard.

"So who was this guy?" I asked, soft enough that I doubted she'd heard.

Mom moved, shaking her head, I guessed. "He told me he was the Tooth Fairy," I said.

Even sitting there with my face pressed against her leg, I could feel Mom smile. "I sure didn't find any prizes," she said. "I'll have to check under the pillow."

"I already looked."

"Nothing?"

I shook my head, my face sticking to her skin.

"Just my luck," she said, sucking in another of those long breaths. She gave my head a pat, different from the others, a this-is-over-now touch.

She moved all of a sudden, and I knew she did not want me seeing her naked. But in the one glimpse I got it was apparent that the bastard gravity had finally noticed she was on his planet. Only a little. Maybe she'd worn her thong last year just in time. While she still could. Maybe that had a lot to do with what was going on.

The shower-curtain rings sang as she whipped it shut behind her. Then the change of the splashing as the water broke and coiled down around her.

A couple of minutes later, she said, "Luce?"

I was standing in front of the mirror, liking the way the fog kept me from seeing myself. "I'm here, Mom."

She let that sink in before saying, "I really am sorry. I am so sorry."

I nodded, invisible in the fog. "Me, too, Mom. But it's okay. We're okay."

CHAPTER FORTY-FIVE

What seemed like hours later, Mom came down the steps, fixed up normal, not date material, just Mom. Like nothing had happened at all between us. But she walked out front, waving for me to follow. We stood on the porch, the day already hot around us.

"This is a day built for driving," she said.

"Driving where?"

"It's a holiday," she said. "We're supposed to be memorializing the dead."

"And here we are without a corpse."

She nodded. "Pity." She looked up and down the street. "Come on. Let's blow this pop stand to hell."

So we drove, windows down, like Tim and I had, only Mom headed north. I thought maybe she'd take the old bootlegger trail running up to Canada, but she stuck to the Fort Benton highway. At last she cut off on the humpy, potholed road leading toward Ryan Dam—the great fall itself. Until then I hadn't known if it was all random, or if she had some sort of idea in mind. The wheat was about four inches high, same as the stubble, and I watched the alternating strips flash past, green, tan, green, tan, live, dead. I leaned back and closed my eyes, the sun and wind on my face, feeling the rush of going. Anywhere.

The lurch of the turn tilted me toward the door, the swoop in my stomach familiar as we dropped down the bluffs to the falls, though we hadn't ventured this far in a long time, and never the two of us alone. When I was a kid, we used to come here a lot, almost every time Dad was home. Mom and Dad had gotten married here.

And before that, there was Lewis and Clark. They'd dragged boats up here all the way from Ohio or someplace, until these falls stopped them in their tracks. Wham. Do not pass go. But instead of cursing and bitching and moaning like normal people; they were thrilled to find them, because it meant they knew where they were. Nobody likes not knowing at least that much. Mom, I figured, had been aiming for this spot ever since climbing into the car.

After she parked and turned off the engine, I sat a minute more, the sun hot on my face, red and bright on my eyelids. The roar of water wasn't as loud as the wind at fifty miles an hour—I mean, I could hear the engine's cooling tick and everything—but it sounded stronger, like all the power in the world.

When I opened my eyes, Mom was looking right at me, smiling.

"Why'd we come here?" I asked, my voice cracking like I was waking up.

"Did I ever tell you—" she started.

"Every time, Mom," I interrupted, though it was really Dad who did the telling. " 'This is where we tied the noose, Luce.' " I said it out loud for her, since he was gone.

Mom gave me the shove she usually gave him. "It's 'knot,' knot-head."

I tried to picture the two of them surrounded by their high school friends. Maybe a sky full of rice. But I couldn't see it. Me doing that in a year or two? Man, I couldn't think of getting married for another *lifetime* or two.

Mom opened her door, and I followed her out, walking down the path to the suspension bridge, then over to the island. Dad would have the whole bridge swaying, Mom and me clutching to the handrails, Mom yelling, "Knock it off, Chuck!"

"What do you think I'm *trying* to do?" he'd shout back.

There were a few people walking the path up to the falls, the island green around them, sprinklers chicka-chicking, the cottonwoods wrapped with chicken wire to fend off the beavers. Mom and I followed the path past the signs about Lewis and Clark, the party they had on finding this place, drinking the last of their booze.

The dam was wide open, more water spilling over than I'd ever seen. The falls were a falls again, the mist reaching us with the wind gusts, wetting our faces. Mom smiled over the novelty of that. Usually, it was like the falls in town, a huge concrete wall, some dry cliffs underneath. A parched reminder of what this place had once been.

We stood there a while, watching the roar, before Mom broke away from the pull of the falls and led the way down the rock stairs, through the pavilion or whatever, all the picnic tables, and out onto the soggy grass, the sprinklers gone quiet.

She stopped on The Spot, the hallowed ground where, when the justice had asked Dad if he would do all the "to have and to hold" stuff, Dad had looked up, startled, and said, "Who? Me?"

Mom almost said something, and I said, " 'Who? Me?' "

She closed her mouth. Raised an eyebrow.

"Come on, Mom. It's like I was there."

She smiled and continued her walk down the island, clear to the other end. It wasn't a spot we—or anyone else—often made it to, the bridge luring you back before you got here, the falls the star attraction.

Before us, the power plant's channel joined the main river in a series of standing waves. They had their own pull, the way they stood there, these tall brownish waves always staying in the same place instead of rushing along like waves are supposed to.

"Okay, smarty-pants," Mom said. "So you know all about the noose. But do you know what else happened on this island?"

She moved over a few feet till she stood on the downstream side of a giant cottonwood, maybe a body's length away from the rocky drop into the river. "On this very spot, right here, where I'm standing?"

I waited. "No," I said, expecting some more Lewis and Clark, a Sacagawea moment.

"You," she said.

"Me?" I braced for the punch line, but Mom stood there gazing out at those standing waves, somewhere a long ways away.

"Are you going to—" I started, but then I got it. Like not *too* stupid.

Me.

I swallowed. The ground she stood on was hardly flat enough, hardly big enough for one person to lie down. Beyond the rush of water, the sheer faces of the cliffs hemmed us in.

It was perfect.

All that water drowning them out, drawing them together, the fury holding its own rhythm, driving them on. I pictured the darkness, the distant line of lights atop the dam, the mosquitoes making them pay. Something they wouldn't notice till later, when developments would make them wish mosquito bites were all they'd come away with.

"That's maybe more than I needed to know," I said, trying to make it sound like a line.

"It was the middle of the night. We had to climb the fence at the bridge. One of the scariest things I've ever done."

"The fence?"

274 | PETE FROMM

"Yes, the *fence*."

I'd known what she meant. It was a serious fence, not just there for looks; tall, with wings leading out into the air over both sides of the bridge.

"Chuck kept giving these whistle blasts. You know, with his fingers in his mouth."

He could crack glass with those. As soon as you stepped onto the island, there was this sign warning you to clear the area immediately in the event of eight sharp whistle blasts. Like you could outrun dam failure. Especially with that fence between you and any chance of safety. And eight? Who'd start counting with number one?

It was something I could picture way too clearly. The smell of the grass; the sharper, sourer smell of the sticky cottonwood buds; the cottonwood fluff blowing around like snow, sticking to their piled clothes.

"Was this before or after?" I asked.

"None of your business," Mom said, smiling.

But I'd done the math years and years ago. It wasn't like they just one day decided to get married, a down-on-your-knee kind of thing. I'd known that forever.

"So, like I said, Mom, why'd we come here?" But I knew. Nobody likes not knowing at least where they are.

CHAPTER FORTY-SIX

Tim and I kept fishing, though, rushing past our tame pecks at the
door, fishing, like watching movies before it, had turned into more of
an excuse to neck and grope than any real pursuit of trout. With
Kenny's postcards pouring in, it made me feel more than ever like
Mom, so, a few days after school got out, I decided to go boy again. It
wasn't this big deal. I didn't think it would stop anything with Tim,
which I didn't really want to stop anyway. I mean, it was fun. And I
knew he didn't mean anything to me. Just this giant guy who'd be going
away soon. Mom again.

Holding the buzzing clipper, my lopped-off hair scattered across
my shoulders, I smiled at the old familiar outline of my rock-hard skull
and ran the motorboat through a few touch-up curves. I might have
made a few outboard noises. I don't know.

It wasn't till I shut off the clipper that I heard the phone ringing.
It was dinnertime, and I figured it was Mom calling to say she wouldn't
be there. I almost didn't answer but, for peace's sake, I made the dash
to her room, bits of hair swirling behind me.

"Hello?"

"Uh, Lainee?" Before I could deny it, he said, "No, this must be
Ruthy."

"Lucy."

"Lucy? Are you sure? I was positive she said you were Ruthy."

"Am I sure? Who is this?"

"I believe you know me as the Tooth Fairy."

I sat back on her bed. "You've got to be kidding."

"Nope. The real name, though, is Bill."

Barnacle Bill, I thought. Dad used to sing this song as he came home, pounding on the door. He'd get his voice all high, warbling, "Who's that knocking at my door? Who's that knocking at my door?" Then, in his big bass, he'd boom, " 'It's only me, from over the sea, says Barnacle Bill the sailor." It was from some cartoon or something.

"I was wondering," said Barnacle, "if your mother is there."

"No, she's not. Would you like to talk to her husband?"

"I'll pass. Just let her know I called. She can reach me at this number."

I repeated the number back to him, like I was writing it down. Then I hung up. He was still talking. Calling me Ruthy again.

When I turned around, Mom was standing in the door, watching me.

I smiled, rubbing my head for luck. "Like seeing an old friend," I said.

"What is your problem?" she asked, startling me.

"No problem at all. Completely maintenance-free."

She leaned against the doorframe. "It's time to grow up, Luce. You're not ten anymore."

"It's easier this way, Mom. I kind of missed it."

"Oh. I can see why you'd need the time. With your killer social schedule. Jumping out of bed every day, checking the calendar, seeing if you're waiting for Dad today or Kenny." Pinching an envelope under her arm, she put her hands out like a scale, bobbing them back and forth. "Dad. Kenny. Dad. Kenny. Or is it Dad, Kenny, Tim now? How *do* you fit it all in?"

I scratched at some of the cut hair on my neck. "That's not what I do."

Mom stepped into the bedroom, waving the manila envelope at me.

"He sent a *letter*?" I asked.

"It's your report card."

I sucked my lip into the corner of my mouth. Tim and I hadn't made a lot of classes there at the end.

She started tapping the report card against her fingertips. "This is great, Luce. Just great. Planning on following me into the telemarketing business?"

I shrugged. "Maybe hairstyling."

"Oh yeah, you've got a real eye there." Without another word, she tossed the card into the wastebasket next to her bed. Starting out of the room, she said, "It's your life. I guess I can't stop you from flushing it down the toilet."

"Kawoosh," I said.

Before I moved a muscle, she was back, jabbing her finger at me. But she didn't know what to say.

"That was Barnacle Bill on the phone. He wants you to call him," I said.

"Who?"

"The Tooth Fairy. 'I've only known him six hours.' Even in that kind of rush, you made an impression."

She gave me a long, long look. "Did he leave a number?"

I lifted my hands in this exaggerated shrug. "Didn't have a pen."

She left, and I followed her down the hallway, but she didn't go for a phone. She ducked into my bathroom and grabbed the clipper, yanking the cord out of the socket like she was hoping to take the wall with her.

"What are you doing?"

I chased her down the stairs, out the front door.

She held the end of the cord in her fist and started twirling the clipper over her head, like she was the roping star in some sort of barbers' rodeo. The cord was miles too long, like you might need to do some clipping in the next block, in a country without electricity.

"Mom!"

Once she really got going, Judging her distance, her speed maxed out, Mom took one step forward, motorboating that old clipper right into our tree, full swing at the end of its cord.

A motorboating disaster. A terrible mishap. Not survivor one.

Bits of black plastic glistened in the lawn. The cord stretched limp from her hand down to the silver body of the clipper. It had bounced way back from the tree. Mom was breathing hard.

"What's *my* problem?" I said.

"I can't believe I let him do that to you all those years."

"I did it, Mom. Me."

"Not anymore. I'm not going to let you go on pretending you're not what you are."

"And that would be?"

"A woman, Lucy."

"A woman?" I asked. "Me?"

"For Christ's sake, Lucy. It's not a dirty word."

"It's whatever you make it," I said. She knew exactly what I meant.

"You didn't have to do that, Mom. You could have called him. It's not like I care."

Without taking her eyes off me, Mom flipped the cord out after the clipper. Then she circled around me back into the house, another silent period starting up for us.

CHAPTER FORTY-SEVEN

The next Friday, Tim stopped by, a borrowed truck idling in the street, a raft in the back. Mom was in the kitchen, almost out the door for work. He was five minutes early.

I walked out and almost made it before Mom called from the porch. "Luce?"

"Oh. I'm gone, Mom. Fishing."

"With?"

I rolled my eyes at Tim. "Time to be introduced, I guess." We plodded up to the porch. "Mom, this is Tim. Shaughnessy. Tim, Mom."

"We've met once before," Tim said. "At the door."

Mom nodded, giving him the eye, up and down. He had shorts on already, sandals, a muscle shirt. I couldn't help a proud little smile.

"How old are you?" Mom asked.

Tim looked surprised. "Nineteen."

"In college?"

"This fall. Missoula. I just graduated. I got a football scholarship."

"No summer job?"

"Mom!"

"I start tomorrow. On my grandparents' ranch out near Belt. I do it every summer."

"How much money do you make?" I asked. "What's your dad do? How many acres is this ranch? Do you drink and drive? Are you aware my daughter is an untouched vessel?"

Mom gave this totally fake laugh. "Isn't she the funniest?"

Tim looked back and forth between the two of us.

"They're getting away out there, Mom."

"Where are you going?"

"Wolf Creek," Tim said. "If that's all right?"

"And you'll be back?"

"Maybe," I said.

"No later than an hour after dark, Mrs. Diamond. You can't fish after dark."

Mom smiled. Tim did sound like he wouldn't know what to do with me if we ran out of light. "Be careful," she said. "Lucy's not much of a swimmer."

"I'm better than you," I said.

"Honey, a brick could outswim me."

"I can swim," Tim said. "I wouldn't let anything happen to her."

He sounded so Dudley Do-Right, Mom and I both smiled. She checked her watch. "Okay. I have to go."

We pulled out, Mom followed as far as the one-way.

"Phew," I said, spinning around to make sure she turned off, stopped following us. "That was close."

When we got back that night, the house dark, Tim and I got pretty heated up out in his truck. I broke it off, saying that she might be home, that she might be spying. But there was nothing like that. No note. No message. No anything. I stood there in the empty hall, my lips tingling, my stomach a little light from the kissing. I should have invited him in. It wasn't like there was anything else to do. Mom didn't roll in until eight the next morning. All showered, her hair still damp, ready to go for the day.

"You racking up so much overtime that Tato put in a shower for you?"

Mom smiled. "I'm not going to start with you."

"Barnacle Bill?" I asked.

She was practically beaming. She practically waltzed through the kitchen. The girls at school would say she wore that "freshly fucked" look. That she wore it well. I said, "You know what you look like? Like you got something to sell and you just made a sale."

She puckered a kiss at me, her makeup, her lipstick, perfect.

" 'I am not like this, Luce. I'm not.' 'He's married, for Christ's sake.' "

"I didn't know him then."

"But I bet you do now. And now he's not married?"

"Hardly."

"How on earth can you be hardly married?"

She looked at me like it was so obvious.

I got up and walked outside. She didn't bother following.

It was so in my face that I didn't talk to her for a week. We walked around each other. I'd wait in my room until she left for work, make myself scarce when she came home. Some days I wouldn't even see her.

Sometimes I'd find an item added to the grocery list on the refrigerator. "Skim milk." "Cottage cheese." "Bread." So I'd know we still cohabited. I thought about adding my own words beside them. "Whore." "Slut." "Bitch." But I didn't want to go Jaimie's route. Instead I went to the store every time I discovered a new item, and scratched the word out so dark it was impossible to tell that anything had ever been written there. Anything but mad, dark scribbles.

Not helping at all, Tim was at his job the whole week, not showing up again until the next Friday afternoon before dinner. He was filthy, bits of straw and grass sticking to his shirt, his skin. "I would have come sooner, but this is the first second I've had off," he said, grinning at me from the porch, huffing like he'd run here all the way from Belt. Just for me.

I pulled him into the house. "We have time to go fishing?" I asked. I mean, I had done not one thing all week.

He kissed me. It felt good, great, exciting, like my life was starting up again. "I don't think so. But we could do something. Take a drive. Get something to eat."

I kissed him back. Hard. "You smell like cow."

"I wanted to make sure I caught you. I'll go home and shower. Won't take an hour."

"Caught me? Where'd you think I'd escape to?"

Tim was, as promised, back in less than an hour, his skin still damp and warm from the shower, his hair dripping onto his shirt collar. I was in a similar boat, having raced up to the shower as soon as he left. I barely had time to scratch on this line of lipstick, a streak of color on my eyelids, which, as soon as I wiped a hole through the fog, I tried to scrub off with a towel. I got most of it, only this faint blue tinge left. The lipstick felt funny, like my lips were bigger than usual. I had to keep myself from licking them.

If Tim said one word, I'd smack him into next week. I felt clown enough without any comments. I still couldn't believe I'd even opened that stupid Christmas present.

Though it was after five, it was a Friday, and I didn't know if I'd see Mom. She didn't call to say she'd be late, and I didn't leave a note. I checked the message machine one last time, just in case, then dashed off to Tim's car.

We went to Ford's, got burgers, curly fries, and weird milk shakes.

I got kiwi, Tim mocha. They weren't as bad as they sounded. But once we drove up and down Tenth a couple of times, finished our food, we didn't know what to do next. We wound up going out to the new mall by the interstate, with all the superstores. The theater had ten screens. Even so, there was nothing there that sounded any good, and after looking at the posters, we stood out in the night, the stars stretching over us.

"What time do you have to be home?" he asked.

"A curfew? Me?"

"I only have till midnight," Tim said, sounding embarrassed.

"Not much time," I said.

"We could drive around."

I agreed, and we walked back to his car. He opened up my door, but before stepping in, I asked, "Mind if I drive?"

"My car?"

"Yours would probably be faster, since I don't have one."

He stood holding the door open for me. "I thought you didn't have a license."

"I don't."

"Well, I don't know, Lucy, it's kind of—"

"I know how to drive," I said.

He pointed to the empty Home Depot lot. "Around the lot," he said. "No more."

The car twisted when I romped on the gas, still in neutral, the engine trying to screw it off the pavement. "Holy shit!"

"This is not your mom's Corvair," he said, smiling.

"You're not just whistling Dixie, Trixie."

I crept over to the Home Depot lot, slalomed through the light poles.

"You're doing great, Lucy. You're a natural."

"It's in my blood," I answered. At the end of the row, I kept going, straight out the exit, into the street.

"Lucy, that's enough."

"Just one trip down Tenth."

"What if we get stopped?"

"What if we don't?"

Halfway down Tenth, I turned onto Fifteenth Street, the one-way heading to the bridge, the Fort Benton highway. It was different at night, with all the traffic, the headlights pointing at me, but I hadn't hit a red light yet, no place for Tim to jump out and pull me from behind the wheel. I could feel him over there, heat simmering off of him.

"Lucy, you said the parking lot."

"Then Tenth."

"Well, we're not on Tenth anymore. Come on. Pull over."

I made all the lights across Central and the one-ways. I couldn't believe it. Another minute more, and we were across the river, out of town. Tim was fuming. "Pull over, Lucy. Pull over *now!*"

"I want to see what it feels like to go fast. Just once."

"Pull over!"

I stepped on the gas, felt the push of acceleration.

"Lucy."

"Don't worry, I'm not going as fast as you did."

"Pull the damn car over!" He had his hand out like he was going to jerk the wheel away from me.

"Seven or eight?" I said.

"Seven or eight what?" he snapped.

"How many times this baby'll roll if you touch that wheel."

He sat back, lowered his hand. "I'm getting pissed, Lucy."

I let the car slow down. "Really?"

"You said the parking lot. You agreed."

"Relax," I said, "we're almost there."

"Where?"

I turned down the road to Ryan Dam, made the run past the wheat fields' stripes out to the bluffs, and dropped down, everything dark except the row of lights across the top of the dam.

I pulled in in front of the footbridge, its cyclone fence gleaming in the headlights. I turned the key, then pulled it out, handing it to Tim. He jerked it out of my hand.

"I want to show you something," I said. We were the only ones there.

He was already out of the car. He came over and opened my door, waiting for me to give up my seat behind the wheel.

I climbed out, not letting him get between me and the car. I pressed up against him, put my arm around him. "I didn't hurt your car," I said. "I just wanted to show you something out here."

He didn't put his arms around me. "I know what's out here. There's nothing you can show me."

"Oh, isn't there?" I said. Taking the chance of letting him get away, I started down the footpath to the gate. "Come on," I called, not sure the next thing I heard wouldn't be the roar of his engine, the squeal of tires, that in another second I wouldn't be starting a hell of a long walk home. I didn't turn to see if he was following.

Then from only a few feet behind me, Tim said, "They lock it at night."

I kept going right up to the gate.

He stopped behind me. "See?"

"When my mom and dad were our age, they used to climb this thing."

Tim studied it. "You're kidding."

I stepped back till we were touching, nuzzling my rear into him.

286 | PETE FROMM

I reached back and found his hands, drew his arms around me. "Want to try it?"

He didn't say anything.

"It'd be fun."

"Or we'd die trying."

"Beats dying not trying."

He finally squeezed me. "I'll go if you go."

I kicked off my sandals. "Thataboy!"

CHAPTER FORTY-EIGHT

Mom was right, the climb around the fence was terrifying. If you fell off the jungle gym, you might break something, or, like Scott Booker, not even that, only bounce. But here, if you were lucky enough to miss the rocks, you'd be twenty feet downstream before you came up for air. And the way I swam, coming up for air was hardly a sure thing. It was dark as a pocket, besides—even if Tim did decide to dive in, there was no saying he'd find me. Then those waves waiting for me at the end of the island. Surf city. After that? The turbines downstream at Morony Dam. Ground into walleye feed.

There was nothing in the climb that stood a lot of thinking. Just white-knuckling the loops of wire, sticking your toes through. Trying to keep moving, keep hanging on. When I finally got around, dropped down to the hard deck of the bridge, I could hardly keep from shouting. My skin buzzed, my hair stood on end. Even more than usual.

Tim dropped down a second later. I hugged him like a python, a boa constrictor. I kissed him like I was trying to crawl down his throat. When we pulled back for breath, I couldn't not give a whoop.

"That's not going to be any easier going back," Tim panted.

I shook my head. "Maybe we can hide till they unlock it tomorrow."

"I'm already late. My folks are not going to be pleased."

I took his hand. "Come here."

He followed, saying we really had to get going.

"I know, I know." I ran him up to the top, to the overlook of the falls. But the dam was shut down. Only the usual little trickle over the side. "Shit," I said, letting Tim's hand drop.

"What's the matter?"

"I was out here the other day. Place was roaring. More water than I'd ever seen. It was like it must have used to be."

"Maybe they were working on something. Had to lower the gates."

"Yeah," I said. "Maybe." I turned away and slumped down the path, the same steps Mom had used.

Tim walked beside me. "That's what you wanted to show me?"

"It was so cool."

"I wish I could have seen it. Who'd you come out here with?"

"Just some boy. I can't keep them all straight."

"What?"

"My mom." I took his hand again. "Do you wish you knew me before?"

"Before what?"

"Before now. Since we were little kids."

He put his arm around me. "I wish I always knew you. That I always will."

We walked the length of the island. I didn't bother him with my parents' wedding details. At the end, I plunked down under Mom and Dad's cottonwood. Sitting on the very ground. I pulled Tim down beside me. We sat staring at the waves, these glistening humps in the starlight.

A mosquito droned. Tim slapped. I couldn't help a smile. I turned and kissed him.

We got all worked up, sliding down till we weren't sitting anymore. I worked my way over him, then under. Our hips started grinding, like they were controlled by some other mind, even with our clothes on.

Rocking back and forth against me, Tim pulled his head back far enough to say, "My folks are probably calling the police."

I nodded, slipping a hand into the tiny, superheated space between our shorts. I felt him right through the denim. I hadn't done that before. He didn't think any more about his folks.

I sat up long enough for him to pull my shirt over my head. Bras held no mystery for him. As he got his first touch, I deshirted him, too. A while later, I was patting my hand around for my shorts, digging in the pockets for the condom I'd slid in after my makeup experiment. Just in case, like the pamphlets said. As little as I wanted to think about Kenny, I knew this was different. I had no idea where Tim's deal had been. I tore open the package and sat up, pointing him skyward to slide it on.

"Lucy," he said. "Lucy."

He sounded urgent enough I looked up, still holding him like that.

"I've never done this before, Lucy."

"One of these?"

"Yeah. That." He swallowed. "And everything."

I looked at him, the pale blob of his face in the dark. "You're kidding."

He shook his head. "Kind of everything but."

I couldn't believe it. "Me, neither," I said, but I laughed. The whole condom thing made it hard to believe that this was some accident. I rolled the thin rubber down. " 'Be prepared,' " I said, my voice all deep. "Bet you didn't know I used to be a Boy Scout." I stroked him, making sure it was on. "I thought you'd be able to show me everything."

He shook his head again.

"We'll be able to teach each other, then," I said. I lay back.

He eased down on his side next to me. He touched a boob like it might explode, though he hadn't been shy before. "Lucy, I—"

I kissed him, slid my hip up tight to his, tipped him over onto me. He started to say one more thing. I wormed my legs around his. Snaked a hand down to show him the way. I drew in a breath as he came in, held him there a minute. I pushed up the tiniest bit.

Tim said, "Lucy," again, but he wasn't asking for anything this time. He wasn't even really talking.

I smiled. We started going, our other minds running the show.

He was trying to hold me and kiss me and feel me and keep up our rhythm all at the same time. I almost had to laugh. He was like a way, way overwound toy. I raked his back with my fingers, holding him, pushing him on.

When it was over, I thought of Mom and Dad, fifteen years ago, lying right here just like this. About to step in front of the wrecking ball but not seeing me yet.

Lying on top of me, Tim started scratching his head furiously, saying he tingled all over like he never knew he could. "Man," he gasped, "I thought lightning was going to come shooting out of my toes!"

I laughed. "I bet you say that to all the girls."

He held me tight. "You are all the girls."

I said, "I'm glad I was your first." And I was. It was cool, knowing that no matter what came after for him, I'd always be there at the start.

"Me, too, Lucy. Man, I can hardly believe it."

"I still can't. That you never. I thought that's all you guys did."

" 'You guys'?"

"Well, those parties. 'To the face!' I just figured—"

"Not me," he said. He gave this kind of laugh. "I was going to wait," he said. "I was, we're, my family . . . Waiting's what you're supposed to do. Till you're married. We're kind of religious."

"Oh," I said. I mean, what could I say? I'd never been in a church or anything. "Are you mad?" I asked.

"Oh, Lucy. No way. I mean, I kind of wish, I mean. No. No way. I just, well, I don't know. I thought maybe I had more control. More than most people, maybe."

"I'm glad you don't," I whispered.

He kissed me. "Me, too, Lucy."

When he started to edge off me, I held the condom to his thing, like the pamphlets said, keeping it from sliding off. Then I peeled it down, twirling it out into the river because I couldn't imagine what the hell else I was supposed to do with it.

Talk about your awkward silences. Tim sat there, like one inch away. I put my arm around his naked back. My boob pushed against his arm. He had to feel that.

"Remember when I asked you about knowing me when I was little?" I said.

"Uh-huh."

"Well, this is as little as you could have gotten. This is where I started." Until then, I'd had no plans of telling him that.

"What?"

I told him what Mom had told me. "That's why they got married."

"And that's why you brought the—that thing? So that wouldn't happen to us?"

Hopefully it was going through the Morony turbines right about now. I nodded.

"You know, if it didn't work, I'd marry you, like your dad did for your mom." He put his arms around me, like that was the most beautiful thing you could say to another person. One second before, it had felt nice to sit there naked, not caring.

I said, "If you knew what you were saying, you wouldn't be saying that."

"What do you mean?"

"That what my parents have is not some fairy tale I've been pining for myself."

"Even without that," he said, "without any baby or anything, I'd do it, Lucy. If you wanted. If you would."

"You'd do what? *Marry* me? Oh, for Christ's sake. Not that again!"

Tim pulled out a handful of grass, threw it into the wind. "Again?"

Oops.

"Kenny?"

"Look, I mean, I really like you and all, but this"—I slapped my hand down on the ground—"this wasn't to trap you into playing house or anything."

"I didn't think it was."

"I mean, we're young, we still have our oats to cook, our birds and bees to sow."

Tim kept tearing up the grass, flitting it into the wind, the river.

"I mean, you're a great guy and all, but hey, variety is the spice. Spice is nice. Maybe even twice. No need for rice." I was an idiot, talking a million miles an hour.

"This wasn't your first time, was it?" Tim said.

I looked at what was left of the grass. I didn't answer.

"It's Kenny, isn't it?"

I brushed my hand over the spiky, torn ends of the blades, like Dad running his palm across the top of my head.

"He's crazy," Tim said. "For ever leaving you here."

"I wish you wouldn't talk about him."

"I don't think I'll make the same mistake."

I closed my eyes.

"Any fool can go to Missoula. Play football," he said.

"And what? Like you're going to stick around here for me? Skip a scholarship, stay in Great Falls. Get a career bagging groceries."

"I can work on the ranch. I think you could—"

"I don't care what you think. You know what? It'd last a few weeks. Waiting three years for me to get out of *high school,* for Christ's sake. You'd be itching to get gone before your second day."

"I think you could come out there with me," he continued.

I laughed. "Your grandparents will let us have a room? Welcome me in?" Like a sailor on watch, I cried, "Religion overboard!"

"We'd have to get married," he admitted.

"Are you out of your mind? Christ, I don't even have a driver's license. I sure as hell don't need a marriage license. Who do you think I am, Rabia Theodora? You going to take me to Alabama next?"

"Who? What are you talking about?"

"Are you afraid of Missoula or something? Afraid you'll be too slow?"

"That's not—"

"Man, you should be twice as afraid of me! Hell, I just made you give up your vows or whatever, your religion thing, the wait and all."

"I did that."

"By yourself?"

"No, but Lucy—"

"We had sex, Tim. That doesn't mean it has to change your life."

"I wouldn't have done it if I wasn't serious about it. About you."

I stood up. "I know, Tim, but man, for crying out loud, that doesn't—you don't have to—I mean, it's not like we have to get married or anything. I mean, we're not Mormons or something. Hutterites."

"You think you know—"

"I *do* know. It's a problem I've been studying my whole life."

Tim stood up, too, sliding into his shorts. He held my shirt up to me. My bra. I took them from his hand. He held my panties, spreading them open for me to step into, like you would dressing a kid. A little sister. I knew he had a big family.

I got my shorts on, but before I could get my shirt on, he hugged me. He brushed his fingers back and forth over my boobs. "Lucy," he whispered.

"Don't, Tim. Don't say one more thing. Don't even think about mentioning the 'L' word."

"I was going to say I think you got some mosquito bites."

That was so obviously untrue that I laughed, letting him get away with it. "I don't even want to think about that fence," I said.

Tim bent down, kissing my boobs.

"Down, boy," I said, pushing him away. Gently.

"But it might be my last time. If I fall off that bridge."

I strapped on my bra and pulled on my shirt as I started for the bridge. Tim was practically tripping over me. "If you fall, it won't be me you're thinking about," I said.

"It will," he said. He meant it.

At the bridge, the fence looming out of the darkness on the other side, I waved him ahead, said, "After you."

He looked puzzled, but he went. I waited until he was halfway across before I let him have it, throwing my weight from side to side, setting the bridge to swinging. He crouched down, clinging to the railings.

"Take it back!" I shouted.

"Take what back?" He was laughing. He turned around and crept back my way.

"All that love stuff!"

"I never said anything about love."

"You were *thinking* it!"

"How do you know what I was thinking?" He was getting close.

"Diamond Girl sees all!" I shouted.

He grabbed me. "Diamond Girl better get her eyes examined." He kissed me like a crazy man.

The fence, after everything else, was nothing.

CHAPTER FORTY-NINE

As soon as we were in the car, Tim behind the wheel, he said, "I have to call my folks."

I laughed. "And tell them what?"

"That I'm late. That I'm all right. That we're on our way."

" 'We're'? You're going to tell them you're with me?"

"I may change some of the facts," he said, not sounding proud about it. He was already punching numbers into his cell phone.

"You're going to wake them up? We can be home in fifteen minutes."

"It's better if they know." A few seconds later, he said, "Dad?"

I put my hand on his leg, ran it up high.

"Sorry, Dad. Sorry to wake you, sorry I'm late. We took a run out to Ryan, and the carb started up again. We got it straightened out, and we're on our way home."

He listened. My hand was way where it shouldn't have been. I wondered if his dad could hear the zipper.

"Yeah. Okay. You, too."

"*You, too*"? That could only be the "L" word. In a good way. I put my hand back in my own lap.

Tim clicked the phone off. "I could barely talk!" he said. He reached for me and started all over again, trying to memorize every inch of me with his hands, his lips. When I got a chance, I sat back against my door. "Now that you've called, they'll be worrying about that carb."

So we drove home. At my house, I only got out of the car by reminding him he'd started the stopwatch with his parents.

"Tomorrow?" he said. "It's my only day off."

I nodded, stepping away from the car.

Leaning over to watch me, he got this serious look. "Lucy, I—"

But before he could say it, I dashed up the walk, not chancing even a wave. I closed the door and waited until I heard his car rumble off up the street. Then, even though I knew I'd started something I didn't want to finish, I couldn't help but smile. "You are dangerous, girl," I said. Putting on a superhero voice, I said, "And, stepping out of her clothes, it's *Diamond Girl*! Is there no man safe? No mother's son?"

Before I started bragging myself up too loud, I ran through the house, checking for signs of Mom. But the place was as empty as a shell.

Despite all my superpowers, I was an uncle sieve. And Dad. Even kryptonite chains couldn't hold him.

The fun ran right out of me. Stepping into the kitchen, seeing the message light blinking all lonely in the dark, I hardly had the heart to push the button. As soon as I heard Kenny's voice, "Hey, Lucy, just wondering what you're doing. M and P," I wished I'd never touched it. M and P. That was this thing he made up. Code he could write on postcards, leave on message machines. How he loved me. *M*adly and *P*assionately.

Knowing I'd stop if I looked at the clock, I picked up the phone. Kenny's dad sounded asleep, though when I apologized, he promised he hadn't been. Kenny sounded even groggier.

We didn't talk about anything. I stretched the cord out enough to sit on the floor, listening to his voice. I couldn't even tell you what he was talking about. It was just this nice noise.

I licked my lips, still a trace of Tim to taste. I whispered, "I love you," like trying out a foreign language.

Kenny was in the middle of some story. He said half the next line before he stopped. "What?"

"You heard me," I said, chewing on my lip but smiling. My stomach danced.

"Oh, man, Lucy, I love you so much," he managed, all out of breath. "Up to the planets, down to the sea." It was what he always said, spreading his arms wide to show me.

"Miss me?"

"Every second."

I smiled. I didn't say it again. Hearing it from him was enough.

Though it had been tugged out of me for all the wrong reasons, I went to bed feeling better. No matter what happened, Tim couldn't touch that.

I stared at the ceiling a long time in the dark. It was hours before I fell asleep.

CHAPTER FIFTY

After our night at the dam, Tim was relentless about keeping to our fishing schedule. We still met every Friday night, at the crack of dawn every Saturday, went out to the rivers, but mostly, well the dam was broken. Fishing wasn't all Tim couldn't get enough of. I got sunburned in places that shouldn't ever see the sun. And Tim? After our first riverside romp, his rear looked like two glowing stoplights.

But eventually, my boobs tanned. Tim's ass. His parents, he said, called him Stranger. He only saw them Saturday nights, when his whole family went to church, so he could be working Sunday morning, letting his grandparents get their crack at church. He said they were all impatient to meet me. I held him off, saying I wanted to let my hair grow out, that I didn't want them thinking I was some kind of freak.

Mom and I were kind of on the stranger path ourselves. No matter how she and Barnacle had started, Mom's promise that she was "not this way," Barnacle was getting to be way more than your average uncle. Every other weekend, two nights in a row, no Mom. The weekends in between were more sporadic. Twice I'd heard him leaving early. Without the stomach to look, I stayed hidden in my room till the coast was clear. Sometimes, coming home from fishing, I'd creep through the house to see if she was home or not, the way I used to when Dad played his game. I'd save her room for last, the tension and suspense building.

In the middle of all this, we had a double-postcard day. Mom got to them first, another Saturday, Tim and me out fishing. So I didn't find them until I'd started my search of the empty house. They were already sitting on the kitchen table, picture side down, Mom not even making me guess if she'd read them. Not that Dad's would have challenged any reader. There was nothing on it besides our address, like he forgot what he was going to write, or knew us so little anymore that he couldn't think of one thing to say.

Kenny's on the other hand, had actual information. Actual questions that needed answering. It was, like, correspondence.

"Lucy. M&P. I've got my driver's license (can you believe)!
M&P. Dad will give me the truck for one week this summer.
M&P. Monday through Friday. M&P. Since you have friends,
you pick. M&P. I am dying to see you!!! M&P.

P.S. M&P!"

I reread, "Since you have friends," wondering how much that had cost him. I was starving, and exhausted, and sore—Tim and I'd hardly thought about fishing—so I sat down hard, wondering how I'd work this. Then I couldn't help smiling, picturing Kenny, perched on phone books behind the wheel, creeping over the pass.

I was juggling men. "Proud of yourself now, Mom?" I muttered, knowing it was me doing this, not Mom, which did not help.

I pushed away from the table to halfheartedly finish my inspection. It wasn't much fun when I knew she wasn't home. But tiptoeing down the hallway, I saw her door cracked, a light on behind it. The house was quiet as death, but I leaned forward to peek through the gap and saw her at the vanity, working on her makeup. Without looking away from the mirror, she said, "Who's there?" Like she wouldn't know.

I pushed open the door. "It's me. Lucy."

She paused, makeup brush hovering above her eye. "Lucy who?"

I stepped into her room.

She swept the brush across the top of her eyelid. "Oh, *that* Lucy. What have you been doing with yourself? Still fishing like there's no tomorrow?"

I shrugged. "Pretty much."

"Just going fishing?" she said, same way you'd say "Going to the falls." "Sounds a little fishy to me."

Finished with her makeup, she worked her way around me to her closet. Billowing out her robe, Mom stepped into a pair of Khaki slacks, pleated, nice. Hangers rattling, she backed out of her closet, shucking her robe and slipping into this sheer flowery summery blouse. Not her usual slinky date material. Pretty subdued. Like she and Barnacle had already tied the noose. She buttoned it up fast, stopping with the button between her boobs. Subdued as it was, she looked like a million bucks.

"You look nice," I said.

She seemed surprised. "Why, thank you," she said cautiously.

Out of nowhere, maybe because we'd just said our first nice things to each other in ages, I asked, "Remember that night at the dam, Mom?"

"It was only a month ago, Luce. Back when we were still friends."

I sighed. "We're still friends, Mom. Don't get so dramatic."

She gave me an eye.

"The night with Dad, I mean. Well, I was wondering—was—did—was there, before Dad—were there, you know, did you, with other guys?"

"This is your business?" she asked, but you could tell it wasn't something she minded thinking about. She studied me in that spooky way, like she was rewinding through the last hours of my life, watching me and Tim going at it. "Why?"

I fished my hand through the perfumes on her dresser. The fancy ones. I shrugged.

She faded away a moment, a smile flashing. "You want my answer," she said, "or his?"

Even though it had happened fifteen years ago, I didn't like hearing that. That she'd been doing this to Dad all along. "I guess I got both."

Mom watched me long seconds before asking, "And how much have you told Kenny about Tim?"

I knocked over a perfume bottle, took some time setting it back up straight.

Mom said, "I'll use that one. Please."

I put the tiny bottle on her palm. "There's nothing to tell."

Mom uncapped it and brushed the top once on each side of her cleavage. The air barely smelled of it. She twisted the cap back in, this gritty glass-on-glass squeak, and held the bottle back out for me.

My hand shook as I took it. "Are you coming home tonight?"

"Don't wait up."

"The kids run away?"

"Actually, they're at their mother's this weekend."

"Lucky you," I said. "I guess you forgot to mention that they're separated."

"A new wrinkle," she said, like it was just this funny thing. She hesitated in the doorway, then said, "See you tomorrow," and was gone.

I stood there a while, lining up her perfumes, before drifting downstairs, forcing myself to look at Kenny's postcard again. "Since you have friends."

I dug around the kitchen like I might stumble across a ready-to-use postcard waiting for me. I wound up with a blank recipe card. After *Here's What's Cooking*, I wrote, "Summer Love."

From the kitchen of: Your wildest dreams.

Ingredients: One truck. One week. One Colonel. One Diamond Girl.

To Prepare: Mix all ingredients. Press together firmly. Add heat. Use care, as ingredients may explode.

I paused. Tim would be gone by the last week of August. Football camp or something. Could I make Kenny wait that long? Without being too obvious?

Maybe last week of July, first of August. Maybe by then I'd have gotten it over with with Tim or could think of some reason not to see him for a week. Maybe I could sneak Kenny in and out on the days Tim was working, never have to mention either to the other.

I muttered, "Bitch," then scribbled, "Last week of July, first of August. Whatever you desire."

I stamped it, addressed it, and stormed out to mail my recipe.

CHAPTER FIFTY-ONE

Kenny and I exchanged a pile of postcards over the next few weeks. His first said, "CAN'T WAIT TO GET COOKING!!!!" The whole rest of the card was filled with exclamation points and "M&P"s. We settled on the last week of July, which dribbled over into August. Each of Kenny's postcards after contained just numbers. The days left until he got here.

The whole time, Tim and I kept after each other like it was our job or something. And though we were doing it every weekend, I couldn't think of any way to let him know Kenny was coming. And I didn't quite have the nerve to wing it, dare Tim to find out if he could.

So, with only one week left, I flat out told him. We were driving home from a day on the Sun River. The fishing had slowed as soon as the morning got hot, which meant that nothing else had. It was deserted out there, and we'd done stuff we hadn't even thought of before. Lying down, standing up, frontward, backward. We were both worn out, frazzled and happy and drained. I figured it was as good a time as any to tell him, and probably better than most.

A few blocks from my house, I picked up his hand, bounced it up and down on my thigh. "Next Monday, Kenny's coming over from Kalispell. His dad's giving him the truck. He's staying till Friday." I talked like I was in a race.

Tim looked straight ahead. He drove the last blocks, then pulled over. He cleared his throat. "Is he staying here?"

"Well, yeah. At his mom's house."

He let out this big, relieved breath.

"What? You thought he'd stay at my house?"

He shrugged.

"I just wanted to let you know," I said, giving him a kiss. "It's no big deal. I didn't want somebody else telling you or something."

He nodded, turning to his window, away from me. "You and him, you used to do things like what we did today?" It sounded like he was being dragged across shattered glass.

I hugged him. "Tim, I don't think *anybody's* done some of the things we did today."

He smiled a little. "Will you promise me something, Luce?"

I waited.

"Will you promise me you won't do anything with him?That you won't ever do anything like that with anyone else but me ever again?"

" 'Ever again'? Doesn't that sound kind of long-range?"

His jaw muscles popped out. I didn't know if he was going to cry or finish me with a quick, merciful head butt.

"A joke," I whispered. When he didn't answer, I went on, "Of course I won't do anything with Kenny. I told you, we're friends. I haven't even seen him in, what, half a year?" I felt about this big. Snakes could slither over me with room to spare.

"Promise?"

He sounded like he was about two. Whatever. "Yes," I said. "I promise."

He hugged me and said, "I love you, Lucy. So much."

That was forbidden territory, and he knew it. But I let it slide this time. Not quite one month and he'd be off to Missoula. I doubted I'd see him more than once or twice after that. Thanksgiving break. Maybe he'd last till Christmas. But with a college full of women, and him knowing what to do with them now, I didn't have big odds on Christmas.

To tell the truth, I was looking forward to the break. God, I was sick of fishing.

Waving good-bye, I walked up to the porch, wondering about the rest of his life, going home, cleaning up, a night with the folks in some church, his whole family, all his little brothers and sisters, and then up at the crack, over the hill to Grandma's house. Outside of what we did together, he was pretty much a complete mystery. Once he was gone, it'd almost be like he never happened at all.

"Home again, home again," I called, not even thinking about whether Mom would be there or not.

She stepped from the kitchen, dressed to leave. "Riggedy jig."

"Oh. You are home. Must be the kids' week with Dad?"

"I'm going out," she said, glancing at her watch, "in about ten minutes."

I nodded, started upstairs.

"Fishing good?"

"Okay."

"I had a call today."

I stopped. She'd said it in her cat-with-a-mouse voice. Dad?

Kenny? "From who?" I asked, hating myself for playing in to her.

"A Mrs. Mary Shaughnessy."

A few seconds passed before it clicked. "Tim's mom?"

"They'd like to meet us. You. Me. She said she's asked Tim to arrange something all summer, but"—she fluttered her hands around her head—"'you know how boys are.'"

"I'll work something out." I started back up the stairs. "Will you be bringing a date?"

Mom raised her voice enough to be heard. "She says Tim has dropped his plans to go to Missoula. May already have lost his football scholarship."

I clutched at the railing. "What?"

"She says he wants to stay here now, close to 'your daughter.' She's hoping we can get together and 'make it all make sense to the two of them.' Maybe 'put it in some perspective for the young people.' The woman talks like a mannequin."

I absolutely gaped.

"You were going to tell me about these plans when?"

"I don't know a thing about it, Mom. He never said one word to me."

"Well, you better say a word or two to him. That's unusual dedication for a fishing partner, wouldn't you say?"

I couldn't come up with an answer before she swung open the door, the weather strip scraping. "See you later, Lucy. Sleep tight."

I ran straight to her room and called Tim. But his mom answered. I hung up. Hard.

CHAPTER FIFTY-TWO

By Friday, instead of calming down, I'd gotten more steamed. It was after noon, but I was still sitting in the kitchen in my Supergirl T-shirt, planning Tim's demise. In a while I'd go up, shower, get ready for him, maybe even a little makeup, just to be perfectly ready to slap his face around to the back of his head. Giving up his scholarship, college, to boink me once a week. Twice.

I heard the front door push timidly open. "Lucy?"

It was Tim, hours early. I jumped up and charged into the hallway.

He had his head poked hopefully through the door. He still wore his ranch clothes, filthy jeans, his hair scrambled with sweat, a dirt line across his forehead from his cowboy hat. When he saw me, his smile grew twice as wide, his eyes dodging down and then back up. He stepped inside.

"Don't you think you should have asked me first?"

He blinked. "You said you were always home. I knew your mom would be working. I didn't think you'd mind."

"Not that, for Christ's sake! Everything you told your mom."

He looked around the hallway like he was reconsidering the whole surprise visit.

"What the hell were you thinking? Or *do* you think? Do you know she called here? Talked to my mom? Wants us all to get together?"

He nodded but said, "I got off early," falling back on the script he'd prepared since leaving the ranch.

"Tim, I never said—Those plans you told your mom, those are not *my* ideas, *my* plans."

He walked up close, reached to touch me. "I know."

"Did you ever think about asking me? At least running it by me before you told the world? Your mom?"

"I tried, but you only made jokes, or got mad."

"Same thing in this house." I turned away from his hand, stalked into the living room. "You have to tell her different. Before we have our little meeting. I am not going to sit around and be blamed for that. I am not going to be a 'young people' having the facts of life spelled out for me. Believe me, I know the fucking facts."

"Lucy. She invited you over for dinner. You and your mom. What's so bad about that?"

"My mom and your mom? You know where my mom is right now?"

He shook his head.

I rolled my eyes. "Forget it. But my mom never said anything about dinner. She never got past the part about you not going to Missoula."

"I told my mom I was thinking about it."

"Because of me."

He shrugged. "Yes."

"Tell her you stopped thinking about it."

"I haven't."

"Well, start."

We faced each other.

"I thought we could have almost a full day today," he said. "I started work this morning at three."

God, talking to him was like trying to derail a train. But he was standing there looking like he'd started at three. All haggard and beat, desperate only for me.

"Are you going to tell her?" I asked.

He saw the opening. He stepped close again. I let him touch my shoulder. "Are you? That I'm not going to let you do it?"

"She'll love you for it."

"Great. All I ever wanted out of life. Your mother's love."

"Give her a chance. You'll like her." He put his other hand on my other shoulder, holding me at arm's length, like he was about to start some football drill. "Lucy, I am not exactly college material. And if I left here, I couldn't stand not being able to see you."

"If you stay, you will *not* see me. Understand that now. I am not putting your life on my conscience, too."

He smiled. "I thought you weren't religious."

"You think only churchgoers have consciences? God, get over yourself."

He squeezed my shoulders. "Maybe you could come to Missoula with me."

I reached out and tapped his forehead with my knuckles. "I'm fifteen. A soph-o-more!"

"Doesn't matter to me."

"It does to me. I don't even think it's legal."

He laughed. "Like you'd care."

I had to smile at that. "You go to Missoula, college boy. We'll see what happens then. Okay? We'll see what happens. If you're so set on things, nothing will change there, right? And what? I'm going to meet somebody here? In Great Falls?"

"You met me here," he said.

I tapped my nose with the tip of my finger.

But he was finally able to understand a little teasing. He smiled, pretend-shook me, his hands closing around my neck. I let him go until he was smiling for real, thinking he had more than a chance. Then he said, "Kenny's coming on Monday."

"I told you, it's no big deal." I wished he was here right now, that we were both doing supersonic death spirals at the very top of the jungle gym, where no one else on earth could reach us. "Don't tell me you're worried about that again?"

He shook his head. "That's why I worked to get off early. So we could have a couple full days together. Before."

I nodded, swept my hands down my shirt. "I've been getting dressed for it all day," I said. "Can't you see?"

His hands slid down from my shoulders, and he moved closer.

What the hell? I stepped back, swept the Supergirl shirt over my head, pitching it toward the couch like they used to throw wineglasses into fireplaces. I held my hands up over my head, throwing a hip to the side. "How'd I do?"

I could see Tim swallow. Literally. His Adam's apple bobbing up and down. I couldn't stop a giggle. I could see his brain flashing all the same pictures Kenny's had.

Boys.

We got after it right there on the couch. I let loose, seeing how crazy I could make him. I already knew this was beyond his wildest dreams, and I thought I'd send him out with a bang. I started making some of the sounds I used to hear Mom make. It was kind of embarrassing, but Tim's eyes about popped out of his head. He thundered on.

I don't know what made me hear the truck pull up. Some old vibration, the sort of thing they say you can remember from the womb. The sound of your parents' voices.

I sat up on top of Tim to see over the back of the couch, out the front window.

He kept going under me, getting close. His hands came up for my boobs. "What?" he said. "Is it Kenny?"

The hope in his voice was so obvious, so infuriating, I wanted to slap him, knowing how much he wanted Kenny to find us exactly like this, get that bone-in-his-throat feeling Tim must have had our night at the dam, knowing Kenny had been there before him.

The sun glared on the window. I squinted to see.

It was Dad, pushing his truck door open with his big, booted foot.

CHAPTER FIFTY-THREE

The air rushed out of me like I'd been punched. "Oh, fuck," I gasped, scrambling for my shirt. "It's my dad! Get out of here, Tim! Out the back! As fast as you can!"

I heard the slam of the truck door. Tim had a leg through his underwear.

"There's no time! Dress in the alley! Run!"

I gave a frantic last look around for any clothes, glimpsed Tim in the kitchen, hopping, a foot stuck in his jeans, his boxers hitched halfway over his tanned butt.

Out front, Dad sang, "Who's that knocking at my door?"

I dashed into the kitchen, pushing Tim toward the door, my shirt and panties under my arm.

The front door screeched. " 'It's only me, from over the sea,' says Barnacle Bill, the sailor."

I shoved Tim into the corner next to the phone, flattening myself against him so Dad couldn't see us from the front hall. Tim wriggled his jeans up. I grabbed his hand, keeping him from the zipper, from making a sound. I held my breath, my heart going a million miles an hour.

I heard Dad's first step in, then another. Then he stopped. "What the . . . Smells like Cupid's gymnasium in here!"

There wasn't even a second of calm before his thoughts straightened around and his outraged bellow of "Mame!" tore the house.

I flinched against Tim, fighting a stinging urge to pee. My eyes watered.

"Mame!" he roared, searing the air from the house, my lungs. Not Lucy. Mame.

I leaned over, my hands trembling as I tried to hold my panties open for my foot. Leaning that way, I buried my face against Tim's chest, like a little kid pulling the blanket over her head. Hiding. Safe. He put his arms around me.

Dad screamed, "Mame!" a last time, and my one hope that he'd charge up the stairs failed. I heard him heading straight for the kitchen like a hound on a scent.

I stepped my other foot into my panties and turned to face him.

He came to a stop, his mouth working, his face falling as if the muscles had been cut.

"It's me, Dad," I squeaked, pulling my panties up, hiding my chest behind my wadded-up shirt, hiding as much of Tim behind me as I could.

Dad stood there. "Luce?" he managed to whisper.

"Dad, I'm—"

"Lucy?" he said again, like he'd taken his own stump upside the head. "Where's your mother?"

"I don't know, Dad. At work. Listen—"

"Mr. Diamond," Tim started, all soft and reasonable. I pushed against him with my elbow, but it was already way too late. It was like Tim's words alone set Dad off. He moved so fast I couldn't swear exactly how I got to the floor. I dropped my shirt. Sat there in my underwear, the linoleum cold against my legs.

I saw Tim straighten after ducking Dad's punch, heard the knuckle-against-wall crunch of Dad's fist, Tim yelling, "Mr. Diamond!" Or maybe "Sir!" I couldn't positively say which.

Either Dad had pushed me out of his way, or Tim, moving quicker than he ever believed he could, had shoved me down to a final few seconds of safety.

Though his fist must have been broken, Dad shot it at Tim's face again. Tim dodged to the side, Dad's other fist glancing off his chest. One of them roared. Maybe both.

Tim came up with both his hands, a blur, landing them against Dad's chest or stomach. Only a push. Not a punch, really.

Dad's feet came off the ground. Dad's. I couldn't believe it.

He landed on his rear, all the way back in the doorway. He sat there trying to get air back into his lungs, gasping and gaping, his eyes wired onto Tim.

Tim shouted, "Mr. Diamond! Mr. Diamond! I don't want to hurt you!"

I scrambled up, started shoving against Tim, but he might as well have been a wall. "Go, Tim! Leave!"

He glanced at me, saying, "Lucy."

"It'll be all right, Tim. I'll be all right. Just go."

"We love each other!" he shouted at Dad.

"We do *not!*" I blurted. "God, Tim, get out of here." I'd never quit pushing on him, and at last I could feel him falter, begin to let me move him.

He said, "Lucy?" once more, but I got him out the door, slammed it between us. I locked it, like the danger was out there.

Dad was still sitting there on the floor, glaring at me, his breath coming back in long, sucking gasps.

"Daddy?" I said, my voice shaking. I picked up my shirt, pinning it against my chest. I bent down to him. "Daddy, are you okay?"

He slapped me. I never saw it coming.

I didn't know where he went when he'd disappear, what he really did, but he didn't feel like a sawyer then, somebody who used anything as easy as a chain saw. He felt like a lumberjack, somebody who chopped through forests with single blows of an ax. Splintered trees with his bare hands. My teeth clanked. My eyes starred. I tasted the metal of blood. Of fear.

I stepped back. A couple of steps. To keep from falling over. I dropped my shirt. Stood there naked before him. I guessed he had to hit somebody right then. Anybody.

He started to heave himself up, started to apologize, "Lucy, I'm sorry, I don't . . ."

There was a hole in the wall next to the phone. Dad's punch gone wild. He had blood on his knuckles. He was still blocking the doorway, but as he gathered himself, I dodged past.

"Lucy," he called, but I made the steps, grabbed the rail. Feeling my way, I reached my door, getting in and closing it, my fingers bumping over the casing, twisting the lock between us. Resting my forehead against the wood, I listened to him climb the stairs behind me.

"Lucy, I'm sorry. Lucy?"

"You stayed away too long, Daddy."

He was quiet. I couldn't even hear him breathe.

"I don't know where you go, but I hope it's worth it. Because you wasted everything here."

"I'm here now," he said.

I sobbed a kind of laugh. Like this was an improvement. Like this would help. Tears, the ones shocked out by his blow, started to flow on their own.

"Luce—" he started.

"God!" I shouted. "It's Lucy! Haven't you ever once thought how 'Luce' makes me sound?"

He was startled. I could almost see the surprise on his face. Right through the door.

"I mean, just think."

"Sorry, Lucy."

"Tip of the ice cube," I said. "You got my whole life to apologize for."

"Now, hang on there."

I laughed. "God! Fuck! And here I was thinking *I'd* ruined your lives. When it was you all along."

"Lucy, stop it."

"*Me? Me* stop?"

"You're trying to spin this on to me the same way Mame does. It wasn't me who got caught here. Let's remember that."

"You have no idea how pathetic you are, do you?"

"You're in a world of trouble, Lucy. Don't make it any worse."

"You can't tell me what to do! Who do you think you are? My dad?" What I meant was that he couldn't start acting like a dad now, not after his history, but in the sudden silence, I realized it didn't sound like that. What I said next blew out of me with the sting of his slap. "God, I can't believe she actually made you think that. All along. For fifteen years. What a buffoon!"

"Luce?"

I snorted out this terrible laugh. "She *told* me, Dad! All about your trip to the dam. How she screwed you there at the end of the island so you'd think I was yours."

"You're mine, all right," he said, but his voice shook, his foundation rocked.

"I'm as much yours as she is!" I shouted. "Less!"

"I don't have to take this, Luce. Not from you."

"My ass! You have to take it for the rest of your life! Run away from *that!*"

He slammed his fist against the door. I jumped. Paint chips dusted down to the carpet. "Maybe," he said real low, "you should tell me what's going on here, Luce."

"We're going on, Dad. Mom and me. You missed our whole lives."

"She knows about this? About—" He couldn't bring himself to say it. "Maybe I'll wait to hear her side of it."

I slid down, sat on the floor, beginning to feel how cold I was. "You'll have to wait a long time."

"Why?"

"She's not coming home tonight."

"I can't hear you."

"Can't or won't?"

He was quiet a while. "What do you think, Lucy? That I'm a complete idiot? Maybe I'm not exactly a rocket surgeon, but you think she's running around on your old man? Making a fool out of me? The cluckold? You think I'm just out there dumb and happy, sending back the bacon?"

I was sorry I'd said anything at all, and I wished he'd just shut up. "That's not what I think. I don't think any of those things."

"Good. Because you know what? You know what? I got a whole other family! Another wife! That's where I go! And when I'm here, she's not out whoring."

"No you don't," I said. "You don't have anything. You're not anything without us. Not one single thing."

"And she stays home," he shouted, drowning me out. "Home with the kids, like mothers are supposed to."

I put my hands over my ears. "And dads?" I said. "What are they supposed to do?"

He wouldn't say.

"Where are these people?" I asked.

"Lethbridge," he said, shaky-sounding.

Lethbridge. Not even that far away. Maybe two hours. Three. Not over the mountains to hell and gone, where the ground was made out of iron. Lethbridge. Dad had taken me to a baseball game once, the Great Falls Dodgers versus the Lethbridge Mounties. He'd stood for the Canadian national anthem. But so did most everybody.

"Are they nice?" I asked.

"Nice? Who?"

"Do they know about us?"

Silence.

I lowered my face into my hands. "I feel so sorry for them."

I felt Dad move. "Lucy?" he said. "I'm sorry."

"You're sorry, all right."

"Lucy."

"Do you know how much we loved you? Do you even know what that means?"

"I know," he said.

"Uh-huh. I used to think you did, too."

"Lucy."

"Just leave, Dad. Go. Don't ever come back. Don't send any more of your stupid bacon. Quit pretending we need you. That you're this force in our lives. Just quit."

He was silent so long, I was afraid he was gone.

"I can't even remember what you look like!" I shouted. "What you sound like! Not even all your fucked-up sayings! Isn't that the gravy on the goddamned cake?"

"Luce."

"Just go!" I shouted. "Go back to Lethbridge. Say hello to the kids for me! The wife!"

"I'm going," he said.

"I'm not even going to tell Mom you were here. You're already so faded out, I'm going to let you vanish. Even your shadow. Poof!"

I heard him going down the stairs.

"Why the hell did you even come back? You're a fucking stranger! A missing person! A ghost!"

I heard his truck start up.

Freezing cold, arms clutched around my naked legs, I lowered my head to my knees and shivered, listening to him drive away.

She stays home with the kids. My brothers and sisters. If he was telling the truth, a big if, I wasn't alone in the world after all. So why was it I could scarcely draw a breath?

CHAPTER FIFTY-FOUR

All I wanted to do, really, was leave. Forever. As easy as Dad. Walk away and never again see this house where we'd wasted so much of our lives waiting for him. Mom and me both. Where, for so long, I'd been such a dumb, happy boy.

Leaving was in my genes, Mom said.

But, instead of getting dressed, doing anything that made sense, I crawled into bed. The whole side of my face ached where he'd hit me, though I thought the pain was not so much from that. It was more like all the crazy things we'd yelled at each other had broken off pieces, leaving behind throbbing hollows the way teeth do. I wondered if what Dad yelled was any truer than what I had; if he really did have another family out there, one who thought he logged down here, who looked for clues in the newspapers he came home with; if his time as an orphan had made him think he had some right to go out and make as many more of his own as he could.

I wondered if all the time he wasn't here with us, he was with them. Staying with them so much more. Years and years more. I wondered if they knew what it was like to get used to him, to kiss him before going to bed at night, to expect to see him still there when they got up in the morning. I wondered if he and that wife gave each other pecks on the cheeks, like parents are supposed to, if he saved the tear-down-the-shower-curtains, no-chains-can-hold-us stuff for Mom. I wondered if he'd stay with them forever now.

For a while, imagining that totally normal family, I bawled like a baby, the whole works, huge racking sobs, like I was suffocating, like I was stuck miles underwater. When I got it together some, I couldn't help asking myself why I'd tried so hard to hurt him. Why I'd lied so hard. Was that something they'd stuck in my genes, too?

Mom showed up right after work, something I hadn't expected. She thumped the front door shut and came trotting straight upstairs. She paused outside my door, saying, "Luce?"

I pretended I was asleep, dead, but she didn't even check. She laughed and went off to her room, calling, "Fish on!" She had no reason to guess I was home.

She showered and changed, and I listened to all the sounds I knew so well, the pull and push of drawers, the drone of the hair dryer; even, once, the clink of perfume bottles, a sharp glassy sound that carried through the house as if there were no walls. Someone alone but with someplace to go.

Then she was gone, too. As gone as Dad.

A while later the phone rang. And rang. I could hear a voice on the machine, a man, somebody deep, but couldn't make out any words. It was like listening to a jetter driving by on the strip, rap blasting, the bass thumping inside your chest, nothing recognizable.

Once the voice was safely gone, I crawled out long enough to use the bathroom. Turning away from the happy angelfish on the shower curtain, I caught a glimpse of myself in the mirror. I grabbed the edge of the countertop, to keep from falling over. My face, where Dad had slapped me, was yellow, purple, the colors swirled, the skin swollen tight and shiny, a spoiled mascara-looking tinge of black settling in below my eye. There was no blood—that had been inside, my tongue constantly fiddling with the teeth-frayed skin.

I sat back hard, lucky to find the toilet. The tears came again. I wouldn't be able to show myself for days. How long? I thought of calling Kenny's mom, guessing she might know the answer. Maybe even Rabia Theodora. Maybe I should call Lethbridge, ask for a Mrs. Diamond there. I didn't really know the kind of people these things happened to.

I looked at my face again, sickly fascinated. It was past makeup. I was sure of that. But I tried anyway. By the time I was done, I looked like a clown who'd been hit by a train. Hard to beat that for funny.

An hour or two later, the phone rang again. The same voice. Dad calling to apologize? I twisted my face into the pillow. A stupider joke had never occurred to me. Then I remembered Kenny and almost jumped out of bed to get the phone, but then sat back. Kenny. God, I'd forgotten all about him.

Mom got back home around ten the next morning. Whoever was calling had kept at it, and I knew I should have erased the messages, but it was too late. Then I heard a man's voice right along with Mom's, a set of heavy steps clodding around downstairs. I listened hard, but I already knew it wasn't Dad. *"It's only me, from over the sea,"* says Barnacle Bill the sailor.

I knew I'd never come out of my room again.

Listening to Mom and Bill downstairs, I saw the smudges of makeup on my pillowcase. I'd be a *drunk* clown now, weaving alongside the train tracks. Beautiful.

I sat petrified, afraid they'd come upstairs, start up one of Mom and Dad's sessions. I didn't know what I'd do, but I would not listen to that. I'd lift Barnacle's keys and take off in his brand-new Suburban. Somewhere. One-way.

For all I knew, this was their standard Saturday. I'd been out so much with Tim, I no longer had any idea what went on around here, what might pass for normal. Maybe Mom was whipping up a picnic lunch and they were on their way out to work on their all-body tans, cast boats into the rapids.

Then I heard yet another man's voice down there. Good God, I thought, not two at once. Or Dad? I sat up straight, waiting for the sound of bodies colliding.

Then I knew what was going on. They were listening to the messages. The machine was still going—the once-reassuring deep rumble of a man's voice that, for my whole life till now, could only have been Dad's—when Mom came charging up the stairs two at a time.

"Lucy?" she was calling. "Lucy?" She sounded scared, which was not something I expected. Ever.

"I'm here, Mom."

"Are you okay? What's going on? What happened?"

"Nothing. What are you talking about?"

She tried the knob, and the door swung open. I couldn't believe I hadn't locked it. But she wasn't supposed to be here.

I turned away from the door, hiding Dad's side of my face. "Hello?" I said. "Is this Russia or something? Where you can just barge in?"

"Tim's called about twenty times. Starting yesterday. Asking if you're all right. Saying he's sorry."

I shrugged. "We didn't do anything this weekend."

"Kenny?"

"I don't know. I just . . ."

Mom came in, walking toward me. I kept turning away. "Do you mind? Does the word 'privacy' mean nothing anymore?"

"Stop," Mom said. "What are you, a top?" She grabbed my shoulder. "Tell me what happened." She craned around, trying to catch my eye. I would have had to be an owl to keep turning my face away. I knew, even before her gasp, that the makeup had been a complete, total waste of time.

"That bastard!" she hissed.

"Mom—"

She took my chin in her fingers, twisted my face to her. "That big, stupid fucking bastard. Did that make him feel like a man?"

Then she was hugging me. She was crying. The two of us, we'd become these sieves.

"What happened, Lucy? What happened?"

"Nothing," I said. "I fell down the stairs. I walked into a door." This was as much her fault as it was his. The two of them, their giant, fucked-up marriage.

"Oh, I know what happened," she said, still holding me in her arms. "Don't think I lived with your dad all those years without learning a thing or two about jealousy."

"He hit you, too?"

"If he thinks he can get away with this." She spun on her heel and was out the door. I followed, but she was already in her room. The phone clanked and jangled as she knocked it off the nightstand. By the time I got there, she was picking it up, beating it back down on the table as if it had tried to get away. She had the headpiece pinned against her shoulder as she yanked at the phone book, tearing pages as she slashed through them.

"Mom? What are you doing? Who are you calling?" You could look him up in the phone book?

Her finger was stabbing down the page. "S."

Shaughnessy.

She thought it was Tim.

I was so slow on the draw, that hadn't even occurred to me.

"No, Mom. Don't. That's not . . ."

She was stabbing at the numbers.

"Mom! You don't—"

"Mary?" Mom said. "This is Lainee Diamond. Lucy's mom."

"Mom!" I whispered. She sounded perfectly calm, though. Perfectly normal.

She was listening. I don't know if she waited for Tim's mom to finish, or if she cut her off. Her words, when she spat them out, were sharp enough to remove flesh. "Do the words 'statutory rape' mean anything to you?"

"Mom!" I shouted. "Stop! Hang up!"

"How about 'assault'?" Mom said, raising her voice over mine.

"You don't know what you're saying, Mom!"

"On your way to church? Well, doesn't that just figure. Don't you hang up on me!" Mom yelled. A second later, she said, "Is that you, you fucking prick? Oh, the father. Are you the one who taught your son to beat on women? You do that to your wife? Keep her in line? Is that why she sounds like a goddamn puppet?"

I could hear Tim's dad sounding far away but stirred up, like bees you're running from. "And what do you know about statutory rape?" Mom asked. "Is that another thing you've got personal experience with?"

From the other end, I caught "no idea what you're talking about."

"My daughter looks like she lost a prizefight!" Mom shrieked, tears springing out again. "That's what the hell I'm talking about. She spends a day with your son, and she looks like she barely escaped with her life, that's what I'm talking about. She's fifteen years old. That's what I'm talking about. And your son is a man, and when she said no, he taught her a lesson, showed her how big and strong he is—"

"Mom! There was nothing like that! Nothing ever! We're friends! We went fishing!" I was pulling on her shoulder, trying to get the phone away from her. "Quit it, Mom! Quit!" I yanked her down onto the bed. At the phone, I yelled, "Don't listen, Mr. Shaughnessy! Tim didn't do anything! I'm all right!" I got both my hands around the phone.

Mom screamed, "You keep him away from her! If my husband was here, you'd be on your way to ID the body! I'll kill him myself!"

I got the phone off her shoulder. She shoved me in the chest. I slipped off the edge of the bed and landed hard on the floor. Right on my ass.

"Mom!" I shouted, hoping to block whatever she was shrieking into the phone.

I scrambled to my knees. Got to the phone jack and yanked, not taking time with the plastic finger. It snapped off with a pop.

Mom was still yelling. Something about police.

I threw the end of the cord at her, remembering how I'd unplugged the phone the last time Dad was home. So boys couldn't call.

Mom looked down at the cord in her lap and let the phone drop away from her ear, her mouth.

"Dad," I started, that close to telling her. Then I saw Bill standing in the doorway, just standing there, watching us, looking worried, almost scared.

"Haven't you done enough?" I shouted at him. "Can't you see what—"

"What?" Mom said. Following my eyes, she turned toward the door.

"Get the fuck out of here!" I screamed. "Leave us the hell alone!"

He backed out of the doorway, out of my sight. It surprised me really, anybody listening to me anymore. "Lainee?" he whispered from out in the hall.

"Please, Bill," Mom said. "I'll call you. Soon." She turned back to me, my face. "Oh, Lucy," she said.

I thought of her screaming into the phone, "If my husband was here," invoking his name, our lethal protector. *If he was here.* I wondered how many times in her life she'd thought that same thing, and I knew that I wasn't ever going to tell her he'd been here, that he'd done this to me. He'd already done so much to us, so much beyond this one stupid bruise, I could spare her at least that.

CHAPTER FIFTY-FIVE

That night, after we went to bed, I listened to Mom call Bill, murmur out her version of the story. She was crying again, and as I got up to shut my door, which she'd left open, I heard her say, "This is not the kind of thing, Bill, not for your daughter, not ever—" I pushed my door closed as softly as I could.

Back in my bed, what I thought about was Tim and his parents, what kind of interview he'd gone through with them. How all this would be handled in a normal family. I ran my tongue across my tattered cheek. Tim would declare complete innocence. Complete ignorance. Right on both counts. They'd shake their heads, dismiss Mom as some kind of lunatic. A hysteric. Same way we'd tossed away Kenny's mom.

They'd finish dressing for church. Go fill a whole pew. Maybe pray for our souls. They'd warn Tim to stay away.

It was for the best, I figured. There was no future in someone like me. Even for Tim, who wasn't exactly sighting in on the moon. He wouldn't be happy about it, but all it had cost him was a few weeks. Three on the outside. Then he'd be gone, too.

On Monday, Mom almost couldn't find the strength to leave me for work, afraid somehow that Tim would come back to finish me off. I wound up prodding her out the door, promising I'd be okay. Same way I had Tim.

Kenny showed up a few hours later. He must have left at dawn. I watched from the couch, him strutting up so proud from his dad's old truck. A driver. A man coming to see his woman. I couldn't keep from smiling.

But when I met him at the door, tried to get my head on his shoulder before he could see my face, he held me away for an instant before wrapping me up. Seeing through my makeup as quick as Mom had, even though she'd helped with this batch, he said, "Tim?"

"God, what does the world have against that guy?" I said. "No. Not Tim."

He didn't believe me. I moved us in to the couch, holding his hand. He looked sick.

"What happened, Lucy?"

"You should see the other guy."

He couldn't smile. "Why did he do it?"

"It was—" I started, but how could I tell him anything without mentioning what had set Dad off in the first place? Cupid's gymnasium. And it didn't make any difference. "He got wanting to be more than friends," I sighed. It was what Kenny'd hear no matter what I said.

I thought *he'd* cry then. There was nothing he could do to avenge me, so he just hugged me, petted my head everywhere but my cheek. I knew there was a part of him dancing inside, knowing I'd fought off unwanted advances; that I'd saved myself, despite gross personal risk, for him.

"You can touch it," I said. "It doesn't hurt anymore. Just looks that way. It's nothing. Nothing but colorful."

When he did, reaching up softer than he ever had, his face looking like it might crumble right there, all these cartoon jigsaws piling down to the floor, I closed my eyes and said, "It was my dad."

"What was?"

"He came home on Friday. One of his surprises. But Mom was at work. We had this huge fight."

"You and your dad?"

"Me and my dad." Trying to stick to the truth, I said, "He wanted to know where Mom was. He kept yelling for her."

Kenny waited.

"She's got this boyfriend. Barnacle Bill. She wasn't coming home that night. What could I tell him?"

"Your mom does? You told your dad that?"

"No. I told him I wasn't his."

Kenny gaped, and I told him how Mom had taken me down to the dam, told me their story, how I'd twisted it around on Dad.

"Why in the world did you do that?"

"He was going crazy. About everything, and it just made me so mad—"

"And you thought it would help, telling him that?"

I shrugged. "I don't know." I thought of what Dad had said in return, but I couldn't tell Kenny that. That Dad might have kids he actually spent time with. What would that make me? "I don't know anything anymore about anything," I said.

He hugged me. "And he hit you? For that? Your dad?"

I nodded. I couldn't keep from lying even when I wanted to. And when I did lie, I couldn't even do it worth a damn anymore. I started to cry, which only made me swear. Kenny held me through all of it. He treated me like I'd been beaten over every inch of my body, not taken one quick slap. We didn't even make love. Just sat there like old people, talking all quiet, like we'd been together forever.

Mom found us like that when she came home for lunch, something she had never done in her working career. We sat up straighter, Kenny making a move to follow her into the kitchen, but I held him back. She buzzed around in there like a TV mom, raising her voice to keep up the chatter, gabbing with Kenny, saying how wonderful it was to see him. She made us all sandwiches, then came back out, singing "To market, to market" like she hadn't in years.

Nobody mentioned the bruise, or risked talking about anything that might lead anywhere. Kenny and I didn't touch the sandwiches until after she was gone.

We moved into the kitchen then, but before we finished eating, the front door opened again. "Now what?" I called, leaning back in my chair to see what she might have forgotten, or if she was going to keep popping in all day, making sure we weren't doing what she would have been.

But it wasn't Mom, and nothing as scary as Dad or another uncle. It was a woman. A little older than Mom. A little heavier. Kind of wild-looking, or desperate, maybe. She stared at me, whispering, "I knocked"—a lie—and took another hesitant step into the hallway. "You?" she asked, sounding like she couldn't believe I was anybody at all.

"Hello?" I said, giving Kenny a what-the-hell glance.

She inched farther in. "It couldn't really be you?"

"It's me. In the flesh." Then, from half my life ago, I took a shot in the dark. "Lola?" Mom's crazy sister?

"Is that what he calls me?"

She made it all the way to the kitchen doorway, squinting at me, at Kenny, taking it all in, a couple of high school kids eating the lunch Mom made for them.

"It's not you. But I saw his truck. I saw—" She stopped. "Your mother." She said it so flatly, so finally, I knew exactly who she was.

"Mrs. Barnacle," I said.

"Where's your mother?" she asked.

"She's at work."

"She's sleeping with my husband."

I worked at a bit of lettuce stuck against my teeth. "I'm sorry to hear that."

"We've got a little boy. A little girl."

"I'm my mom's girl."

I wondered if I should be afraid, if she'd come here to do Mom some harm. But she looked too unsure, too tail-between-her-legs to be dangerous.

"She's ruining our lives," she said.

I nodded. "It's this thing we do," I said, not to sound smart-ass but to begin to explain.

"She looks like you, doesn't she?" she asked. She didn't care about anything I might say.

"My mom? She looks like a mom."

She stood there worrying her fingers. She'd hardly taken her eyes off of me. "I'm a mom," she answered in a way that meant there was no flattery left in the word. "That's what's going on here. Just because he thinks he can, that she's younger and—and not tied down, and doesn't have these kids holding her back every second, and—"

"She has a kid," I said. "She's tied down."

"You don't look like you've tied anybody down in a long time."

I lowered my eyes. "True enough."

Kenny said, "I'm tied to her like glue."

The woman kept staring at me until I had to ask, "Is there something we can do for you?"

"I need to talk to your mother. I need to make her stop."

"She's at work."

"You're not going to tell me it's not her, are you?"

It hadn't even occurred to me. "I don't know who your husband is. I don't know who you are."

"I'm the wife. He's the man. She's the other woman." She took a quick look around, maybe seeing something besides me. "Do you have a father?"

"Everybody's got a father."

She almost smiled, or maybe grimaced. Something. It made me notice she had tears on her cheeks. I didn't know how long they'd been there. The whole time?

"I just wondered how many families she was tearing apart."

"This one's been in shreds for years."

She nodded like it was what she'd expected. "Tell her she can't have mine," she said. "I'm sorry about yours, but she can't have mine."

"I'll let her know."

She walked away. I watched till the door closed. I was still kicked back on my chair legs. I set the front legs down on the floor. Kenny studied his sandwich.

"Well," I said.

We went back to the couch. As soon as my butt touched down, I jumped up and locked the front door. Sitting beside Kenny, I said, "I think that's enough visitors for one day."

"It's not your fault," he said. "What your mom does doesn't have anything to do with you."

I let him hold me. I didn't believe a word he said.

In a little while, we went upstairs and made love, Kenny treating me the same way even then, as if the bruises went through and through. To tell the truth, after as wild as me and Tim had gotten, it was kind of nice, being treated that way, as if the slightest jarring might break something beyond fixing. To have something beyond sex.

He held me forever afterward, telling me how much he loved me. Sappy as it sounds, that felt so good it almost made me cry. I even said it back.

CHAPTER FIFTY-SIX

For old time's sake, Kenny and I walked over to the park and climbed to the very top of the jungle gym. We were still there when Mom came home. Instead of missing us, she pulled right over, same way I had the day Scott educated us about the undeniables.

Walking to the base of the gym, she put a foot on the bottom bar, like she might climb up. Tilting her head back, she shielded her eyes against the brightness of the sky. "This is one place I did not expect to see the two of you."

We sat silent, wondering what to say. "We had to come here," I said at last. "Mrs. Bill is looking for you. Barnacle's wife." Somehow I couldn't not tell her.

Even as high as we were, or maybe because of that, I could see how Mom had to shift her weight, how the news staggered her, how she had to find a whole new balance. "She came to the house?" she asked.

"Right after you left."

She started rubbing at her forehead with the hand that had been blocking the sun. She stepped back until she could lean against the car. "So, how's the vacation so far, Kenny?"

"Seeing Lucy is worth anything."

She nodded, looking up the block to our porch, imagining who knows what of that scene. "I'm sorry you had to see anything else, Kenny. I apologize for that."

"No apology necessary," he said.

She was picking her lip. "Kenny, maybe you ought to go let your mom know you're home, all right? Lucy and I have a few things we need to talk over. Why don't you kids come on down from there?"

We clambered down like a couple of circus monkeys. Kenny took off down the block without even a "See you." He'd reached his porch before Mom sat down on the jungle gym's lowest bar and said, "Tell me what happened, Luce." She looked gray, like somebody held prisoner in the dark for years, and seeing her like that rattled me. Mom was not somebody who bowed down to every breeze. Tornadoes left her unruffled.

I sat down on the next bar over and toed some of the wood chips the city had replaced the old dirt with. I told her everything. Even trying to get the words right. Right up to "Tell her she can't have mine."

That made Mom kind of laugh. "Believe me, honey, I do not want your family." She twisted her hands back and forth over the polished steel bar. "Bill says she is out-and-out crazy. Completely unbalanced."

"And he lets his kids stay with her?"

She said, "She's their mother." She white-knuckled the bar she was sitting on. "Honey, I want you to believe something for me," she said, looking down at the dusty gray wood chips. "That woman's problems are not mine. I mean I did not cause them. She and Bill were finished long before I met him. He's working on getting the divorce right now. She just isn't mentally ready to face that yet. That's what you saw, and I'm sorry that you did. You and Kenny both. It's not something you should ever have to worry about."

I tipped back, following the crisscrossing rows of steel into the plain flat blue of the sky. "A divorce, huh?"

"I have nothing to do with that."

Only that you're fucking him, I wanted to shout. I rocked forward and said, "What then, Mom? You and Barnacle going to tie the noose?"

Mom goggle-eyed me, then just cracked up. Full-blown case of the giggles. Couldn't quit. She had to pull a Kleenex out of her sleeve to keep the tears from ruining her eyes. She had to stand up, walk a circle around in the wood chips, as if otherwise she would have fallen right off the bar.

When she started to wind down, I said, "Did I say something funny?"

"Marry?" she gasped. "Oh, Lucy." She whooped and sighed a few more times, said, "Married?" again, like it was this huge punch line. If you knew her as well as I did, you could see how she was forcing the whole act; how, without her even wanting it, the picture of her and Barnacle married had developed, the idea of someone like Barnacle always around for her, never leaving, clinging to her like lint.

Wiping her eyes, shaking her head, she started for home across the street. "Married," she sighed one more time. "Fool me once, shame on you. Fool me twice, shame on me."

I followed, the two of us walking past the car, leaving it there. "If he'll abandon one wife," I said, "he'll abandon another."

"You always could find the silver lining," she said, putting an arm across my shoulders.

CHAPTER FIFTY-SEVEN

As soon as I got Mom up onto our porch, I said, "I'm going to Kenny's," but over there, I didn't even make the porch. "You just missed them," Mrs. Bahnmiller called from her chair. "I think they went out for dinner."

I stood on the sidewalk, chewing my lip.

She eyed me. She could see my house from here. Tally the comings and goings of Tim's car. Before she could say another word, I turned tail.

When I came through our front door, Mom was on the kitchen phone, shouting. I went into this reflex crouch, like I was about to do some sort of kung fu flip and save the day. But then I heard, "For Christ's sake, you saw her face! Wasn't that enough for her to go through? And now your wife shows up saying who knows what to her? You keep her away from here, Bill! I won't have her dragging your laundry out in front of Lucy!"

Your laundry? Like what, Mom, you didn't wear any of those clothes yourself?

"I don't give a damn what you have to do! I'm telling you how it has to be."

I went upstairs. I had no interest in hearing another word.

The rest of that week, Mom went off to work every morning, Kenny showing up a few minutes later, and we had the mornings to ourselves.

Once we figured out that Mom was going to be home for every lunch, I started making sure we were out of the house before noon. After she was safely back at work, we'd come home and make love in the afternoons. It was like spring break in a way, only smashed into half days, and somehow not quite as exciting knowing we weren't fooling anyone. There was still a tinge of fear to everything, though, with Tim out there, Dad, Mrs. Barnacle. Mom came home every night, minutes after five. Nobody said a word about Bill or his wife. Kenny went home for dinner. Mom and I sat around.

The night before Kenny had to go back to Kalispell, his mom had us over for dinner. Me and Mom. I asked Mom if she was going to bring Barnacle along, but she gave me her razor-lipped, aren't-you-cute smile.

Dinner was fine. Kenny's mom was. Quiet. Nobody drank. Nobody shouted "fuck" at anybody. The house was unrecognizably clean. She must have worked on it all year.

I didn't say two words. This was our life now. Eating dinner with somebody we thought only months ago, was so crazy, so far below us, we wouldn't have handed her a glass of water if she was on fire.

Mom and I walked home together afterward. I was already planning on sneaking out as soon as she was asleep, but as we climbed up the porch steps, Mom said, "Don't plan on crawling through any windows tonight, Luce. If you're not pregnant yet, I'm sure not going to let it happen on my watch."

"You, too, Mom," I snapped back.

"My chances, Luce, are even slimmer than yours."

We banged up to our bedrooms, and twice, before I fell asleep, I heard Mom pad down the hall to check on me. What on earth, I wondered, did she think we did all day? She, of all people, should have known you didn't need darkness for any boinking.

The next morning, Kenny stopped by on his way out, tiny behind the wheel of his dad's truck. He asked me again to come with him.

"Good one," I told him. "You're a barrel of monkeys."

"You could go to school in Kalispell. I know Dad would let you stay with us." He'd been at this all week. Ever since seeing my eye. I wasn't sure he didn't still think Tim did it.

I looked at our house. Mom, believe it or not, was staying home late for this, out of nowhere shooting for parent-of-the-year awards. She was inside making a sandwich for Kenny to take on the road. Really, what she was doing was keeping her eye on us, like we might get to street-humping the way she and Dad did when he was leaving.

Putting a foot up on the running board, I leaned in and gave Kenny a kiss, buckled his seat belt around him. "Thanks for coming, Kenny," I said. Mom was coming toward us, her hands full of plastic bags, cans of pop. Putting some meat on his bones. "You saved my life."

There was almost no trace of a bruise left on my face. A new blank slate.

"Only a couple of months, you'll have your license, too," he said.

"Yeah, and I think Dad's buying me a Corvette. Having it delivered."

He shrugged. "You never know."

"No. Sometimes you do."

Mom passed the food to Kenny. He said he'd be able to drive to Alaska and back with leftovers. Then she put her arm around my waist, stepping back and pulling me with her. We should have been holding a pitchfork. "You drive safe," she said to Kenny. "You're still a rookie out there."

I jerked out of her grasp, and stepped back in for one more kiss. "Bye, Kenny. Thanks."

He whispered, "M and P." I said it back. We talked like postcards. What had I done to him?

I moved away, and he started the truck and eased off down the street. Started signaling for the turn about a mile before he was there. Nothing but caution. But he signaled left for the left. He didn't know everything he thought he did.

I turned on Mom. "What the hell was that all about? Am I four again?"

"I just wanted to stand with you."

"You just wanted to interrupt. Same as all week."

She looked surprised. Hurt. "You're the one always saying you're only friends."

I wished I'd taken the time to put on one of her nothing-to-doubt outfits, that I could go back inside and strip out of it, show her who was the one in the house who had someone left to say good-bye to. I started up the walk.

"Do you want to go to Tracy's?"

"This is my life, Mom. Not yours."

"What the hell is this about? I made him a sandwich!"

"You butted in, okay? I have a life, Mom. And it's mine. Not *yours*. Not *ours*. *Mine!*"

She stood there looking all puzzled and offended.

"I keep my nose out of whatever it is you think you're doing, don't I?" I said.

She raised her hands, a quick, back-off gesture.

"You better get to work," I said.

"Going," she said, moving toward her car.

"Should I bother making dinner?"

"I thought we were on this 'don't ask, don't tell' kind of thing."

"Whatever."

"Whatever," she answered, slamming her door so hard the windows rattled. I banged the gate shut, the hinges somehow hanging on, the gate not dropping onto the lawn the way I'd hoped.

She was back that night at 5:05. Maybe she had no place else to go. We did not speak.

But the next night, Friday, me safely alone, watching the hours wind out past five, I was strangely disappointed to know the whole show had been only for Kenny. Or maybe it had been Mrs. Bill's show, derailing Mom for all of a few days. When I heard the Corvair pull into the drive before nine o'clock, I had to jump up to see, to believe.

Mom walked in right past me, sitting down at the kitchen table. Hard, like somebody looking not to hit the floor.

I made sure Barnacle wasn't right behind her, then stood in the doorway. "I'm gobsmacked," I said, one of Dad's favorites. I wasn't sure it was a real word.

Mom barely raised her head to me.

I tapped my watch, held it to my ear like it ticked. "It is Friday, isn't it?"

"It's Friday."

"Well, um, pardon me, but what are you doing here?"

"Am I in your way? Don't I live here, too?"

"Well, no. Not really. Not exactly. You do visit now and then."

"Stop it," she said, "you're killing me."

"Oh, now, the two of you didn't have a fight, did you? You go and call him this instant. Tell him you're sorry."

"Quit it, Luce. You're not funny."

"Go on," I said, waving her toward the phone. "You go kiss and make up."

"Quit!" she shouted.

I stepped back, surprised.

Mom pulled the salt and pepper close, then pushed them away. "He moved back in with his wife."

I could hear the stove clock's uneven hum. "You mean the mother? The out-and-out-crazy one?"

"That's who I mean."

I pictured the heavyset woman in the hallway that day, her lost-dog look. "How come?"

"You'd have to ask him."

"Wow," I said. "Barnacle Bill. Lost at sea. And here I was thinking you guys were noose material."

I wasn't trying to be mean.

She shook her head like I was this tiny kid, somebody who'd never know a single thing about love, about what adults did with each other. To each other.

"Don't worry," I said, my hackles up that fast, even though she did look pretty miserable. "There's plenty of other sailors in the sea. You, of all people, should know that."

She kept rearranging the salt and pepper shakers. "Shut up, Lucy. Just, for once, shut up."

We never said that. It was like this huge rule.

I lifted my fingers to my lips. Pulled the zipper shut. Twisted and threw away the key.

And that's how it went for weeks, Mom coming home every night like that. You could have set watches by her. Weekends we were back to cleaning. One Sunday she was inside working on toilets or something, while I was out doing the yard, plowing along behind the mower, deafened by the roar, trying not to breath in the blue fumes of the exhaust, broken ends of grass stuck all over my bare legs.

It wasn't till I turned the corner and doubled back on my tracks that I saw Tim sitting behind the wheel of the ranch truck, watching me. I hadn't seen him since Dad. Only a couple of messages I hadn't had the heart to return.

I kept mowing, circling and circling, running out of lawn. I had no idea what to say to him. When I had no place left to go, I shut down the mower and rattled it back into the garage. He was still sitting there. I could hear the truck idling.

When I came out, squinting in the sun, he was walking up the driveway. Like he meant to trap me in the garage, its sweltering, gas-stinking darkness.

"Hi," I said.

He nodded, like guys do.

"Off to Mizzou?"

He nodded again.

"Good. Tear 'em up over there. I'm glad you're going."

"I thought you would be. Rapist wife beater and all."

"I'm not your wife," I said, but even I knew that wasn't funny. "That was a mistake. Mom wouldn't listen to me."

The last time I'd seen him, I'd been shoving him out the kitchen door, Dad gasping like a guppy on the floor, gearing himself up for one last punch.

"It was my dad that hit me," I said. To tell the truth, it was good being able to say that to someone who'd know it was true.

I walked past him into the front yard and sat down in the cut grass, leaning against the tree. Tim sat down on the other side of the tree. Not next to me. We couldn't see each other. I told him everything, about Dad, about Mom, about her phone call. About how I'd tried to stop her.

"But you didn't try to fix anything after that."

I shook my head. "You're better off without it."

"Without what?"

"Me."

"I don't see it."

"You will."

"In our house, love's not this thing you ignore, try to make go away."

I looked at his truck, filled with his college stuff. He didn't know anything about love. About me. He'd never think to tell me M and P. I was just this lost soul his whole Christian deal said he had to be kind to after what Justin did. Then a body, his first. "You're all packed," I said.

"My folks think I'm on the road."

"You'd have a few more Hail Marys if they knew you were here."

"They were pretty upset," he said. "But really, once they got over the call, I think it was a relief for them." He sat there, letting that sink in. Then he edged his way around the tree. I edged away, too, like we were playing a kid's game. Like a couple of squirrels.

He grabbed my hand, stopping me. "Lucy?"

I sat.

"You were glad, too, weren't you? To get it over with. As glad as my folks. That's why you never called, never told them the truth."

"Come on, Tim, it's not like we—"

"You know what the difference was? Between you and them? My folks felt bad about it."

"Tim."

"There's only one thing I'd take back," he said. "I wish I never told you that first time. That it was my first. I wish you didn't know that about me."

"Forgotten," I said.

He gave a snort. "I don't want you thinking you're somebody special over that."

"Don't worry about it."

"I do worry about it."

"You'll get past it. As soon as you find some college girl, I'll be like this—"

"I just wish I'd kept my mouth shut," Tim snapped. "That's all I'm saying. I told you way too much about everything. I—"

"You don't have a clue, do you? You don't even know why we got together in the first place. Do you have some vague memory of that? Think hard. I split up you and Haven. Same as I broke up him and Tilton. I showed him how much his friends thought he was worth."

Tim's face twisted into this huge, dumb *What?* "He and Jaimie were history before we even knew who you were."

"Ha."

Tim stood up. "You don't think I'm very smart, do you?"

"No smarter than you do."

"I know you're quicker than me. That you can make fun of any-thing. But you know what? That's all you can do. You got a mean streak that'd shame a grizzly bear."

"That's *all* I can do?" I laughed. "How's the tan on your ass?"

"Fading," he answered, shaking his head and walking down to the truck.

"No shit it's fading. It'll be a long time till it sees the sun again."

"You're proud of that?" he asked, standing with his hand on the door latch. "Man, Lucy. Any animal can do that. I mean, we're all born with the parts."

"Well, you're going into politics for a long while now."

He got that lost look.

"Spending your time shaking hands with the unemployed."

He gave a totally unamused sort of laugh. "You know," he said, "I think you're right. It is for the best. I can't believe what I almost did." He opened the door and climbed in. Fired it up. "Happy now?" he asked.

"Overjoyed." I slapped the side of his truck. "Adios, amoebas."

He shook his head. "Have a nice life," he said, starting off. "I hope you aren't always so miserable."

I jumped into the street after him, shouting, "Hey, Flash, misery loves company! How the fuck could *I* be miserable?"

He went around the corner, and I turned back to the house. There was Mom, standing on the porch, watching everything.

Still in the middle of the street, I said, "You, too, Mom. You should have married Barnacle when you had the chance. Now it's you and me, baby. Just the two of us."

Mom kept looking at me like she didn't recognize me or something.

Then I realized what I was doing. Standing in the middle of the street. Alone. Shouting. For no reason at all, on the verge of tears. I dashed past Mom into the house, up the stairs. By the time I hit the bathroom, I knew I couldn't hold it back. I turned on faucets, tub and sink, drowning everything out, then sat down on the throne and let go, the big underwater sobs. I pictured Tim driving away, actually missing me, actually sorry it was over. Me. His only wish that I didn't know I was first. I held on to the edge of the counter and buried my face in my arms, wondering how in the hell I'd gotten like this. I cried like it was me, not Tim, who was saying good-bye to a whole part of our lives.

CHAPTER FIFTY-EIGHT

School, when it started again, was more an invisibility training course than ever. Kenny was gone, Tim, Rabia; even Jaimie and Justin, who was off to Bozeman, where he could still knock heads against his old pal Tim on the football field. I marched around with my shoulders hunched, my head down, no eye contact. My hair had grown back enough to not make me stand out much. I went entire days without saying a word.

And home. Not until Barnacle was out of the picture—Mom and me always bumping into each other, standing back to let the other get by, no risk of touching, of talking—did I see how much we'd been gone. I started staying in my room, my territory again reduced to a few square yards. We didn't have a truce so much as this uneasy cease-fire, both of us wary of each other's talents as snipers.

We got so out of the practice of talking that the night I wandered into her room, caught her sitting at her dresser in front of her perfume bottles, she flinched. She watched in her mirror, waiting.

"I'm going to get my driver's license on my birthday," I told her. "I was wondering about a car. What I'll do for wheels."

"Were you?" she asked, absently fingering her perfume bottles.

"Hey," I said. "You know why women wear makeup and perfume?"

She raised an eyebrow.

"Because they're ugly and they stink."

She snapped a bottle down against the glass top of her dresser. "Is there something wrong with you? Something that allows you to think that is one bit funny?"

"Just something Dad told me once."

"Ah," she said, as if I'd explained everything. She opened a perfume bottle, waved the stopper under her nose, closed her eyes. "So, after deciding to spend your summer 'fishing' instead of working, you're wondering about a car. Good thinking." She put the perfume bottle down with the others. The smell made me think of my locker.

"I was wondering if I'd be able to have the car some weekends."

"Run off to Kalispell to see your paramour?"

"To see Kenny. I was thinking about it."

We never mentioned Dad at all anymore.

"We'll talk about it when you have your license, honey." She pushed herself up and swung around me, out into the hall.

"Mom," I called after her. "It's only a couple of weeks." I followed her down the stairs.

She slipped into her chair in the kitchen, each of us as hemmed in as any animal in any zoo, only shifting from one perch to the next. "Who knows what can happen in a couple of weeks?" she said, tossing it off like we had all these delicious possibilities.

Two nights before my birthday, after like twenty days in a row of stewing in our house, Mom got a phone call. Right in the middle of dinner. All I heard was her intake of breath, the way she let it out in a laugh, the first I'd heard out of her since her fake cackling on the jungle gym. I thought for sure it must be Dad, maybe an early call for my birthday.

She said, "You have got to be kidding me! You're where?"

Dad on his way here? I pushed my chair back and waited for her to hand over the phone. I couldn't believe he'd called, and I wanted to hear what he'd say, whether he'd pretend his last visit never happened. I got butterflies just thinking of his voice, the way he'd jumble up half of everything he said. It made me sick how much I wanted to hear him.

"Ron," Mom said, almost a sigh, as if it were a name she thought she'd never have the chance to say again. She laughed some more. "Don't even think of telling me how many years it's been!"

I walked out to the living room. Some ancient uncle crawling out of the woodwork.

My stomach still fluttered from that one second of hoping I was going to talk to Dad. I kicked the couch. Dad, the only person in the world who had ever hit me. I kicked it again.

The next night Mom didn't come home. At all. No call. No nothing. To tell the truth, with Barnacle overboard and this Ron guy an apparent transient, I got a little worried. I even tried her emergency number a few times.

She still wasn't home in the morning, though it was a Friday, a workday. So, of course, there were no shouts of "Happy birthday!" No prizes sitting in my place at the kitchen table. I hadn't been expecting any, but still.

There wasn't even a postcard from Dad. Only me echoing around the house, wondering if there was something I should be doing. I wondered if maybe telling Dad I wasn't his had put his last obligation out of its misery.

Waiting till after she'd have to be at work, I tried Mom's emergency number one more time. No answer. I went upstairs, through her room. All her clothes and everything were still there. Her drawers full.

I trimmed a fingernail with my teeth. Another one. Who the hell was Ron?

I thumped back down to the kitchen. Stared at the phone. When I didn't have any nails left to chew, I called Tato.

He told me she'd quit. Yesterday.

I sat down at the table. Just sat there. Would she really bolt? Thinking of the last few months, I whispered, "Why on earth would she stay?"

My breathing got fast, and I got all sweaty. I gnawed my lip ragged. What were we going to do without any money? What was *I* going to do? Dropping my head into my hands, I rubbed at my temples. I'd get a job, I figured. Doing something. School was probably history. Maybe a GED, someday. I'd have to start reading the mail, the bills and stuff, not only postcards. Stay in the house till I got kicked out. Maybe Mrs. B. would take me in for the company. Mrs. Theodora. Maybe she missed

Rabia that much. Maybe I'd have to snag a jetter of my own.

Every scary thing that had ever happened to me—Justin squashing me down, "Suit yourself," Dad smacking my head full of stars—hadn't been half as scary as this. I couldn't stand thinking about it anymore. I was already way too late for school. I tried chewing on the stubs of my nails. "Happy birthday," I whispered, having to start twice to get it out. "Happy birthday to me."

I pushed back my chair and, snagging the spare car key the way I had when Kenny and I went up to the bus station, I walked down to Mom's office, found her car parked out front, all abandoned-looking, two parking tickets stuck under the windshield. Pitching those under the car, I drove it over to the courthouse and took my driver's test. Sticking to my original plan because I couldn't think of a single other thing to do.

I tried to pretend I was celebrating, but it seemed like I'd need the license sooner rather than later. To start my working life. My life of self-support. I didn't even know if the house was paid for. I sure didn't think Dad was sending any more checks. If Mom had blown town, where was I going to live?

Would she really do that to me?

Stuffing the temp license in my pocket, I left the courthouse and drove back to Mom's spot. The tickets were lying in the gutter, and I stuffed them back under the wiper. Looking up at the telemarketing world headquarters, I lost my nerve and walked down the block toward home. But the license in my pocket made walking slower, Great Falls suddenly twice as big, twice as empty. I turned around but only walked past headquarters again. After walking up and down the block a couple of times, I finally pushed through the glass doors, whacked the old buffalo on the rump. Upstairs, the secretary or whatever wouldn't let me see Tato. It didn't help that I couldn't remember his real name.

Even I knew you didn't get a job by asking for Mr. Potato Head. "I know he's got an opening," I insisted. She gave me an application, telling me I'd have to fill it out like everybody else.

With the application in my pocket along with my new license, I climbed back into the Corvair. I hesitated before turning the key, thinking about leaving the car for Mom, like somehow that might make it easier for her to come home, like she couldn't walk the twenty blocks herself, have Uncle Ron give her a lift. Then I started it up. If she'd left me behind, I'd be needing it a lot more than she would. I drove one block toward home before realizing how dead a place it would be, with no one coming back to it except me. So, without planning it, or making any turns I thought about, I wound up on the river road, admitting that I had no place to go and pulling over above Rainbow Falls. I remembered how Kenny and I had gone to the falls that first day, the day we kissed, how everything had changed after that, and I figured this was a place it made sense to be.

I spent the last of the day sitting behind the wheel above the falls, most of the cliffs dry and gray, the water trickling through. It was sunny out, bright but cold, the air north of us funny, the world simply ending, ground and sky fusing into one dense wall, like a dust storm or a forest fire was galloping around loose up there. Storm coming for sure, the wind already picking up, shifting around to the north, burring the shine off the flat water above the dam. A minute later, it started whitecapping. Another winter ripping down as I was about to become a street person.

Before it got completely dark, I rolled up the window and backed out into the dusk, trying to shake the shivers, not wanting to think about what would be waiting for me at home. The emptiness there. The rest of my life.

CHAPTER FIFTY-NINE

When I came around the corner, instead of the black hole I expected, our house was lit up like a casino. Easing into the driveway, I craned at the windows, fearing some sort of uncle convention, but there was no one I could see. I crept into the garage and walked around out front, onto the porch, opened the door as slowly as I could. The stereo was on. I couldn't remember the last time Mom had listened to anything.

I walked down the hall to the kitchen, keeping my jacket on, chilled to the core.

Mom smiled as soon as she saw me. "Happy birthday, Lucy," she said, seeming normal, seeming nice.

There was a cake on the table, a box of candles almost empty beside it, a few spilling out, maybe half a dozen candles stabbed into the frosting. Mom had the rest in her hand. She was still wearing what she'd worn to work yesterday. Rumpled, maybe, but still way nicer than me in my usual old jeans, T-shirt, sweatshirt, Dad's huge old Carhart over the top. "Nice outfit," I said. "I can see why you'd want to keep wearing it."

Smiling like I hadn't said a word, she turned to the counter, pulled a little box off, and set it next to the cake. "I didn't have time to wrap it."

"These birthdays do sneak up on a person."

She couldn't quite keep from flashing me a look.

"Where have you been?" I asked, like it was making conversation, nothing I needed to know.

"I met a friend I haven't seen in years," she admitted so easily I felt like slapping her, if just for Dad's sake, like he was actually out there working his tail off for us.

She stabbed more candles into the cake, working on a pattern spelling out "16."

"I called Tato," I said.

She punched in a candle out of line. "Why, honey, would you do that?"

"I didn't know where you were. I was worried."

She nodded, swept some hair back from her face. "I bet that wasn't a call that settled your nerves."

I sort of chuckled. "No, not exactly."

"I was going to tell you. It was sudden."

"I guess so."

"Tato—Mr. Rolanski," she corrected, "got these ideas I couldn't get out of his head. I was telling Ron about it, and he thinks I have a strong case for a sexual-harassment suit."

"Ron's a lawyer?"

"He knows about things."

"And that's how you're thinking we'll live? Off the money from the Tato suit?"

"Could be a hefty chunk of change."

"I spent all day wondering if the house was paid for. I tried to get your job."

Mom squinted at me, puzzled. She really needed glasses.

"You don't come home," I explained. "I find out you quit your job. You still don't come home."

"You thought I'd blown the coop?"

"I figured it was best to start making plans." It seemed embarrassing now.

"You have an overactive imagination." She started on the candles again. "The house has been paid for forever. You know that. How do you think we've lived here? Only thing you'd have to worry about is taxes."

"Good to know," I said.

"Well, this has gotten a little deep. Come on over and blow out your candles. Make a wish. Open your present."

"You in a rush or something?"

"Just to watch you."

"Uh-huh."

She struck a match. Her hand trembled over the candles, but she got them all.

"Who is Ron?"

"No one you know."

"Uncle Ron?"

She shook out the match, the flame licking against her fingertips. "Blow out the candles, Luce."

"Do you want some dinner first?"

"The candles will melt all over the frosting."

"I haven't eaten all day."

"It's your birthday, Luce. For crying out loud. You can splurge once a year. Have cake."

"For dinner? 'Let them eat cake?' "

"Exactly."

"You know what happened after that?" I dropped the edge of my hand across the back of my neck. "Thwap. Gack."

"Blow out the candles, or it might happen before."

I blew.

Mom lopped out a dinner-size piece for me, a sliver for herself.

As I sat down, I saw the Albertson's box stashed behind the garbage pail, Mom hiding it like I might for one second think she'd made this cake herself. Dad, when I was a kid, used to stop at the bakery, letting me watch them frost the cake, build the flowers, squirt on the leaves. He'd flirt with the decorators as they worked, all these stout old women, and I loved how they loved him. They even got to know my name.

Mom nibbled at her skinny piece standing up.

"You don't have to stay, Mom. If you got a date or something."

She whipped out a chair, dropped herself down, all dramatic. "I don't have a date," she said. "I was thinking about seeing a lawyer."

"Ron's idea?"

"He says the sooner the better."

"I don't think lawyers pull night shifts."

"Are you going to open your present?"

"What is it?" It was an old line of mine. Always trying to find out before time.

"Open it, Nosey Posey."

For a second there, we almost had it again.

My mouth was full of cake. Too much frosting, like always with storebought. My name wasn't on it or anything. Just a thick frosting flower on each corner.

I slid the box over, tipped off the lid.

A pair of leather gloves, the leather barely thicker than a condom, holes cut out on the back of each knuckle, patterns of tiny ones ticking across the back of the hands.

Mom beamed. "Driving gloves. Did you get your license?"

I scooched forward, pulled the wadded, creased, and flattened paper out of my pocket, set it on the table.

"No picture?"

"They'll mail it when it's ready."

"It's reassuring to know that at least you were driving legally."

Putting down my fork, I said, "Without you, I thought I'd at least need wheels." I slid my hands into the gloves. They smoothed down against my skin like Lycra, smelled like fresh pigskin. I flexed my fists. "I think we need a real Corvette for gloves like this."

Mom laughed. "One step at a time. Do you like them?"

I knew they were something she'd picked up that afternoon on her way home, maybe asking Uncle Ron to stop at Kaufman's after he drove her downtown to pick up her car, found it missing. The men's store. First place she saw. I pictured the glove display up front, easy to see, fast. In and out. No need for Ron to plug the meter. "They're great, Mom."

She stood up, clasping her hands beneath her chin, like she'd been agonizing over this gift for months, on pins and needles till she knew I liked it.

I still had half my piece of cake left. "Go ahead, Mom. You can go."

"I don't know why you keep insisting I leave."

"Night's not as young as it used to be. Neither are you."

"Lucy, I—"

I whistled a few bars of "Back in the Saddle Again."

She slapped a hand against the table. "I am trying here!"

I looked at my plate, the blob of cake. I couldn't hold it in: "It didn't take you long, did it? Horse Teeth. Poof! Then, even though 'I am not like this,' Barnacle sweeps you right off your feet. When he walks the plank, shazam, another love of your life appears. 'Hey Rocky, watch me pull an uncle out of my hat.' "

Her lips were a slash across her face. "What is it about me, exactly, that you hate so much?"

"God, where would I start?"

She glared at me; maybe, who knows, counting to ten, trying some twelve-step thing to keep from killing me. "Do you think, Lucy, for even one second that I am not aware of my failings as a mother?"

"Nobody could know that much."

"Oh, I know all right. Even without you spelling it out for me. Even without you having to handle Bill's wife sniffing around. You'd be better off without me, wouldn't you? You know it as well as I do. Better. That's what you've been thinking, isn't it?"

"You know what I've been thinking? I've been wondering if I'm even Dad's kid."

She took a step back. "What on earth? What the hell is that supposed to mean?"

I shrugged. "I'm sixteen now, and I think I should know."

Her hands were in fists. "Know what?"

"Well, you had me so young and all. All these uncles creeping around. Maybe I was this mistake. Something Dad agreed to take on. Or maybe something he didn't even know about."

"I should slap your face right off your head."

"Maybe that dam run wasn't some once-in-a-lifetime stunt. Maybe that's why he's gone all the time!"

Mom reared back like I was giving her actual shoves.

"Maybe that's why he can't ever use the telephone like a normal human being. God, even Mr. Crauder called Kenny a few times!" I'd gotten to shouting somehow, and when I stopped, the house buzzed silent around us.

"How do you come up with this shit?"

"Boy, I can't even begin to imagine."

"Do you lie awake at night wondering how you can hurt me the worst?"

"Of course, Mom. It's always about you. You're all anybody ever thinks about."

She didn't say a word. Only gave a shout and spun around, stomping out of the room.

"At least take a shower! You smell like Cupid's gymnasium!"

The front door slammed.

CHAPTER SIXTY

Mom was home before ten, but I was already safely in my room. I listened to her slamming drawers, climbing up and down the stairs, back and forth. She cranked the radio on again, letting me know she wasn't hiding anything. I kept listening for another set of steps, another voice, but she was as alone as me. What the hell was she doing? Packing? Letting me hear her leave? I couldn't quite tell, and though I was itching with curiosity, I knew that was what she wanted, and I wasn't about to open the door to let her know she knew me that well. She was still at it when I fell asleep, worn out from the strain of ignoring her.

In the morning, though I woke early, I smelled coffee. Dad home? I smiled, the way you do at any ridiculous idea, and shook my head, trying to wake up the rest of the way. Walking down the stairs, I had to step around a heap of suitcases at the bottom, stacked so I couldn't miss them, so I'd have to ask, so my life would be thrown into turmoil and doubt.

Mom was sitting in the kitchen, sipping her coffee. Except that she was now dressed like me, sweatshirt and all, she looked like she'd never been to bed at all.

" 'Morning," I said.

She was good enough that she didn't bat an eye at my walking past all her carefully piled evidence.

I snagged a banana from the clump on the counter. "School day," I said. "A mind is a terrible thing to lose. Waste. Whatever. Will you be home when I get back?"

"Counting the minutes."

I walked out the door, calling, "To market, to market."

I went through the motions at school, same as any day. There was a note for me to go to the office, and the women there were all smiles, not saying a word about yesterday's absence. They gave me a blue glass vase full of roses, red edged with white. I turned way redder than the flowers, opening the note just far enough to see Kenny's writing, about a million M&Ps. Dad's old coat was just wide enough to let me pretend I was hiding them till I got them in my locker, and then later to sneak them out of school.

I carried Kenny's roses home, knowing he'd sent them to school to stake his claim, to let all the boys see I was taken, but I couldn't stop smiling anyway, every time I looked at them, smelled them.

By the time I reached the jungle gym, I could see the Corvair parked out in front of our house, not hidden away in the garage. At least, I thought, she hasn't disappeared. Unless Ron took her, the car left out as her parting gift.

But Mom was inside, stripping my postcards off the refrigerator. Laying them into a box on the table.

"Those are mine," I said, clutching my roses to my chest.

"I'm aware of that."

"So?"

"You don't display souvenirs forever, Lucy. You store them now and then, make room for new events in your life."

"What kind of events are you planning?"

"A trip. A vacation."

"Now?"

"Another birthday present." She folded the box lids over each other, squishing the last one in. Finally looking at me, she said, "Nice flowers." Then she hefted the box up and staggered past me to the front door. I watched from the porch as she worked the key into the lock on the front of the car, popping open the trunk and dropping in the box. The trunk was the biggest thing about the Corvair. We'd hardly ever used it.

Coming back up the steps, Mom smiled at me, stopping just long enough to reach for the card on the flowers. I pulled them away, and she shrugged and kept going into the house.

"We're taking my souvenirs on a vacation?"

"They're so excited, they can hardly stand it."

I stood out on the porch, wondering if I should be mad or afraid. She came back by, a suitcase dragging down each arm.

"Mom. I give. What are you doing?"

"We, honey. We."

"Okay, you win. What are *we* doing?"

She came back to the house for more. "It's a surprise," she said, her false, traffic-stopping smile stretched tight.

On the next load, I set Kenny's flowers down on the porch and grabbed a bag from Mom, jerking it out of her hand. She kept going.

I carried it to the car's gaping trunk and threw it in after the others. "What?" I sighed, like I was so tired of packing this way.

"He has spent his whole life out there, and you've been, where, Helena? It's your turn now," she said. "*Our* turn."

"What, Mom? Our turn for what?"

She was on her way to the house again. "To be the ones not waiting," she said, like I'd missed something obvious.

"Why can't we not wait here?"

I tried to jump in front of her, get a glimpse of what was happening on her face, but she kept rushing up the porch steps, up the stairs.

Her room looked like a trailer court after the tornado. Stuff everywhere, drawers yanked all the way out. She stopped in the middle, surveying, then sidestepped me again, marching to my room, an empty gym bag dangling from her hand. By the time I caught up, she was stuffing my underwear into it.

"Mom!" I shouted.

But she already had my condoms, and she stuffed them into the bag without comment, then jumped to my bed, lifted the mattress, and swept out my birth-control pills, throwing them into the bag as well.

I felt furious and guilty at the same time, caught and spied on. "What the hell do you think you're doing?"

She was in my closet, throwing a few shirts into the bag.

I grabbed her from behind, hauling her out backward, spinning her around.

She blinked. "What?"

The one guess I could come up with was that she was hauling me to Dad. Letting him take his turn with me. I thought of him, miles from nowhere, a chain saw in his hand, nothing but hundreds of miles of dark, damp forest before him, acres of stumps and slash behind. Or sitting in a cozy house in Lethbridge, a gaggle of kids around his feet. "Where do you think I'm going?"

"We are getting you out of this godforsaken place, Lucy. We should have done it years ago."

I snorted. "Come on, Mom. Like this is for *me*. Like it has not one thing to do with you. Like you're not clearing the decks, ready for action."

"What decks? What action?"

"The uncles-of-love cavalcade. Finally round-the-clock."

For maybe a full minute, she didn't say anything. Then she reached down to the floor of my closet for another gym bag and started stuffing jeans into it. "You're too young to even realize that everything I have ever done has been for you."

"That's a joke, right?"

"I might agree with you there. A bad one."

"I'm not going anywhere, Mom. You're not. You're not dumping me on Dad."

She bolted up. Inches from me. Her hair flying in my face. "You pretend we don't even live together. You treat me like this complete piece of shit. This is not my job, Lucy! This is not what I signed on for. Here I am trying to take you to Mexico for a fresh start, but if you want to go to *him* now, fine! Find out how much *he* likes being the brunt of his daughter's goddamn charm!"

I just stood there, gobsmacked. Mexico? My room looked exactly like hers now.

A duffel bag in each hand—what she'd apparently decided were my life's belongings—Mom tore away, down the stairs. I walked down after her, counting the steps one last time. At the door, I grabbed Dad's old Stihl cap, scrunched it down on my head. I picked up Kenny's roses from the porch.

The gate of our picket fence was lying flat in the walk. She'd done it at last.

Mom was slamming down the trunk lid. Jumping up, landing on it with her rear. Holding tight to my stupid flowers, I sat down on it beside her, heard the solid click. "Mexico?" I said quietly.

"I have spent my last day waiting," she hissed through her teeth. "My absolute last." She sprang off the trunk and, going back to the passenger door, whipped it open for me like it was a temporary setback that we were without a chauffeur.

"Do you even know where he is?" I asked, afraid both that she did and that she didn't.

"Who?"

"Dad."

"He has nothing to do with this."

I slid off the trunk and walked over to her. "Can I at least drive?"

Maybe I could detour us back here after she calmed down.

She pointed at the passenger seat. "Get in."

"Remember, I've got a real live driver's license. And those hot gloves."

Mom shook the door for me. "I know. You're a big girl now. Sixteen and never been kissed. Whooee."

I slipped past her into the passenger seat, cradling my vase, my roses. The blind leading the deaf.

Mom leaned in, saying, "Buckle up." Same old joke.

That's when I saw the bruises on her neck. Hickeys. On my mom.

"Mom?" I started, then fell back on the old lines. "No belts in the Corvair, Mom."

She moved back out. "Trust, Luce," she answered. "Makes the world go round."

Maybe they were fingerprints, I pretended. Maybe old Ron was a little rougher than she remembered. Maybe that's why we were going to Dad.

Mom sat down. Pushed the key in. "And they're off!" she cried.

CHAPTER SIXTY-ONE

Mom crossed over the nearest bridge without saying a word. We shot up the hill, out of the river's cut, past the TV stations' flashing towers, and into the gathering darkness. The wind of yesterday's dry storm rocked the car, whistling around the windows, Kenny's flowers making everything smell too close. Mom cranked the heater, every rustle of her movements making me cringe, thinking this time she was settling in to say something, that I'd have to tell her she was headed north. That Mexico was the other direction. That the only thing up this way was Dad.

But she was settling in to nothing beyond the drive. We weren't, as far as I knew, taking the straightest shot to Lethbridge. Maybe she knew more about his whereabouts than I did. Or maybe, after all these years, she'd just jumped on the quickest route out of town, would worry about directions, destinations, later.

Not until we reached Havre, the Bear Paws rising up in the gloom, then falling behind, did I break the silence. "It was a joke, Mom."

"What's that?"

"About not being his kid. I know I am."

She shook her head. "God. After a lifetime of his lousy jokes. Figures the two of us would have to breed to create one worse."

"Me?"

Mom took her eyes off the road long enough to skewer me with one of her looks. "And you say I think it's all about me."

I sat back. Looked out the window at the night. "What about school?"

"They have schools. Even in Mexico."

"Mom. A few more minutes, we'll be in Canada."

"We've got a stop to make first."

"And this, Mexico, moving, this is something you never thought to ask me about?"

"Lucy," she said, like "Don't start," but then she took this whole new tack. "Chuck started leaving when you were a baby. I was nearly your age. About as old as you are right now. Try to picture that. To remember that."

"I know, Mom." If she was going to go through all that again, I might open my door and step out, see how long I'd last on my own at sixty miles an hour.

"When you were about two, I—your dad, he was gone again, and that was not something I had ever planned on. Being alone. I, well, there was someone, and we, I . . ." She sighed. "My whole life long, I let your dad convince me I'd made this terrible mistake, that I was an eyelash away from losing everything." She gave a parched chuckle. " 'Losing what?' I should have asked."

"Ron?"

She nodded. I could barely see it in the dash lights.

"And now you think you got this big second-chance thing?"

She dipped her head, some kind of shrug and nod both.

It was a while before I got the nerve to open my mouth again. Could get my lips wet enough to speak. The headlights were already catching signs warning about the closeness of Canada, the port of entry. "Where are we going, Mom? If Mexico's really the target, Dad would envy the navigation."

I doubted she had any clearer idea of where we were going than I did, but maybe all this darkness—the narrow, deserted two-lane, no matter where it was going—felt right to her. "Do you even know where Dad is?"

"That's not where we're going," she said, and then she stood on the brakes, peeling us off the highway across a patch of gravel. I grabbed the dash, Kenny's vase, thinking that she couldn't stand it anymore, had decided to finish us off.

But it was nothing as dramatic as that. Nothing dramatic at all. Just this tiny roadside café, a couple of lonely gas pumps, a low little building around the back, a motel for the chronically desperate. A semi out by the highway—its parking lights on, engine rattling, that ready to get the hell back on the road—was the only customer.

Mom jerked back the parking brake. "You must be starved," she said, opening her door and stepping out. I chased her into the wind, the gritty blast of dust and gravel making the café a place to run for.

Muscling the door open against the wind gave us enough time to read the COOK WANTED sign. Mom tapped it. "See, Luce," she said, shouting above the wind, "opportunity's always knocking."

Inside, there was the one trucker eating, and one skinny guy working behind the counter. After a glance, the truck driver went back to his burger, but the guy working let his smile grow and grow, like he was seeing his long-lost best friend or something, like he'd won some sort of way long-shot bet. Still grinning, he whispered, "Hola, Lola."

My jaw dropped, and he said it again, louder this time, almost yelling it, like something he'd been dying to say all his life. "Hola, Lola!"

I glanced at Mom, caught her return smile gleaming. Felt this sick tremor down low in my stomach.

"Hola, Ron," she said.

He looked kind of sunbaked and had tattoos trailing out of both shirt sleeves, but other than that, he really wasn't *not* handsome enough. He was tall but thin, more Kenny than Dad. He had a head of black hair, a little too long, with this cowlick kind of thing dangling down in front, almost to his eyes, which was supposed to look like an accident.

Mom caught me looking at it and leaned in to me. "He mousses that. Don't let him fool you for an instant." But she'd already pulled into Fool City. Set the parking brake hard.

I guessed the only kind of moose this guy had ever heard of was the kind you shoot at, but Mom knew these things. I nodded. "Maybe trying to impress the trucker," I whispered. But I didn't have the sort of luck that would make this guy turn out gay.

Ron—Tattoo—clapped his hands together. "I called Cabo again today. If you're anteing up, the deal is done."

I said, "Huh?"

Mom said, "Deal me in."

"Ha!" he crowed. "I knew it!"

"That's more than I can say," Mom answered.

"And little Lola? Will she be waiting the tables?" He said it with this weird beaner accent, leetle Lola, zee tables. Half Speedy Gonzales, half Pepe Le Pew.

"No," I said, though I had no idea what they were talking about.

Mom gave me a playful backhand to the shoulder. "That will be up to her. She's all grown up now."

She slipped behind the counter. Rather than giving her a hug or anything, Ron tied an apron around her waist. "A night of training," he said.

I stood staring at the two of them, waiting for the punch line. But Mom only said, "Honey, Lucy, this is Ron. Ron, Lucy."

He started to say, "I've heard a lot," but I spun around and shoved through the door. I didn't want to hear one thing about whatever plan they'd dreamed up for us.

The door opened behind me before it got all the way closed, and I turned to give Mom a going-over, but it was the trucker, giving me the eye. "Looks like you're staying a while," he said. "Unless you're going my way?"

I headed into the wind for the Corvair. "I wouldn't be going your way if I *lived* here." I slammed the door behind me, pressing down the locks. I pulled my roses into my lap. Trying to keep them from freezing to death, I drew my knees up tight to the vase, folded my arms around them. I was not stopping here, I swore to myself. I'd steal the keys and go introduce myself to Kenny's dad, if that's what it took.

I wasn't out there two minutes before Mom, still wearing her apron, came out and rapped her knuckles against the window. When I unlocked the door, she drove us around back to the motel rooms: a line of four doors in a building the size of a railroad car. "I could take the job here, if that's what you'd like. Instead of going to Mexico. The room is part of the benefits package." She was practically giggling. "And we can eat in the café. Free."

Still waiting for the punch line, I said, "Mom, we don't have to do this. We aren't at the bottom of the barrel yet. We're practically still skimming cream."

She got the key in the door. "But won't it be nice standing on our own two footloose feet?" she said, flopping down on the bed, nearly disappearing in the sag of mattress.

I slumped beside her, and we stared at our feet, dangling out there off the bed. I didn't point out that there were four of them. That Ron's would make six.

"Mom, there's only one bed."

"I don't mind. We'll be snug as bugs."

"Snug as pigs," I said. "Bugs in a blanket."

Mom didn't bite. I said, "Really, Mom. What's going on?"

She took a big breath. "Ron's a chef, and—"

"A *chef*? Come on, Mom. Here?"

"In Mexico. Cabo San Lucas. The place he worked burned down. He's up here now, he's from up here, helping out his father until he got this deal put together. He's buying his own restaurant down there. He's going to call it A la Deriva. It means 'at drift on the tides.' "

Mom didn't know a single word of any foreign language. For all she knew, it could mean "I'm stealing your wife." "And he wants you to go with him?"

"Us, Lucy. Both of us."

I couldn't think of a word to say. "We can't go to Mexico, Mom. Come on."

"We can do anything," she answered, bouncing up off the bed and heading for the door. "Think about it, Luce. I know it's out of the blue, but think about it. I've got to run. Ron's going to show me some tricks of the trade."

"I don't think I'd use the word 'tricks' if I were you."

She spun, her finger pointed at me like a weapon. Her mouth was open, a threat dangling there, but she snapped it shut. Twisting behind her back, fumbling with the doorknob before getting the door open, she kept her eye on me until she was ready to disappear. "We got ourselves a clean slate, Luce. We can do anything, go anywhere. We can be anybody." Then she was gone.

I sat alone on the bed, too stunned to move. But then I thought, if Ron was in fact a chef, it would take him all of two seconds to realize Mom would be better left in Canada than brought anywhere near his own restaurant. No need to panic.

I looked around the room, about the size of a smallish closet. No TV. No phone. One electric baseboard I'd set Kenny's flowers in front of. The warmest spot. I sank back on my elbows, stared at the ceiling, the walls. I wondered how long I'd have to stay here before Mom lost her nerve, got us back on the road home or even to Dad. Maybe that would take more nerve. In all the years, it was the one thing we'd never done. *It's no place for a girl, Mame.*

There was a cigarette hole burned in the shade. I struggled up out of the bed and bent down to it, pretending it was a bullet hole, that anything could happen here. I peered though its tiny circle, spying on the gravel parking lot, the back of the café, the Dumpster. Like someone out there might see me if I wasn't so sneaky.

I walked around the room. Twice. Four seconds burned. I did another few laps. Checked out the bathroom. Hitting the light, I saw the stains, blurted, "Gross!," and snapped the light back off. Maybe it was the water staining the toilet bowl, the shower stall. Iron in the ground.

After another few laps, one more try sitting on the boa constrictor of a bed, I crawled back up, whispered, "Fuck this," and battled my way upwind to the café. Showdown at the Totally Not OK Café.

There were no cars out front, nothing to tempt any passersby, if there were any. The wind slammed the door shut behind me, but as I caught my breath, I could already see there wasn't a soul in the place. Nobody. Nowhere.

"Mom?" I asked, my voice tiny. I licked my lips. "Mom?" I said again, louder.

I could almost see it, her ditching me here for Tattoo, figuring she'd gotten me close enough, that I'd have as much chance finding Dad on my own.

Then Mom came out from the back, her apron filthy around her waist, her hair flying everywhere. No bothering with hair nets on the Montana/Canadian border. A billow of smoke followed her out the stainless door.

"Little excitement here," she said fast, noticing me, waving me back behind the door, snagging a fire extinguisher from beneath the counter.

I followed, wondering if she'd heard me calling for her or if she was just out to retrieve the extinguisher.

Dad would be howling. One shift and the place was on fire.

I was only a second behind, but it was all over by the time I pushed past the steel door. Mom and Tattoo were breathless, leaning against a counter, laughing as hard as Dad'd be. There was smoke everywhere but no fire. The tattoo on Ron's arm had palm trees in it. I didn't look long enough to know what else.

" 'Hold on,' " he was saying, a fair imitation of Mom. " 'I'll get it.' " He could hardly spit it out. He patted her back, then took hold of her arm like he was the only thing keeping them both from collapsing on the spot. His fingers pressed into where she was getting soft, up above her elbow, and it occurred to me that Mom had probably caught more than one glimpse of the day heads would stop turning her way.

She was stamping her foot, patting her hair flat, holding her hand to her mouth. I started coughing in the smoke myself. "I thought it was water," Mom squeaked out. "I thought that's what it was there for."

Tattoo turned to me. "Oil!" he crowed. "She pours the oil bucket on the fire. To put it out!" He had nice eyes. He was going to die laughing. Just not soon enough.

"I thought that's what it was there for," Mom said again, wiping her eyes.

"Could've burned the whole place to the ground," he said.

I stepped from foot to foot, waiting for him to let go of her. "Who were you cooking for?"

They stopped, still blinking back smoke and tears. "For us," Mom said. "The three of us."

"Customers been pretty thin lately," Tattoo said.

"Lately?" Like since the last ice age. With Mom cooking, thin was really going to be the rage.

Ron couldn't keep a lid on it, a laugh burbling back up every time you thought he was finished. He was a laugher. The worst thing he could have been. I glanced at the grill, the blackened chips of something, brown-black lumps off to the side, volcanoey-looking. "What were you making?"

"Burgers and 'browns," Mom answered, like she'd been slinging hash for years.

"House specialty," Ron added, his eyes crinkling up again. A definite laugher. I knew Mom didn't stand a chance of coming to her senses. But Dad, no matter what else, was still the world's best laugher. It was a cinch, seeing it happening again right before my eyes, to see what had suckered Mom for Dad when they were both so young, before finding out about his love of postcards. It was still suckering her for Ron.

Chuckling, Ron scraped the grill clean and started fresh. He over-explained each step to Mom. She bummed a smoke off of him and leaned back against the counter, taking a drag, winking at me, laughing with Ron.

Out in the booth, Ron smashed the last of his hash browns between the tines of his fork, polishing his plate like it was a contest. He'd been going on and on about his restaurant. He told Mom maybe she'd start out serving the drinks, what with all the inflammables in the kitchen. He told me I could do the same, that the two of us together would draw business from all over the peninsula. Catching me staring, Mom smiled, rolled her eyes. Ron slurped his fork clean, setting it on the shining plate, and gave it a spin. You hardly needed to wash it.

"Clean-plate club," I whispered, one of Dad's. I watched Mom, expecting it to cattle-prod her or something, but it slicked off her like Teflon.

I wondered if Ron had his own room out in the railroad-box motel or if I'd have to sleep in the car. "You grew up here?" I asked. "This is your place?"

Ron shook his head. "This place is a ticket to nowhere."

Yeah, I thought. And you're the driver.

Then he was back to his restaurant. A la Deriva. Right down on the beach. Lobsters and Coronas. Shrimp and tall, salty margaritas. Like it was something anybody might do. At drift on the tides.

Mom sat straight, though, really seeing it. Outside, Canada's fall gales plinked gravel against the glass door, rattling a loose window, but Mom had a trace of sea breeze riffling her hair, tropical sun glinting off the ocean chop, blinding her.

"Where did you say?" I interrupted Ron. "Where in Mexico?" I wouldn't have taken any bets that this guy could say what direction Mexico was, even if you ruled out east and west. North. "Which coast?"

Mom said, "Lucy!" but Ron held a hand up to stop her and actually looked at me instead of Mom. "I've been there, Lucy. I've been most everywhere."

I'd seen Mexico on a map, and that was as close as I wanted to get. One long strip of scorched brown dirt. Scorpions. Gila monsters. This guy covered with palm trees.

As soon as my own plate was clean, Mom sent me back to our room. So she and Ron could clean the kitchen, she said. Talk about lame.

I locked myself in and fell back on the bed, the grease of dinner sitting in me like a lump. "We've got some big decisions ahead of us," she'd said. "You better sleep on it." I wanted to ask her what it was she planned sleeping on, but I kept my mouth shut.

Because there was absolutely nothing else to do, I fell asleep. Clothes on, bed still made, everything. I turned over once, awake long enough to know that Mom wasn't back. I mean, you couldn't roll over without hitting somebody if they were there to hit. My feet hurt, and I kicked off my shoes without untying them, wrestled out of my clothes.

I wondered about lying there naked with Uncle Ron on the loose, but I pulled up the starchy-smelling sheet and thin blankets and rolled over to face the wall, trying to pretend none of this was happening.

CHAPTER SIXTY-TWO

Sometime later, middle of the night, I woke up with my skin all prickles, somehow knowing I wasn't alone anymore, the air in the room as close and dark as the inside of a glove. "Hello?" I whispered, praying there was no one there to answer. I heard a shuffle, then breathing. "Mom?" I squeaked.

"It's me, honey."

"Jesus," I gasped. "You scared me to death."

She took a step, bumping into the bed and sitting down, sagging me into her. "Honey?" she asked, her hands on me, feeling around, trying to find where I was. She touched my shoulder, my face. She stank like cigarettes and booze, which wasn't that common, no matter what else she did.

"You okay, Mom?"

"Honey, we're going to Mexico," she said, like a lifelong prayer had been answered. "Can you believe it? Us? Me?" I tried to sit up, but Mom held me down. "We're leaving now. You've got to pack."

"Pack? Why on earth would I have *un*packed?"

"We'll be the hostesses," she went on. "Ron says we've got the figures of dynamite hostesses."

"Dynamite doesn't need a hostess."

"He'll teach us to cook."

I struggled out from under her. "So he can collect the fire insurance?"

She petted my cheek. "Shhh," she said. "It's what I want to believe right now. And you're old enough to—"

"I'm sixteen, Mom. Just." What she *wanted* to believe. Not what she believed.

"It's your decision, but come with us, Luce. Ron says you'll love it down there. And I know you will, too. The beach. The sun. You and I, we can get a new start with each other."

"We can't swim, Mom."

"You don't have to swim. But we could learn. And the sunsets, Luce, the smell of the ocean, not the refinery, a breeze coming off the sea, not these goddamn dry gales. Not forty fucking below. The place full of these rich, beautiful people coming to our restaurant, wanting to know us. No farmers in their cowboy hats, bitching about the moisture. Not surrounded by jetters hunkered in their silos waiting to send us all to kingdom come."

"Mom, get a grip on yourself. You're having a midlife thing. That's okay. Whatever. But we're not going to Mexico."

"I am," she answered, so matter-of-factly that I knew she was. "And I want you to come with me."

"And if I don't?"

"You could have a whole new life, Lucy! Escape Great Falls! I mean, what's to miss? All your perfume-toting school chums?"

"I don't need a new life, Mom. I need new parents."

She went silent, and when I was about to say I was sorry, she pressed her car keys into my hand. Like a blessing. Last rites. "I left Dad's address in the car. Directions. A map. There's money there, too."

"Dad? You think that'd be an improvement?"

She breathed heavy, then said, "No, the money's in my purse. Shit, where's my purse?" She stood up, leaving me alone in the bed.

"Mom?"

"Maybe living with him, you'll stop hating me so much."

"I don't hate you, Mom."

She knocked something over, searching.

"Turn on the light, Mom. It's okay."

"I think I broke it," she said. Then she cried, "There!" like it'd been this treasure hunt. I heard her purse zip open.

"Maybe you ought to slide in here, Mom." I scooted over, patting the mattress hard enough she'd hear. "Bugs in a blanket. You know?"

She sat down on the very edge of the bed, almost missing it. "Don't start talking like him, Luce."

"But Mom."

"Luce, it's time for you to use that new license of yours. That's what it's for."

"I guess I missed that day in driver's ed." Mom didn't say anything. I went on, "You're leaving right now? How much have you been drinking?"

"Ron showed me how to make a margarita."

I imagined the two of them in that little wind-blasted café, sipping umbrella drinks, dreaming about making up their lost fifteen years. Lost because, back then, Mom couldn't leave me behind.

"Mom, you're not making sense. You're—"

"Well, what does make sense?" she blurted. "Sitting home waiting for your dad to blow through? Every day watching how much I disgust you? How many more years of that?"

"But Mom—"

"No buts, Luce. I've never asked you for anything but your understanding."

"Mom. Einstein couldn't understand this. NASA couldn't."

She chuckled. " 'If they can put one man on the moon, why can't they put them all there?' "

"They faked the whole thing, anyway. Filmed it in Arizona. Built a whole movie set."

"Now we're both talking like him," she said, her breath stuttering. "Shit, Luce, don't put me through this."

Something light feathered against my face. I jerked back, but I heard Mom fumbling and realized it was the money from her wallet, that she was fishing it out, throwing it at me blind.

"What are you going to do without money, Mom?"

"I've saved some back."

"What am I going to do?"

"You'll be fine. You'll be with Dad tomorrow. We're close now."

"I don't even know where he is. You don't. You don't know anything you think you know about him."

After a moment, Mom asked, "What's that supposed to mean, Luce?" I could feel her staring down at me in the darkness, and I understood how a mouse felt, knowing everything out there is after it. Owls. Coyotes. Wolves.

"I told him I wasn't his kid," I whispered.

She breathed once, then again. "When did you do this?"

"He called on my birthday. After you left."

Mom kind of chuckled. "I wondered where the hell that came from. Don't worry, Luce, he didn't believe you."

"I made him believe me."

"Lucy, there is no way—"

"He told me he has another family. In Canada."

That stopped her. "He said that?"

I nodded in the dark, nothing she could see.

"Wow. Don't tell me you believed him?"

"I don't know."

"Oh, Luce, I thought if you'd learned one thing, it'd be that he was never meant to be married in the first place. He's not married to anybody else. He doesn't have another family. It's the last thing he'd ever do. And even if, what do you think the chances are of him finding a second woman dumb enough to marry him?"

"But how will I—"

"The two of you are going to have to kiss and make up. It'll do you good, apologizing for once." She did that chuckle thing again. "That must have been a hell of a pissing match. Not his kid. Another family. Like the two of you don't have enough real shit to throw at each other."

"What'll I do when he leaves again? With you off with Tattoo? What'll *you* do? When Tattoo finds another one built like a hostess? A younger one? When he leaves you in Mexico?" I was almost shouting.

Mom laughed once more, nothing funny about it. "Shit, Luce," she said. "They all leave you. I thought you'd've learned *that* much. But right now he's the one waiting. For me, Luce. He's waiting for *me*."

It dawned on me that I'd been listening to the steady rumble of some kind of big engine the whole time Mom had been in the room.

"I have to go, Luce."

"No you don't. You don't *have* to do anything."

"Say hello to your dad for me."

"What else should I say to him?" I asked, trying to wound, anything to slow her down.

"Don't get that way, Luce. He'll know what I'm doing. Same thing he's been doing since he said 'I do.' Looking for another life."

"You already have a life, Mom. *We* do."

"Waiting's not a life, Luce."

"I'll tell Dad you ran off with a tattoo-covered fry cook!"

"Come on," she said like a sigh. "You know what he'll say."

She was right. I could see him standing there pulling on his chin, taking in my news, saying, "Well, ain't that the gravy on the cake." Or maybe, no matter what Mom said, he'd be rushing me off his porch, getting me away from his front door, hiding me from the wife and kids, pushing me back toward the Corvair, pulling money out of his pocket, begging me to disappear.

Even as desolate as that made me feel—Dad giving me the bum's rush, sweeping me back into his distant past—I knew that it was way more likely he'd be standing alone in the doorway of some broken-down trailer, the razor-edged chain he'd been sharpening still dangling from his blackened fingers, so surprised was he by anyone tapping at his door, let alone me. I pictured how the news about Mom would stagger him, how he'd start worrying at the oily chain like a rosary, shaving off curls of his hardened skin, not even feeling it. I guessed he'd look the same way he had that day Tim dropped him to the floor, stunned and gasping, his legs cut out from under him at last. His life collapsing forever to the tiny dot it would be without even the theory of us to come back to. If he got out any words at all, I doubted there'd be fun enough left in him to mangle a single one. I doubted he'd be able to say much more than "What do we do now, Luce?"

"Mom!" I shouted, wanting to show her the disaster of that surprise reunion.

She whispered, "Shh, Lucy, shh," like I was her baby again. "Please come with me."

I looked out at the space she filled in the darkness beside me, and said, "I'm not going anywhere, Mom. Not with you. Not with him. I'm not running. And I'm not waiting. I'm staying."

"Here?"

"Here's as good as anywhere."

"God, what have I done to you?"

"Nothing, Mom. You can still—"

She shushed me again. "It's time then, Luce. For both of us." She started that hollow laugh, saying, "Bon voy-a-ee," the way she used to, then, "I'll send you a postcard." But that killed the laughing dead.

"God," she gasped. "I can't believe I said that. I'll send you huge, long letters, Luce. Honest. I promise. Pages and pages."

Then, like she'd just promised me the world, Mom reached a cupped hand out for my cheek. But she'd lost me in the dark, and she touched my naked breast instead, a soft, loving caress, cut short as soon as she realized. In all my grappling and groping, I'd never once been touched like that; nothing quite so, I don't know, full of love or something, safety. Certainly never by her. I found I couldn't breathe.

"Jesus, Luce," Mom stammered, standing up quick, the bed bouncing with only me left in it. "I'm sorry."

I felt myself blushing, there in the pitch black. "No, Mom, it's—"

She opened the door fast, a flash of murky light, Tattoo's truck or muscle car or whatever loud and powerful-sounding. "I have to go, Luce. Please don't hate me. But if I don't go now, I never will."

"Mom!"

She said quick, "I love you, Luce. I do," then the room went dark as she shut the door. I heard the truck door open and slam so fast it was practically all one sound. Mom running to keep from stopping.

"Mom!" I shouted, though it was too late. I was already left behind, that last whisper of hers fading into the dark.

I slumped back into the grip of the bed. All I could feel was the tingling run her fingers left on my breast. I could see why she might want to run for that. Why missing it might have made her crazy like it had. But lying back down alone, Mom's car keys still clenched in my hand, I wondered if I'd ever feel anything as good or close again.

As cool as I was, that's all I wanted. My mom.

CHAPTER SIXTY-THREE

I stayed there all night, wide awake, adding up where I was. Who I was. All my attractive options. I had the car, but I'd lose the house, I guessed, unless I went back. I figured it wouldn't be long before Mom came dragging home from however close she'd gotten to Mexico. She'd need it then to hole up in and lick her wounds, and I knew I didn't want to be around for that. Even if she never came back, Great Falls seemed like one giant step backward. Like a kid climbing down the ladder from the high dive, showing everybody she'd lost her nerve.

There was always Dad, the address Mom had left in the car. But no matter which way I found him, all alone or with another family, I couldn't see myself staying with him. I mean, he'd done enough without me going looking for more.

And Kenny. His dad. Kalispell. He'd take me in a second. At least he said he would, that his dad wouldn't mind. But that seemed more like a step sideways than forward. Like Rabia, like Mom, finding a man to take care of them. Poor old Kenny was only a boy. A kid. Our whole thing really something kids did. Playing grown-ups.

Thinking of us that way tightened up my throat, but I knew the game was over now. That I'd landed here in the real thing.

So, I had the car and whatever money Mom had thrown at me. The last thing I could face was turning on the lights to add it up. I doubted it'd be end-of-the-rainbow material, anyway.

Across the parking lot, I knew, was a job. Double shifts, probably, what with Tattoo blowing out. A veritable gold mine.

The wind rattled the windows, the shade with the cigarette burn waving in the drafts. I pulled the blankets up tighter. Could a person stay here? Live here?

I fought my way out of the bed's grasp. Drawing in a breath, ducking my head, I hit the lights. It would be temporary. A stepping stone to my big, beautiful life. The cauldron out of which would emerge the Truly Incredible, Amazing Diamond Girl!

The first things I saw after the dazzle of the lights were my duffel bags sitting by the door. A box. Mom must have carried them in. Maybe that was what woke me, their thumping onto the floor. Maybe she'd planned to leave without saying a word. Stealing out into the night. Tossing them onto the bed, I zipped them open, pulled back the cardboard lid of the box to get started.

I broke out laughing, a laugh I fought to keep from disintegrating into tears. At the top of one of the bags was Dad's jackalope. In the box, Kenny's rows and rows of taped-together postcards. I'd forgotten how I'd watched her lay those in, the last few nights blending into this jangled snarl, no one single thing I could have worked free.

I lifted them out, standing there naked, covered with goose bumps—I swear I could see my breath—with a jackalope and fifty bucks' worth of postcards in my hands. My life.

There was a nail in the wall that the jackalope kind of hung on. Not for long, maybe, but for now.

Kenny's cards I had to leave stretched over the little three-legged table. I figured I'd swipe some tape from the café, if they had any. More nails if I needed to. I pinned them down with his vase, my roses, which weren't looking like they'd traveled all that well.

Dawn still a long way off, I stepped into the shower, trying not to look at the stains. Though it smelled like Yellowstone, the eggy stink of geysers, the water was about as hot, and for the first time since I'd climbed into the car beside Mom, I warmed up. Back out, I rubbed a splotch of mirror free of fog and looked myself in the eye. At least it wasn't black anymore. I said, "Come on. You, at least, can cook. They'll hire you in a second. It's not like they'll have a line of applicants. Like they'll have this cook-off." I wasn't nearly as sure as I tried to sound, facing an interview with Tattoo's dad.

I had to make sure.

Going back to my bed, buck-ass naked and feeling it, like some Scott Booker might be panting beside a peephole that very second, I dumped out the bags, scattering everything across the crumple of blankets. Jeans and T-shirts, sweatshirts. Not exactly job-interview outfits. Still hardly believing the way Mom had pulled them right out of their hiding spots, I stashed my birth-control pills and condoms in the nightstand. Like I was moving in. Then I retreated to what was left of the steamy heat of the bathroom with my Christmas makeup and a handful of clothes.

There was a heater in the wall I hadn't seen before. Tiny wire coils that glowed red almost as soon as I twisted the knob. The damp room filled with the smell of burned dust.

Mom's Christmas earrings fell out of the makeup kit. I put them on the glass shelf above the sink and skittered into my underwear, pulled on a T-shirt, jeans.

The fog was gone, and I looked at myself full on. A kid. Not somebody who'd been around the block, let alone around a kitchen.

Trying to think like Mom, I stenciled in a line around my eyes, globbed on some mascara. Now I looked worse. Like a kid trying to look old. A girl with something to sell. I smudged some color across my eyelids, onto my cheeks. Mom could do this in her sleep. A frantic woman who couldn't cook a hole in the ground, dragging a kid along besides, she'd get hired without even asking.

I took one of Mom's earrings. The spike looked sharp enough. Holding my breath and biting down, I shoved it through the top of my ear. Well, into it, anyway. My eyes watered. My ear bled. I tried again. The post bent; nothing up there but cartilage. I kept after it until I had a hole worn through my ear. I mangled the earring so bad I had to use the other. One earring through the top of my ear instead of the bottom. It stung like hell, but I kind of liked the look. It went with my hair, which looked like I'd combed it with a hurricane. If my ear stopped bleeding, I could look like somebody who might be hiding a personality, not some lunatic on the lam. Though I wasn't sure it made me look any more employable.

If only I had some tattoos. I could claim I was their long-lost grandkid.

I stood on tiptoe, trying to see below my neck. Thinking about it a good long while, I slipped my arms out of my sleeves. I knew how Mom would get this job.

I popped the clasp of my bra, thinking about Kenny, his leaden fingers groping, unable to ever get it, even after I'd shown him the workings, let him practice on the empty bra. I shrugged out of the shoulder straps, slipped it off completely. I stood on tiptoe again. My nipples pushed out their buttons. "Let him see your résumé," I whispered, trying to imitate Mom the way Ron had.

Finding the nail file in the makeup kit, I sawed away at the seams of my sleeves, tore them off. I looked tougher now, my arms strong, seams of their own that I flexed, proud of my body like I hadn't been since the jungle-gym days.

I thought about ripping the collar off, tearing open the front in a long cleavage "V" like Mom would sport, but the tight shirt, my nakedness clear beneath, did more than enough. I didn't want to go completely Mom, not in my first hours without her.

Peeking out the cigarette hole in the shade, I saw it was still dark outside, no business picking up yet.

Facing the room, I stashed all my clothes back into the duffels, leaving my bra lying on the bed in case I lost my nerve, came to my senses, whatever. I made the bed, stashing the fistful of Mom's money under the pillow.

Home sweet home.

Thumbing my jacket over my shoulder, Dad's beat-up, oversize old Carhart, I cracked the door. It was about a million below out there, but that would only add to my swinging-free, nipple-in-your-eye look.

Shivering, I chewed on my lip a moment more, wondering if I shouldn't hop in the car, turn it around, make a home for myself in Great Falls, my own personal orphanage, waiting until Mom or Dad came drifting back through.

"Waiting's not a life, Luce," I whispered.

I dashed.

The wind, shot through with tiny pellets of snow, knocked a grunt out of me, this force trying to drive me back into the room, into my old life. I put my head down and ran around the Dumpster, around the corner of the café, where it could really get a grip on me.

The door was locked, and with the wind battering me, whipping tears out of my eyes, I nearly gave up and started to cry. But through the blur, I saw that in their hurry, Mom and Tattoo had left the key in the door. Fumbling with it, I pictured Tattoo laughing, Mom tugging at him, saying, "Come on, they're getting away out there!," maybe leaning in to give him a love bite or two of his own, Tattoo leaving the key, figuring he'd done enough just getting it locked.

I fell inside, the wind nailing the door shut behind me. A few low lights behind the counters glowed bright enough for me to move around, find the real light switches.

I shrugged into my coat, my whole tits-like-warheads look wasted. What an idiot. I found a thermostat, cranked it up to sixty-six. Another light switch turned on the outside light: CAFÉ.

Genius in advertising.

I fumbled around awhile, finding things, figuring out how some of this industrial stuff worked. I got coffee going. The smell alone was worth it.

Going up close to the front window, blocking out the glare with my hands, I could make out the palest streaks in the east, dawn on its way. I shivered again, more from nerves than cold. The shit was nearing the fan. I slipped my coat over the back of a chair. Gave my boobs a bounce. "Boys," I said, "do your duty."

I sure as hell hoped it wasn't Tattoo's mom who showed up, some rasty old woman who let her son look like that. Some ranch wife trying to survive. I pictured myself like a cartoon, getting bounced out the door, my ass springy, making skidding, screeching noises every time it hit the pavement.

On the counter was Tattoo's pack of cigarettes. Camels. The kind Mom had been smoking as we watched Tattoo teach us the intimacies of his grill. One left. I pulled it out, held it between my fingers, took a practice puff.

Maybe it'd make me look older.

I turned on the grill. Ready for action. Found some matches.

My first toke set me to coughing, but I got over it. I poured myself a cup of coffee and stood there looking at it, its steaming, oily black surface. Feeling the tears trying to well up again, I sloshed some of my coffee off into the sink, then poured in the cream, the sugar. Making ice cream all by myself, clinging to that one part of my old life like a scraggly weed at the edge of an impossibly high cliff. I was glad they didn't have the paper hats the waitresses wore at Tracy's. That I wouldn't have to picture myself at seventy, still here, still pouring out coffee.

Taking a sip, I cleared my throat, wiped my eyes. "You are not going to be here when you are seventy," I said out loud. "No way. You're not going to be here when you're *seventeen*." I'd work here long enough to get my feet on the ground. Get myself a bankroll. Get used to the idea that I was somebody whose mother would leave her in a place like this. "Okay, eighteen. I promise."

I thought of Mom on her way to Mexico, Dad who knows where, doing whatever he wanted. "There's a whole world out there, Luce," I whispered. I could set sail from here to anywhere. Go someplace nobody knew me. Pretend I was whoever I wanted to be. Like Rabia and her makeover, only this time playing for real, for keeps.

I leaned against the counter, stuck out a hip, blew out a puff of smoke. "Baby," I said, "this joint is open for business."

I held my pose for a long, long time. Nobody showed up to see. I had the jitters so bad, I was afraid I was going to throw up. I started to think. Why would anybody be happy to find me sitting here smoking cigarettes, drinking their coffee? I stubbed out the smoke, went and found cleaning supplies. There was plenty to do.

I was mopping when I heard the door open. Its tinny bell. I spun around, trying to get into some stance, something that would show me off, make me look like something you wouldn't automatically put out with the trash.

There was this old guy dressed all in white, bald as a cue, a white sailor hat perched on his head like Popeye. Big old jean jacket, the long kind, what Dad called a pig-farmer coat. His eyes were the bulgy kind, and now they were practically standing outside his head. He took one look around his place, at the till, then came back around to me. He checked me out, up and down, making me feeler nakeder than I'd ever been. Skinned.

"Who the hell are you?" he rasped.

"Your new cook." Shit. I had to swallow and say it again, bring my voice down out of the stratosphere.

He still had his key in his hand, like he'd done the same simple routine every morning of his life until this very second. He looked like a rancher who'd maybe lost his place or let his wife talk him into something other than that empty, windblown life, so gave her this instead, like it was much of a change.

"My cook," he said. "Can you cook?"

"Better than your last," I answered, though he didn't know yet about Mom.

"How'd you get in here?"

"Your old cook eloped last night."

He muttered something that didn't sound good while he lifted his cap and ran his fingers over his shiny scalp. "Jesus H. Christ," he said. He looked around again, smelling the coffee, I hoped. Then his gaze came back to me. He hadn't moved a step in from the door.

"You are the owner, aren't you?" I asked.

"Supposed to be. Though I always guessed that'd mean I'd know what was going on."

He finally took a step in. Put his keys in his pocket. "Ron off to Mexico?"

I nodded.

"A la Deriva," he said, looking like he might have to spit. He walked behind the counter and poured himself a cup of coffee. He sniffed at it. Took a sip like it might be poison. He smiled. "You can make coffee, anyway." He glanced around. "Place is cleaner than Ron ever left it in his life."

"I'm a white tornado," I said.

"And you can cook?"

I nodded, catching him looking at my rear. Everywhere I'd wanted him to. But I couldn't pull this off, I knew that now. "Listen," I said, trying one last-ditch time to be Mom, "you're free to look. Looks are free. It's a free country. But looking is all. One touch, even once, even an accident, and you won't want to see what the next blue plate will be."

His eyes shot up to mine, narrowed. "There's no call for talk like that, miss."

Miss?

He rubbed his hand up over his head again. Swiped his cap back on straight. "Okay. I'll give you a try. You cleaned the place, I owe you for that already." He shook his head. "Lord, Norma will kill me."

I jumped behind the counter and topped off his cup for him.

"I'm not a customer," he grumbled. "I can get my own coffee in my own place." He waved me toward the kitchen. "Go get ready for our rush," he said in a way that made it clear a rush was something this place had never seen.

I stood in the kitchen doorway ready to jump. "I'm staying out back," I said. "There's no phone there."

"I know."

"They even give you a phone call in jail."

He kind of smiled. "Pay phone's all I got." He pointed at it and walked over to the till, popped it open. "The son of a bitch." He pulled out his wallet, started stocking the register with a few bills. "You'll have to call collect."

"I've got my own money." I still hadn't had the nerve to count up what Mom had tossed at me. "Till payday."

Stepping out from behind the counter, he cranked the thermostat, though up or down I couldn't tell. He gave a long look around, like he was trying to remember this place the way it was before I happened. Reaching back around the counter, he popped the till again. He pulled a ten out and held it toward me. "Buy yourself some underwear."

I blushed then. I could feel the heat, and I damn near cracked, told this total stranger everything, and walked out the door to the Corvair. But I picked up his ten, looked at it, and said, "Been a while since you bought any underwear."

He shook his big, heavy head, pulled out another ten, pushing it my way. "Miss," he said, "I ain't ever bought any underwear." Then he smiled. "And it's been longer than that since I let myself think about the kind you're needing."

I smiled back. Last night Mom had picked too quick.

"Maybe you got some other clothes?" he asked. "Something with all its pieces. To put on before the wife gets here."

I nodded. Abandoning my post, I headed for the door. As I passed him, he brushed at his ear, the hair growing out thick and gray. "Did you know your ear's bleeding?"

I reached up to touch it, then stopped myself.

"Might want to lose the ring," he said.

"Nope. My mother gave it to me."

He made that face again, like he might spit. "Your mother?"

I nodded.

"She got something to do with Ron's elopement?"

I shrugged. "For a while, anyway."

"She give you that haircut, too?"

"Nope. That's my dad's."

His eyes widened, wondering, I guessed, what exactly he was taking on here. "Probably looks better on him," he said.

"Thanks." I put my hand on the door. I was embarrassed looking like this, like he'd caught me playing dress-up. I talked so it wouldn't be so quiet, the wind so loud. "Where are we, anyway?"

He grinned. "The middle of nowhere, kid."

"Here at last."

Then, as if we'd settled something, he shrugged out of his coat, hung it up on the chrome stand beside the door, the kind with the wide curlicue arms. His T-shirt was bleached as white as his pants. On his arm he had an ancient blue tattoo. An anchor. The letters "USN" still readable above it. Tattoos must run in the family. "Name's Gerald, kid," he told me. "Most call me Popeye, though. For short."

"No way."

"I was in the navy. In the war. About your age when I signed up. Ever hear of Pearl Harbor?"

"I saw the movie." I pointed at his arm. "United States Navy?"

He grinned. "*Until* I *See Norma.* Least that's what she says."

I smiled back. He'd known her way back then, and here they were, still this team. Mom had picked *way* too quick.

"And you?" he asked. "You have a name yourself?"

"Lucy," I said. "Just Lucy. Nothing for short."

I was still standing there, dangling off the door handle, when Popeye said, "I wouldn't waste much time getting too moved in back there, Lucy. Don't bother doing a lot of prettying the place up."

"Okay," I said. I bit my lip, wondering what I'd done wrong in just one second.

"Norma," he said, bobbing his head, doing his lift-the-hat, rub-the-scalp thing. "She's been taking in orphans her whole life. Gophers, cats, anything. Had a meadowlark once that lived eight years. Has to be some kind of record. Once she raised up an antelope. An antelope, for the love of Mike. It moved off with the herd the next spring, but we saw it around for a few years afterward."

I kept looking. Listening.

He squared his cap. "Those rooms back there. They're all right if you're trying to catch a few hours, keep yourself on the road, but they're no place to live."

"I'm not afraid of a room."

"Didn't say you were. But Norma, she's going to like the cut of your jib. So you might as well get used to the idea of staying with us. She doesn't take to 'no' all that well."

"We'll see," I said. "I got some figuring of my own to do."

He smiled, like he was saying, "You haven't met my Norma yet. You don't know what you're up against."

Then, my future maybe taking this new detour, I said, "Is there a Middle of Nowhere High? A school bus?"

He nodded. "Yup. Norma even drives the damn thing. Got to say, though, you don't look much like you'll fit in."

"We'll see," I said. "I just might." Like a thumb in an asshole, Dad would say. I opened the door, the wind stinging. I held my arm up quick, blocking what I could.

Crossing the parking lot, I started to imagine my one phone call. To Kenny. So at least one person in the world would know where I was. The one person who'd care. I'd tell him I knew I could win a stare-down with Norma, but I'd have to decide whether I wanted to. And if I did decide to make my own stand in the motel, I'd tell him it was all or nothing. That I wasn't accepting any goddamn visitors, that my life wasn't running on that kind of waiting schedule.

I collapsed against the door, the wind pummeling me until I got it open and fell into the thin, welcoming heat. Looking over the room, I moved the rickety table with Kenny's postcards in front of the window, arranged his flowers so they'd block the hole in the shade.

I could see Kenny rushing up here, the two of us filling this tiny room, the collapsed bed, playing grown-ups for keeps. People, for once, would be trying to peer *in* through that cigarette hole—not people looking out, hoping for some sort of life to pass by and sweep them up, but people peering in, trying to see what we had, envying it, maybe, even. Like they might have looked once at Mom and Dad, when they were so young, standing beneath the falls the explorers rejoiced over, so positive they knew exactly where they were, the sky full of rice, everything still out there ahead of them.

I mean, wouldn't that be the icing on the cake? After that, anything else would just be gravy.